WORTH POCKET COMPANIONS

MYSTERY & SUSPENSE

Short Stories by Great Writers

WORTH POCKET COMPANIONS

Other titles in the series

CRIME

ROMANCE

TRAVEL & ADVENTURE

Mystery & Suspense

Short Stories by Great Writers

Selected by

ROSEMARY GRAY

WORTH POCKET COMPANIONS

First published in 2012 by
Worth Press Limited, Cambridge, UK
www.worthpress.co.uk

The reset text, concept, design and production
specification copyright © Worth Press Limited 2012

A catalogue record for this book is available
from the British Library

ISBN 978 1 84931 068 0

Cover design Bradbury & Williams
Typeset in Great Britain by Antony Gray
Printed and bound in China by Imago

1

Contents

EDITH WHARTON

Edith Wharton was born in 1862 into a wealthy New York family. In 1885 she married a Boston socialite; the couple travelled widely and settled in France in 1907, but the marriage was unhappy and they divorced in 1913. Her first major novel was *The House of Mirth* (1905); many short stories, travel books, memoirs and novels followed, including *Ethan Frome* (1911), *The Reef* (1912) and *The Age of Innocence* (1920). Wharton was decorated for her humanitarian work during the First World War. She died in France in 1937.

A Bottle of Perrier

1

A two days' struggle over the treacherous trails in a well-intentioned but short-winded 'flivver', and a ride of two more on a hired mount of unamiable temper, had disposed young Medford, of the American School of Archaeology at Athens, to wonder why his queer English friend, Henry Almodham, had chosen to live in the desert.

Now he understood.

He was leaning against the roof parapet of the old building, half Christian fortress, half Arab palace, which had been Almodham's pretext; or one of them. Below, in an inner court, a little wind, rising as the sun sank, sent through a knot of palms the rain-like rattle so cooling to the pilgrims of the desert. An ancient fig tree, enormous, exuberant, writhed over a white-washed well-head, sucking life from what appeared to be the only source of moisture within the walls. Beyond these, on every side, stretched away the mystery of the sands, all golden with promise, all livid with menace, as the sun alternately touched or abandoned them.

Young Medford, somewhat weary after his journey from the coast, and awed by his first intimate sense of the omnipresence of the desert, shivered and drew back. Undoubtedly, for a scholar and a misogynist, it was a wonderful refuge; but one would have to be, incurably, both.

'Let's take a look at the house,' Medford said to himself, as if speedy contact with man's handiwork were necessary to his reassurance.

The house, he already knew, was empty save for the quick cosmopolitan manservant, who spoke a sort of palimpsest Cockney lined with Mediterranean tongues and desert dialects – English, Italian or Greek, which was he? – and two or three burnoused underlings who, having carried Medford's bags to his room, had relieved the palace of their gliding presences. Mr Almodham, the servant told him, was away; suddenly summoned by a friendly chief to visit some unexplored ruins to the south, he had ridden off at dawn, too hurriedly to write, but leaving messages of excuse and regret. That evening late he might be back, or next morning. Meanwhile Mr Medford was to make himself at home.

Almodham, as young Medford knew, was always making these archaeological explorations; they had been his ostensible reason for settling in that remote place, and his desultory search had already resulted in the discovery of several early Christian ruins of great interest.

Medford was glad that his host had not stood on ceremony, and rather relieved, on the whole, to have the next few hours to himself. He had had a malarial fever the previous summer, and in spite of his cork helmet he had probably caught a touch of the sun; he felt curiously, helplessly tired, yet deeply content.

And what a place it was to rest in! The silence, the remoteness, the illimitable air! And in the heart of the wilderness green leafage, water, comfort – he had already caught a glimpse of wide wicker chairs under the palms – a humane and welcoming habitation. Yes, he began to understand Almodham. To anyone sick of the Western fret and fever the very walls of this desert fortress exuded peace.

As his foot was on the ladder-like stair leading down from the roof, Medford saw the manservant's head rising towards him. It rose slowly and Medford had time to remark that it was sallow, bald on the top, diagonally dented with a long white scar, and ringed with thick ash-blond hair. Hitherto Medford had noticed only the man's face – youngish, but sallow also – and been chiefly struck by its wearing an odd expression which could best be defined as surprise.

The servant, moving aside, looked up, and Medford perceived that his air of surprise was produced by the fact that his intensely blue eyes were rather wider open than most eyes, and fringed with thick ash-blond lashes; otherwise there was nothing noticeable about him.

'Just to ask – what wine for dinner, sir? Champagne, or – '

'No wine, thanks.'

The man's disciplined lips were played over by a faint flicker of deprecation or irony, or both. 'Not any at all, sir?'

Medford smiled back. 'It's not out of respect for Prohibition.' He was sure that the man, of whatever nationality, would understand that; and he did.

'Oh, I didn't suppose, sir – '

'Well, no; but I've been rather seedy, and wine's forbidden.'

The servant remained incredulous. 'Just a little light Moselle, though, to colour the water, sir?'

'No wine at all,' said Medford, growing bored. He was still in the stage of convalescence when it is irritating to be argued with about one's dietary. 'Oh – what's your name, by the way?' he added, to soften the curtness of his refusal.

'Gosling,' said the other unexpectedly, though Medford didn't in the least know what he had expected him to be called.

'You're English, then?'

'Oh, yes, sir.'

'You've been in these parts a good many years, though?'

Yes, he had, Gosling said; rather too long for his own liking; and added that he had been born in Malta. 'But I know England well too.' His deprecating look returned. 'I will confess, sir, I'd like to have 'ad a look at Wembley.* Mr Almodham 'ad promised me – but there – ' As if to minimise the abandon of this confidence, he followed it up by a ceremonious request for Medford's keys, and an enquiry as to when he would like to dine. Having received a reply, he still lingered, looking more surprised than ever. 'Just a mineral water, then, sir?'

'Oh, yes – anything.'

'Shall we say a bottle of Perrier?'

Perrier in the desert! Medford smiled assentingly, surrendered his keys and strolled away.

The house turned out to be smaller than he had imagined, or at least the habitable part of it; for above this towered mighty dilapidated walls of yellow stone, and in their crevices clung plaster chambers, one above the other, cedar-beamed, crimson-shuttered but crumbling. Out of this jumble of masonry and stucco, Christian and Moslem, the latest tenant of the fortress had chosen a cluster of rooms tucked into an angle of the ancient keep. These apartments opened on the uppermost court, where the palms chattered and the fig tree coiled above the well. On the broken marble pavement, chairs and a low table were grouped, and a few geraniums and blue morning-glories had been coaxed to grow between the slabs.

A white-skirted boy with watchful eyes was watering the plants; but at Medford's approach he vanished like a wisp of vapour.

* A famous exhibition took place at Wembley in 1924.

There was something vaporous and insubstantial about the whole scene; even the long arcaded room opening on the court, furnished with saddlebag cushions, divans with gazelle skins and rough indigenous rugs; even the table piled with old copies of *The Times* and ultra-modern French and English reviews – all seemed, in that clear mocking air, born of the delusion of some desert wayfarer.

A seat under the fig tree invited Medford to doze, and when he woke the hard blue dome above him was gemmed with stars and the night breeze gossiped with the palms.

Rest – beauty – peace. Wise Almodham!

2

Wise Almodham! Having carried out – with somewhat disappointing results – the excavation with which an archaeological society had charged him twenty-five years ago, he had lingered on, taken possession of the Crusaders' stronghold, and turned his attention from ancient to medieval remains. But even these investigations, Medford suspected, he prosecuted only at intervals, when the enchantment of his leisure did not lie on him too heavily.

The young American had met Henry Almodham at Luxor the previous winter; had dined with him at old Colonel Swordsley's, on that perfumed starlit terrace above the Nile; and, having somehow awakened the archaeologist's interest, had been invited to look him up in the desert the following year.

They had spent only that one evening together, with old Swordsley blinking at them under memory-laden lids, and two or three charming women from the Winter Palace chattering and exclaiming; but the two men had ridden back to Luxor together in the moonlight, and during that ride Medford fancied he had puzzled out the essential lines of Henry Almodham's character. A nature saturnine yet sentimental; chronic indolence alternating with spurts of highly intelligent activity; gnawing self-distrust soothed by intimate self-appreciation; a craving for complete solitude coupled with the inability to tolerate it for long.

There was more, too, Medford suspected: a dash of Victorian romance, gratified by the setting, the remoteness, the inaccessibility of his retreat, and by being known as *the* Henry Almodham – 'the one who lives in a Crusaders' castle, you know' – the gradual imprisonment in a pose assumed in youth, and into which middle age had slowly stiffened; and something deeper, darker, too, perhaps, though the young man doubted that; probably just the fact that living in that particular way had brought healing to an old wound, an old mortification, something which years ago had touched a vital part and left him writhing. Above all, in Almodham's hesitating movements and the dreaming look of his long well-featured brown face with its shock of grey hair, Medford detected an inertia, mental and moral, which life in this castle of romance must have fostered and excused.

'Once here, how easy not to leave!' he mused, sinking deeper into his deep chair.

'Dinner, sir,' Gosling announced.

The table stood in an open arch of the living-room; shaded candles made a rosy pool in the dusk. Each time he emerged into their light the servant, white-jacketed, velvet-footed, looked more competent and more surprised than ever. Such dishes, too – the cook also a Maltese? Ah, they were geniuses, these Maltese! Gosling bridled, smiled his acknowledgment, and started to fill the guest's glass with Chablis.

'No wine,' said Medford patiently.

'Sorry, sir. But the fact is – '

'You said there was Perrier?'

'Yes, sir; but I find there's none left. It's been awfully hot, and Mr Almodham has been and drank it all up. The new supply isn't due till next week. We 'ave to depend on the caravans going south.'

'No matter. Water, then. I really prefer it.'

Gosling's surprise widened to amazement. 'Not water, sir? Water – in these parts?'

Medford's irritability stirred again. 'Something wrong with your water? Boil it then, can't you? I won't – ' He pushed away the half-filled wineglass.

'Oh – boiled? Certainly, sir.' The man's voice dropped almost to a whisper. He placed on the table a succulent mess of rice and mutton, and vanished.

Medford leaned back, surrendering himself to the night, the coolness, the ripple of wind in the palms.

One agreeable dish succeeded another. As the last appeared, the diner began to feel the pangs of thirst, and at the same moment a beaker of water was placed at his elbow. 'Boiled, sir, and I squeezed a lemon into it.'

'Right. I suppose at the end of the summer your water gets a bit muddy?'

'That's it, sir. But you'll find this all right, sir.'

Medford tasted. 'Better than Perrier.' He emptied the glass, leaned back and groped in his pocket. A tray was instantly at his hand with cigars and cigarettes.

'You don't – smoke sir?'

Medford, for answer, held up his cigar to the man's light. 'What do you call this?'

'Oh, just so. I meant the other style.' Gosling glanced discreetly at the opium pipes of jade and amber laid out on a low table.

Medford shrugged away the invitation – and wondered. Was that perhaps Almodham's other secret – or one of them? For he began to think there might be many; and all, he was sure, safely stored away behind Gosling's vigilant brow.

'No news yet of Mr Almodham?'

Gosling was gathering up the dishes with dexterous gestures. For a moment he seemed not to hear. Then – from beyond the candle gleam – 'News, sir? There couldn't 'ardly be, could there? There's no wireless in the desert, sir; not like London.' His respectful tone tempered the slight irony. 'But tomorrow evening ought to see him riding in.' Gosling paused, drew nearer, swept one of his swift hands across the table in pursuit of the last crumbs, and added tentatively: 'You'll surely be able, sir, to stay till then?'

Medford laughed. The night was too rich in healing; it sank on his spirit like wings. Time vanished, fret and trouble were no more. 'Stay, I'll stay a year if I have to!'

'Oh – a year?' Gosling echoed it playfully, gathered up the dessert dishes and was gone.

3

Medford had said that he would wait for Almodham a year; but the next morning he found that such arbitrary terms had lost their meaning. There were no time measures in a place like this. The silly face of his watch told its daily tale to emptiness. The wheeling of the constellations over those ruined walls marked only the revolutions of the earth; the spasmodic motions of man meant nothing.

The very fact of being hungry, that stroke of the inward clock, was minimised by the slightness of the sensation – just the ghost of a pang, that might have been quieted by dried fruit and honey. Life had the light monotonous smoothness of eternity.

Towards sunset Medford shook off this queer sense of other-whereness and climbed to the roof. Across the desert he spied for Almodham. Southward the Mountains of Alabaster hung like a blue veil lined with light. In the west a great column of fire shot up, spraying into plumy cloudlets which turned the sky to a fountain of rose-leaves, the sands beneath to gold.

No riders specked them. Medford watched in vain for his absent host till night fell, and the punctual Gosling invited him once more to table.

In the evening Medford absently fingered the ultra-modern reviews – three months old, and already so stale to the touch – then tossed them aside, flung himself on a divan and dreamed. Almodham must spend a lot of time dreaming; that was it. Then, just as he felt himself sinking down into torpor, he would be off on one of these dashes across the desert in quest of unknown ruins. Not such a bad life.

Gosling appeared with Turkish coffee in a cup cased in filigree.

'Are there any horses in the stable?' Medford suddenly asked.

'Horses? Only what you might call pack-horses, sir. Mr Almodham has the two best saddle-horses with him.'

'I was thinking I might ride out to meet him.'

Gosling considered. 'So you might, sir.'

'Do you know which way he went?'

'Not rightly, sir. The *caid*'s man was to guide them.'

'Them? Who went with him?'

'Just one of our men, sir. They've got the two thoroughbreds. There's a third, but he's lame.' Gosling paused. 'Do you know the trails, sir? Excuse me, but I don't think I ever saw you here before.'

'No,' Medford acquiesced, 'I've never been here before.'

'Oh, then' – Gosling's gesture added: 'In that case, even the best thoroughbred wouldn't help you.'

'I suppose he may still turn up tonight?'

'Oh, easily, sir. I expect to see you both breakfasting here tomorrow morning,' said Gosling cheerfully.

Medford sipped his coffee. 'You said you'd never seen me here before. How long have you been here yourself?'

Gosling answered instantly, as though the figures were never long out of his memory: 'Eleven years and seven months altogether, sir,'

'Nearly twelve years! That's a longish time.'

'Yes, it is.'

'And I don't suppose you often get away?'

Gosling was moving off with the tray. He halted, turned back, and said with sudden emphasis: 'I've never once been away. Not since Mr Almodham first brought me here.'

'Good Lord! Not a single holiday?'

'Not one, sir.'

'But Mr Almodham goes off occasionally. I met him at Luxor last year.'

'Just so, sir. But when he's here he needs me for himself; and when he's away he needs me to watch over the others. So you see – '

'Yes, I see. But it must seem to you devilish long.'

'It seems long, sir.'

'But the others? You mean they're not – wholly trustworthy?'

'Well, sir, they're just Arabs,' said Gosling with careless contempt.

'I see. And not a single old reliable among them?'

'The term isn't in their language, sir.'

Medford was busy lighting his cigar. When he looked up he found that Gosling still stood a few feet off.

'It wasn't as if it 'adn't been a promise, you know, sir,' he said, almost passionately.

'A promise?'

'To let me 'ave my holiday, sir. A promise – agine and agine.'

'And the time never came?'

'No, sir, the days just drifted by – '

'Ah. They would, here. Don't sit up for me,' Medford added. 'I think I shall wait up – wait for Mr Almodham.'

Gosling's stare widened. 'Here, sir? Here in the court?'

The young man nodded, and the servant stood still regarding him, turned by the moonlight to a white spectral figure, the unquiet ghost of a patient butler who might have died without his holiday.

'Down here in the court all night, sir? It's a lonely spot. I couldn't 'ear you if you was to call. You're best in bed, sir. The air's bad. You might bring your fever on again.'

Medford laughed and stretched himself in his long chair. 'Decidedly,' he thought, 'the fellow needs a change.' Aloud he remarked: 'Oh, I'm all right. It's you who are nervous, Gosling. When Mr Almodham comes back I mean to put in a word for you. You shall have your holiday.'

Gosling still stood motionless. For a minute he did not speak. 'You would, sir, you would?' He gasped it out on a high cracked note, and the last word ran into a laugh – a brief shrill cackle, the laugh of one long unused to such indulgences. 'Thank you, sir. Good-night, sir.' He was gone.

4

'You do boil my drinking-water, always?' Medford questioned, his hand clasping the glass without lifting it.

The tone was amicable, almost confidential; Medford felt that since his rash promise to secure a holiday for Gosling he and Gosling were on terms of real friendship.

'Boil it? Always, sir. Naturally.' Gosling spoke with a slight note of reproach, as though Medford's question implied a slur – unconscious, he hoped – on their newly established relation. He scrutinised Medford with his astonished eyes, in which a genuine concern showed itself through the glaze of professional indifference.

'Because, you know, my bath this morning – '

Gosling was in the act of receiving from the hands of a gliding Arab a fragrant dish of couscous. Under his breath he hissed to the native: 'You damned aboriginy, you, can't even 'old a dish steady? Ugh!' The Arab vanished before the imprecation, and Gosling, with a calm deliberate hand, set the dish before Medford. 'All alike, they are.' Fastidiously he wiped a trail of grease from his linen sleeve.

'Because, you know, my bath this morning simply stank,' said Medford, plunging fork and spoon into the dish.

'Your bath, sir?' Gosling stressed the word. Astonishment, to the exclusion of all other emotion, again filled his eyes as he rested them on Medford. 'Now, I wouldn't 'ave 'ad that 'appen for the world,' he said self-reproachfully.

'There's only the one well here, eh? The one in the court?'

Gosling aroused himself from absorbed consideration of the visitor's complaint. 'Yes, sir; only the one.'

'What sort of a well is it? Where does the water come from?'

'Oh, it's just a cistern, sir. Rainwater. There's never been any other here. Not that I ever knew it to fail; but at this season sometimes it does turn queer. Ask any o' them Arabs, sir; they'll tell you. Liars as they are, they won't trouble to lie about that.'

Medford was cautiously tasting the water in his glass. 'This seems all right,' he pronounced.

Sincere satisfaction was depicted on Gosling's countenance. 'I seen to its being boiled myself, sir. I always do. I 'ope that Perrier'll turn up tomorrow, sir.'

'Oh, tomorrow – ' Medford shrugged, taking a second helping. 'Tomorrow I may not be here to drink it.'

'What – going away, sir?' cried Gosling.

Medford, wheeling round abruptly, caught a new and incomprehensible look in Gosling's eyes. The man had seemed to feel a sort of dog-like affection for him; had wanted, Medford could have sworn, to keep him on, persuade him to patience and delay; yet now, Medford could equally have sworn, there was relief in his look, satisfaction, almost, in his voice.

'So soon, sir?'

'Well, this is the fifth day since my arrival. And as there's no news yet of Mr Almodham, and you say he may very well have forgotten all about my coming – '

'Oh, I don't say that, sir; not forgotten! Only, when one of those old piles of stones takes 'old of him, he does forget about

18

the time, sir. That's what I meant. The days drift by – 'e's in a dream. Very likely he thinks you're just due now, sir.' A small thin smile sharpened the lustreless gravity of Gosling's features. It was the first time that Medford had seen him smile.

'Oh, I understand. But still – ' Medford paused. Through the spell of inertia laid on him by the drowsy place and its easeful comforts his instinct of alertness was struggling back. 'It's odd – '

'What's odd?' Gosling echoed unexpectedly, setting the dried dates and figs on the table.

'Everything,' said Medford.

He leaned back in his chair and glanced up through the arch at the lofty sky from which noon was pouring down in cataracts of blue and gold. Almodham was out there somewhere under that canopy of fire, perhaps, as the servant said, absorbed in his dream. The land was full of spells.

'Coffee, sir?' Gosling reminded him. Medford took it.

'It's odd that you say you don't trust any of these fellows – these Arabs – and yet that you don't seem to feel worried at Mr Almodham's being off God knows where, all alone with them.'

Gosling received this attentively, impartially; he saw the point. 'Well, sir, no – you wouldn't understand. It's the very thing that can't be taught, when to trust 'em and when not. It's 'ow their interests lie, of course, sir; and their religion, as they call it.' His contempt was unlimited. 'But even to begin to understand why I'm not worried about Mr Almodham, you'd 'ave to 'ave lived among them, sir, and you'd 'ave to speak their language.'

'But I – ' Medford began. He pulled himself up short and bent above his coffee.

'Yes, sir.'

'But I've travelled among them more or less.'

'Oh, travelled!' Even Gosling's intonation could hardly conciliate respect with derision in his reception of this boast.

'This makes the fifth day, though,' Medford continued argumentatively. The midday heat lay heavy even on the shaded side of the court, and the sinews of his will were weakening.

'I can understand, sir, a gentleman like you 'aving other engagements – being pressed for time, as it were,' Gosling reasonably conceded.

He cleared the table, committed its freight to a pair of Arab arms that just showed and vanished, and finally took himself off while Medford sank into the divan. A land of dreams . . .

The afternoon hung over the place like a great velarium of cloth-of-gold stretched across the battlements and drooping down in ever slacker folds upon the heavy-headed palms. When at length the gold turned to violet, and the west to a bow of crystal clasping the desert sands, Medford shook off his sleep and wandered out. But this time, instead of mounting to the roof, he took another direction.

He was surprised to find how little he knew of the place after five days of loitering and waiting. Perhaps this was to be his last evening alone in it. He passed out of the court by a vaulted stone passage which led to another walled enclosure. At his approach two or three Arabs who had been squatting there rose and melted out of sight. It was as if the solid masonry had received them.

Beyond, Medford heard a stamping of hoofs, the stir of a stable at nightfall. He went under another archway and found himself among horses and mules. In the fading light an Arab was rubbing down one of the horses, a powerful young chestnut. He too seemed about to vanish; but Medford caught him by the sleeve.

'Go on with your work,' he said in Arabic.

The man, who was young and muscular, with a lean Bedouin face, stopped and looked at him.

'I didn't know your excellency spoke our language.'

'Oh, yes,' said Medford.

The man was silent, one hand on the horse's restless neck, the other thrust into his woollen girdle. He and Medford examined each other in the faint light.

'Is that the horse that's lame?' Medford asked.

'Lame?' The Arab's eyes ran down the animal's legs. 'Oh, yes; lame,' he answered vaguely.

Medford stooped and felt the horses knees and fetlocks. 'He seems pretty fit. Couldn't he carry me for a canter this evening if I felt like it?'

The Arab considered; he was evidently perplexed by the weight of responsibility which the question placed on him.

'Your excellency would like to go for a ride this evening?'

'Oh, just a fancy. I might or I might not.' Medford lit a cigarette and offered one to the groom, whose white teeth flashed his gratification. Over the shared match they drew nearer and the Arab's diffidence seemed to lessen.

'Is this one of Mr Almodham's own mounts?' Medford asked.

'Yes, sir; it's his favourite,' said the groom, his hand passing proudly down the horse's bright shoulder.

'His favourite? Yet he didn't take him on this long expedition?'

The Arab fell silent and stared at the ground.

'Weren't you surprised at that?' Medford queried.

The man's gesture declared that it was not his business to be surprised.

The two remained without speaking while the quick blue night descended.

At length Medford said carelessly: 'Where do you suppose your master is at this moment?'

The moon, unperceived in the radiant fall of day, had now suddenly possessed the world, and a broad white beam lay full on the Arab's white smock, his brown face and the turban of camel's hair knotted above it. His agitated eyeballs glistened like jewels.

'If Allah would vouchsafe to let us know!'

'But you suppose he's safe enough, don't you? You don't think it's necessary yet for a party to go out in search of him?'

The Arab appeared to ponder this deeply. The question must have taken him by surprise. He flung a brown arm about the horse's neck and continued to scrutinise the stones of the court.

'When the master is away, Mr Gosling is our master.'

'And he doesn't think it necessary?'

The Arab sighed: 'Not yet.'

'But if Mr Almodham were away much longer – '

The man was again silent, and Medford continued: 'You're the head groom, I suppose?'

'Yes, excellency.'

There was another pause. Medford half turned away; then over his shoulder: 'I suppose you know the direction Mr Almodham took? The place he's gone to?'

'Oh, assuredly, excellency.'

'Then you and I are going to ride after him. Be ready an hour before daylight. Say nothing to anyone – Mr Gosling or anybody else. We two ought to be able to find him without other help.'

The Arab's face was all a responsive flash of eyes and teeth. 'Oh, sir, I undertake that you and my master shall meet before tomorrow night. And none shall know of it.'

'He's as anxious about Almodham as I am,' Medford thought; and a faint shiver ran down his back. 'All right. Be ready,' he repeated.

He strolled back and found the court empty of life, but fantastically peopled by palms of beaten silver and a white marble fig tree.

'After all,' he thought irrelevantly, 'I'm glad I didn't tell Gosling that I speak Arabic.'

He sat down and waited till Gosling, approaching from the living-room, ceremoniously announced for the fifth time that dinner was served.

5

Medford sat up in bed with the jerk which resembles no other. Someone was in his room. The fact reached him not by sight or sound – for the moon had set, and the silence of the night was complete – but by a peculiar faint disturbance of the invisible currents that enclose us.

He was awake in an instant, caught up his electric hand-lamp and flashed it into two astonished eyes. Gosling stood above the bed.

'Mr Almodham – he's back?' Medford exclaimed.

'No, sir; he's not back.' Gosling spoke in low controlled tones. His extreme self-possession gave Medford a sense of danger – he couldn't say why, or of what nature. He sat upright, looking hard at the man.

'Then what's the matter?'

'Well, sir, you might have told me you talk Arabic' – Gosling's tone was now wistfully reproachful – 'before you got 'obnobbing with that Selim. Making randyvoos with 'im by night in the desert.'

Medford reached for his matches and lit the candle by the bed. He did not know whether to kick Gosling out of the room or to listen to what the man had to say; but a quick movement of curiosity made him determine on the latter course.

'Such folly! First I thought I'd lock you in. I might 'ave.' Gosling drew a key from his pocket and held it up. 'Or again I might 'ave let you go. Easier than not. But there was Wembley.'

'Wembley?' Medford echoed. He began to think that the man was going mad. One might, so conceivably, in that place of postponements and enchantments! He wondered whether Almodham himself were not a little mad – if, indeed, Almodham were still in a world where such a fate is possible.

'Wembley. You promised to get Mr Almodham to give me

an 'oliday – to let me go back to England in time for a look at Wembley. Every man 'as 'is fancies, 'asn't he, sir? And that's mine. I've told Mr Almodham so, agine and agine. He'd never listen, or only make believe to; say: "We'll see, now, Gosling, we'll see" – and no more 'eard of it. But you was different, sir. You said it, and I knew you meant it – about my 'oliday. So I'm going to lock you in.' Gosling spoke composedly, but with an under-thrill of emotion in his queer Mediterranean-Cockney voice.

'Lock me in?'

'Prevent you somehow from going off with that murderer. You don't suppose you'd ever 'ave come back alive from that ride, do you?'

A shiver ran over Medford, as it had the evening before when he had said to himself that the Arab was as anxious as he was about Almodham. He gave a slight laugh.

'I don't know what you're talking about. But you're not going to lock me in.'

The effect of this was unexpected. Gosling's face was drawn up into a convulsive grimace and two tears rose to his pale eyelashes and ran down his cheeks.

'You don't trust me, after all,' he said plaintively.

Medford leaned on his pillow and considered. Nothing as queer had ever before happened to him. The fellow looked almost ridiculous enough to laugh at; yet his tears were certainly not simulated. Was he weeping for Almodham, already dead, or for Medford, about to be committed to the same grave?

'I should trust you at once,' said Medford, 'if you'd tell me where your master is.'

Gosling's face resumed its usual guarded expression, though the trace of the tears still glittered on it.

'I can't do that, sir.'

'Ah, I thought so!'

'Because – 'ow do I know?'

24

Medford thrust a leg out of bed. One hand, under the blanket, lay on his revolver.

'Well, you may go now. Put that key down on the table first. And don't try to do anything to interfere with my plans. If you do I'll shoot you,' he added concisely.

'Oh, no, you wouldn't shoot a British subject; it makes such a fuss. Not that I'd care – I've often thought of doing it myself. Sometimes in the sirocco season. That don't scare me. And you shan't go.'

Medford was on his feet now, the revolver visible. Gosling eyed it with indifference.

'Then you do know where Mr Almodham is? And you're determined that I shan't find out?' Medford challenged him.

'Selim's determined,' said Gosling, 'and all the others are. They all want you out of the way. That's why I've kept 'em to their quarters – done all the waiting on you myself. Now will you stay here? For God's sake, sir! The return caravan is going through to the coast the day after tomorrow. Join it, sir – it's the only safe way! I darsn't let you go with one of our men, not even if you was to swear you'd ride straight for the coast and let this business be.'

'This business? What business?'

'This worrying about where Mr Almodham is, sir. Not that there's anything to worry about. The men all know that. But the plain fact is they've stolen some money from his box, since he's been gone, and if I hadn't winked at it they'd 'ave killed me; and all they want is to get you to ride out after 'im, and put you safe away under a 'eap of sand somewhere off the caravan trails. Easy job. There; that's all, sir. My word it is.'

There was a long silence. In the weak candlelight the two men stood considering each other.

Medford's wits began to clear as the sense of peril closed in on him. His mind reached out on all sides into the enfolding mystery, but it was everywhere impenetrable. The odd thing was that, though he did not believe half of what Gosling had told him, the man yet inspired him with a queer sense of confidence as far as their mutual relation was concerned. 'He may be lying about Almodham, to hide God knows what; but I don't believe he's lying about Selim.'

Medford laid his revolver on the table. 'Very well,' he said. 'I won't ride out to look for Mr Almodham, since you advise me not to. But I won't leave by the caravan; I'll wait here till he comes back.'

He saw Gosling whiten under his sallowness. 'Oh, don't do that, sir; I couldn't answer for them if you was to wait. The caravan'll take you to the coast the day after tomorrow as easy as if you was riding in Rotten Row.'

'Ah, then you know that Mr Almodham won't be back by the day after tomorrow?' Medford caught him up.

'I don't know anything, sir.'

'Not even where he is now?'

Gosling reflected. 'He's been gone too long, sir, for me to know that,' he said from the threshold.

The door closed on him.

Medford found sleep unrecoverable. He leaned in his window and watched the stars fade and the dawn break in all its holiness. As the stir of life rose among the ancient walls he marvelled at the contrast between that fountain of purity welling up into the heavens and the evil secrets clinging bat-like to the nest of masonry below.

He no longer knew what to believe or whom. Had some enemy of Almodham's lured him into the desert and bought the connivance of his people? Or had the servants had some reason of their own for spiriting him away, and was Gosling possibly telling the truth when he said that the same fate would befall Medford if he refused to leave?

Medford, as the light brightened, felt his energy return. The very impenetrableness of the mystery stimulated him. He would stay, and he would find out the truth.

6

It was always Gosling himself who brought up the water for Medford's bath; but this morning he failed to appear with it, and when he came it was to bring the breakfast tray. Medford noticed that his face was of a pasty pallor, and that his lids were reddened as if with weeping. The contrast was unpleasant, and a dislike for Gosling began to shape itself in the young man's breast.

'My bath?' he queried.

'Well, sir, you complained yesterday of the water – '

'Can't you boil it?'

'I 'ave, sir.'

'Well, then – '

Gosling went out sullenly and presently returned with a brass jug. 'It's the time of year – we're dying for rain,' he grumbled, pouring a scant measure of water into the tub.

Yes, the well must be pretty low, Medford thought. Even boiled, the water had the disagreeable smell that he had noticed the day before, though of course, in a slighter degree. But a bath was a necessity in that climate. He splashed the few cupfuls over himself as best as he could.

He spent the day in rather fruitlessly considering his situation. He had hoped the morning would bring counsel, but it brought only courage and resolution, and these were of small use without enlightenment. Suddenly he remembered that the caravan going south from the coast would pass near the castle that afternoon. Gosling had dwelt on the date often enough, for it was the caravan which was to bring the box of Perrier water.

'Well, I'm not sorry for that,' Medford reflected, with a slight shrinking of the flesh. Something sick and viscous, half smell, half substance, seemed to have clung to his skin since his morning bath, and the idea of having to drink that water again was nauseating.

But his chief reason for welcoming the caravan was the hope

of finding in it some European, or at any rate some native official from the coast, to whom he might confide his anxiety. He hung about, listening and waiting, and then mounted to the roof to gaze northward along the trail. But in the afternoon glow he saw only three Bedouins guiding laden pack mules towards the castle.

As they mounted the steep path he recognised some of Almodham's men, and guessed at once that the southward caravan trail did not actually pass under the walls and that the men had been out to meet it, probably at a small oasis behind some fold of the sand-hills. Vexed at his own thoughtlessness in not foreseeing such a possibility, Medford dashed down to the court, hoping the men might have brought back some news of Almodham, though, as the latter had ridden south, he could at best only have crossed the trail by which the caravan had come. Still, even so, someone might know something, some report might have been heard – since everything was always known in the desert.

As Medford reached the court, angry vociferations, and retorts as vehement, rose from the stable-yard. He leaned over the wall and listened. Hitherto nothing had surprised him more than the silence of the place. Gosling must have had a strong arm to subdue the shrill voices of his underlings. Now they had all broken loose, and it was Gosling's own voice – usually so discreet and measured – which dominated them.

Gosling, master of all the desert dialects, was cursing his subordinates in a half-dozen.

'And you didn't bring it – and you tell me it wasn't there, and I tell you it was, and that you know it, and that you either left it on a sand-heap while you were jawing with some of those slimy fellows from the coast, or else fastened it on to the horse so carelessly that it fell off on the way – and all of you too sleepy to notice. Oh, you sons of females I wouldn't soil my lips by naming! Well, back you go to hunt it up, that's all.'

'By Allah and the tomb of his Prophet, you wrong us unpardonably. There was nothing left at the oasis, nor yet dropped off on the way back. It was not there, and that is the truth in its purity.'

'Truth! Purity! You miserable lot of shirks and liars, you – and the gentleman here not touching a drop of anything but water – as you profess to do, you liquor-swilling humbugs!'

Medford drew back from the parapet with a smile of relief. It was nothing but a case of Perrier – the missing case – which had raised the passions of these grown men to the pitch of frenzy! The anti-climax lifted a load from his breast. If Gosling, the calm and self-controlled, could waste his wrath on so slight a hitch in the working of the commissariat, he at least must have a free mind. How absurd this homely incident made Medford's speculations seem!

He was at once touched by Gosling's solicitude, and annoyed that he should have been so duped by the hallucinating fancies of the East.

Almodham was off on his own business; very likely the men knew where and what the business was; and even if they had robbed him in his absence, and quarrelled over the spoils, Medford did not see what he could do. It might even be that his eccentric host – with whom, after all, he had had but one evening's acquaintance – repenting an invitation too rashly given, had ridden away to escape the boredom of entertaining him. As this alternative occurred to Medford it seemed so plausible that he began to wonder if Almodham had not simply withdrawn to some secret suite of that intricate dwelling, and were waiting there for his guest's departure.

So well would this explain Gosling's solicitude to see the visitor off – so completely account for the man's nervous and contradictory behaviour – that Medford, smiling at his own obtuseness, hastily resolved to leave on the morrow. Tranquillised by this decision, he lingered about the court till dusk fell, and then, as usual, went up to the roof. But today his eyes, instead of raking the horizon, fastened on the clustering edifice of which, after six days' residence, he knew so little. Aerial chambers, jutting out at capricious angles, baffled him with closely shuttered windows, or here and there with the enigma of painted panes. Behind which window was his host concealed, spying, it might be, at this very moment on the movements of his lingering guest?

The idea that that strange moody man, with his long brown face and shock of white hair, his half-guessed selfishness and tyranny, and his morbid self-absorption, might be actually within a stone's throw, gave Medford, for the first time, a sharp sense of isolation. He felt himself shut out, unwanted – the place, now that he imagined someone might be living in it unknown to him, became lonely, inhospitable, dangerous.

'Fool that I am – he probably expected me to pack up and go as soon as I found he was away!' the young man reflected. Yes; decidedly he would leave the next morning.

Gosling had not shown himself all the afternoon. When at length, belatedly, he came to set the table, he wore a look of sullen, almost surly, reserve which Medford had not yet seen on his face. He hardly returned the young man's friendly, 'Hello – dinner?' and when Medford was seated handed him the first dish in silence. Medford's glass remained unfilled till he touched its brim.

'Oh, there's nothing to drink, sir. The men lost the case of Perrier – or dropped it and smashed the bottles. They say it never came. 'Ow do I know, when they never open their 'eathen lips but to lie?' Gosling burst out with sudden violence.

He set down the dish he was handing, and Medford saw that he had been obliged to do so because his whole body was shaking as if with fever.

'My dear man, what does it matter? You're going to be ill,' Medford exclaimed, laying his hand on the servant's arm. But the latter, muttering: 'Oh, God, if I'd only 'a' gone for it myself,' jerked away and vanished from the room.

Medford sat pondering; it certainly looked as if poor Gosling were on the edge of a breakdown. No wonder, when Medford himself was so oppressed by the uncanniness of the place. Gosling reappeared after an interval, correct, close-lipped, with the dessert and a bottle of white wine. 'Sorry, sir.'

To pacify him, Medford sipped the wine and then pushed his chair away and returned to the court. He was making for the fig tree by the well when Gosling, slipping ahead, transferred his chair and wicker table to the other end of the court.

'You'll be better here – there'll be a breeze presently,' he said. 'I'll fetch your coffee.'

He disappeared again, and Medford sat gazing up at the pile of masonry and plaster, and wondering whether he had not been moved away from his favourite corner to get him out of – or into? – the angle of vision of the invisible watcher. Gosling, having brought the coffee, went away and Medford sat on.

At length he rose and began to pace up and down as he smoked. The moon was not up yet, and darkness fell solemnly on the ancient walls. Presently the breeze arose and began its secret commerce with the palms.

Medford went back to his seat; but as soon as he had resumed it he fancied that the gaze of his hidden watcher was jealously fixed on the red spark of his cigar. The sensation became increasingly distasteful; he could almost feel Almodham reaching out long ghostly arms from somewhere above him in the darkness. He moved back into the living-room, where a shaded light hung from the ceiling; but the room was airless, and finally he went out again and dragged his seat to its old place under the fig tree. From there the windows which he suspected could not command him, and he felt easier, though the corner was out of the breeze and the heavy air seemed tainted with the exhalation of the adjoining well.

'The water must be very low,' Medford mused. The smell, though faint, was unpleasant; it smirched the purity of the night. But he felt safer there, somehow, farther from those unseen eyes which seemed mysteriously to have become his enemies.

'If one of the men had knifed me in the desert, I shouldn't wonder if it would have been at Almodham's orders,' Medford thought. He drowsed.

When he woke the moon was pushing up its ponderous orange disk above the walls, and the darkness in the court was less dense. He must have slept for an hour or more. The night was delicious, or would have been anywhere but there. Medford felt a shiver of his old fever and remembered that Gosling had warned him that the court was unhealthy at night.

'On account of the well, I suppose. I've been sitting too close to it,' he reflected. His head ached, and he fancied that the sweetish foulish smell clung to his face as it had after his bath. He stood up and approached the well to see how much water was left in it. But the moon was not yet high enough to light those depths, and he peered down into blackness.

Suddenly he felt both shoulders gripped from behind and forcibly pressed forward, as if by someone seeking to push him over the edge. An instant later, almost coinciding with his own swift resistance, the push became a strong tug backwards, and he swung round to confront Gosling, whose hands immediately dropped from his shoulders.

'I thought you had the fever, sir – I seemed to see you pitching over,' the man stammered.

Medford's wits returned. 'We must both have it, for I fancied you were pitching me,' he said with a laugh.

'Me, sir?' Gosling gasped. 'I pulled you back as 'ard as ever – '

'Of course. I know.'

'Whatever are you doing here, anyhow, sir? I warned you it was un'ealthy at night,' Gosling continued irritably.

Medford leaned against the well-head and contemplated him. 'I believe the whole place is unhealthy.'

Gosling was silent. At length he asked: 'Aren't you going up to bed, sir?'

'No,' said Medford, 'I prefer to stay here.'

Gosling's face took on an expression of dogged anger. 'Well, then, I prefer that you shouldn't.'

Medford laughed again. 'Why? Because it's the hour when Mr Almodham comes out to take the air?'

The effect of this question was unexpected. Gosling dropped back a step or two and flung up his hands, pressing them to his lips as if to stifle a low outcry.

'What's the matter?' Medford queried. The man's antics were beginning to get on his nerves.

'Matter?' Gosling still stood away from him, out of the rising slant of moonlight.

'Come! Own up that he's here and have done with it!' cried Medford impatiently.

'Here? What do you mean by "here"? You 'aven't seen 'im, 'ave you?' Before the words were out of the man's lips he flung up his arms again, stumbled forward and fell in a heap at Medford's feet.

Medford, still leaning against the well-head, smiled down contemptuously at the stricken wretch. His conjecture had been the right one, then; he had not been Gosling's dupe after all.

'Get up, man. Don't be a fool! It's not your fault if I guessed that Mr Almodham walks here at night – '

'Walks here!' wailed the other, still cowering.

'Well, doesn't he? He won't kill you for owning up will he?'

'Kill me? Kill me? I wish I'd killed *you*!' Gosling half got to his feet, his head thrown back in ashen terror. 'And I might 'ave, too, so easy! You felt me pushing of you over, didn't you? Coming 'ere spying and sniffing – ' His anguish seemed to choke him.

Medford had not changed his position. The very abjectness of the creature at his feet gave him an easy sense of power. But Gosling's last cry had suddenly deflected the course of his speculations. Almodham was here, then; that was certain; but just where was he, and in what shape? A new fear scuttled down Medford's spine.

'So you did want to push me over?' he said. 'Why? As the quickest way of joining your master?'

The effect was more immediate than he had foreseen.

Gosling, getting to his feet, stood there bowed and shrunken in the accusing moonlight.

'Oh, God – and I 'ad you 'arf over! You know I did! And then – it was what you said about Wembley. So help me, sir, I felt you meant it, and it 'eld me back.' The man's face was again wet with tears, but this time Medford recoiled from them as if they had been drops splashed up by a falling body from the foul waters below.

Medford was silent. He did not know if Gosling were armed or not, but he was no longer afraid; only aghast, and yet shudderingly lucid.

Gosling continued to ramble on half deliriously: 'And if only that Perrier 'ad of come. I don't believe it'd ever 'ave crossed your mind, if only you'd 'ave had your Perrier regular, now would it? But you say 'e walks – and I knew he would! Only – what was I to do with him, with you turning up like that the very day?'

Still Medford did not move.

'And 'im driving me to madness, sir, sheer madness, that same morning. Will you believe it? The very week before you come, I was to sail for England and 'ave my 'oliday, a 'ole month, sir – and I was entitled to six, if there was any justice – a 'ole month in 'Ammersmith, sir, in a cousin's 'ouse, and the chance to see Wembley thoroughly; and then 'e 'eard you was coming, sir, and 'e was bored and lonely 'ere, you understand – 'e 'ad to have new excitements provided for 'im or 'e'd go off 'is bat – and when 'e 'eard you was coming, 'e come out of his black mood in a flash and was 'arf crazy with pleasure, and said, "I'll keep 'im 'ere all winter – a remarkable young man, Gosling – just my kind." And when I says to him: "And 'ow about my 'oliday?" he stares at me with those stony eyes of 'is and says: "Oliday? Oh, to be sure; why next year – we'll see what can be done about it next year." Next year, sir, as if 'e was doing me a favour! And that's the way it 'ad been for nigh on twelve years.

'But this time, if you 'adn't 'ave come I do believe I'd 'ave got away, for he was getting used to 'aving Selim about 'im and his 'ealth was never better – and, well, I told 'im as much, and 'ow a man 'ad his rights after all, and my youth was going, and me that 'ad served him so well chained up 'ere like 'is watchdog, and always next year and next year – and, well, sir, 'e just laughed, sneering-like, and lit 'is cigarette. "Oh, Gosling, cut it out," 'e says.

'He was standing on the very spot where you are now, sir; and he turned to walk into the 'ouse. And it was then I 'it 'im. He was a heavy man, and he fell against the well kerb. And just when you were expected any minute – oh, my God!'

Gosling's voice died out in a strangled murmur.

Medford, at his last words, had unvoluntarily shrunk back a few feet. The two men stood in the middle of the court and stared at each other without speaking. The moon, swinging high above the battlements, sent a searching spear of light down into the guilty darkness of the well.

CHARLES DICKENS

Charles Dickens (1812–70) was perhaps the greatest novelist of
the nineteenth century. All his novels are still in print and they
present a rich canvas of life and behaviour at all levels of
contemporary society. Many of his works, such as *Oliver Twist*,
Great Expectations, *David Copperfield*, *A Tale of Two Cities* and
A Christmas Carol, have been filmed, televised and presented as
both straight plays and musicals, revealing the power and the
timelessness of his writing.

The Black Veil

One winter's evening, towards the close of the year 1800, or
within a year or two of that time, a young medical practitioner,
recently established in business, was seated by a cheerful fire in
his little parlour, listening to the wind which was beating the
rain in pattering drops against the window or rumbling dismally
in the chimney. The night was wet and cold; he had been
walking through mud and water the whole day, and was now
comfortably reposing in his dressing-gown and slippers, more
than half asleep and less than half awake, revolving a thousand
matters in his wandering imagination. First, he thought how
hard the wind was blowing and how the cold, sharp rain would
be at that moment beating in his face if he were not comfortably
housed at home. Then, his mind reverted to his annual Christmas visit to his native place and dearest friends; he thought how
glad they would all be to see him, and how happy it would make
Rose if he could only tell her that he had found a patient at last,
and hoped to have more and to come down again, in a few

months' time, and marry her, and take her home to gladden his lonely fireside and stimulate him to fresh exertions. Then he began to wonder when his first patient would appear or whether he was destined, by a special dispensation of providence, never to have any patients at all; and then he thought about Rose again, and dropped to sleep and dreamed about her, till the tones of her sweet merry voice sounded in his ears and her soft tiny hand rested on his shoulder.

There *was* a hand upon his shoulder, but it was neither soft nor tiny, its owner being a corpulent round-headed boy who, in consideration of the sum of one shilling per week and his food, was let out by the parish to carry medicine and messages. As there was no demand for the medicine, however, and no necessity for the messages, he usually occupied his unemployed hours – averaging fourteen a day – in abstracting peppermint drops, taking animal nourishment and going to sleep.

'A lady, sir – a lady!' whispered the boy, rousing his master with a shake.

'What lady?' cried our friend, starting up, not quite certain that his dream was an illusion and half expecting that it might be Rose herself. 'What lady? Where?'

'*There*, sir!' replied the boy, pointing to the glass door leading into the surgery, with an expression of alarm which the very unusual apparition of a customer might have tended to excite.

The surgeon looked towards the door and started himself, for an instant, on beholding the appearance of his unlooked-for visitor.

It was a singularly tall woman, dressed in deep mourning and standing so close to the door that her face almost touched the glass. The upper part of her figure was carefully muffled in a black shawl, as if for the purpose of concealment; and her face was shrouded by a thick black veil. She stood perfectly erect; her figure was drawn up to its full height, and though the surgeon *felt* that the eyes beneath the veil were fixed on him,

37

she stood perfectly motionless, and evinced, by no gesture whatever, the slightest consciousness of his having turned towards her.

'Do you wish to consult me?' he enquired, with some hesitation, holding open the door. It opened inwards, and therefore the action did not alter the position of the figure, which still remained motionless on the same spot.

She slightly inclined her head, in token of acquiescence.

'Pray walk in,' said the surgeon.

The figure moved a step forward; and then, turning its head in the direction of the boy – to his infinite horror – appeared to hesitate.

'Leave the room, Tom,' said the young man, addressing the boy, whose large round eyes had been extended to their utmost width during this brief interview. 'Draw the curtain, and shut the door.'

The boy drew a green curtain across the glass part of the door, retired into the surgery, closed the door after him, and immediately applied one of his large eyes to the keyhole on the other side.

The surgeon drew a chair to the fire and motioned the visitor to a seat. The mysterious figure slowly moved towards it. As the blaze shone upon the black dress, the surgeon observed that the bottom of it was saturated with mud and rain.

'You are very wet,' he said.

'I am,' said the stranger, in a low deep voice.

'And you are ill?' added the surgeon, compassionately, for the tone was that of a person in pain.

'I am,' was the reply – 'very ill; not bodily, but mentally. It is not for myself, or on my own behalf,' continued the stranger, 'that I come to you. If I laboured under bodily disease, I should not be out, alone, at such an hour or on such a night as this; and if I were afflicted with it, twenty-four hours hence, God knows how gladly I would lie down and pray to die. It is for another that I beseech your aid, sir. I may be mad to ask it for him – I think I am; but, night after night, through the long dreary hours of watching and weeping, the thought has been ever present to my mind; and though even I see the hopelessness of human assistance availing him, the bare thought of laying him in his grave without it makes my blood run cold!' And a shudder, such as the surgeon well knew art could not produce, trembled through the speaker's frame.

There was a desperate earnestness in this woman's manner that went to the young man's heart. He was young in his profession and had not yet witnessed enough of the miseries which are daily presented before the eyes of its members to have grown comparatively callous to human suffering.

'If,' he said, rising hastily, 'the person of whom you speak be in so hopeless a condition as you describe, not a moment is to be lost. I will go with you instantly. Why did you not obtain medical advice before?'

'Because it would have been useless before – because it is useless even now,' replied the woman, clasping her hands passionately.

The surgeon gazed, for a moment, on the black veil, as if to ascertain the expression of the features beneath it: its thickness, however, rendered such a result impossible.

'You *are* ill,' he said, gently, 'although you do not know it. The fever which has enabled you to bear, without feeling it, the fatigue you have evidently undergone, is burning within you now. Put that to your lips,' he continued, pouring out a glass of water – 'compose yourself for a few moments, and then tell me, as calmly as you can, what the disease of the patient is and how long he has been ill. When I know what it is necessary I should know to render my visit serviceable to him, I am ready to accompany you.'

The stranger lifted the glass of water to her mouth, without raising the veil; put it down again untasted; and burst into tears.

'I know,' she said, sobbing aloud, 'that what I say to you now

39

seems like the ravings of fever. I have been told so before, less kindly than by you. I am not a young woman; and they do say that as life steals on towards its final close, the last short remnant, worthless as it may seem to all beside, is dearer to its possessor than all the years that have gone before, connected though they be with the recollection of old friends long since dead and young ones – children perhaps – who have fallen off from and forgotten one as completely as if they had died too. My natural term of life cannot be many years longer and should be dear on that account; but I would lay it down without a sigh – with cheerfulness – with joy – if what I tell you now were only false or imaginary. Tomorrow morning he of whom I speak will be I *know*, though I would fain think otherwise, beyond the reach of human aid; and yet, tonight, though he is in deadly peril, you must not see and could not serve him.'

'I am unwilling to increase your distress,' said the surgeon, after a short pause, 'by making any comment on what you have just said, or appearing desirous to investigate a subject you are so anxious to conceal; but there is an inconsistency in your statement which I cannot reconcile with probability. This person is dying tonight, and I cannot see him when my assistance might possibly avail; you apprehend it will be useless tomorrow, and yet you would have me see him then! If he be, indeed, as dear to you as your words and manner would imply, why not try to save his life before delay and the progress of his disease render it impracticable?'

'God help me!' exclaimed the woman, weeping bitterly, 'how can I hope strangers will believe what appears incredible, even to myself? You will *not* see him then, sir?' she added, rising suddenly.

'I did not say that I declined to see him,' replied the surgeon; 'but I warn you that if you persist in this extraordinary procrastination, and the individual dies, a fearful responsibility rests with you.'

'The responsibility will rest heavily somewhere,' replied the stranger bitterly. 'Whatever responsibility rests with me, I am content to bear and ready to answer.'

'As I incur none,' continued the surgeon, 'by acceding to your request, I will see him in the morning, if you leave me the address. At what hour can he be seen?'

'*Nine*,' replied the stranger.

'You must excuse my pressing these enquiries,' said the surgeon, 'but is he in your charge now?'

'He is not,' was the rejoinder.

'Then if I gave you instructions for his treatment through the night, you could not assist him?'

The woman wept bitterly, as she replied, 'I could not.'

Finding that there was but little prospect of obtaining more information by prolonging the interview, and anxious to spare the woman's feelings, which, subdued at first by a violent effort, were now irrepressible and most painful to witness, the surgeon repeated his promise of calling in the morning at the appointed hour. His visitor, after giving him a direction to an obscure part of Walworth, left the house in the same mysterious manner in which she had entered it.

It will be readily believed that so extraordinary a visit produced a considerable impression on the mind of the young surgeon; and that he speculated a great deal and to very little purpose on the possible circumstances of the case. In common with the generality of people, he had often heard and read of singular instances in which a presentiment of death, at a particular day or even minute, had been entertained and realised. At one moment he was inclined to think that the present might be such a case; but, then, it occurred to him that all the anecdotes of the kind he had ever heard were of persons who had been troubled with a foreboding of their own death. This woman, however, spoke of another person – a man; and it was impossible to suppose that a mere dream or delusion of fancy would induce her to speak of his approaching dissolution with such terrible certainty as she had spoken. It could not be that the man was to be murdered in the morning, and that the woman, originally a consenting party, and bound to secrecy by an oath, had relented, and, though unable to prevent the commission of some outrage on the victim, had determined to prevent his death if possible by the timely interposition of medical aid? The idea of such things happening within two miles of the metropolis appeared too wild and preposterous to be entertained beyond the instant. Then his original impression that the woman's intellects were disordered recurred; and, as it was the only mode of solving the difficulty with any degree of satisfaction, he obstinately made up his mind to believe that she was mad. Certain misgivings upon this point, however, stole upon his thoughts at the time, and presented themselves again and again through the long dull course of a sleepless night; during which, in spite of all his efforts to the contrary, he was unable to banish the black veil from his disturbed imagination.

The back part of Walworth, at its greatest distance from town, is a straggling miserable place enough, even in these days; but, five-and-thirty years ago, the greater portion of it was little better than a dreary waste, inhabited by a few scattered people of questionable character, whose poverty prevented their living in any better neighbourhood or whose pursuits and mode of life rendered its solitude desirable. Very many of the houses which have since sprung up on all sides were not built until some years afterwards; and the great majority even of those which were sprinkled about, at irregular intervals, were of the rudest and most miserable description.

The appearance of the place through which he walked in the morning was not calculated to raise the spirits of the young surgeon, or to dispel any feeling of anxiety or depression which the singular kind of visit he was about to make had awakened. Striking off from the high road, his way lay across a marshy common, through irregular lanes, with here and there a ruinous and dismantled cottage fast falling to pieces with decay and neglect. A stunted tree or pool of stagnant water, roused into a sluggish action by the heavy rain of the preceding night, skirted the path occasionally; and, now and then, a miserable patch of garden-ground, with a few old boards knocked together for a summerhouse and old palings imperfectly mended with stakes pilfered from the neighbouring hedges, bore testimony at once to the poverty of the inhabitants and the little scruple they entertained in appropriating the property of other people to their own use. Occasionally, a filthy-looking woman would make her appearance from the door of a dirty house, to empty the contents of some cooking utensil into the gutter in front or to scream after a little slipshod girl who had contrived to stagger a few yards from the door under the weight of a sallow infant almost as big as herself; but scarcely anything was stirring around; and so much of the prospect as could be faintly traced through the cold damp mist which hung heavily over it presented a lonely and dreary appearance perfectly in keeping with the objects we have described.

After plodding wearily through the mud and mire; making many enquiries for the place to which he had been directed; and receiving as many contradictory and unsatisfactory replies in return; the young man at length arrived before the house which had been pointed out to him as the object of his destination. It was a small low building, one storey above the ground, with even a more desolate and unpromising exterior than any he had yet passed. An old yellow curtain was closely drawn across the window upstairs, and the parlour shutters were closed, but not fastened. The house was detached from any other, and, as it stood at an angle of a narrow lane, there was no other habitation in sight.

When we say that the surgeon hesitated and walked a few paces beyond the house before he could prevail upon himself to lift the knocker, we say nothing that need raise a smile upon the face of the boldest reader. The police of London were a very different body in that day; the isolated position of the suburbs, when the rage for building and the progress of improvement had not yet begun to connect them with the main body of the city and its environs, rendered many of them (and this in particular) a place of resort for the worst and most depraved characters. Even the streets in the gayest parts of London were imperfectly lighted at that time; and such places as these were left entirely to the mercy of the moon and stars. The chances of detecting desperate characters, or of tracing them to their haunts, were thus rendered very few, and their offences naturally increased in boldness as the consciousness of comparative security became the more impressed upon them by daily experience. Added to these considerations, it must be remembered that the young man had spent some time in the public hospitals of the metropolis; and, although neither Burke nor Bishop had then gained a horrible notoriety, his own observation might have suggested to him how easily the atrocities to which the former has since given his name might be committed. Be this as it may, whatever reflection made him hesitate, he *did* hesitate: but, being a young man of strong mind and great personal courage, it was only for an instant – he stepped briskly back and knocked gently at the door.

A low whispering was audible, immediately afterwards, as if some person at the end of the passage were conversing stealthily with another on the landing above. It was succeeded by the noise of a pair of heavy boots upon the bare floor. The door-chain was softly unfastened; the door opened; and a tall, ill-favoured man, with black hair and a face, as the surgeon often declared afterwards, as pale and haggard as the countenance of any dead man he ever saw, presented himself.

'Walk in, sir,' he said in a low tone.

The surgeon did so, and the man having secured the door

again, by the chain, led the way to a small back parlour at the extremity of the passage.

'Am I in time?'

'Too soon!' replied the man. The surgeon turned hastily round, with a gesture of astonishment not unmixed with alarm, which he found it impossible to repress.

'If you'll step in here, sir,' said the man, who had evidently noticed the action – 'if you'll step in here, sir, you won't be detained five minutes, I assure you.'

The surgeon at once walked into the room. The man closed the door and left him alone.

It was a little cold room, with no other furniture than two deal chairs and a table of the same material. A handful of fire, unguarded by any fender, was burning in the grate, which brought out the damp if it served no more comfortable purpose, for the unwholesome moisture was stealing down the walls in long slug-like tracks. The window, which was broken and patched in many places, looked into a small enclosed piece of ground almost covered with water. Not a sound was to be heard, either within the house or without. The young surgeon sat down by the fireplace to await the result of his first professional visit.

He had not remained in this position many minutes when the noise of some approaching vehicle struck his ear. It stopped; the street-door was opened; a low talking succeeded, accompanied with a shuffling noise of footsteps along the passage and on the stairs, as if two or three men were engaged in carrying some heavy body to the room above. The creaking of the stairs, a few seconds afterwards, announced that the newcomers having completed their task, whatever it was, were leaving the house. The door was again closed, and the former silence was restored.

Another five minutes had elapsed, and the surgeon had resolved to explore the house in search of someone to whom he might make his errand known, when the room-door opened and his last night's visitor, dressed in exactly the same manner, with the veil lowered as before, motioned him to advance. The singular height of her form, coupled with the circumstance of her not speaking, caused the idea to pass across his brain for an instant that it might be a man disguised in woman's attire. The hysteric sobs which issued from beneath the veil, and the convulsive attitude of grief of the whole figure, however, at once exposed the absurdity of the suspicion; and he hastily followed.

The woman led the way upstairs to the front room and paused at the door to let him enter first. It was scantily furnished with an old deal box, a few chairs, and a tent bedstead, without hangings or cross-rails, which was covered with a patchwork counterpane. The dim light admitted through the curtain which he had noticed from the outside rendered the objects in the room so indistinct, and communicated to all of them so uniform a hue, that he did not, at first, perceive the object on which his eye at once rested when the woman rushed frantically past him and flung herself on her knees by the bedside.

Stretched upon the bed, closely enveloped in a linen wrapper and covered with blankets, lay a human form, stiff and motionless. The head and face, which were those of a man, were uncovered, save by a bandage which passed over the head and under the chin. The eyes were closed. The left arm lay heavily across the bed and the woman held the passive hand.

The surgeon gently pushed the woman aside and took the hand in his.

'My God!' he exclaimed, letting it fall involuntarily – 'the man is dead!'

The woman started to her feet and beat her hands together.

'Oh! don't say so, sir,' she exclaimed, with a burst of passion amounting almost to frenzy. 'Oh! don't say so, sir! I can't bear it! Men have been brought to life before, when unskilful people have given them up for lost; and men have died who might have been restored if proper means had been resorted to. Don't let him lie here, sir, without one effort to save him! This very moment life may be passing away. Do try, sir – do, for heaven's sake!' – And while speaking, she hurriedly chafed first the forehead and then the breast of the senseless form before her; and then wildly beat the cold hands, which, when she ceased to hold them, fell listlessly and heavily back on the coverlet.

'It is of no use, my good woman,' said the surgeon, soothingly, as he withdrew his hand from the man's breast. 'Stay – undraw that curtain!'

'Why?' said the woman, starting up.

'Undraw that curtain!' repeated the surgeon in an agitated tone.

'I darkened the room on purpose,' said the woman, throwing herself before him as he rose to undraw it. – 'Oh! sir, have pity on me! If it can be of no use, and he is really dead, do not expose that form to other eyes than mine!'

'This man died no natural or easy death,' said the surgeon. 'I *must* see the body!' With a motion so sudden that the woman hardly knew that he had slipped from beside her, he tore open the curtain, admitted the full light of day and returned to the bedside.

'There has been violence here,' he said, pointing towards the body and gazing intently on the face from which the black veil was now, for the first time, removed. In the excitement of a minute before, the female had thrown off the bonnet and veil, and now stood with her eyes fixed upon him. Her features were those of a woman about fifty, who had once been handsome. Sorrow and weeping had left traces upon them which not time itself would ever have produced without their aid; her face was deadly pale; and there was a nervous contortion of the lip and an unnatural fire in her eye which showed too plainly that her bodily and mental powers had nearly sunk beneath an accumulation of misery.

47

'There has been violence here,' said the surgeon, preserving his searching glance.

'There has!' replied the woman.

'This man has been murdered.'

'That I call God to witness he has,' said the woman, passionately; 'pitilessly, inhumanly murdered!'

'By whom?' said the surgeon, seizing the woman by the arm.

'Look at the butchers' marks, and then ask me!' she replied.

The surgeon turned his face towards the bed and bent over the body which now lay full in the light of the window. The throat was swollen and a livid mark encircled it. The truth flashed suddenly upon him.

'This is the man who was hanged this morning!' he exclaimed, turning away with a shudder.

'It is,' replied the woman, with a cold, unmeaning stare.

'Who was he?' enquired the surgeon.

'*My son*,' rejoined the woman; and fell senseless at his feet.

It was true. A companion, equally guilty with himself, had been acquitted for want of evidence; and this man had been left for death, and executed. To recount the circumstances of the case, at this distant period, must be unnecessary, and might give pain to some persons still alive. The history was an everyday one. The mother was a widow without friends or money, and had denied herself necessaries to bestow them on her orphan boy. That boy, unmindful of her prayers and forgetful of the sufferings she had endured for him – incessant anxiety of mind and voluntary starvation of body – had plunged into a career of dissipation and crime. And this was the result; his own death by the hangman's hands, and his mother's shame and incurable insanity.

For many years after this occurrence, and when profitable and arduous avocations would have led many men to forget that such a miserable being existed, the young surgeon was a daily visitor at the side of the harmless madwoman; not only soothing her by his presence and kindness, but alleviating the rigour of her condition by pecuniary donations for her comfort and support, bestowed with no sparing hand. In the transient gleam of recollection and consciousness which preceded her death, a prayer for his welfare and protection, as fervent as mortal ever breathed, rose from the lips of this poor friendless creature. That prayer flew to heaven and was heard. The blessings he was instrumental in conferring have been repaid to him a thousandfold; but, amid all the honours of rank and station which have since been heaped upon him, and which he has so well earned, he can have no reminiscence more gratifying to his heart than that connected with the black veil.

ARTHUR CONAN DOYLE

Sir Arthur Conan Doyle (1859–1930) was a Scottish physician and author, most noted for his stories about the detective Sherlock Holmes, generally considered without equal in the field of crime fiction. He was a prolific writer whose other works include science-fiction stories, plays, romances, poetry, non-fiction and historical novels. Conan Doyle was also a fervent advocate of justice and personally investigated two closed cases, which led to two men being exonerated from the crimes of which they were accused.

The New Catacomb

'Look here, Burger,' said Kennedy, 'I do wish that you would confide in me.'

The two famous students of Roman remains sat together in Kennedy's comfortable room overlooking the Corso. The night was cold, and they had both pulled up their chairs to the unsatisfactory Italian stove which threw out a zone of stuffiness rather than of warmth.

Outside under the bright winter stars lay the modern Rome, the long, double chain of the electric lamps, the brilliantly lighted cafés, the rushing carriages and the dense throng upon the footpaths. But inside, in the sumptuous chamber of the rich young English archaeologist, there was only old Rome to be seen. Cracked and time-worn friezes hung upon the walls, grey old busts of senators and soldiers with their fighting heads and their hard, cruel faces peered out from the corners. On the centre table, amidst a litter of inscriptions, fragments and ornaments, there stood the famous reconstruction by Kennedy of the Baths of Caracalla, which excited such interest and admiration when it was exhibited in Berlin.

Amphorae hung from the ceiling, and a litter of curiosities strewed the rich red Turkey carpet. And of them all there was not one which was not of the most unimpeachable authenticity, and of the utmost rarity and value; for Kennedy, though little more than thirty, had a European reputation in this particular branch of research, and was, moreover, provided with that long purse which either proves to be a fatal handicap to the student's energies, or, if his mind is still true to its purpose, gives him an enormous advantage in the race for fame. Kennedy had often been seduced by whim and pleasure from his studies, but his mind was an incisive one, capable of long and concentrated efforts which ended in sharp reactions of sensuous languor. His handsome face, with its high, white forehead, its aggressive nose, and its somewhat loose and sensuous mouth, was a fair index of the compromise between strength and weakness in his nature.

Of a very different type was his companion, Julius Burger. He came of a curious blend, a German father and an Italian mother, with the robust qualities of the North mingling strangely with the softer graces of the South. Blue Teutonic eyes lightened his sun-browned face, and above them rose a square, massive forehead, with a fringe of close yellow curls lying round it. His strong, firm jaw was clean-shaven, and his companion had frequently remarked how much it suggested those old Roman busts which peered out from the shadows in the corners of his chamber. Under its bluff German strength there lay always a suggestion of Italian subtlety, but the smile was so honest, and the eyes so frank, that one understood that this was only an indication of his ancestry, with no actual bearing upon his character.

In age and in reputation he was on the same level as his English companion, but his life and his work had both been far more arduous. Twelve years before he had come as a poor student to Rome, and had lived ever since upon some small endowment for research which had been awarded to him by the University of Bonn.

Painfully, slowly and doggedly, with extraordinary tenacity and single-mindedness, he had climbed from rung to rung of the ladder of fame, until now he was a member of the Berlin Academy, and there was every reason to believe that he would shortly be promoted to the chair of the greatest of German universities. But the singleness of purpose which had brought him to the same high level as the rich and brilliant Englishman, had caused him in everything outside their work to stand infinitely below him. He had never found a pause in his studies in which to cultivate the social graces. It was only when he spoke of his own subject that his face was filled with life and soul. At other times he was silent and embarrassed, too conscious of his own limitations in larger subjects and impatient of that small talk which is the conventional refuge of those who have no thoughts to express.

And yet for some years there had been an acquaintanceship which appeared to be slowly ripening into a friendship between these two very different rivals. The base and origin of this lay in the fact that in their own studies each was the only one of the younger men who had knowledge and enthusiasm enough properly to appreciate the other. Their common interests and pursuits had brought them together, and each had been attracted by the other's knowledge. And then gradually something had been added to this. Kennedy had been amused by the frankness and simplicity of his rival, while Burger in turn had been fascinated by the brilliancy and vivacity which had made Kennedy such a favourite in Roman society. I say 'had', because just at the moment the young Englishman was somewhat under a cloud.

A love affair, the details of which had never quite come out, had indicated a heartlessness and callousness upon his part which shocked many of his friends. But in the bachelor circles of students and artists in which he preferred to move there is no very rigid code of honour in such matters, and though a head might be shaken or a pair of shoulders shrugged over the flight of two and the return of one, the general sentiment was probably one of curiosity and perhaps of envy rather than of reprobation.

'Look here, Burger,' said Kennedy, looking hard at the placid face of his companion, 'I do wish that you would confide in me.'

As he spoke he waved his hand in the direction of a rug which lay upon the floor.

On the rug stood a long, shallow fruit-basket of the light wickerwork which is used in the Campagna, and this was heaped with a litter of objects, inscribed tiles, broken inscriptions, cracked mosaics, torn papyri, rusty metal ornaments, which to the uninitiated might have seemed to have come straight from a dustman's bin, but which a specialist would have speedily recognised as unique of their kind.

The pile of odds and ends in the flat wickerwork basket supplied exactly one of those missing links of social development which are of such interest to the student. It was the German who had brought them in, and the Englishman's eyes were hungry as he looked at them.

'I won't interfere with your treasure-trove, but I should very much like to hear about it,' he continued, while Burger very deliberately lit a cigar. 'It is evidently a discovery of the first importance. These inscriptions will make a sensation throughout Europe.'

'For every one here there are a million there!' said the German. 'There are so many that a dozen savants might spend a lifetime over them, and build up a reputation as solid as the Castle of St Angelo.'

Kennedy was thinking, with his fine forehead wrinkled and his fingers playing with his long, fair moustache.

'You have given yourself away, Burger!' said he at last. 'Your words can only apply to one thing. You have discovered a new catacomb.'

'I had no doubt that you had already come to that conclusion from an examination of these objects.'

'Well, they certainly appeared to indicate it, but your last remarks make it certain. There is no place except a catacomb which could contain so vast a store of relics as you describe.'

'Quite so. There is no mystery about that. I *have* discovered a new catacomb.'

'Where?'

'Ah, that is my secret, my dear Kennedy! Suffice it that it is so situated that there is not one chance in a million of anyone else coming upon it. Its date is different from that of any known catacomb, and it has been reserved for the burial of the highest Christians, so that the remains and the relics are quite different from anything which has ever been seen before. If I was not aware of your knowledge and of your energy, my friend, I would not hesitate, under the pledge of secrecy, to tell you everything about it. But as it is I think that I must certainly prepare my own report of the matter before I expose myself to such formidable competition.'

Kennedy loved his subject with a love which was almost a mania – a love which held him true to it, amidst all the distractions which come to a wealthy and dissipated young man. He had ambition, but his ambition was secondary to his mere abstract joy and interest in everything which concerned the old life and history of the city. He yearned to see this new underworld which his companion had discovered.

'Look here, Burger,' said he, earnestly, 'I assure you that you can trust me most implicitly in the matter. Nothing would induce me to put pen to paper about anything which I see until I have your express permission. I quite understand your feeling, and I think it is most natural, but you have really nothing whatever to fear from me. On the other hand, if you don't tell me I shall make a systematic search, and I shall most certainly discover it. In that case, of course, I should make what use I liked of it, since I should be under no obligation to you.'

Burger smiled thoughtfully over his cigar.

'I have noticed, friend Kennedy,' said he, 'that when I want information over any point you are not always so ready to supply it.'

'When did you ever ask me anything that I did not tell you? You remember, for example, my giving you the material for your paper about the temple of the Vestals.'

'Ah, well, that was not a matter of much importance. If I were to question you upon some intimate thing, would you give me an answer, I wonder! This new catacomb is a very intimate thing to me, and I should certainly expect some sign of confidence in return.'

'What you are driving at I cannot imagine,' said the Englishman, 'but if you mean that you will answer my question about the catacomb if I answer any question which you may put to me, I can assure you that I will certainly do so.'

'Well, then,' said Burger, leaning luxuriously back in his settee, and puffing a blue tree of cigar-smoke into the air, 'tell me all about your relations with Miss Mary Saunderson.'

Kennedy sprang up in his chair and glared angrily at his impassive companion.

'What the devil do you mean?' he cried. 'What sort of a question is this? You may mean it as a joke, but you never made a worse one.'

'No, I don't mean it as a joke,' said Burger, simply. 'I am really rather interested in the details of the matter. I don't know much about the world and women and social life and that sort of thing, and such an incident has the fascination of the unknown for me. I know you, and I knew her by sight – I had even spoken to her once or twice. I should very much like to hear from your own lips exactly what it was which occurred between you.'

'I won't tell you a word.'

'That's all right. It was only my whim to see if you would give up a secret as easily as you expected me to give up my secret of the new catacomb. You wouldn't, and I didn't expect you to. But why should you expect otherwise of me? There's St John's clock striking ten. It is quite time that I was going home.'

'No, wait a bit, Burger,' said Kennedy; 'this is really a ridiculous caprice of yours to wish to know about an old love affair which has burned out months ago. You know we look upon a man who kisses and tells as the greatest coward and villain possible.'

'Certainly,' said the German, gathering up his basket of curiosities, 'when he tells anything about a girl which is previously unknown, he must be so. But in this case, as you must be aware, it was a public matter which was the common talk of Rome, so that you are not really doing Miss Mary Saunderson any injury by discussing her case with me. But still, I respect your scruples; and so good-night!'

'Wait a bit, Burger,' said Kennedy, laying his hand upon the other's arm; 'I am very keen upon this catacomb business, and I can't let it drop quite so easily. Would you mind asking me something else in return – something not quite so eccentric this time?'

'No, no; you have refused, and there is an end of it,' said Burger, with his basket on his arm. 'No doubt you are quite right not to answer, and no doubt I am quite right also – and so again, my dear Kennedy, good-night!'

The Englishman watched Burger cross the room, and he had his hand on the handle of the door before his host sprang up with the air of a man who is making the best of that which cannot be helped. 'Hold on, old fellow,' said he. 'I think you are behaving in a most ridiculous fashion, but still, if this is your condition, I suppose that I must submit to it. I hate saying anything about a girl, but, as you say, it is all over Rome, and I don't suppose I can tell you anything which you do not know already. What was it you wanted to know?'

The German came back to the stove, and, laying down his basket, he sank into his chair once more. 'May I have another cigar?' said he. 'Thank you very much! I never smoke when I work, but I enjoy a chat much more when I am under the influence of tobacco. Now, as regards this young lady, with whom you had this little adventure. What in the world has become of her?'

'She is at home with her own people.'

'Oh, really – in England?'

'Yes.'

'What part of England – London?'

'No, Twickenham.'

'You must excuse my curiosity, my dear Kennedy, and you must put it down to my ignorance of the world. No doubt it is quite a simple thing to persuade a young lady to go off with you for three weeks or so, and then to hand her over to her own family at – what did you call the place?'

'Twickenham.'

'Quite so – at Twickenham. But it is something so entirely outside my own experience that I cannot even imagine how you set about it. For example, if you had loved this girl your love could hardly disappear in three weeks, so I presume that you could not have loved her at all. But if you did not love her why should you make this great scandal which has damaged you and ruined her?'

Kennedy looked moodily into the red eye of the stove. 'That's a logical way of looking at it, certainly,' said he. 'Love is a big word, and it represents a good many different shades of feeling. I liked her, and – well, you say you've seen her – you know how charming she can look. But still I am willing to admit, looking back, that I could never have really loved her.'

'Then, my dear Kennedy, why did you do it?'

'The adventure of the thing had a great deal to do with it.'

'What! You are so fond of adventures!'

'Where would the variety of life be without them? It was for an adventure that I first began to pay my attentions to her. I've chased a good deal of game in my time, but there's no chase like that of a pretty woman. There was the piquant difficulty of it also, for, as she was the companion of Lady Emily Rood, it was almost impossible to see her alone. On the top of all the other obstacles which attracted me, I learned from her own lips very early in the proceedings that she was engaged.'

'Mein Gott! To whom?'

'She mentioned no names.'

'I do not think that anyone knows that. So that made the adventure more alluring, did it?'

'Well, it did certainly give a spice to it. Don't you think so?'

'I tell you that I am very ignorant about these things.'

'My dear fellow, you can remember that the apple you stole from your neighbour's tree was always sweeter than that which fell from your own. And then I found that she cared for me.'

'What – at once?'

'Oh, no, it took about three months of sapping and mining. But at last I won her over. She understood that my judicial separation from my wife made it impossible for me to do the right thing by her – but she came all the same, and we had a delightful time, as long as it lasted.'

'But how about the other man?'

Kennedy shrugged his shoulders. 'I suppose it is the survival of the fittest,' said he. 'If he had been the better man she would not have deserted him. Let's drop the subject, for I have had enough of it!'

'Only one other thing. How did you get rid of her in three weeks?'

'Well, we had both cooled down a bit, you understand. She absolutely refused, under any circumstances, to come back to face the people she had known in Rome. Now, of course, Rome is necessary to me, and I was already pining to be back at my work – so there was one obvious cause of separation. Then, again, her old father turned up at the hotel in London, and there was a scene, and the whole thing became so unpleasant that really – though I missed her dreadfully at first – I was very glad to slip out of it. Now, I rely upon you not to repeat anything of what I have said.'

'My dear Kennedy, I should not dream of repeating it. But all that you say interests me very much, for it gives me an insight into your way of looking at things, which is entirely different from mine, for I have seen so little of life. And now you want to know about my new catacomb. There's no use my trying to describe it, for you would never find it by that. There is only one thing, and that is for me to take you there.'

'That would be splendid.'

'When would you like to come?'

'The sooner the better. I am all impatience to see it.'

'Well, it is a beautiful night – though a trifle cold. Suppose we start in an hour. We must be very careful to keep the matter to ourselves. If anyone saw us hunting in couples they would suspect that there was something going on.'

'We can't be too cautious,' said Kennedy. 'Is it far?'

'Some miles.'

'Not too far to walk?'

'Oh, no, we could walk there easily.'

'We had better do so, then. A cabman's suspicions would be aroused if he dropped us both at some lonely spot in the dead of the night.'

'Quite so. I think it would be best for us to meet at the gate of the Appian Way at midnight. I must go back to my lodgings for the matches and candles and things.'

'All right, Burger! I think it is very kind of you to let me into this secret, and I promise you that I will write nothing about it until you have published your report. Goodbye for the present! You will find me at the gate at twelve.'

The cold, clear air was filled with the musical chimes from that city of clocks as Burger, wrapped in an Italian overcoat, with a lantern hanging from his hand, walked up to the rendez-vous. Kennedy stepped out of the shadow to meet him.

'You are ardent in work as well as in love!' said the German, laughing.

'Yes; I have been waiting here for nearly half an hour.'

'I hope you left no clue as to where we were going.'

'Not such a fool! By Jove, I am chilled to the bone! Come on, Burger, let us warm ourselves by a spurt of hard walking.'

Their footsteps sounded loud and crisp upon the rough stone paving of the disappointing road which is all that is left of the most famous highway of the world. A peasant or two going home from the wine-shop, and a few carts of country produce coming up to Rome, were the only things which they met. They swung along, with the huge tombs looming up through the darkness upon each side of them, until they had come as far as the Catacombs of St Calixtus, and saw against a rising moon the great circular bastion of Cecilia Metella in front of them. Then Burger stopped with his hand to his side. 'Your legs are longer than mine, and you are more accustomed to walking,' said he, laughing. 'I think that the place where we turn off is somewhere here. Yes, this is it, round the corner of the trattoria. Now, it is a very narrow path, so perhaps I had better go in front, and you can follow.' He had lit his lantern, and by its light they were enabled to follow a narrow and devious track which wound across the marshes of the Campagna. The great aqueduct of old Rome lay like a monstrous caterpillar across the moonlit landscape, and their road led them under one of its huge arches, and past the circle of crumbling bricks which marks the old arena. At last Burger stopped at a solitary wooden cow-house, and he drew a key from his pocket.

'Surely your catacomb is not inside a house!' cried Kennedy.

'The entrance to it is. That is just the safeguard which we have against anyone else discovering it.'

'Does the proprietor know of it?'

'Not he. He had found one or two objects which made me almost certain that his house was built on the entrance to such a place. So I rented it from him, and did my excavations for myself. Come in, and shut the door behind you.'

It was a long, empty building, with the mangers of the cows along one wall. Burger put his lantern down on the ground, and shaded its light in all directions save one by draping his overcoat round it. 'It might excite remark if anyone saw a light in this lonely place,' said he. 'Just help me to move this boarding.' The flooring was loose in the corner, and plank by plank the two savants raised it and leaned it against the wall. Below there was a square aperture and a stair of old stone steps which led away down into the bowels of the earth.

'Be careful!' cried Burger, as Kennedy, in his impatience, hurried down them. 'It is a perfect rabbits' warren below, and if you were once to lose your way there, the chances would be a hundred to one against your ever coming out again. Wait until I bring the light.'

'How do you find your own way if it is so complicated?'

'I had some very narrow escapes at first, but I have gradually learned to go about. There is a certain system to it, but it is one which a lost man, if he were in the dark, could not possibly find out. Even now I always spin out a ball of string behind me when I am going far into the catacomb. You can see for yourself that it is difficult, for every one of these passages divides and sub-divides a dozen times before you go a hundred yards.' They had descended some twenty feet from the level of the byre, and they were standing now in a square chamber cut out of the soft tufa.

The lantern cast a flickering light, bright below and dim above, over the cracked brown walls. In every direction were the black openings of passages which radiated from this common centre.

'I want you to follow me closely, my friend,' said Burger. 'Do not loiter to look at anything upon the way, for the place to which I will take you contains all that you can see, and more. It will save time for us to go there direct.' He led the way down one of the corridors, and the Englishman followed closely at his heels. Every now and then the passage bifurcated, but Burger was evidently following some secret marks of his own, for he neither stopped nor hesitated. Everywhere along the walls, packed like the berths upon an emigrant ship, lay the Christians of old Rome. The yellow light flickered over the shrivelled features of the mummies, and gleamed upon rounded skulls and long white arm-bones crossed over fleshless chests. And everywhere as he passed Kennedy looked with wistful eyes upon inscriptions, funeral vessels, pictures, vestments, utensils, all lying as pious hands had placed them so many centuries ago. It was apparent to him, even in those hurried, passing glances, that this was the earliest and finest of the catacombs, containing such a storehouse of Roman remains as had never before come at one time under the observation of the student. 'What would happen if the light went out?' he asked, as they hurried on.

'I have a spare candle and a box of matches in my pocket. By the way, Kennedy, have you any matches?'

'No; you had better give me some.'

'Oh, that is all right. There is no chance of our separating.'

'How far are we going? It seems to me that we have walked at least a quarter of a mile.'

'More than that, I think. There is really no limit to the tombs – at least, I have never been able to find any. This is a very difficult place, so I think that I will use our ball of string.' He fastened one end of it to a projecting stone and he carried the coil in the breast of his coat, paying it out as he advanced.

Kennedy saw that it was no unnecessary precaution, for the passages had become more complex and tortuous than ever, with a perfect network of intersecting corridors. But these all ended in one large circular hall with a square pedestal of tufa topped with a slab of marble at one end of it. 'By Jove!' cried Kennedy in an ecstasy, as Burger swung his lantern over the marble. 'It is a Christian altar – probably the first one in existence. Here is the little consecration cross cut upon the corner of it. No doubt this circular space was used as a church.'

'Precisely,' said Burger. 'If I had more time I should like to show you all the bodies which are buried in these niches upon the walls, for they are the early popes and bishops of the Church, with their mitres, their croziers, and full canonicals. Go over to that one and look at it!' Kennedy went across, and stared at the ghastly head which lay loosely on the shredded and mouldering mitre.

'This is most interesting,' said he, and his voice seemed to boom against the concave vault. 'As far as my experience goes, it is unique. Bring the lantern over, Burger, for I want to see them all.' But the German had strolled away, and was standing in the middle of a yellow circle of light at the other side of the hall.

'Do you know how many wrong turnings there are between this and the stairs?' he asked. 'There are over two thousand. No doubt it was one of the means of protection which the Christians adopted. The odds are two thousand to one against a man getting out, even if he had a light; but if he were in the dark it would, of course, be far more difficult.'

'So I should think.'

'And the darkness is something dreadful. I tried it once for an experiment. Let us try it again!' He stooped to the lantern, and in an instant it was as if an invisible hand was squeezed tightly over each of Kennedy's eyes. Never had he known what darkness was. It seemed to press upon him and to smother him. It was a solid obstacle against which the body shrank from advancing. He put his hands out to push it back from him. 'That will do, Burger,' said he, 'let's have the light again.'

But his companion began to laugh, and in that circular room the sound seemed to come from every side at once. 'You seem uneasy, friend Kennedy,' said he.

'Go on, man, light the candle!' said Kennedy, impatiently.

'It's very strange, Kennedy, but I could not in the least tell by the sound in which direction you stand. Could you tell where I am?'

'No; you seem to be on every side of me.'

'If it were not for this string which I hold in my hand I should not have a notion which way to go.'

'I dare say not. Strike a light, man, and have an end of this nonsense.'

'Well, Kennedy, there are two things which I understand that you are very fond of. The one is adventure, and the other is an obstacle to surmount. The adventure must be the finding of your way out of this catacomb. The obstacle will be the darkness and the two thousand wrong turns which make the way a little difficult to find. But you need not hurry, for you have plenty of time, and when you halt for a rest now and then, I should like you just to think of Miss Mary Saunderson, and whether you treated her quite fairly.'

'You devil, what do you mean?' roared Kennedy. He was running about in little circles and clasping at the solid blackness with both hands.

'Goodbye,' said the mocking voice, and it was already at some distance. 'I really do not think, Kennedy, even by your own showing that you did the right thing by that girl. There was only one little thing which you appeared not to know, and I can supply it. Miss Saunderson was engaged to a poor, ungainly devil of a student, and his name was Julius Burger.' There was a rustle somewhere – the vague sound of a foot striking a stone – and then there fell silence upon that old Christian church – a stagnant heavy silence which closed round Kennedy and shut him in like water round a drowning man.

Some two months afterwards the following paragraph made the round of the European press:

One of the most interesting discoveries of recent years is that of the new catacomb in Rome, which lies some distance to the east of the well-known vaults of St Calixtus. The finding of this important burial-place, which is exceedingly rich in most interesting early Christian remains, is due to the energy and sagacity of Dr Julius Burger, the young German specialist, who is rapidly taking the first place as an authority upon ancient Rome. Although the first to publish his discovery, it appears that a less fortunate adventurer had anticipated Dr Burger. Some months ago Mr Kennedy, the well-known English student, disappeared suddenly from his rooms in the Corso, and it was conjectured that his association with a recent scandal had driven him to leave Rome. It appears now that he had in reality fallen a victim to that fervid love of archaeology which had raised him to a distinguished place among living scholars. His body was discovered in the heart of the new catacomb, and it was evident from the condition of his feet and boots that he had tramped for days through the tortuous corridors which make these subterranean tombs so dangerous to explorers. The deceased gentleman had, with inexplicable rashness, made his way into this labyrinth without, as far as can be discovered, taking with him either candles or matches, so that his sad fate was the natural result of his own temerity. What makes the matter more painful is that Dr Julius Burger was an intimate friend of the deceased. His joy at the extraordinary find which he has been so fortunate as to make has been greatly marred by the terrible fate of his comrade and fellow-worker.

RICHARD HARRIS BARHAM

Richard Harris Barham (1788–1845) was a humorous poet and a son of a country gentleman. He was born at Canterbury, educated at St Paul's School and Brasenose College, Oxford, took holy orders, held various incumbencies and was divinity lecturer and minor canon of St Paul's. It is not, however, as a churchman that he is remembered, but as the author of the *Ingoldsby Legends,* a series of comic and serio-comic pieces in verse, sparkling with wit and full of striking and often grotesque turns of expression, which appeared first in *Bentley's Miscellany,* and were published collectively in three series (1840–7). He also wrote, in *Blackwood's Magazine,* a novel, *My Cousin Nicholas.*

The Spectre of Tappington

'It is very odd, though; what can have become of them?' said Charles Seaforth, as he peeped under the valance of an old-fashioned bedstead in an old-fashioned apartment of a still more old-fashioned manor-house; ' 'tis confoundedly odd and I can't make it out at all. Why, Barney, where are they! and where the devil are you?'

No answer was returned to this appeal; and the lieutenant, who was, in the main, a reasonable person – at least as reasonable a person as any young gentleman of twenty-two in 'the service' can fairly be expected to be – cooled when he reflected that his servant could scarcely reply extempore to a summons which it was impossible he should hear.

An application to the bell was the considerate result; and the footsteps of as tight a lad as ever put pipe-clay to belt sounded along the gallery.

'Come in!' said his master. An ineffectual attempt upon the door reminded Mr Seaforth that he had locked himself in. 'By heaven! this is the oddest thing of all,' said he, as he turned the key and admitted Mr Maguire into his dormitory.

'Barney, where are my pantaloons?'

'Is it the breeches?' asked the valet, casting an enquiring eye round the apartment – 'is it the breeches, sir?'

'Yes; what have you done with them?'

'Sure then your honour had them on when you went to bed, and it's hereabout they'll be, I'll be bail;' and Barney lifted a fashionable tunic from a cane-backed armchair, proceeding in his examination. But the search was vain: there was the tunic aforesaid; there was a smart-looking kerseymere waistcoat; but the most important article of all in a gentleman's wardrobe was still wanting.

'Where *can* they be?' asked the master, with a strong accent on the auxiliary verb.

'Divil if I knows,' said the man.

'It *must* have been the devil, then, after all, who has been here and carried them off!' cried Seaforth, staring full into Barney's face. Mr Maguire was not devoid of the superstition of his countrymen, still he looked as if he did not quite subscribe to the *sequitur*.

His master read incredulity in his countenance. 'Why, I tell you, Barney, I put them there, on that armchair, when I got into bed; and, by heaven! I distinctly saw the ghost of the old fellow they told me of come in at midnight, put on my pantaloons, and walk away with them.'

'Maybe so,' was the cautious reply.

'I thought, of course, it was a dream; but then – where the devil are the breeches?'

The question was more easily asked than answered. Barney renewed his search, while the lieutenant folded his arms and, leaning against the washstand, sank into a reverie.

'After all, it must be some trick of my laughter-loving cousins,' said Seaforth.

'Ah! then, the ladies!' chimed in Mr Maguire, though the observation was not addressed to him; 'and, will it be Miss Caroline, or Miss Fanny, that's stole your honour's things?'

'I hardly know what to think of it,' pursued the bereaved lieutenant, still speaking in soliloquy, with his eye resting dubiously on the chamber-door. 'I locked myself in, that's certain; and – but there must be some other entrance to the room – pooh! I remember – the private staircase; how could I be such a fool?' and he crossed the chamber to where a low oaken doorcase was dimly visible in a distant corner. He paused before it. Nothing now interfered to screen it from observation; but it bore tokens of having been at some earlier period concealed by tapestry, remains of which yet clothed the walls on either side the portal.

'This way they must have come,' said Seaforth; 'I wish with all my heart I had caught them!'

'Och! the kittens!' sighed Mr Barney Maguire.

But the mystery was yet as far from being solved as before. True there *was* the 'other door'; but then that too, on examination, was even more firmly secured than the one which opened on the gallery – two heavy bolts on the inside effectually prevented any *coup de main* on the lieutenant's bivouac from that quarter. He was more puzzled than ever; nor did the minutest inspection of the walls and door throw any light upon the subject: one thing only was clear – the breeches were gone!

'It is *very* singular,' said the lieutenant.

Tappington (generally called Tapton) Everard is an antiquated but commodious manor-house in the eastern division of the county of Kent. A former proprietor had been high-sheriff in the days of Elizabeth, and many a dark and dismal tradition was yet extant of the licentiousness of his life, and the enormity of his offences. The Glen, which the keeper's daughter was seen to enter but never known to quit, still frowns darkly as of yore; while an ineradicable bloodstain on the oaken stair yet bids defiance to the united energies of soap and sand. But it is with one particular apartment that a deed of more especial atrocity is said to be connected.

A stranger guest – so runs the legend – arrived unexpectedly at the mansion of the 'Bad Sir Giles'. They met in apparent friendship; but the ill-concealed scowl on their master's brow told the domestics that the visit was not a welcome one; the banquet, however, was not spared; the wine-cup circulated freely – too freely, perhaps – for sounds of discord at length reached the ears of even the excluded serving-men, as they were doing their best to imitate their betters in the lower hall. Alarmed, some of them ventured to approach the parlour; one, an old and favoured retainer of the house, went so far as to break in upon his master's privacy. Sir Giles, already high in oath, fiercely enjoined his absence, and he retired; not, however, before he had distinctly heard from the stranger's lips a menace that 'there was that within his pocket which could disprove the knight's right to issue that or any other command within the walls of Tapton'.

The intrusion, though momentary, seemed to have produced a beneficial effect; the voices of the disputants fell, and the conversation was carried on thenceforth in a more subdued tone, till, as evening closed in, the domestics, when summoned to attend with lights, found not only cordiality restored, but that a still deeper carouse was meditated. Fresh stoups, and from the choicest bins, were produced; not was it till at a late, or rather early hour, that the revellers sought their chambers.

The one allotted to the stranger occupied the first floor of the eastern angle of the building, and had once been the favourite apartment of Sir Giles himself. Scandal ascribed this preference to the facility which a private staircase, communicating with the grounds, had afforded him, in the old knight's time, of following his wicked courses unchecked by parental observation; a consideration which ceased to be of weight when the death of his father left him uncontrolled master of his estate and actions. From that period Sir Giles had established himself in what were called the 'state apartments', and the 'oaken chamber' was rarely tenanted, save on occasions of extraordinary festivity, or when the yule-log drew an unusually large accession of guests around the Christmas hearth.

On this eventful night it was prepared for the unknown visitor, who sought his couch heated and inflamed from his midnight orgies, and in the morning was found in his bed a swollen and blackened corpse. No marks of violence appeared upon the body; but the livid hue of the lips, and certain dark-coloured spots visible on the skin, aroused suspicions which those who entertained them were too timid to express. Apoplexy, induced by the excesses of the preceding night, Sir Giles's confidential leech pronounced to be the cause of his sudden dissolution. The body was buried in peace; and though some shook their heads as they witnessed the haste with which the funeral rites were hurried on, none ventured to murmur. Other events arose to distract the attention of the retainers; men's minds became occupied by the stirring politics of the day; while the near approach of that formidable armada, so vainly arrogating to itself a title which the very elements joined with human valour to disprove, soon interfered to weaken, if not obliterate, all remembrance of the nameless stranger who had died within the walls of Tapton Everard.

Years rolled on: the 'Bad Sir Giles' had himself long since gone to his account, the last, as it was believed, of his immediate line; though a few of the older tenants were sometimes heard to speak of an elder brother, who had disappeared in early life, and never inherited the estate. Rumours, too, of his having left a son in foreign lands were at one time rife; but they died away;

nothing occurring to support them, the property passed un-challenged to a collateral branch of the family, and the secret, if secret there were, was buried in Denton churchyard, in the lonely grave of the mysterious stranger.

One circumstance alone occurred, after a long intervening period, to revive the memory of these transactions. Some work-men employed in grubbing an old plantation, for the purpose of raising on its site a modern shrubbery, dug up, in the execution of their task, the mildewed remnants of what seemed to have been once a garment. On more minute inspection, enough remained of silken slashes and a coarse embroidery, to identify the relics as having once formed part of a pair of trunk hose; while a few papers which fell from them, altogether illegible from damp and age, were by the unlearned rustics conveyed to the then owner of the estate.

Whether the squire was more successful in deciphering them was never known; he certainly never alluded to their contents; and little would have been thought of the matter but for the inconvenient memory of one old woman, who declared she heard her grandfather say that when the 'stranger guest' was poisoned, though all the rest of his clothes were there, his breeches, the supposed repository of the supposed documents, could never be found. The master of Tapton Everard smiled when he heard Dame Jones's hint of deeds which might impeach the validity of his own title in favour of some unknown descendant of some unknown heir; and the story was rarely alluded to, save by one or two miracle-mongers, who had heard that others had seen the ghost of old Sir Giles, in his nightcap, issue from the postern, enter the adjoining copse, and wring his shadowy hands in agony, as he seemed to search vainly for something hidden among the evergreens. The stranger's death-room had, of course, been occasionally haunted from the time of his decease; but the periods of visitation had latterly become very rare – even Mrs Botherby, the housekeeper, being forced to admit that, during her long sojourn at the manor, she had never 'met with anything worse than herself'; though, as the old lady afterwards added upon mature reflection, 'I must say I think I saw the devil *once.*'

Such was the legend attached to Tapton Everard and such the story which the lively Caroline Ingoldsby detailed to her equally mercurial cousin, Charles Seaforth, lieutenant in the Hon. East India Company's second regiment of Bombay Fencibles, as arm in arm they promenaded a gallery decked with some dozen grim-looking ancestral portraits and, among others, with that of the redoubted Sir Giles himself. The gallant commander had that very morning paid his first visit to the house of his maternal uncle, after an absence of five years passed with his regiment on the arid plains of Hindustan, whence he was now returned on a three years' furlough. He had gone out a boy – he returned a man; but the impression made upon his youthful fancy by his favourite cousin remained unimpaired, and to Tapton he directed his steps, even before he sought the home of his widowed mother – comforting himself in this breach of filial decorum by the reflection that, as the manor was so little out of his way, it would be unkind to pass, as it were, the door of his relatives, without just looking in for a few hours.

But he found his uncle as hospitable, and his cousin more charming than ever; and the looks of one, and the requests of the other, soon precluded the possibility of refusing to lengthen the 'few hours' into a few days, though the house was at the moment full of visitors.

The Peterses were there from Ramsgate; and Mr, Mrs and the two Miss Simpkinsons, from Bath, had come to pass a month with the family; and Tom Ingoldsby had brought down his college friend the Hon. Augustus Sucklethumbkin, with his groom and pointers, to take a fortnight's shooting. And then there was Mrs Ogleton, the rich young widow, with her large black eyes, who, people did say, was setting her cap at the young squire, though Mrs Botherby did not believe it; and, above all, there was Mademoiselle Pauline, her *femme de chambre*, who *mon-Dieu*'d everything and everybody, and cried, '*Quel horreur!*' at Mrs Botherby's cap. In short, to use the last-named and much-respected lady's own expression, the house was 'choke-full' to the very attics – all save the 'oaken chamber', which, as the lieutenant expressed a most magnanimous disregard of ghosts, was forthwith appropriated to his particular accommodation. Mr Maguire meanwhile was fain to share the apartment of Oliver Dobbs, the squire's own man: a jocular proposal of joint occupancy having been first indignantly rejected by 'Mademoiselle', though preferred with the 'laste taste in life' of Mr Barney's most insinuating brogue.

'Come, Charles, the urn is absolutely getting cold; your breakfast will be quite spoiled: what can have made you so idle?' Such was the morning salutation of Miss Ingoldsby to the *militaire* as he entered the breakfast-room half an hour after the latest of the party.

'A pretty gentleman, truly, to make an appointment with,' chimed in Miss Frances. 'What is become of our ramble to the rocks before breakfast?'

'Oh! the young men never think of keeping a promise now,' said Mrs Peters, a little ferret-faced woman with underdone eyes.

'When I was a young man,' said Mr Peters, 'I remember I always made a point of – '

'Pray how long ago was that?' asked Mr Simpkinson from Bath.

'Why, sir, when I married Mrs Peters, I was – let me see – was – '

'Do pray hold your tongue, P., and eat your breakfast!' interrupted his better half, who had a mortal horror of chronological references; 'it's very rude to tease people with your family affairs.'

The lieutenant had by this time taken his seat in silence – a good-humoured nod, and a glance, half-smiling, half-inquisitive, being the extent of his salutation. Smitten as he was, and in the immediate presence of her who had made so large a hole in his heart, his manner was evidently *distrait*, which the fair Caroline in her secret soul attributed to his being solely occupied by her *agrémens*: how would she have bridled had she known that they only shared his meditations with a pair of breeches!

Charles drank his coffee and spiked some half-dozen eggs, darting occasionally a penetrating glance at the ladies, in hope of detecting the supposed waggery by the evidence of some furtive smile or conscious look. But in vain; not a dimple moved indicative of roguery, nor did the slightest elevation of eyebrow rise confirmative of his suspicions. Hints and insinuations passed unheeded – more particular enquiries were out of the question – the subject was unapproachable.

In the meantime, 'patent cords' were just the thing for a morning's ride; and, breakfast ended, away cantered the party over the downs, till, every faculty absorbed by the beauties, animate and inanimate, which surrounded him, Lieutenant Seaforth of the Bombay Fencibles bestowed no more thought upon his breeches than if he had been born on the top of Ben Lomond.

Another night had passed away; the sun rose brilliantly, forming with his level beams a splendid rainbow in the far-off west, whither the heavy cloud, which for the last two hours had been pouring its waters on the earth, was now flying before him.

'Ah! then, and it's little good it'll be the claning of ye,' apostrophised Mr Barney Maguire, as he deposited, in front of his master's washstand, a pair of 'bran new' jockey boots, one of Hoby's primest fits, which the lieutenant had purchased on his

way through town. On that very morning had they come for the
first time under the valet's depurating hand, so little soiled,
indeed, from the turfy ride of the preceding day, that a less
scrupulous domestic might, perhaps, have considered the
application of 'Warren's Matchless', or oxalic acid, altogether
superfluous. Not so Barney: with the nicest care had he removed
the slightest impurity from each polished surface, and there they
stood, rejoicing in their sable radiance. No wonder a pang shot
across Mr Maguire's breast, as he thought on the work now cut
out for them, so different from the light labours of the day
before; no wonder he murmured with a sigh, as the scarce dried
window-panes disclosed a road now inch deep in mud. 'Ah!
then, it's little good the claning of ye!' – for well had he learned
in the hall below that eight miles of stiff clay soil lay between the
manor and Bolsover Abbey, whose picturesque ruins,

Like ancient Rome, majestic decay,

the party had determined to explore. The master had already
commenced dressing, and the man was fitting straps upon a
light pair of crane-necked spurs, when his hand was arrested by
the old question – 'Barney, where are the breeches?'

They were nowhere to be found!

Mr Seaforth descended that morning, whip in hand, and
equipped in a handsome green riding-frock, but no 'breeches
and boots to match' were there: loose jean trousers, sur-
mounting a pair of diminutive Wellingtons, embraced, somewhat incongruously, his nether man, the 'patent cords' being,
like yesterday's pantaloons, absent without leave. The 'top-
boots' had a holiday.

'A fine morning after the rain,' said Mr Simpkinson from
Bath.

'Just the thing for the 'ops,' said Mr Peters. 'I remember
when I was a boy – '

'Do hold your tongue, P.,' said Mrs Peters – advice which that exemplary matron was in the constant habit of administering to 'her P.' as she called him, whenever he prepared to vent his reminiscences. Her precise reason for this it would be difficult to determine, unless, indeed, the story be true which a little bird had whispered into Mrs Botherby's ear – Mr Peters, though now a wealthy man, had received a liberal education at a charity school, and was apt to recur to the days of his muffin-cap and leathers. As usual, he took his wife's hint in good part and 'paused in his reply'.

'A glorious day for the ruins!' said young Ingoldsby. 'But, Charles, what the deuce are you about? you don't mean to ride through our lanes in such toggery as that?'

'Lassy me!' said Miss Julia Simpkinson, 'won't you be very wet?'

'You had better take Tom's cab,' quoth the squire.

But this proposition was at once overruled; Mrs Ogleton had already nailed the cab, a vehicle of all others the best adapted for a snug flirtation.

'Or drive Miss Julia in the phaeton?' No; that was the post of Mr Peters, who, indifferent as an equestrian, had acquired some fame as a whip while travelling through the midland counties for the firm of Bagshaw, Snivelby and Ghrimes.

'Thank you, I shall ride with my cousins,' said Charles, with as much nonchalance as he could assume – and he did so: Mr Ingoldsby, Mrs Peters, Mr Simpkinson from Bath, and his eldest daughter with her album, following in the family coach. The gentleman-commoner 'voted the affair damned slow', and declined the party altogether in favour of the gamekeeper and a cigar. 'There was "no fun" in looking at old houses!' Mrs Simpkinson preferred a short *séjour* in the still-room with Mrs Botherby, who had promised to initiate her in that grand *arcanum*, the transmutation of gooseberry jam into guava jelly.

*

'Did you ever see an old abbey before, Mr Peters?'

'Yes, miss, a French one; we have got one at Ramsgate; he teaches the Miss Joneses to parley-voo, and is turned of sixty.'

Miss Simpkinson closed her album with an air of ineffable disdain.

Mr Simpkinson from Bath was a professed antiquary, and one of the first water; he was master of Gwillim's *Heraldry* and Mills's *History of the Crusades*; knew every plate in the *Monasticon*; had written an essay on the origin and dignity of the office of overseer; and had settled the date of a Queen Anne's farthing. An influential member of the Antiquarian Society, to whose *Beauties of Bagnigge Wells* he had been a liberal subscriber, procured him a seat on the board of that learned body, since which happy epoch Sylvanus Urban had not a more indefatigable correspondent. His inaugural essay on the president's cocked hat was considered a miracle of erudition; and his account of the earliest application of gilding to gingerbread, a masterpiece of antiquarian research.

His eldest daughter was of a kindred spirit: if her father's mantle had not fallen upon her, it was only because he had not thrown it off himself; she had caught hold of its tail, however, while it yet hung upon his honoured shoulders. To souls so congenial, what a sight was the magnificent ruin of Bolsover! its broken arches, its mouldering pinnacles and the airy tracery of its half-demolished windows. The party were in raptures: Mr Simpkinson began to meditate an essay, and his daughter an ode; even Seaforth, as he gazed on these lonely relics of the olden time, was betrayed into a momentary forgetfulness of his love and losses; the widow's eyeglass turned from her *cicisbeo*'s whiskers to the mantling ivy; Mrs Peters wiped her spectacles; and 'her P.' supposed the central tower 'had once been the county jail'. The squire was a philosopher, and had been there often before, so he ordered out the cold tongue and chickens.

'Bolsover Priory,' said Mr Simpkinson, with the air of a

connoisseur – 'Bolsover Priory was founded in the reign of Henry VI, about the beginning of the eleventh century. Hugh de Bolsover had accompanied that monarch to the Holy Land, in the expedition undertaken by way of penance for the murder of his young nephews in the Tower. Upon the dissolution of the monasteries, the veteran was enfeoffed in the lands and manor to which he gave his own name of Bowlsover, or Bee-owls-over (by corruption Bolsover) – a Bee in chief, over three Owls, all proper, being the armorial ensigns borne by this distinguished crusader at the siege of Acre.'

'Ah! that was Sir Sidney Smith,' said Mr Peters; 'I've heard tell of him, and all about Mrs Partington, and – '

'P., be quiet, and don't expose yourself!' sharply interrupted his lady. P. was silenced, and betook himself to the bottled stout.

'These lands,' continued the antiquary, 'were held in grand sergeantry by the presentation of three white owls and a pot of honey – '

'Lassy me! how nice!' said Miss Julia.

Mr Peters licked his lips.

'Pray give me leave, my dear – owls and honey, whenever the king should come a rat-catching into this part of the country.'

'Rat-catching!' ejaculated the squire, pausing abruptly in the mastication of a drumstick.

'To be sure, my dear sir: don't you remember the rats once came under the forest laws – a minor species of venison? "Rats and mice, and such small deer", eh? – Shakespeare, you know. Our ancestors ate rats ["The nasty fellows!" shuddered Miss Julia, in a parenthesis]; and owls, you know, are capital mousers – '

'I've seen a howl,' said Mr Peters: 'there's one in the Soho-logical Gardens – a little hook-nosed chap in a wig, only its feathers and – '

Poor P. was destined never to finish a speech.

'*Do* be quiet!' cried the authoritative voice; and the would-be naturalist shrank into his shell, like a snail in the 'Sohological Gardens'.

'You should read Blount's *Jocular Tenures*, Mr Ingoldsby,' pursued Simpkinson. 'A learned man was Blount! Why, sir, His Royal Highness the Duke of York once paid a silver horseshoe to Lord Ferrers – '

'I've heard of him,' broke in the incorrigible Peters; 'he was hanged at the Old Bailey on a silk rope for shooting Dr Johnson.'

The antiquary vouchsafed no notice of the interruption; but taking a pinch of snuff, continued his harangue.

'A silver horseshoe, sir, which is due from every scion of royalty who rides across one of his manors; and if you look into the penny county histories, now publishing by an eminent friend of mine, you will find that Langhale in County Norfolk was held by one Baldwin *per saltum, sufflatum et pettum*; that is, he was to come every Christmas into Westminster Hall, there to take a leap, cry hem! and – '

'Mr Simpkinson, a glass of sherry?' cried Tom Ingoldsby hastily.

'Not any, thank you, sir. This Baldwin, surnamed Le – '

'Mrs Ogleton challenges you, sir; she insists upon it,' said Tom still more rapidly, at the same time filling a glass, and forcing it on the *sçavan*, who, thus arrested in the very crisis of his narrative, received and swallowed the potation as if it had been physic.

'What on earth has Miss Simpkinson discovered there?' continued Tom; 'something of interest. See how fast she is writing.'

The diversion was effectual; everyone looked towards Miss Simpkinson, who, far too ethereal for 'creature comforts', was seated apart on the dilapidated remains of an altar-tomb, committing eagerly to paper something that had strongly impressed her; the air – the eye in a 'fine frenzy rolling' – all betokened that the divine *afflatus* was come. Her father rose, and stole silently towards her.

'What an old boar!' muttered young Ingoldsby; alluding, perhaps, to a slice of brawn which he had just begun to operate upon, but which, from the celerity with which it disappeared, did not seem so very difficult of mastication.

But what had become of Seaforth and his fair Caroline all this while? Why, it so happened that they had been simultaneously stricken with the picturesque appearance of one of those high and pointed arches, which that eminent antiquary, Mr Horseley Curties, has described in his *Ancient Records*, as 'a *Gothic* window of the *Saxon* order'; and then the ivy clustered so thickly and so beautifully on the other side that they went round to look at that; and then their proximity deprived it of half its effect, and so they walked across to a little knoll, a hundred yards off, and in crossing a small ravine, they came to what in Ireland they call 'a bad step' and Charles had to carry his cousin over it; and then when they had to come back, she would not give him the trouble again for the world, so they followed a better but more circuitous route, and there were hedges and ditches in the way, and stiles to get over and gates to get through, so that an hour or more had elapsed before they were able to rejoin the party.

'Lassy me!' said Miss Julia Simpkinson, 'how long you have been gone!'

And so they had. The remark was a very just as well as a very natural one. They were gone a long while, and a nice cosy chat they had; and what do you think it was all about, my dear miss?

'O, lassy me! love, no doubt, and the moon and eyes and nightingales and – '

Stay, stay, my sweet young lady; do not let the fervour of your feelings run away with you! I do not pretend to say, indeed, that one or more of these pretty subjects might not have been introduced; but the most important and leading topic of the conference was – Lieutenant Seaforth's breeches.

'Caroline,' said Charles, 'I have had some very odd dreams since I have been at Tappington.'

'Dreams, have you?' – smiled the young lady, arching her taper neck like a swan in pluming. 'Dreams, have you?'

'Ay, dreams – or dream, perhaps, I should say; for, though repeated, it was still the same. And what do you imagine was its subject?'

'It is impossible for me to divine,' said the tongue; 'I have not the least difficulty in guessing,' said the eye, as plainly as ever eye spoke.

'I dreamt – of your great-grandfather!'

There was a change in the glance – 'My great-grandfather?'

'Yes, the old Sir Giles, or Sir John, you told me about the other day: he walked into my bedroom in his short cloak of murrey-coloured velvet, his long rapier and his Raleigh-looking hat and feather, just as the picture represents him; but with one exception.'

'And what was that?'

'Why, his lower extremities, which were visible, were those of a skeleton.'

'Well?'

'Well, after taking a turn or two about the room, and looking round him with a wistful air, he came to the bed's foot, stared at me in a manner impossible to describe – and then he – he laid hold of my pantaloons; whipped his long bony legs into them in a twinkling; and strutting up to the glass, seemed to view himself in it with great complacency. I tried to speak, but in vain. The effort, however, seemed to excite his attention; for, wheeling about, he showed me the grimmest-looking death's-head you can well imagine, and with an indescribable grin strutted out of the room.'

'Absurd, Charles! How can you talk such nonsense?'

'But, Caroline – the breeches are really gone.'

*

On the following morning, contrary to his usual custom, Seaforth was the first person in the breakfast-parlour. As no one else was present, he did precisely what nine young men out of ten so situated would have done; he walked up to the mantelpiece, established himself upon the rug, and subducting his coattails one under each arm, turned towards the fire that portion of the human frame which is considered equally indecorous to present to a friend or an enemy. A serious, not to say anxious, expression was visible upon his good-humoured countenance, and his mouth was fast buttoning itself up for an incipient whistle when little Flo, a tiny spaniel of the Blenheim breed – the pet object of Miss Julia Simpkinson's affections – bounced out from beneath a sofa and began to bark at – his pantaloons.

They were cleverly 'built', of a light-grey mixture, a broad stripe of the most vivid scarlet traversing each seam in a perpendicular direction from hip to ankle – in short, the regimental costume of the Royal Bombay Fencibles. The animal, educated in the country, had never seen such a pair of breeches in her life – *Omne ignotum pro magnifico!* The scarlet streak, inflamed as it was by the reflection of the fire, seemed to act on Flora's nerves as the same colour does on those of bulls and turkeys; she advanced at the *pas de charge*, and her vociferation, like her amazement, was unbounded. A sound kick from the disgusted officer changed its character and induced a retreat at the very moment when the mistress of the pugnacious quadruped entered to the rescue.

'Lassy me! Flo, what *is* the matter?' cried the sympathising lady, with a scrutinising glance levelled at the gentleman.

It might as well have lighted on a feather-bed. His air of imperturbable unconsciousness defied examination; and as he would not, and Flora could not, expound, that injured individual was compelled to pocket up her wrongs. Others of the household soon dropped in and clustered round the board dedicated to the most sociable of meals; the urn was paraded 'hissing hot' and the cups which 'cheer, but do not inebriate' steamed, redolent of hyson and pekoe; muffins and marmalade, newspapers and Finnon haddies, left little room for observation on the character of Charles's warlike 'turn-out'. At length a look from Caroline, followed by a smile that nearly ripened to a titter, caused him to turn abruptly and address his neighbour. It was Miss Simpkinson, who, deeply engaged in sipping her tea and turning over her album, seemed, like a female Chrononotonthologos, 'immersed in cogibundity of cogitation'. An interrogatory on the subject of her studies drew from her the confession that she was at that moment employed in putting the finishing touches to a poem inspired by the romantic shades of Bolsover. The entreaties of the company were of course urgent. Mr Peters, 'who liked verses', was especially persevering, and Sappho at length compliant. After a preparatory hem! and a glance at the mirror to ascertain that her look was sufficiently sentimental, the poetess began:

> 'There is a calm, a holy feeling,
>   Vulgar minds can never know,
> O'er the bosom softly stealing –
>   Chasten'd grief, delicious woe!
> Oh! how sweet at eve regaining
>   Yon lone tower's sequester'd shade –
> Sadly mute and uncomplaining – '

'You! – yeough! – yeough! – yow! – yow!' yelled a hapless sufferer from beneath the table. It was an unlucky hour for quadrupeds, and if 'every dog will have his day', he could not have selected a more unpropitious one than this. Mrs Ogleton, too, had a pet – a favourite pug, whose squab figure, black muzzle and tortuosity of tail, that curled like a head of celery in a salad-bowl, bespoke his Dutch extraction. 'Yow! yow yow!' continued the brute – a chorus in which Flo instantly joined. Sooth to say, pug had more reason to express his dissatisfaction than was given him by the muse of Simpkinson; the other only barked for company.

Scarcely had the poetess got through her first stanza, when Tom Ingoldsby, in the enthusiasm of the moment, became so lost in the material world that, in his abstraction, he unwarily laid his hand on the tap of the urn. Quivering with emotion, he gave it such an unlucky twist that the full stream of its scalding contents descended on the gingerbread hide of the unlucky Cupid. The confusion was complete; the whole economy of the table disarranged – the company broke up in most admired disorder – and 'vulgar minds will never know' anything more of Miss Simpkinson's ode till they peruse it in some forthcoming Annual.

Seaforth profited by the confusion to take the delinquent who had caused this 'stramash' by the arm, and to lead him to the lawn, where he had a word or two for his private ear. The conference between the young gentlemen was neither brief in its duration nor unimportant in its result. The subject was what the lawyers call tripartite, embracing the information that Charles Seaforth was over head and ears in love with Tom Ingoldsby's sister; secondly, that the lady had referred him to 'papa' for his sanction; thirdly and lastly, his nightly visitations, and consequent bereavement. At the two first items Tom smiled auspiciously – at the last he burst out into an absolute guffaw.

'Steal your breeches! Miss Bailey over again, by Jove,' shouted Ingoldsby. 'But a gentleman, you say – and Sir Giles too. I am not sure, Charles, whether I ought not to call you out for aspersing the honour of the family.'

'Laugh as you will, Tom – be as incredulous as you please. One fact is incontestable – the breeches are gone! Look here – I am reduced to my regimentals; and if these go, tomorrow I must borrow of you!'

Rochefoucault says there is something in the misfortunes of our very best friends that does not displease us; assuredly we can, most of us, laugh at their petty inconveniences, till called upon to supply them. Tom composed his features on the instant and replied with more gravity, as well as with an expletive, which, if my Lord Mayor had been within hearing, might have cost him five shillings.

'There is something very queer in this, after all. The clothes, you say, have positively disappeared. Somebody is playing you a trick; and, ten to one, your servant has a hand in it. By the way, I heard something yesterday of his kicking up a bobbery in the kitchen and seeing a ghost, or something of that kind, himself. Depend upon it, Barney is in the plot.'

It now struck the lieutenant at once, that the usually buoyant spirits of his attendant had of late been materially sobered down, his loquacity obviously circumscribed, and that he, the said lieutenant, had actually rung his bell three separate times that very morning before he could procure his attendance. Mr Maguire was forthwith summoned and underwent a close examination. The 'bobbery' was easily explained. Mr Oliver Dobbs had hinted his disapprobation of a flirtation carrying on between the gentleman from Munster and the lady from the Rue St Honoré. Mademoiselle had boxed Mr Maguire's ears, and Mr Maguire had pulled Mademoiselle upon his knee, and the lady had *not* cried *Mon Dieu!* And Mr Oliver Dobbs said it was very wrong; and Mrs Botherby said it was 'scandalous' and what ought not to be done in any moral kitchen; and Mr Maguire had got hold of the Honourable Augustus Sucklethumbkin's powder-flask, and had put large pinches of the best Double Dartford into Mr Dobbs's tobacco-box; and Mr Dobbs's pipe had exploded and set fire to Mrs Botherby's Sunday cap; and Mr Maguire had put it out with the slop-basin, 'barring the wig'; and then they were all so 'cantankerous', that Barney had gone to take a walk in the garden; and then – then Mr Barney had seen a ghost.

'A what? you blockhead!' asked Tom Ingoldsby.

'Sure then, and it's meself will tell your honour the rights of it,' said the ghost-seer. 'Meself and Miss Pauline, sir – or Miss Pauline and meself, for the ladies come first, anyhow – we got tired of the hobstroppylous scrimmaging among the ould servants that didn't know a joke when they seen one: and we went out to look at the comet, that's the roryboryalehouse, they calls him in this country – and we walked upon the lawn – and divil of any alehouse there was there at all; and Miss Pauline said it was bekase of the shrubbery maybe, and why wouldn't we see it better beyonst the trees? and so we went to the trees, but sorrow a comet did meself see there, barring a big ghost instead of it.'

'A ghost? And what sort of a ghost, Barney?'

'Och, then, divil a lie I'll tell your honour. A tall ould gentleman, he was, all in white, with a shovel on the shoulder of him, and a big torch in his fist – though what he wanted with that it's meself can't tell, for his eyes were like gig-lamps, let alone the moon and the comet, which wasn't there at all – and "Barney," says he to me – 'cause why he knew me – "Barney," says he, "what is it you're doing with the colleen there, Barney?" – Divil a word did I say. Miss Pauline screeched, and cried murther in French, and ran off with herself; and of course meself was in a mighty hurry after the lady, and had no time to stop palavering with him anyway: so I dispersed at once, and the ghost vanished in a flame of fire!'

Mr Maguire's account was received with avowed incredulity by both gentlemen; but Barney stuck to his text with unflinching pertinacity. A reference to Mademoiselle was suggested, but abandoned as neither party had a taste for delicate investigations.

'I'll tell you what, Seaforth,' said Ingoldsby, after Barney had received his dismissal, 'that there is a trick here is evident; and Barney's vision may possibly be part of it. Whether he is most knave or fool, you best know. At all events I will sit up with you tonight, and see if I can convert my ancestor into a visiting acquaintance. Meanwhile your finger on your lip!'

'Twas now the very witching time of night,
When churchyards yawn, and graves give up their dead.

Gladly would I grace my tale with decent horror and therefore I do beseech the 'gentle reader' to believe that if all the *succedanea* to this mysterious narrative are not in strict keeping he will ascribe it only to the disgraceful innovations of modern degeneracy upon the sober and dignified habits of our ancestors. I can introduce him, it is true, into an old and high-roofed chamber, its walls covered on three sides with black oak wainscoting, adorned with carvings of fruit and flowers long anterior to those of Grinling Gibbons; the fourth side is clothed with a curious remnant of dingy tapestry, once elucidatory of some scriptural history, but of which not even Mrs Botherby could determine. Mr Simpkinson, who had examined it carefully, inclined to believe the principal figure to be either Bathsheba, or Daniel in the lions' den; while Tom Ingoldsby decided in favour of the King of Bashan. All, however, was conjecture, tradition being silent on the subject.

A lofty arched portal led into and a little arched portal led out of this apartment; they were opposite each other and each possessed the security of massy bolts on its interior. The bedstead, too, was not one of yesterday but manifestly coeval with days ere Seddon was and when a good four-post 'article' was deemed worthy of being a royal bequest. The bed itself, with all appurtenances of palliasse, mattresses, etc., was of far later date, and looked most incongruously comfortable; the casements, too, with their little diamond-shaped panes and iron binding, had given way to the modern heterodoxy of the sash-window. Nor was this all that conspired to ruin the costume, and render the room a meet haunt for such 'mixed spirits' only as could condescend to don at the same time an Elizabethan doublet and Bond Street inexpressibles.

With their green morocco slippers on a modern fender, in front of a disgracefully modern grate, sat two young gentlemen, clad in 'shawl-pattern' dressing-gowns and black silk stocks, much at variance with the high cane-backed chairs which supported them. A bunch of abomination, called a cigar, reeked in the left-hand corner of the mouth of one and in the right-hand corner of the mouth of the other – an arrangement happily adapted for the escape of the noxious fumes up the chimney, without that unmerciful 'funking' each other which a less scientific disposition of the weed would have induced. A small pembroke table filled up the intervening space between them, sustaining, at each extremity, an elbow and a glass of toddy – thus in 'lonely pensive contemplation' were the two worthies occupied, when the 'iron tongue of midnight had tolled twelve'.

'Ghost-time's come!' said Ingoldsby, taking from his waistcoat pocket a watch like a gold half-crown, and consulting it as though he suspected the turret-clock over the stable of mendacity.

'Hush!' said Charles; 'did I not hear a footstep?'

There was a pause – there *was* a footstep – it sounded distinctly – it reached the door – it hesitated, stopped, and – passed on.

Tom darted across the room, threw open the door, and became aware of Mrs Botherby toddling to her chamber, at the other end of the gallery, after dosing one of the housemaids with an approved julep from the Countess of Kent's *Choice Manual*.

'Good-night, sir!' said Mrs Botherby.

'Go to the devil!' said the disappointed ghost-hunter.

An hour – two – rolled on and still no spectral visitation; nor did aught intervene to make night hideous; and when the turret-clock sounded at length the hour of three, Ingoldsby, whose patience and grog were alike exhausted, sprang from his chair, saying, 'This is all infernal nonsense, my good fellow. Deuce of any ghost shall we see tonight; it's long past the canonical hour. I'm off to bed; and as to your breeches, I'll insure them for the next twenty-four hours at least at the price of the buckram.'

'Certainly! Oh! thank'ee – to be sure!' stammered Charles, rousing himself from a reverie, which had degenerated into an absolute snooze.

'Good-night, my boy! Bolt the door behind me; and defy the Pope, the Devil and the Pretender!'

Seaforth followed his friend's advice and the next morning came down to breakfast dressed in the habiliments of the preceding day. The charm was broken, the demon defeated; the light greys with the red stripe down the seams were yet *in rerum natura* and adorned the person of their lawful proprietor.

Tom felicitated himself and his partner of the watch on the result of their vigilance; but there is a rustic adage which warns us against self-gratulation before we are quite 'out of the wood'. Seaforth was yet within its verge.

A rap at Tom Ingoldsby's door the following morning startled him as he was shaving – he cut his chin.

'Come in, and be damned to you!' said the martyr, pressing his thumb on the scarified epidermis. The door opened, and exhibited Mr Barney Maguire.

'Well, Barney, what is it?' quoth the sufferer, adopting the vernacular of his visitant.

'The master, sir – '

'Well, what does he want?'

'The loanst of a breeches, plase your honour.'

'Why you don't mean to tell me – By heaven, this is too good!' shouted Tom, bursting into a fit of uncontrollable laughter. 'Why, Barney, you don't mean to say the ghost has got them again?'

Mr Maguire did not respond to the young squire's risibility – the cast of his countenance was decidedly serious.

'Faith, then, it's gone they are, sure enough! Hasn't meself been looking over the bed, and under the bed, and *in* the bed, for the matter of that; and divil a ha'p'orth of breeches is there to the fore at all – I'm bothered entirely!'

'Hark'ee! Mr Barney,' said Tom, incautiously removing his thumb and letting a crimson stream 'incarnadine the multitudinous' lather that plastered his throat – 'this may be all very well with your master, but you don't humbug *me*, sir – tell me instantly, what have you done with the clothes?'

This abrupt transition from 'lively to severe' certainly took Maguire by surprise and he seemed for an instant as much disconcerted as it is possible to disconcert an Irish gentleman's gentleman.

'Me? is it meself, then, that's the ghost to your honour's thinking?' said he, after a moment's pause and with a slight shade of indignation in his tones; 'is it I would stale the master's things – and what would I do with them?'

'That you best know – what your purpose is I can't guess, for I don't think you mean to "stale" them, as you call it; but that you are concerned in their disappearance, I am satisfied. Confound this blood! – give me a towel, Barney.'

Maguire acquitted himself of the commission. 'As I've a sowl, your honour,' said he solemnly, 'little it is meself knows of the matter: and after what I've seen – '

'What you've seen! Why, what *have* you seen? – Barney, I don't want to enquire into your flirtations; but don't suppose you can palm off your saucer eyes and gig-lamps upon me!'

'Then, as sure as your honour's standing there, I saw him; and why wouldn't I, when Miss *Pauline* was to the fore as well as meself and – '

'Get along with your nonsense – leave the room, sir!'

'But the master?' said Barney, imploringly; 'and without a breeches? – sure he'll be catching cowld! – '

'Take that, rascal!' replied Ingoldsby, throwing a pair of pantaloons at, rather than to, him; 'but don't suppose, sir, you shall carry on your tricks here with impunity; recollect there is such a thing as a treadmill, and that my father is a county magistrate.'

Barney's eye flashed fire – he stood erect, and was about to speak; but, mastering himself, not without an effort, he took up the garment and left the room as perpendicular as a Quaker.

'Ingoldsby,' said Charles Seaforth, after breakfast, 'this is now past a joke; today is the last of my stay; for, notwithstanding the ties which detain me, common decency obliges me to visit home after so long an absence. I shall come to an immediate explanation with your father on the subject nearest my heart and depart while I have a change of dress left. On his answer will my return depend! In the meantime tell me candidly – I ask it in all seriousness and as a friend – am I not a dupe to your well-known propensity for hoaxing? have you not a hand in – '

'No, by heaven, Seaforth; I see what you mean: on my honour, I am as much mystified as yourself; and if your servant – '

'Not he – if there be a trick, he at least is not privy to it.'

'If there *be* a trick? why, Charles, do you think – '

'I know not *what* to think, Tom. As surely as you are a living man, so surely did that spectral anatomy visit my room again last night, grin in my face, and walk away with my trousers; nor was I able to spring from my bed or break the chain which seemed to bind me to my pillow.'

'Seaforth!' said Ingoldsby, after a short pause, 'I will – But hush! here are the girls and my father – I will carry off the females and leave you a clear field with the governor: carry your point with him and we will talk about your breeches afterwards.'

Tom's diversion was successful; he carried off the ladies *en masse* to look at a remarkable specimen of the class *Dodecandria Monogynia* – which they could not find; while Seaforth marched boldly up to the encounter and carried 'the governor's' out-works by a *coup de main*. I shall not stop to describe the progress of the attack; suffice it that it was as successful as could have been wished, and that Seaforth was referred back again to the lady. The happy lover was off at a tangent; the botanical party was soon overtaken; and the arm of Caroline, whom a vain endeavour to spell out the Linnaean name of a daffy-down-dilly had detained a little in the rear of the others, was soon firmly locked in his own.

> What was the world to them,
> Its noise, its nonsense, and its 'breeches' all?

Seaforth was in the seventh heaven; he retired to his room that night as happy as if no such thing as a goblin had ever been heard of and personal chattels were as well fenced in by law as real property. Not so Tom Ingoldsby: the mystery – for mystery there evidently was – had not only piqued his curiosity, but ruffled his temper. The watch of the previous night had been unsuccessful, probably because it was undisguised. Tonight he would 'ensconce himself' – not indeed 'behind the arras' – for the little that remained was, as we have seen, nailed to the wall – but in a small closet which opened from one corner of the room, and by leaving the door ajar would give to its occupant a view of all that might pass in the apartment. Here did the young ghost-hunter take up a position, with a good stout sapling under his arm, a full half-hour before Seaforth retired for the night. Not even his friend did he let into his confidence, fully determined that if his plan did not succeed, the failure should be attributed to himself alone.

At the usual hour for separation for the night, Tom saw from his concealment the lieutenant enter his room and after taking a few turns in it, with an expression so joyous as to betoken that his thoughts were mainly occupied by his approaching happiness, proceed slowly to disrobe himself. The coat, the waistcoat, the black silk stock, were gradually discarded; the green morocco slippers were kicked off and then – ay, and then – his countenance grew grave; it seemed to occur to him all at once that this was his last state, nay, that the very breeches he had on were not his own – that tomorrow morning was his last and that if he lost *them* . . . A glance showed that his mind was made up; he replaced the single button he had just subducted, and threw himself upon the bed in a state of transition – half chrysalis, half grub.

Wearily did Tom Ingoldsby watch the sleeper by the flickering light of the night-lamp, till the clock striking one induced him to increase the narrow opening which he had left for the purpose of observation. The motion, slight as it was, seemed to attract Charles's attention; for he raised himself suddenly to a sitting posture, listened for a moment, and then stood upright upon the floor. Ingoldsby was on the point of discovering himself, when, the light flashing full upon his friend's countenance, he perceived that, though his eyes were open, 'their sense was shut' – that he was yet under the influence of sleep. Seaforth advanced slowly to the washstand, lit his candle at the lamp that stood on it, then, going back to the bed's foot, appeared to search eagerly for something which he could not find. For a few moments he seemed restless and uneasy, walking round the apartment and examining the chairs, till, coming fully in front of a large swing-glass that flanked the dressing-table, he paused as if contemplating his figure in it. He now returned towards the bed, put on his slippers and, with cautious and stealthy steps, proceeded towards the little arched doorway that opened on the private staircase.

As he drew the bolts, Tom Ingoldsby emerged from his hiding-place; but the sleepwalker heard him not; he proceeded softly downstairs, followed at a due distance by his friend; opened the door which led out upon the gardens and stood at once among the thickest of the shrubs, which there clustered round the base of a corner turret and screened the postern from common observation. At this moment Ingoldsby had nearly spoiled all by making a false step; the sound attracted Seaforth's attention – he paused and turned; and, as the full moon shed her light directly upon his pale and troubled features, Tom marked, almost with dismay, the fixed and rayless appearance of his eyes –

> There was no speculation in those orbs
> That he did glare withal.

The perfect stillness preserved by his follower seemed to reassure him; he turned aside and from the midst of a thickset laurustinus drew forth a gardener's spade, shouldering which he proceeded with greater rapidity into the midst of the shrubbery. Arrived at a certain point where the earth seemed to have been recently disturbed, he set himself heartily to the task of digging, till, having thrown up several shovelfuls of mould, he stopped, flung down his tool, and very composedly began to disencumber himself of his pantaloons.

Up to this moment Tom had watched him with a wary eye; he now advanced cautiously and, as his friend was busily engaged in disentangling himself from his garment, made himself master of the spade. Seaforth, meanwhile had accomplished his purpose: he stood for a moment with

> His streamers waving in the wind,

occupied in carefully rolling up the small-clothes into as compact a form as possible, and all heedless of the breath of heaven, which might certainly be supposed at such a moment, and in such a plight, to 'visit his frame too roughly'.

He was in the act of stooping low to deposit the pantaloons in the grave which he had been digging for them, when Tom Ingoldsby came close behind him, and with the flat side of the spade –

The shock was effectual – never again was Lieutenant Seaforth known to act the part of a somnambulist. One by one, his breeches – his trousers – his pantaloons – his silk-net tights – his patent cords – his showy greys with the broad red stripe of the Bombay Fencibles, were brought to light – rescued from the grave in which they had been buried, like the strata of a Christmas pie; and after having been well aired by Mrs Botherby, they became once again effective.

The family, the ladies especially, laughed – the Peterses laughed – the Simpkinsons laughed – Barney Maguire cried, 'Botheration!' and Ma'mselle Pauline, *'Mon Dieu!'*

Charles Seaforth, unable to face the quizzing which awaited him on all sides, started off two hours earlier than he had proposed – he soon returned, however, and having, at his father-in-law's request, given up the occupation of Rajah-hunting and shooting Nabobs, led his blushing bride to the altar.

Mr Simpkinson from Bath did not attend the ceremony, being engaged at the Grand Junction meeting of *sçavans*, then congregating from all parts of the known world in the city of Dublin. His essay, demonstrating that the globe is a great custard, whipped into coagulation by whirlwinds and cooked by electricity – a little too much baked in the Isle of Portland and a thought underdone about the Bog of Allen – was highly spoken of and narrowly escaped obtaining a Bridgewater prize.

Miss Simpkinson and her sister acted as bridesmaids on the occasion; the former wrote an *epithalamium* and the latter cried, 'Lassy me!' at the clergyman's wig. Some years have since rolled on; the union has been crowned with two or three tidy little off-shoots from the family tree, of whom Master Neddy is 'grand-papa's darling' and Mary Anne mamma's particular 'Sock'. I shall only add, that Mr and Mrs Seaforth are living together quite as happily as two good-hearted, good-tempered bodies, very fond of each other, can possibly do; and that, since the day of his marriage, Charles has shown no disposition to jump out of bed or ramble out of doors o' nights – though from his entire devotion to every wish and whim of his young wife, Tom insinuates that the fair Caroline does still occasionally take advantage of it so far as to 'slip on the breeches'.

BRAM STOKER

Abraham Stoker was born near Dublin in 1847. He was virtually bedridden with an unidentified illness until the age of seven. After graduating from Trinity College, he followed his father into a career as a civil servant in Dublin Castle, writing journalism and short stories in his spare time. In 1876 he met the actor Henry Irving and two years later became manager of Irving's Lyceum Theatre in London. Through Oscar Wilde's parents, Stoker met his wife Florence Balcombe. He wrote many books of which only *Dracula* (1897) is widely remembered. He died in 1912.

The Judge's House

When the time for his examination drew near Malcolm Malcolmson made up his mind to go somewhere to read by himself. He feared the attractions of the seaside, and also he feared completely rural isolation, for of old he knew its charms, and so he determined to find some unpretentious little town where there would be nothing to distract him. He refrained from asking suggestions from any of his friends for he argued that each would recommend some place of which he had knowledge, and where he had already acquaintances. As Malcolmson wished to avoid friends he had no wish to encumber himself with the attention of friends' friends, and so he determined to look out for a place for himself. He packed a portmanteau with some clothes and all the books he required, and then took a ticket for the first name on the local timetable which he did not know.

When at the end of a three hours' journey he alighted at Benchurch, he felt satisfied that he had so far obliterated his tracks as to be sure of having a peaceful opportunity of pursuing his studies. He went straight to the one inn which the sleepy little place contained, and put up for the night. Benchurch was a market town, and once in three weeks was crowded to excess, but for the remainder of the twenty-one days it was as attractive as a desert. Malcolmson looked around the day after his arrival to try to find quarters more isolated than even so quiet an inn as the Good Traveller afforded. There was only one place which took his fancy, and it certainly satisfied his wildest ideas regarding quiet; in fact, quiet was not the proper word to apply to it – desolation was the only term conveying any suitable idea of its isolation. It was an old rambling heavy-built house of the Jacobean style, with imposing gables and windows, unusually small, set higher than was customary in such houses, and it was surrounded with a high brick wall massively built. Indeed, on examination, it looked more like a fortified house than an ordinary dwelling. But all these things pleased Malcolmson. 'Here,' he thought, 'is the very spot I have been looking for, and if I can only get opportunity of using it I shall be happy.' His joy was increased when he realised beyond doubt that it was not at present inhabited.

From the post-office he got the name of the agent, who was rarely surprised at the application to rent a part of the old house. Mr Carnford, the local lawyer and agent, was a genial old gentleman and frankly confessed his delight at anyone being willing to live in the house.

'To tell you the truth,' said he, 'I should be only too happy, on behalf of the owners, to let anyone have the house rent free for a term of years if only to accustom the people here to see it inhabited. It has been so long empty that some kind of absurd prejudice has grown up about it, and this can be best put down by its occupation – if only,' he added with a sly glance at Malcolmson, 'by a scholar like yourself, who wants it quiet for a time.'

Malcolmson thought it needless to ask the agent about the 'absurd prejudice'; he knew he would get more information, if he should require it, on that subject from other quarters. He paid his three months' rent, got a receipt, and the name of an old woman who would probably undertake to 'do' for him, and came away with the keys in his pocket. He then went to the landlady of the inn, who was a cheerful and most kindly person, and asked her advice as to such stores and provisions as he would be likely to require. She threw up her hands in amazement when he told her where he was going to settle himself.

'Not in the Judge's House!' she said, and grew pale as she spoke. He explained the locality of the house, saying that he did not know its name. When he had finished she answered: 'Aye, sure enough – sure enough the very place! It is the Judge's House sure enough.'

He asked her to tell him about the place, why so called, and what there was against it. She told him that it was so called locally because it had been many years before – how long she could not say, as she was herself from another part of the country, but she thought it must have been a hundred years or more – the abode of a judge who was held in great terror on account of his harsh sentences and his hostility to prisoners at assizes. As to what there was against the house itself she could not tell. She had often asked, but no one could inform her; but there was a general feeling that there was *something*, and for her own part she would not take all the money in Drinkwater's Bank to stay in the house an hour by herself. Then she apologised to Malcolmson for her disturbing talk.

'It is too bad of me, sir, and you – and a young gentleman, too – if you will pardon me saying it, going to live there all alone. If you were my boy – and you'll excuse me for saying it – you wouldn't sleep there a night, not if I had to go there myself and pull the big alarm bell that's on the roof!'

The good creature was so manifestly in earnest, and was so kindly in her intentions, that Malcolmson, although amused, was touched. He told her kindly how much he appreciated her interest in him, and added: 'But, my dear Mrs Witham, indeed you need not be concerned about me! A man who is reading for the Mathematical Tripos has too much to think of to be disturbed by any of these mysterious *somethings*, and his work is of too exact and prosaic a kind to allow of his having any corner in his mind for mysteries of any sort. Harmonical progression, permutations and combinations and elliptic functions have sufficient mysteries for me!'

Mrs Witham kindly undertook to see after his commissions, and he went himself to look for the old woman who had been recommended to him. When he returned to the Judge's House with her, after an interval of a couple of hours, he found Mrs Witham herself waiting with several men and boys carrying parcels, and an upholsterer's man with a bed in a cart, for she said, though tables and chairs might be all very well, a bed that hadn't been aired for mayhap fifty years was not proper for young bones to lie on. She was evidently curious to see the inside of the house; and though manifestly so afraid of the *somethings* that at the slightest sound she clutched on to Malcolmson, whom she never left for a moment, went over the whole place.

After his examination of the house, Malcolmson decided to take up his abode in the great dining-room, which was big enough to serve for all his requirements; and Mrs Witham, with the aid of the charwoman, Mrs Dempster, proceeded to arrange matters. When the hampers were brought in and unpacked, Malcolmson saw that with much kind forethought she had sent from her own kitchen sufficient provisions to last for a few days. Before going she expressed all sorts of kind wishes; and at the door turned and said: 'And perhaps, sir, as the room is big and draughty it might be well to have one of those big screens put round your bed at night – though, truth to tell, I would die myself if I were to be so shut in with all kinds of – of *things*, that put their heads round the sides, or over the top, and look on me!' The image which she had called up was too much for her nerves, and she fled incontinently.

Mrs Dempster sniffed in a superior manner as the landlady disappeared, and remarked that for her own part she wasn't afraid of all the bogies in the kingdom.

'I'll tell you what it is, sir,' she said: 'bogies is all kinds and sorts of things – except bogies! Rats and mice, and beetles; and creaky doors, and loose slates, and broken panes, and stiff drawer handles that stay out when you pull them and then fall down in the middle of the night. Look at the wainscot of the room! It is old – hundreds of years old! Do you think there's no rats and beetles there! And do you imagine, sir, that you won't see none of them! Rats is bogies, I tell you, and bogies is rats; and don't you get to think anything else!'

'Mrs Dempster,' said Malcolmson gravely, making her a polite bow, 'you know more than a Senior Wrangler! And let me say that, as a mark of esteem for your indubitable soundness of head and heart, I shall, when I go, give you possession of this house, and let you stay here by yourself for the last two months of my tenancy, for four weeks will serve my purpose.'

'Thank you kindly, sir!' she answered, 'but I couldn't sleep away from home a night. I am in Greenhow's Charity, and if I slept a night away from my rooms I should lose all I have got to live on. The rules is very strict; and there's too many watching for a vacancy for me to run any risks in the matter. Only for that, sir, I'd gladly come here and attend on you altogether during your stay.'

'My good woman,' said Malcolmson hastily, 'I have come here on purpose to obtain solitude; and believe me I am grateful to the late Greenhow for having so organised his admirable charity – whatever it is – that I am perforce denied the opportunity of suffering from such a form of temptation! St Anthony himself could not be more rigid on the point!'

The old woman laughed harshly. 'Ah, you young gentlemen,' she said, 'you don't fear for naught; and belike you'll get all the solitude you want here.' She set to work with her cleaning; and by nightfall, when Malcolmson returned from his walk – he always had one of his books to study as he walked – he found the room swept and tidied, a fire burning in the old hearth, the lamp lit, and the table spread for supper with Mrs Witham's excellent fare. 'This is comfort, indeed,' he said, as he rubbed his hands.

When he had finished his supper, and lifted the tray to the other end of the great oak dining-table, he got out his books again, put fresh wood on the fire, trimmed his lamp, and set himself down to a spell of real hard work. He went on without pause till about eleven o'clock, when he knocked off for a bit to fix his fire and lamp, and to make himself a cup of tea. He had always been a tea-drinker, and during his college life had sat late at work and had taken tea late. The rest was a great luxury to him and he enjoyed it with a sense of delicious, voluptuous ease. The renewed fire leaped and sparkled and threw quaint shadows through the great old room; and as he sipped his hot tea he revelled in the sense of isolation from his kind. Then it was that he began to notice for the first time what a noise the rats were making.

'Surely,' he thought, 'they cannot have been at it all the time I was reading. Had they been, I must have noticed it!' Presently, when the noise increased, he satisfied himself that it was really new. It was evident that at first the rats had been frightened at the presence of a stranger, and the light of fire and lamp; but as the time went on they had grown bolder and were now disporting themselves as was their wont.

How busy they were! and hark to the strange noises! Up and down behind the old wainscot, over the ceiling and under the floor they raced, and gnawed, and scratched! Malcolmson smiled to himself as he recalled to mind the saying of Mrs Dempster, 'Bogies is rats, and rats is bogies!' The tea began to have its effect of intellectual and nervous stimulus, he saw with joy another long spell of work to be done before the night was past, and in the sense of security which it gave him, he allowed himself the luxury of a good look round the room. He took his lamp in one hand and went all around, wondering that so quaint and beautiful an old house had been so long neglected. The carving of the oak on the panels of the wainscot was fine, and on and round the doors and windows it was beautiful and of rare merit. There were some old pictures on the walls, but they were coated so thick with dust and dirt that he could not distinguish any detail of them, though he held his lamp as high as he could over his head. Here and there as he went round he saw some crack or hole blocked for a moment by the face of a rat with its bright eyes glittering in the light, but in an instant it was gone, and a squeak and a scamper followed.

The thing that most struck him, however, was the rope of the great alarm bell on the roof, which hung down in a corner of the room on the right-hand side of the fireplace. He pulled up close to the hearth a great high-backed carved oak chair, and sat down to his last cup of tea. When this was done, he made up the fire and went back to his work, sitting at the corner of the table, having the fire to his left. For a while the rats disturbed him somewhat with their perpetual scampering, but he got accustomed to the noise as one does to the ticking of a clock or to the roar of moving water; and he became so immersed in his work that everything in the world, except the problem which he was trying to solve, passed away from him.

He suddenly looked up; his problem was still unsolved, and there was in the air that sense of the hour before the dawn, which is so dread to doubtful life. The noise of the rats had ceased. Indeed it seemed to him that it must have ceased but lately and that it was the sudden cessation which had disturbed him. The fire had fallen low, but still it threw out a deep red glow. As he looked he started in spite of his *sang froid*.

There on the great high-backed carved oak chair by the right side of the fireplace sat an enormous rat, steadily glaring at him with baleful eyes. He made a motion to it as though to hunt it away, but it did not stir. Then he made the motion of throwing something. Still it did not stir, but showed its great white teeth angrily, and its cruel eyes shone in the lamplight with an added vindictiveness.

Malcolmson felt amazed, and seizing the poker from the hearth ran at it to kill it. Before, however, he could strike it, the rat, with a squeak that sounded like the concentration of hate, jumped upon the floor, and, running up the rope of the alarm bell, disappeared in the darkness beyond the range of the green-shaded lamp. Instantly, strange to say, the noisy scampering of the rats in the wainscot began again.

By this time Malcolmson's mind was quite off the problem; and as a shrill cockcrow outside told him of the approach of morning, he went to bed and to sleep.

He slept so sound that he was not even waked by Mrs Dempster coming in to make up his room. It was only when she had tidied up the place and got his breakfast ready and tapped on the screen which closed in his bed that he woke. He was a little tired still after his night's hard work, but a strong cup of tea soon freshened him up, and, taking his book, he went out for his morning walk, bringing with him a few sandwiches lest he should not care to return till dinner time. He found a quiet walk between high elms some way outside the town and here he spent the greater part of the day studying his Laplace.

On his return he looked in to see Mrs Witham and to thank her for her kindness. When she saw him coming through the diamond-paned bay-window of her sanctum she came out to meet him and asked him in. She looked at him searchingly and shook her head as she said: 'You must not overdo it, sir. You are paler this morning than you should be. Too late hours and too hard work on the brain isn't good for any man! But tell me, sir, how did you pass the night? Well, I hope? But, my heart! sir, I was glad when Mrs Dempster told me this morning that you were all right and sleeping sound when she went in.'

'Oh, I was all right,' he answered, smiling, 'the *somethings* didn't worry me, as yet. Only the rats; and they had a circus, I tell you, all over the place. There was one wicked looking old devil that sat up on my own chair by the fire, and wouldn't go till I took the poker to him, and then he ran up the rope of the alarm bell and got to somewhere up the wall or the ceiling – I couldn't see where, it was so dark.'

'Mercy on us,' said Mrs Witham, 'an old devil, and sitting on a chair by the fireside! Take care, sir! take care! There's many a true word spoken in jest.'

'How do you mean? 'Pon my word, I don't understand.'

'An old devil! *The* old devil, perhaps. There! sir, you needn't laugh,' for Malcolmson had broken into a hearty peal. 'You young folks thinks it easy to laugh at things that makes older ones shudder. Never mind, sir! never mind! Please God, you'll laugh all the time. It's what I wish you myself!' and the good lady beamed all over in sympathy with his enjoyment, her fears gone for a moment.

'Oh, forgive me!' said Malcolmson presently. 'Don't think me rude but the idea was too much for me – that the old devil himself was on the chair last night!' And at the thought he laughed again. Then he went home to dinner.

This evening the scampering of the rats began earlier; indeed it had been going on before his arrival, and only ceased while his presence by its freshness disturbed them. After dinner he sat by the fire for a while and had a smoke; and then, having cleared his table, began to work as before. Tonight the rats disturbed him more than they had done on the previous night. How they scampered up and down and under and over! How they squeaked, and scratched, and gnawed! How they, getting bolder by degrees, came to the mouths of their holes and to the chinks and cracks and crannies in the wainscoting till their eyes shone like tiny lamps as the firelight rose and fell. But to him, now doubtless accustomed to them, their eyes were not wicked; only their playfulness touched him. Sometimes the boldest of them made sallies out on the floor or along the mouldings of the wainscot. Now and again as they disturbed him Malcolmson made a sound to frighten them, smiting the table with his hand or giving a fierce 'Hsh, hsh' so that they fled straightway to their holes.

And so the early part of the night wore on; and despite the noise Malcolmson got more and more immersed in his work.

All at once he stopped, as on the previous night, being overcome by a sudden sense of silence. There was not the faintest sound of gnaw, or scratch, or squeak. The silence was as of the grave. He remembered the odd occurrence of the previous night, and instinctively he looked at the chair standing close by the fireside. And then a very odd sensation thrilled through him.

There, on the great old high-backed carved oak chair beside the fireplace sat the same enormous rat, steadily glaring at him with baleful eyes.

Instinctively he took the nearest thing to his hand, a book of logarithms, and flung it at it. The book was badly aimed and the rat did not stir, so again the poker performance of the previous night was repeated; and again the rat, being closely pursued, fled up the rope of the alarm bell. Strangely, too, the departure of this rat was instantly followed by the renewal of the noise made by the general rat community. On this occasion, as on the previous one, Malcolmson could not see at what part of the room the rat disappeared, for the green shade of his lamp left the upper part of the room in darkness, and the fire had burned low.

On looking at his watch he found it was close on midnight; and, not sorry for the *divertissement*, he made up his fire and made himself his nightly pot of tea. He had got through a good spell of work, and thought himself entitled to a cigarette; and so he sat on the great carved oak chair before the fire and enjoyed it. Whilst smoking he began to think that he would like to know where the rat disappeared to, for he had certain ideas for the morrow not entirely disconnected with a rat-trap. Accordingly he lit another lamp and placed it so that it would shine well into the right-hand corner of the wall by the fire-place. Then he got all the books he had with him, and placed them handy to throw at the vermin. Finally he lifted the rope of the alarm bell and placed the end of it on the table, fixing the extreme end under the lamp. As he handled it he could not help noticing how pliable it was, especially for so strong a rope, and one not in use. 'You could hang a man with it,' he thought to himself. When his preparations were made he looked around, and said complacently: 'There now, my friend, I think we shall learn something of you this time!' He began his work again, and though as before somewhat disturbed at first by the noise of the rats, soon lost himself in his propositions and problems.

Again he was called to his immediate surroundings suddenly. This time it might not have been the sudden silence only which took his attention; there was a slight movement of the rope, and the lamp moved. Without stirring, he looked to see if his pile of books was within range, and then cast his eye along the rope. As he looked he saw the great rat drop from the rope on to the oak armchair and sit there glaring at him. He raised a book in his right hand, and taking careful aim, flung it at the rat. The latter, with a quick movement, sprang aside and dodged the missile. He then took another book, and a third, and flung them one after another at the rat, but each time unsuccessfully. At last, as he stood with a book poised in his hand to throw, the rat squeaked and seemed afraid. This made Malcolmson more than ever eager to strike, and the book flew and struck the rat a resounding blow. It gave a terrified squeak, and turning on its pursuer a look of terrible malevolence, ran up the chairback and made a great jump to the rope of the alarm bell and ran up it like lightning. The lamp rocked under the sudden strain, but it was a heavy one and did not topple over. Malcolmson kept his eyes on the rat, and saw it by the light of the second lamp leap to a moulding of the wainscot and disappear through a hole in one of the great pictures which hung on the wall, obscured and invisible through its coating of dirt and dust.

'I shall look up my friend's habitation in the morning,' said the student, as he went over to collect his books. 'The third picture from the fireplace; I shall not forget.' He picked up the books one by one, commenting on them as he lifted them. '*Conic Sections* he does not mind, nor *Cycloidal Oscillations*, nor the *Principia*, nor *Quaternions*, nor *Thermodynamics*. Now for the book that fetched him!' Malcolmson took it up and looked at it. As he did so he started, and a sudden pallor overspread his face. He looked round uneasily and shivered slightly, as he murmured to himself, 'The Bible my mother gave me! What an odd coincidence.'

He sat down to work again, and the rats in the wainscot renewed their gambols. They did not disturb him, however; somehow their presence gave him a sense of companionship. But he could not attend to his work, and after striving to master the subject on which he was engaged gave it up in despair, and went to bed as the first streak of dawn stole in through the eastern window.

He slept heavily but uneasily, and dreamed much; and when Mrs Dempster woke him late in the morning he seemed ill at ease, and for a few minutes did not seem to realise exactly where he was. His first request rather surprised the servant.

'Mrs Dempster, when I am out today I wish you would get

the steps and dust or wash those pictures – specially that one the third from the fireplace – I want to see what they are.'

Late in the afternoon Malcolmson worked at his books in the shaded walk, and the cheerfulness of the previous day came back to him as the day wore on, and he found that his reading was progressing well. He had worked out to a satisfactory conclusion all the problems which had as yet baffled him, and it was in a state of jubilation that he paid a visit to Mrs Witham at the Good Traveller. He found a stranger in the cosy sitting-room with the landlady, who was introduced to him as Dr Thornhill. She was not quite at ease, and this, combined with the doctor's plunging at once into a series of questions, made Malcolmson come to the conclusion that his presence was not an accident, so without preliminary he said: 'Dr Thornhill, I shall with pleasure answer you any question you may choose to ask me if you will answer me one question first.'

The doctor seemed surprised, but he smiled and answered at once. 'Done! What is it?'

'Did Mrs Witham ask you to come here and see me and advise me?'

Dr Thornhill for a moment was taken aback, and Mrs Witham got fiery red and turned away; but the doctor was a frank and ready man, and he answered at once and openly: 'She did: but she didn't intend you to know it. I suppose it was my clumsy haste that made you suspect. She told me that she did not like the idea of your being in that house all by yourself, and that she thought you took too much strong tea. In fact, she wants me to advise you if possible to give up the tea and the very late hours. I was a keen student in my time so I suppose I may take the liberty of a college man, and without offence, advise you not quite as a stranger.'

Malcolmson with a bright smile held out his hand. 'Shake! as they say in America,' he said. 'I must thank you for your kindness and Mrs Witham too, and your kindness deserves a return on my part. I promise to take no more strong tea – no tea at all till you let me – and I shall go to bed tonight at one o'clock at the latest. Will that do.'

'Capital,' said the doctor. 'Now tell us all that you noticed in the old house;' and so Malcolmson then and there told in minute detail all that had happened in the last two nights. He was interrupted every now and then by some exclamation from Mrs Witham, till finally when he told of the episode of the Bible the landlady's pent-up emotions found vent in a shriek; and it was not till a stiff glass of brandy and water had been administered that she grew composed again. Dr Thornhill listened with a face of growing gravity, and when the narrative was complete and Mrs Witham had been restored he asked: 'The rat always went up the rope of the alarm bell?'

'Always.'

'I suppose you know,' said the doctor after a pause, 'what the rope is?'

'No!'

'It is,' said the doctor slowly, 'the very rope which the hangman used for all the victims of the judge's judicial rancour!' Here he was interrupted by another scream from Mrs Witham, and steps had to he taken for her recovery. Malcolmson, having looked at his watch and found that it was close to his dinner hour, had gone home before her complete recovery.

When Mrs Witham was herself again she almost assailed the doctor with angry questions as to what he meant by putting such horrible ideas into the poor young man's mind. 'He has quite enough there already to upset him,' she added.

Dr Thornhill replied: 'My dear madam, I had a distinct purpose in it! I wanted to draw his attention to the bell rope, and to fix it there. It may be that he is in a highly overwrought state and has been studying too much, although I am bound to say that he seems as sound and healthy a young man, mentally and bodily, as ever I saw – but then the rats – and that suggestion of

the devil . . . ' The doctor shook his head and went on, 'I would
have offered to go and stay the night with him but I felt sure it
would have been a cause of offence. He may get in the night
some strange fright or hallucination; and if he does I told him
to pull that rope. All alone as he is it will give us warning, and
we may reach him in time to be of service. I shall be sitting up
pretty late tonight and shall keep my ears open. Do not be
alarmed if Benchurch gets a surprise before morning.'

'Oh, doctor, what do you mean? What do you mean?'

'I mean this: that possibly – nay more, probably – we shall hear
the great alarm bell from the Judge's House tonight,' and the
doctor made about as effective an exit as could be thought of.

When Malcolmson arrived home he found that it was a little
after his usual time, and Mrs Dempster had gone away – the
rules of Greenhow's Charity were not to be neglected. He was
glad to see that the place was bright and tidy with a cheerful
fire and a well-trimmed lamp. The evening was colder than
might have been expected in April, and a heavy wind was
blowing with such rapidly increasing strength that there was
every promise of a storm during the night. For a few minutes
after his entrance the noise of the rats ceased; but so soon as
they became accustomed to his presence they began again. He
was glad to hear them, for he felt once more the sense of
companionship in their noise, and his mind ran back to the
strange fact that they only ceased to manifest themselves when
that other – the great rat with the baleful eyes – came upon the
scene. The reading-lamp only was lit and its green shade kept
the ceiling and the upper part of the room in darkness, so that
the cheerful light from the hearth spreading over the floor and
shining on the white cloth laid over the end of the table was
warm and cheery. Malcolmson sat down to his dinner with a
good appetite and a buoyant spirit. After his dinner and a
cigarette he sat steadily down to work, determined not to let
anything disturb him, for he remembered his promise to the

doctor, and made up his mind to make the best of the time at his disposal.

For an hour or so he worked all right, and then his thoughts began to wander from his books. The actual circumstances around him, the calls on his physical attention and his nervous susceptibility were not to be denied. By this time the wind had become a gale, and the gale a storm. The old house, solid though it was, seemed to shake to its foundations, and the storm roared and raged through its many chimneys and its queer old gables, producing strange, unearthly sounds in the empty rooms and corridors. Even the great alarm bell on the roof must have felt the force of the wind, for the rope rose and fell slightly, as though the bell were moved a little from time to time, and the limber rope fell on the oak floor with a hard and hollow sound.

As Malcolmson listened to it he bethought himself of the doctor's words, 'It is the rope which the hangman used for the victims of the judge's judicial rancour,' and he went over to the corner of the fireplace and took it in his hand to look at it. There seemed a sort of deadly interest in it, and as he stood there he lost himself for a moment in speculation as to who these victims were and the grim wish of the judge to have such a ghastly relic ever under his eyes. As he stood there, the swaying of the bell on the roof still lifted the rope now and again; but presently there came a new sensation – a sort of tremor in the rope, as though something was moving along it.

Looking up instinctively, Malcolmson saw the great rat coming slowly down towards him, glaring at him steadily. He dropped the rope and started back with a muttered curse, and the rat, turning, ran up the rope again and disappeared, and at the same instant Malcolmson became conscious that the noise of the rats, which had ceased for a while, began again.

All this set him thinking, and it occurred to him that he had not investigated the lair of the rat or looked at the pictures, as he had intended. He lit the other lamp without the shade and, holding it up, went and stood opposite the third picture from the fireplace on the right-hand side where he had seen the rat disappear on the previous night.

At the first glance he started back so suddenly that he almost dropped the lamp, and a deadly pallor overspread his face. His knees shook and heavy drops of sweat came on his forehead and he trembled like an aspen. But he was young and plucky, and pulled himself together, and after the pause of a few seconds stepped forward again, raised the lamp, and examined the picture which had been dusted and washed and now stood out clearly.

It was of a judge dressed in his robes of scarlet and ermine. His face was strong and merciless, evil, crafty and vindictive, with a sensual mouth and a hooked nose of ruddy colour, shaped like the beak of a bird of prey. The rest of the face was of a cadaverous colour. The eyes were of peculiar brilliance and had a terribly malignant expression. As he looked at them, Malcolmson grew cold, for he saw there the very counterpart of the eyes of the great rat. The lamp almost fell from his hand when he saw the rat with its baleful eyes peering out through the hole in the corner of the picture and noted the sudden cessation of the noise of the other rats. However, he pulled himself together and went on with his examination of the picture.

The judge was seated in a great high-backed carved oak chair on the right-hand side of a great stone fireplace where, in the corner, a rope hung down from the ceiling, its end lying coiled on the floor. With a feeling of something like horror, Malcolmson recognised the scene of the room as it stood and gazed around him in an awestruck manner as though he expected to find some strange presence behind him. Then he looked over to the corner of the fireplace – and with a loud cry he let the lamp fall from his hand.

There, in the judge's armchair, with the rope hanging behind, sat the rat with the judge's baleful eyes, now intensified and with a fiendish leer. Save for the howling of the storm without there was silence.

The fallen lamp recalled Malcolmson to himself. Fortunately it was of metal, and so the oil was not spilt. However, the practical need of attending to it settled at once his nervous apprehensions. When he had turned it out, he wiped his brow and thought for a moment.

'This will not do,' he said to himself. 'If I go on like this I shall become a crazy fool. This must stop! I promised the doctor I would not take tea. Faith, he was pretty right! My nerves must have been getting into a queer state. Funny I did not notice it. I never felt better in my life. However, it is all right now, and I shall not be such a fool again.'

Then he mixed himself a good stiff glass of brandy and water and resolutely sat down to his work.

It was nearly an hour later when he looked up from his book, disturbed by the sudden stillness. Without, the wind howled and roared louder than ever, and the rain drove in sheets against the windows, beating like hail on the glass; but within there was no sound whatever save the echo of the wind as it roared in the great chimney, and now and then a hiss as a few raindrops found their way down the chimney in a lull of the storm. The fire had fallen low and had ceased to flame, though it threw out a red glow. Malcolmson listened attentively, and presently heard a thin, squeaking noise, very faint. It came from the corner of the room where the rope hung down, and he thought it was the creaking of the rope on the floor as the swaying of the bell raised and lowered it. Looking up, however, he saw in the dim light the great rat clinging to the rope and gnawing it. The rope was already nearly gnawed through – he could see the lighter colour where the strands were laid bare. As he looked the job was completed, and the severed end of the rope fell clattering on the oaken floor, whilst for an instant the great rat remained like a knob or tassel at the end of the rope, which now began to sway to and fro. Malcolmson felt for a moment another pang of terror as he thought that now the possibility of calling the outer world to his assistance was cut off, but an intense anger took its place, and seizing the book he was reading he hurled it at the rat. The blow was well aimed, but before the missile could reach it the rat dropped off and struck the floor with a soft thud. Malcolmson instantly rushed over towards it, but it darted away and disappeared in the darkness of the shadows of the room.

Malcolmson felt that his work was over for the night, and determined then and there to vary the monotony of the proceedings by a hunt for the rat, taking off the green shade of the lamp so as to ensure a wider spreading light. As he did so the gloom of the upper part of the room was relieved, and in the new flood of light, great by comparison with the previous darkness, the pictures on the wall stood out boldly. From where he stood, Malcolmson saw right opposite to him the third picture on the wall from the right of the fireplace. He rubbed his eyes in surprise, and then a great fear began to come upon him. In the centre of the picture was a great irregular patch of brown canvas, as fresh as when it was stretched on the frame. The background was as before, with chair and chimney-corner and rope, but the figure of the judge had disappeared.

Malcolmson, almost in a chill of horror, turned slowly round, and then he began to shake and tremble like a man in a palsy. His strength seemed to have left him, and he was incapable of action or movement, hardly even of thought. He could only see and hear.

There, on the great high-backed carved oak chair, sat the judge in his robes of scarlet and ermine, with his baleful eyes glaring vindictively and a smile of triumph on the resolute, cruel mouth as he lifted with his hands a *black cap*. Malcolmson felt as if the blood was running from his heart, as one does in moments of prolonged suspense. There was a singing in his ears. Without, he could hear the roar and howl of the tempest, and through it, swept on the storm, came the striking of midnight by the great chimes in the market-place. He stood for a space of time that seemed to him endless, still as a statue and with wide-open, horror-struck eyes, breathless. As the clock struck, so the smile of triumph on the judge's face intensified, and at the last stroke of midnight he placed the black cap on his head.

Slowly and deliberately the judge rose from his chair and picked up the piece of rope of the alarm bell which lay on the floor, drew it through his hands as if he enjoyed its touch, and then deliberately began to knot one end of it, fashioning it into a noose. This he tightened and tested with his foot, pulling hard at it till he was satisfied and then making a running noose of it, which he held in his hand. Then he began to move along the table on the opposite side to Malcolmson, keeping his eyes on him until he had passed him, when with a quick movement he stood in front of the door. Malcolmson then began to feel that he was trapped, and tried to think of what he should do. There was some fascination in the judge's eyes, which he never took off him, and he had, perforce, to look. He saw the judge approach – still keeping between him and the door – and raise the noose and throw it towards him as if to entangle him. With a great effort he made a quick movement to one side, and saw the rope fall beside him, and heard it strike the oaken floor. Again the judge raised the noose and tried to ensnare him, ever keeping his baleful eyes fixed on him, and each time by a mighty effort the student just managed to evade it. So this went on for many times, the judge seeming never discouraged nor discomposed at failure, but playing as a cat does with a mouse. At last in despair, which had reached its climax, Malcolmson cast a quick glance round him. The lamp seemed to have blazed up, and there was a fairly good light in the room. At the many rat holes and in the chinks and crannies of the wainscot he saw the rats' eyes; and this aspect, that was purely physical, gave him a gleam of comfort. He looked up and saw that the rope of the great alarm bell was laden with rats. Every inch of it was covered with them, and more and more were pouring through the small circular hole in the ceiling whence it emerged, so that with their weight the bell was beginning to sway.

Hark! it had swayed till the clapper had touched the bell. The sound was but a tiny one, but the bell was only beginning to sway and it would increase.

At the sound the judge, who had been keeping his eyes fixed on Malcolmson, looked up, and a scowl of diabolical anger overspread his face. His eyes fairly glowed like hot coals, and he stamped his foot with a sound that seemed to make the house shake. A dreadful peal of thunder broke overhead as he raised the rope again, while the rats kept running up and down the bell-rope as though working against time. This time, instead of throwing it, he drew close to his victim, and held open the noose as he approached. As he came closer there seemed something paralysing in his very presence, and Malcolmson stood rigid as a corpse. He felt the judge's icy fingers touch his throat as he adjusted the rope. The noose tightened – tightened. Then the judge, taking the rigid form of the student in his arms, carried him over and placed him standing in the oak chair, and stepping up beside him, put his hand up and caught the end of the swaying rope of the alarm bell. As he raised his hand the rats fled squeaking, and disappeared through the hole in the ceiling. Taking the end of the noose which was round Malcolmson's neck he tied it to the hanging bell-rope, and then descending, pulled away the chair.

When the alarm bell of the Judge's House began to sound a crowd soon assembled. Lights and torches of various kinds appeared, and soon a silent crowd was hurrying to the spot. They knocked loudly at the door, but there was no reply. Then they burst in the door, and poured into the great dining-room, the doctor at the head.

There at the end of the rope of the great alarm hell hung the body of the student, and on the face of the judge in the picture was a malignant smile.

STEPHEN CRANE

Stephen Crane was born in Newark, New Jersey, in 1871, the youngest son of a Methodist minister. After failing to settle at university, Crane moved to New York where he worked as a journalist and wrote his first novel *Maggie: A Girl of the Streets* in 1893. His second novel, *The Red Badge of Courage*, was far more successful, critically and commercially, and after its publication in 1895 he travelled as a newspaper correspondent to Mexico, to Cuba and to Greece. In 1897 he settled in England, where he met Joseph Conrad and Henry James. He died in Germany in 1900, aged twenty-eight.

An Illusion in Red and White

Nights on the Cuban blockade were long, at times exciting, often dull. The men on the small leaping dispatch boats became as intimate as if they had all been buried in the same coffin. Correspondents, who in New York had passed as fairly good fellows, sometimes turned out to be perfect rogues of vanity and selfishness, but still more often the conceited chumps of Park Row became the kindly and thoughtful men of the Cuban blockade. Also each correspondent told all he knew, and some-times more. For this gentle tale I am indebted to one of the brightening stars of New York journalism.

'Now, this is how I imagine it happened. I don't say it happened this way, but this is how I imagine it happened. And it always struck me as being a very interesting story. I hadn't been on the paper very long, but just about long enough to get a good show, when the city editor suddenly gave me this sparkling murder assignment.

'It seems that up in one of the back counties of New York State a farmer had taken a dislike to his wife; and so he went into the kitchen with an axe, and in the presence of their four little children he just casually rapped his wife on the nape of the neck with the head of this axe. It was early in the morning, but he told the children they had better go to bed. Then he took his wife's body out in the woods and buried it.

'This farmer's name was Jones. The widower's eldest child was named Freddy. A week after the murder, one of the long-distance neighbours was rattling past the house in his buckboard when he saw Freddy playing in the road. He pulled up, and asked the boy about the welfare of the Jones family.

' "Oh, we're all right," said Freddy, "only ma – she ain't – she's dead."

' "Why, when did she die?" cried the startled farmer. "What did she die of?"

' "Oh," answered Freddy, "last week a man with red hair and big white teeth and real white hands came into the kitchen, and killed ma with an axe."

'The farmer was indignant with the boy for telling him this strange childish nonsense, and drove off much disgruntled. But he recited the incident at a tavern that evening, and when people began to miss the familiar figure of Mrs Jones at the Methodist Church on Sunday mornings, they ended by having an investigation. The calm Jones was arrested for murder, and his wife's body was lifted from its grave in the woods and buried by her own family.

'The chief interest now centred upon the children. All four declared that they were in the kitchen at the time of the crime, and that the murderer had red hair. The hair of the virtuous Jones was grey. They said that the murderer's teeth were large and white. Jones only had about eight teeth, and these were small and brown. They said the murderer's hands were white. Jones's hands were the colour of black walnuts. They lifted their dazed, innocent faces, and crying, simply because the mysterious excitement and their new quarters frightened them, they repeated their heroic legend without important deviation, and without the parroty sameness which would excite suspicion.

'Women came to the jail and wept over them and made little frocks for the girls and little breeches for the boys, and idiotic detectives questioned them at length. Always they upheld the theory of the murderer with red hair, big white teeth and white hands. Jones sat in his cell, his chin sullenly on his first vest button. He knew nothing about any murder, he said. He thought his wife had gone on a visit to some relatives. He had had a quarrel with her, and she had said that she was going to leave him for a time, so that he might have proper opportunities for cooling down. Had he seen the blood on the floor? Yes, he had seen the blood on the floor. But he had been cleaning and skinning a rabbit at that spot on the day of his wife's dis-appearance. He had thought nothing of it. What had his children said when he returned from the fields? They had told him that their mother had been killed by an axe in the hands of a man with red hair, big white teeth and white hands. To questions as to why he had not informed the police of the county, he answered that he had not thought it a matter of sufficient importance. He had cordially hated his wife, anyhow, and he was glad to be rid of her. He decided afterwards that she had run off; and he had never credited the fantastic tale of the children.

'Of course, there was very little doubt in the minds of the majority that Jones was guilty, but there was a fairly strong following who insisted that Jones was a coarse and brutal man, and perhaps weak in his head – yes – but not a murderer. They pointed to the children and declared that children could never lie, and these kids, when asked, said that the murder had been committed by a man with red hair, large white teeth and white hands. I myself had a number of interviews with the children, and I was amazed at the convincing power of their little story. Shining in the depths of the limpid up-turned eyes, one could fairly see tiny mirrored images of men with red hair, big white teeth and white hands.

'Now, I'll tell you how it happened – how I imagine it was done. Some time after burying his wife in the woods Jones strolled back into the house. Seeing nobody, he called out in the familiar fashion, "Mother!" Then the kids came out whimpering. "Where is your mother?" said Jones. The children looked at him blankly. "Why, pa," said Freddy, "you came in here, and hit ma with the axe; and then you sent us to bed." "Me?" cried Jones "I haven't been near the house since breakfast-time."

'The children did not know how to reply. Their meagre little sense informed them that their father had been the man with the axe, but he denied it, and to their minds everything was a mere great puzzle with no meaning whatever, save that it was mysteriously sad and made them cry.

' "What kind of a looking man was it?" said Jones.

'Freddy hesitated. "Now – he looked a good deal like you, pa."

' "Like me?" said Jones. "Why, I thought you said he had red hair?"

' "No, I didn't," replied Freddy. "I thought he had grey hair, like yours."

' "Well," said Jones, "I saw a man with kind of red hair going along the road up yonder, and I thought maybe that might have been him."

'Little Lucy, the second child, here piped up with intense conviction. "His hair was a little teeny bit red. I saw it."

' "No," said Jones. "The man I saw had very red hair. And what did his teeth look like? Were they big and white?"

' "Yes," answered Lucy, "they were."

'Even Freddy seemed to incline to think it.

' "His teeth may have been big and white."

'Jones said little more at that time. Later he intimated to the children that their mother had gone off on a visit, and although they were full of wonder, and sometimes wept because of the oppression of an incomprehensible feeling in the air, they said nothing. Jones did his chores. Everything was smooth.

'The morning after the day of the murder, Jones and his children had a breakfast of hominy and milk.

' "Well, this man with red hair and big white teeth, Lucy," said Jones. "Did you notice anything else about him?"

'Lucy straightened in her chair, and showed the childish desire to come out with brilliant information which would gain her father's approval.

' "He had white hands – hands all white – "

' "How about you, Freddy?"

' "I didn't look at them much, but I think they were white," answered the boy.

' "And what did little Martha notice?" cried the tender parent. "Did she see the big bad man?"

'Martha, aged four, replied solemnly, "His hair was all yed, and his hand was white – all white."

' "That's the man I saw up the road," said Jones to Freddy.

' "Yes, sir, it seems like it must have been him," said the boy, his brain now completely muddled.

'Again Jones allowed the subject of his wife's murder to lapse. The children did not know that it was a murder, of course. Adults were always performing in a way to make children's heads swim. For instance, what could be more incomprehensible than that a man with two horses, dragging a queer thing, should walk all day making the grass turn down and the earth turn up? And why did they cut the long grass and put it in a barn? And what was a cow for? Did the water in the well like to be there? All these actions and things were grand, because they were associated with the high estate of grown-up people, but they were deeply mysterious. If then, a man with red hair, big white teeth and white hands should hit their mother on the nape of the neck with an axe, it was merely a phenomenon of grown-up life. Little Henry, the baby, when he had a want, howled and pounded the table with his spoon. That was all of life to him. He was not concerned with the fact that his mother had been murdered.

'One day Jones said to his children suddenly, "Look here; I wonder if you could have made a mistake. Are you absolutely sure that the man you saw had red hair, big white teeth and white hands?"

'The children were indignant with their father. "Why, of course, pa, we ain't made no mistake. We saw him as plain as day."

'Later young Freddy's mind began to work like ketchup. His nights were haunted with terrible memories of the man with the red hair, big white teeth and white hands, and the prolonged absence of his mother made him wonder and wonder. Presently he quite gratuitously developed the theory that his mother was dead. He knew about death. He had once seen a dead dog; also dead chickens, rabbits and mice. One day he asked his father, "Pa, is ma ever coming back?"

'Jones said: "Well, no; I don't think she is." This answer confirmed the boy in his theory. He knew that dead people did not come back.

'The attitude of Jones towards this descriptive legend of the man with the axe was very peculiar. He came to be in opposition to it. He protested against the convictions of the children, but he could not move them. It was the one thing in their lives of which they were stonily and absolutely positive.

'Now that really ends the story. But I will continue for your amusement. The jury hung Jones as high as they could, and they were quite right because Jones confessed before he died. Freddy is now a highly respected driver of a grocery waggon in

Ogdensburg. When I was up there a good many years afterwards people told me that when he ever spoke of the tragedy at
all he was certain to denounce the alleged confession as a lie.
He considered his father a victim of the stupidity of juries, and
someday he hopes to meet the man with the red hair, big white
teeth and white hands, whose image still remains so distinct in
his memory that he could pick him out in a crowd of ten
thousand.'

EDGAR ALLAN POE

Edgar Poe was born in Boston in 1809 to travelling actors David Poe and Elizabeth Arnold Hopkins. His mother died in December 1811 and his father died or disappeared soon afterwards, leading to Edgar's being brought up by John Allan, a prosperous Virginian merchant. Five of his formative years were spent with the Allans in England. On their return to the States, Edgar attended the University of Virginia before enlisting as a private soldier. He published his first poems in 1827 but it was not until he was discharged from the army and won a literary prize for his tale 'MS Found in a Bottle' that he started to achieve fame as a short-story writer. He gained the position of editor at the *Southern Literary Messenger* and distinguished himself writing journalism, literary criticism, stories and poems. He had his greatest successes in 1845 when 'The Raven' and a new collection of his *Tales* were published to national acclaim. His wife Virginia, a cousin whom he had married when she was only thirteen, died early and this led to the depression and reliance on drink that have scarred his reputation and dominated the interpretation of his work. He himself died in mysterious circumstances in 1849 and the details of his biography remain controversial and disputed.

The Oblong Box

Some years ago, I engaged passage from Charleston, South Carolina, to the city of New York, in the fine packet-ship *Independence*. We were to sail on the fifteenth of the month (June), weather permitting, and on the fourteenth I went on board to arrange some matters in my stateroom.

I found that we were to have a great many passengers,

including a more than usual number of ladies. On the list were several of my acquaintances and among other names I was rejoiced to see that of Mr Cornelius Wyatt, a young artist, for whom I entertained feelings of warm friendship. He had been a fellow-student at Columbia University, where we were very much together. He had the ordinary temperament of genius, and was a compound of misanthropy, sensibility and enthusiasm. To these qualities he united the warmest and truest heart which ever beat in a human bosom.

I observed that his name was carded upon *three* staterooms; and, upon again referring to the list of passengers, I found that he had engaged passage for himself, wife and two sisters – his own. The staterooms were sufficiently roomy, and each had two berths, one above the other. These berths, to be sure, were so exceedingly narrow as to be insufficient for more than one person; still, I could not comprehend why there were three staterooms for these four persons. I was, just at that epoch, in one of those moody frames of mind which make a man abnormally inquisitive about trifles; and I confess, with shame, that I busied myself in a variety of ill-bred and preposterous conjectures about this matter of the supernumerary stateroom. It was no business of mine, to be sure; but with none the less pertinacity did I occupy myself in attempts to resolve the enigma. At last I reached a conclusion which wrought in me great wonder why I had not arrived at it before. 'It is a servant, of course,' I said; 'what a fool I am not sooner to have thought of so obvious a solution!' And then I again repaired to the list – but here I saw distinctly that *no* servant was to come with the party; although, in fact, it had been the original design to bring one – for the words 'and servant' had been first written and then over-scored. 'Oh, extra baggage, to be sure,' I now said to myself – 'something he wishes not to be put in the hold – something to be kept under his own eye – ah, I have it – a painting or so – and this is what he has been bargaining about with Nicolino, the Italian Jew.' This idea satisfied me, and I dismissed my curiosity for the nonce.

Wyatt's two sisters I knew very well, and most amiable and clever girls they were. His wife he had newly married, and I had never yet seen her. He had often talked about her in my presence, however, and in his usual style of enthusiasm. He described her as of surpassing beauty, wit and accomplishment. I was, therefore, quite anxious to make her acquaintance.

On the day on which I visited the ship (the fourteenth), Wyatt and party were also to visit it – so the captain informed me – and I waited on board an hour longer than I had designed, in hope of being presented to the bride; but then an apology came: 'Mrs W. was a little indisposed, and would decline coming on board until tomorrow, at the hour of sailing.'

The morrow having arrived, I was going from my hotel to the wharf, when Captain Hardy met me and said that, 'owing to circumstances' (a stupid but convenient phrase), he rather thought the *Independence* would not sail for a day or two, and that when all was ready, he would send up and let me know. This I thought strange, for there was a stiff southerly breeze; but as 'the circumstances' were not forthcoming, although I pumped for them with much perseverance, I had nothing to do but to return home and digest my impatience at leisure.

I did not receive the expected message from the captain for nearly a week. It came at length, however, and I immediately went on board. The ship was crowded with passengers, and everything was in the bustle attendant upon making sail. Wyatt's party arrived in about ten minutes after myself. There were the two sisters, the bride and the artist – the latter in one of his customary fits of moody misanthropy. I was too well used to these, however, to pay them any special attention. He did not even introduce me to his wife; this courtesy devolving, perforce, upon his sister Marian – a very sweet and intelligent girl, who, in a few hurried words, made us acquainted.

Mrs Wyatt had been closely veiled; and when she raised her veil, in acknowledging my bow, I confess that I was very profoundly astonished. I should have been much more so, however, had not long experience advised me not to trust, with too implicit a reliance, the enthusiastic description of my friend, the artist, when indulging in comments upon the loveliness of women. When beauty was the theme, I well knew with what facility he soared into the regions of the purely ideal.

The truth is, I could not help regarding Mrs Wyatt as a decidedly plain-looking woman. If not positively ugly, she was not, I think, very far from it. She was dressed, however, in exquisite taste – and then I had no doubt that she had captivated my friend's heart by the more enduring graces of the intellect and soul. She said very few words, and passed at once into her stateroom with Mr W.

My old inquisitiveness now returned. There was *no* servant – *that* was a settled point. I looked, therefore, for the extra baggage. After some delay, a cart arrived at the wharf with an oblong pine box, which was everything that seemed to be expected. Immediately upon its arrival we made sail, and in a short time were safely over the bar and standing out at sea.

The box in question was, as I say, oblong. It was about six feet in length by two and a half in breadth; I observed it attentively, and like to be precise. Now this shape was *peculiar*; and no sooner had I seen it, than I took credit to myself for the accuracy of my guessing. I had reached the conclusion, it will be remembered, that the extra baggage of my friend, the artist, would prove to be pictures, or at least a picture – for I knew he had been for several weeks in conference with Nicolino; and now here was a box which, from its shape, *could* possibly contain nothing in the world but a copy of Leonardo's *Last Supper*; and a copy of this very *Last Supper*, done by Rubini the younger, at Florence, I had known, for some time, to be in the possession of Nicolino. This point, therefore, I considered as sufficiently settled. I chuckled excessively when I thought of my acumen. It was the first time I had ever known Wyatt to keep from me any of his artistical secrets; but here he evidently intended to steal a march upon me, and smuggle a fine picture to New York, under my very nose, expecting me to know nothing of the matter. I resolved to quiz him well, now and hereafter.

One thing, however, annoyed me not a little. The box did *not* go into the extra stateroom. It was deposited in Wyatt's own; and there, too, it remained, occupying very nearly the whole of the floor – no doubt to the exceeding discomfort of the artist and his wife; this the more especially as the tar or paint with which it was lettered in sprawling capitals emitted a strong, disagreeable, and, to *my* fancy, a peculiarly disgusting odour. On the lid were painted the words – 'Mrs Adelaide Curtis, Albany, New York. Charge of Cornelius Wyatt, Esq. This side up. To be handled with care.'

Now, I was aware that Mrs Adelaide Curtis, of Albany, was the artist's wife's mother; but then I looked upon the whole address as a mystification, intended especially for myself. I made up my mind, of course, that the box and contents would never get farther north than the studio of my misanthropic friend in Chambers Street, New York.

For the first three or four days we had fine weather, although the wind was dead ahead, having chopped round to the north-ward immediately upon our losing sight of the coast. The passengers were, consequently, in high spirits, and disposed to be social. I must except, however, Wyatt and his sisters, who behaved stiffly and, I could not help thinking, uncourteously to the rest of the party. *Wyatt's* conduct, I did not so much regard. He was gloomy, even beyond his usual habit – in fact he was *morose* – but in him I was prepared for eccentricity. For the sisters, however, I could make no excuse. They secluded themselves in their staterooms during the greater part of the passage, and absolutely refused, although I repeatedly urged them, to hold communication with any person on board.

Mrs Wyatt herself was far more agreeable. That is to say, she was *chatty*; and to be chatty is no slight recommendation at sea. She became *excessively* intimate with most of the ladies; and, to my profound astonishment, evinced no equivocal disposition to coquet with the men. She amused us all very much. I say '*amused*' – and scarcely know how to explain myself. The truth is, I soon found that Mrs W. was far oftener laughed *at* than *with*. The gentlemen said little about her; but the ladies, in a little while, pronounced her 'a good-hearted thing, rather indifferent-looking, totally uneducated, and decidedly vulgar'. The great wonder was how Wyatt had been entrapped into such a match. Wealth was the general solution – but this I knew to be no solution at all; for Wyatt had told me she neither brought him a dollar nor had any expectations from any source whatever. He had married, he said, for love, and for love only; and his bride was far more than worthy of his love. When I thought of these expressions, on the part of my friend, I confess that I felt indescribably puzzled. Could it be possible that he was taking leave of his senses? What else could I think? *He*, so refined, so intellectual, so fastidious, with so exquisite a perception of the faulty, and so keen an appreciation of the beautiful! To be sure, the lady seemed especially fond of *him* – particularly so in his absence – when she made herself ridiculous by frequent quotations of what had been said by her 'beloved husband, Mr Wyatt'. The word 'husband' seemed for ever – to use one of her own delicate expressions – for ever 'on the tip of her tongue'. In the meantime, it was observed by all on board, that he avoided *her* in the most pointed manner, and, for the most part, shut himself up alone in his stateroom, where, in fact, he might have been said to live altogether, leaving his wife at full liberty to amuse herself as she thought best, in the public society of the main cabin.

My conclusion, from what I saw and heard, was that the artist, by some unaccountable freak of fate, or perhaps in some fit of enthusiastic and fanciful passion, had been induced to unite himself with a person altogether beneath him, and that the natural result, entire and speedy disgust, had ensued. I pitied him from the bottom of my heart – but could not, for that reason, quite forgive his incommunicativeness in the matter of the *Last Supper*. For this I resolved to have my revenge.

One day he came upon deck, and, taking his arm as had been my wont, I sauntered with him backwards and forwards. His gloom, however (which I considered quite natural under the circumstances), seemed entirely unabated. He said little, and that moodily, and with evident effort. I ventured a jest or two, and he made a sickening attempt at a smile. Poor fellow! – as I thought of his wife, I wondered that he could have heart to put on even the semblance of mirth. At last I ventured a home thrust. I determined to commence a series of covert insinuations, or innuendoes, about the oblong box – just to let him perceive, gradually, that I was *not* altogether the butt, or victim, of his little bit of pleasant mystification. My first observation was by way of opening a masked battery. I said something about the 'peculiar shape of *that* box'; and, as I spoke the words, I smiled knowingly, winked, and touched him gently with my forefinger in the ribs.

The manner in which Wyatt received this harmless pleasantry convinced me at once that he was mad. At first he stared at me as if he found it impossible to comprehend the witticism of my remark; but as its point seemed slowly to make its way into his brain, his eyes in the same proportion seemed protruding from their sockets. Then he grew very red – then hideously pale – then, as if highly amused with what I had insinuated, he began a loud and boisterous laugh, which, to my astonishment, he kept up with gradually increasing vigour for ten minutes or more. In conclusion, he fell flat and heavily upon the deck. When I ran to uplift him, to all appearance he was dead.

I called assistance, and with much difficulty, we brought him to himself. Upon reviving, he spoke incoherently for some time. At length we bled him and put him to bed. The next morning he was quite recovered, so far as regarded his mere bodily health. Of his mind I say nothing, of course. I avoided him during the rest of the passage, by advice of the captain, who seemed to coincide with me altogether in my views of his insanity, but cautioned me to say nothing on this head to any person on board.

Several circumstances occurred immediately after this fit of Wyatt's, which contributed to heighten the curiosity with which I was already possessed. Among other things, this: I had been nervous, drunk too much strong green tea and slept ill at night – in fact, for two nights I could not be properly said to have slept at all. Now, my stateroom opened into the main cabin, or dining-room, as did those of all the single men on board. Wyatt's three rooms were in the after-cabin, which was separated from the main one by a slight sliding door, never locked even at night. As we were almost constantly on a wind, and the breeze was not a little stiff, the ship heeled to leeward very considerably; and whenever her starboard side was to leeward, the sliding door between the cabins slid open, and so remained, nobody taking the trouble to get up and shut it. But my berth was in such a position that when my own stateroom door was open, as well as the sliding door in question (and my own door was *always* open on account of the heat), I could see into the after-cabin quite distinctly, and just at that portion of it, too, where were situated the staterooms of Mr Wyatt. Well, during two nights (*not* consecutive), while I lay awake, I clearly saw Mrs W., about eleven o'clock upon each night, steal cautiously from the stateroom of Mr W., and enter the extra room, where she remained until daybreak, when she was called by her husband and went back. That they were virtually separated was clear. They had separate apartments – no doubt in contemplation of a more permanent divorce; and here after all, I thought, was the mystery of the extra stateroom.

There was another circumstance, too, which interested me much. During the two wakeful nights in question, and immediately after the disappearance of Mrs Wyatt into the extra stateroom, I was attracted by certain singular, cautious, subdued noises in that of her husband. After listening to them for some time, with thoughtful attention, I at length succeeded perfectly in translating their import. They were sounds occasioned by the artist in prising open the oblong box by means of a chisel and mallet – the latter being apparently muffled or deadened by some soft woollen or cotton substance in which its head was enveloped.

In this manner I fancied I could distinguish the precise moment when he fairly disengaged the lid – also, that I could determine when he removed it altogether, and when he deposited it upon the lower berth in his room; this latter point I knew, for example, by certain slight taps which the lid made in striking against the wooden edges of the berth, as he endeavoured to lay it down very gently – there being no room for it on the floor. After this there was a dead stillness, and I heard nothing more, upon either occasion, until nearly daybreak; unless, perhaps, I may mention a low sobbing or murmuring sound, so very much suppressed as to be nearly inaudible – if, indeed, the whole of this latter noise were not rather produced by my own imagination. I say it seemed to resemble sobbing or sighing – but, of course, it could not have been either. I rather think it was a ringing in my own ears. Mr Wyatt, no doubt, according to custom, was merely giving the rein to one of his hobbies – indulging in one of his fits of artistic enthusiasm. He had opened his oblong box in order to feast his eyes on the pictorial treasure within. There was nothing in this, however, to make him sob. I repeat, therefore, that it must have been simply a freak of my own fancy, distempered by good Captain Hardy's green tea. Just before dawn, on each of the two nights of which I speak, I distinctly heard Mr Wyatt replace the lid upon the oblong box, and force the nails into their old places, by means of the muffled mallet. Having done this, he issued from his stateroom, fully dressed, and proceeded to call Mrs W. from hers.

We had been at sea seven days, and were now off Cape Hatteras, when there came a tremendously heavy blow from the south-west. We were, in a measure, prepared for it, however, as the weather had been holding out threats for some time. Everything was made snug, alow and aloft; and as the wind steadily freshened, we lay to, at length, under spanker and foretopsail, both double-reefed.

In this trim we rode safely enough for forty-eight hours – the ship proving herself an excellent sea-boat, in many respects, and shipping no water of any consequence. At the end of this period, however, the gale had freshened into a hurricane, and our after-sail split into ribbons, bringing us so much in the trough of the water that we shipped several prodigious seas, one immediately after the other. By this accident we lost three men overboard with the caboose, and nearly the whole of the larboard bulwarks. Scarcely had we recovered our senses before the foretopsail went into shreds, when we got up a storm staysail, and with this did pretty well for some hours, the ship heading the sea much more steadily than before.

The gale still held on, however, and we saw no signs of its abating. The rigging was found to be ill-fitted and greatly strained; and on the third day of the blow, about five in the afternoon, our mizzen mast, in a heavy lurch to windward, went by the board. For an hour or more we tried in vain to get rid of it on account of the prodigious rolling of the ship; and, before we had succeeded, the carpenter came aft and announced four feet of water in the hold. To add to our dilemma, we found the pumps choked and nearly useless.

All was now confusion and despair – but an effort was made to lighten the ship by throwing overboard as much of her cargo as could be reached, and by cutting away the two masts that remained. This we at last accomplished – but we were still unable to do anything at the pumps; and, in the meantime, the leak gained on us fast.

At sundown, the gale had sensibly diminished in violence, and as the sea went down with it, we still entertained faint hopes of saving ourselves in the boats. At eight o'clock the clouds broke away to windward, and we had the advantage of a full moon – a piece of good fortune which served wonderfully to cheer our drooping spirits.

After incredible labour we succeeded, at length, in getting the long-boat over the side without material accident, and into this we crowded the whole of the crew and most of the passengers. This party made off immediately, and after undergoing much suffering, finally arrived, in safety, at Ocracoke Inlet, on the third day after the wreck.

Fourteen passengers, with the captain, remained on board, resolving to trust their fortunes to the jolly-boat at the stern. We lowered it without difficulty, although it was only by a miracle that we prevented it from swamping as it touched the water. It contained, when afloat, the captain and his wife, Mr Wyatt and party, a Mexican officer, wife, four children, and myself, with a negro valet.

We had no room, of course, for anything except a few positively necessary instruments, some provisions, and the clothes upon our backs. No one had thought of even attempting to save anything more. What must have been the astonishment of all then, when, having proceeded a few fathoms from the ship,

Mr Wyatt stood up in the stern-sheets, and coolly demanded of Captain Hardy that the boat should be put back for the purpose of taking in his oblong box!

'Sit down, Mr Wyatt,' replied the captain, somewhat sternly, 'you will capsize us if you do not sit quite still. Our gunwale is almost in the water now.'

'The box!' vociferated Mr Wyatt, still standing – 'the box, I say! Captain Hardy, you cannot, you *will* not refuse me. Its weight will be but a trifle – it is nothing – mere nothing. By the mother who bore you – for the love of heaven – by your hope of salvation, I *implore* you to put back for the box!'

The captain, for a moment, seemed touched by the earnest appeal of the artist; but he regained his stern composure, and merely said, 'Mr Wyatt, you are mad. I cannot listen to you. Sit down, I say, or you will swamp the boat. Stay – hold him – seize him! – he is about to spring overboard! There – I knew it – he is over!'

As the captain said this, Mr Wyatt, in fact, sprang from the boat, and as we were yet in the lee of the wreck, succeeded, by almost superhuman exertion, in getting hold of a rope which hung from the fore-chains. In another moment he was on board, and rushing frantically down into the cabin.

In the meantime, we had been swept astern of the ship, and being quite out of her lee, were at the mercy of the tremendous sea which was still running. We made a determined effort to put back, but our little boat was like a feather in the breath of the tempest. We saw at a glance that the doom of the unfortunate artist was sealed.

As our distance from the wreck rapidly increased, the madman (for as such only could we regard him) was seen to emerge from the companionway, up which, by dint of a strength that appeared gigantic, he dragged, bodily, the oblong box. While we gazed in the extremity of astonishment, he passed, rapidly, several turns of a three-inch rope, first around the box and then around his body. In another instant both body and box were in the sea – disappearing suddenly, at once and for ever.

We lingered awhile sadly upon our oars, with our eyes riveted upon the spot. At length we pulled away. The silence remained unbroken for an hour. Finally, I hazarded a remark.

'Did you observe, captain, how suddenly they sank? Was not that an exceedingly singular thing? I confess that I entertained some feeble hope of his final deliverance, when I saw him lash himself to the box, and commit himself to the sea.'

'They sank as a matter of course,' replied the captain, 'and that like a shot. They will soon rise again, however – *but not till the salt melts*.'

'The salt!' I ejaculated.

'Hush!' said the captain, pointing to the wife and sisters of the deceased. 'We must talk of these things at some more appropriate time.'

We suffered much, and made a narrow escape; but fortune befriended us, as well as our mates in the long boat. We landed, in fine, more dead than alive, after four days of intense distress, upon the beach opposite Roanoke Island. We remained here a week, were not ill-treated by the wreckers, and at length obtained a passage to New York.

About a month after the loss of the *Independence*, I happened to meet Captain Hardy in Broadway. Our conversation turned, naturally, upon the disaster, and especially upon the sad fate of poor Wyatt. I thus learned the following particulars.

The artist had engaged passage for himself, wife, two sisters and a servant. His wife was, indeed, as she had been represented, a most lovely and most accomplished woman. On the morning of the fourteenth of June (the day on which I first visited the ship), the lady suddenly sickened and died. The young husband was frantic with grief – but circumstances imperatively forbade his deferring his voyage to New York. It was necessary to take to her mother the corpse of his adored wife, and on the other hand, the universal prejudice which would prevent his doing so openly was well known. Nine-tenths of the passengers would have abandoned the ship rather than take passage with a dead body.

In this dilemma, Captain Hardy arranged that the corpse, being first partially embalmed, and packed, with a large quantity of salt, in a box of suitable dimensions, should be conveyed on board as merchandise. Nothing was to be said of the lady's decease; and, as it was well understood that Mr Wyatt had engaged passage for his wife, it became necessary that some person should personate her during the voyage. This the deceased's lady's-maid was easily prevailed on to do. The extra stateroom, originally engaged for this girl, during her mistress's life, was now merely retained. In this stateroom the pseudo wife slept, of course, every night. In the daytime she performed, to the best of her ability, the part of her mistress – whose person, it had been carefully ascertained, was unknown to any of the passengers on board.

My own mistakes arose, naturally enough, through too careless, too inquisitive and too impulsive a temperament. But of late, it is a rare thing that I sleep soundly at night. There is a countenance which haunts me, turn as I will. There is an hysterical laugh which will for ever ring within my ears.

OSCAR WILDE

Oscar Fingal O'Flahertie Wills Wilde (1854–1900) was an Irish-born poet, dramatist and novelist. At Oxford, Wilde founded an aesthetic movement that advocated art for art's sake. At the height of his success, he began an affair with the young Lord Alfred Douglas, whose father, the Marquis of Queensberry, accused Wilde of being a 'somdomite' (*sic*). Tried and found guilty of homosexual practices, Wilde was sentenced to imprisonment (1895–97) with hard labour. After his release, he lived in Paris until his death. Celebrated among his works are *The Importance of Being Earnest* and *The Portrait of Dorian Gray*; *The Ballad of Reading Gaol* and *De Profundis* (1905) are the fruits of his imprisonment.

The Sphinx without a Secret

One afternoon I was sitting outside the Café de la Paix, watching the splendour and shabbiness of Parisian life, and wondering over my vermouth at the strange panorama of pride and poverty that was passing before me, when I heard someone call my name. I turned round and saw Lord Murchison. We had not met since we had been at college together, nearly ten years before, so I was delighted to come across him again, and we shook hands warmly. At Oxford we had been great friends. I had liked him immensely, he was so handsome, so high-spirited, and so honourable. We used to say of him that he would be the best of fellows if he did not always speak the truth, but I think we really admired him all the more for his frankness. I found him a good deal changed. He looked anxious and puzzled, and seemed to be in doubt about something. I felt it could not be modern scepticism, for Murchison was the stoutest of Tories, and believed in the Pentateuch as firmly as he believed in the House of Peers; so I concluded that it was a woman, and asked him if he was married yet.

'I don't understand women well enough,' he answered.

'My dear Gerald,' I said, 'women are meant to be loved, not to be understood.'

'I cannot love where I cannot trust,' he replied.

'I believe you have a mystery in your life, Gerald,' I exclaimed; 'tell me about it.'

'Let us go for a drive,' he answered, 'it is too crowded here. No, not a yellow carriage, any other colour – there, that dark green one will do;' and in a few moments we were trotting down the boulevard in the direction of the Madeleine.

'Where shall we go to?' I said.

'Oh, anywhere you like!' he answered – 'to the restaurant in the Bois; we will dine there, and you shall tell me all about yourself.'

'I want to hear about you first,' I said. 'Tell me your mystery.'

He took from his pocket a little silver-clasped morocco case, and handed it to me. I opened it. Inside there was the photograph of a woman. She was tall and slight, and strangely picturesque with her large vague eyes and loosened hair. She looked like a *clairvoyante*, and was wrapped in rich furs.

'What do you think of that face?' he said. 'Is it truthful?'

I examined it carefully. It seemed to me the face of someone who had a secret, but whether that secret was good or evil I could not say. Its beauty was a beauty moulded out of many mysteries – the beauty, in fact, which is psychological, not plastic – and the faint smile that just played across the lips was far too subtle to be really sweet.

'Well,' he cried impatiently, 'what do you say?'

'She is the Gioconda in sables,' I answered. 'Let me know all about her.'

'Not now,' he said; 'after dinner,' and began to talk of other things.

When the waiter brought us our coffee and cigarettes I reminded Gerald of his promise. He rose from his seat, walked two or three times up and down the room, and, sinking into an armchair, told me the following story: 'One evening,' he said, 'I was walking down Bond Street about five o'clock. There was a terrific crush of carriages, and the traffic was almost stopped. Close to the pavement was standing a little yellow brougham which, for some reason or other, attracted my attention. As I passed by there looked out from it the face I showed you this afternoon. It fascinated me immediately. All that night I kept thinking of it, and all the next day. I wandered up and down that wretched Row, peering into every carriage, and waiting for the yellow brougham; but I could not find *ma belle inconnue*, and at last I began to think she was merely a dream. About a week afterwards I was dining with Madame de Rastail. Dinner was for eight o'clock; but at half-past eight we were still waiting in the drawing-room. Finally the servant threw open the door and announced Lady Alroy. It was the woman I had been looking for. She came in very slowly, looking like a moonbeam in grey lace, and, to my intense delight, I was asked to take her in to dinner. After we had sat down, I remarked quite innocently, "I think I caught sight of you in Bond Street some time ago, Lady Alroy." She grew very pale, and said to me in a low voice, "Pray do not talk so loud; you may be overheard." I felt miserable at having made such a bad beginning, and plunged recklessly into the subject of the French plays. She spoke very little, always in the same low musical voice, and seemed as if she was afraid of someone listening. I fell passionately, stupidly in love, and the indefinable atmosphere of mystery that surrounded her excited my most ardent curiosity. When she was going away, which she did very soon after dinner, I asked her if I might call and see her. She hesitated for a moment, glanced round to see if anyone

was near us, and then said, "Yes; tomorrow at a quarter to five."
I begged Madame de Rastail to tell me about her; but all that I
could learn was that she was a widow with a beautiful house in
Park Lane, and as some scientific bore began a dissertation on
widows, as exemplifying the survival of the matrimonially fittest,
I left and went home.

'The next day I arrived at Park Lane punctual to the
moment, but was told by the butler that Lady Alroy had just
gone out. I went down to the club quite unhappy and very
much puzzled, and after long consideration wrote her a letter,
asking if I might be allowed to try my chance some other
afternoon. I had no answer for several days, but at last I got a
little note saying she would be at home on Sunday at four and
with this extraordinary postscript: "Please do not write to me
here again; I will explain when I see you." On Sunday she
received me, and was perfectly charming; but when I was going
away she begged of me, if I ever had occasion to write to her
again, to address my letter to Mrs Knox, care of Whittaker's
Library, Green Street. 'There are reasons," she said, "why I
cannot receive letters in my own house."

'All through the season I saw a great deal of her, and the
atmosphere of mystery never left her. Sometimes I thought
that she was in the power of some man, but she looked so
unapproachable that I could not believe it. It was really very
difficult for me to come to any conclusion, for she was like one
of those strange crystals that one sees in museums, which are
at one moment clear and at another clouded. At last I determined to ask her to be my wife: I was sick and tired of the
incessant secrecy that she imposed on all my visits, and on the
few letters I sent her. I wrote to her at the library to ask her if
she could see me the following Monday at six. She answered
yes, and I was in the seventh heaven of delight. I was infatuated
with her: in spite of the mystery, I thought then – in
consequence of it, I see now. No; it was the woman herself I

loved. The mystery troubled me, maddened me. Why did chance put me in its track?'

'You discovered it, then?' I cried.

'I fear so,' he answered. 'You can judge for yourself. When Monday came round I went to lunch with my uncle, and about four o'clock found myself in the Marylebone Road. My uncle, you know, lives in Regent's Park. I wanted to get to Piccadilly, and took a short cut through a lot of shabby little streets. Suddenly I saw in front of me Lady Alroy, deeply veiled and walking very fast. On coming to the last house in the street, she went up the steps, took out a latchkey, and let herself in. "Here is the mystery," I said to myself; and I hurried on and examined the house. It seemed a sort of place for letting lodgings. On the doorstep lay her handkerchief, which she had dropped. I picked it up and put it in my pocket. Then I began to consider what I should do. I came to the conclusion that I had no right to spy on her, and I drove down to the club. At six I called to see her. She was lying on a sofa, in a tea-gown of silver tissue looped up by some strange moonstones that she always wore. She was looking quite lovely. "I am so glad to see you," she said; "I have not been out all day." I stared at her in amazement, and pulling the handkerchief out of my pocket, handed it to her. "You dropped this in Cumnor Street this afternoon, Lady Alroy," I said very calmly. She looked at me in terror, but made no attempt to take the handkerchief. "What were you doing there?" I asked. "What right have you to question me?" she answered. "The right of a man who loves you," I replied; "I came here to ask you to be my wife." She hid her face in her hands, and burst into floods of tears. "You must tell me," I continued. She stood up, and, looking me straight in the face, said, "Lord Murchison, there is nothing to tell you." – "You went to meet someone," I cried; "this is your mystery." She grew dreadfully white, and said, "I went to meet no one." – "Can't you tell the truth?" I exclaimed. "I have told it,' she replied. I was mad, frantic; I don't know what I said, but I said terrible things to her. Finally I rushed out of the house. She wrote me a letter the next day; I sent it back unopened, and started for Norway with Alan Colville. After a month I came back, and the first thing I saw in the *Morning Post* was the death of Lady Alroy. She had caught a chill at the opera, and had died in five days of congestion of the lungs. I shut myself up and saw no one. I had loved her so much, I had loved her so madly. Good God! how I had loved that woman!'

'You went to the street, to the house in it?' I said.

'Yes,' he answered. 'One day I went to Cumnor Street. I could not help it; I was tortured with doubt. I knocked at the door, and a respectable looking woman opened it to me. I asked her if she had any rooms to let. "Well, sir," she replied, "the drawing-rooms are supposed to be let; but I have not seen the lady for three months, and as rent is owing on them, you can have them." – "Is this the lady?" I said, showing the photograph. "That's her, sure enough," she exclaimed; "and when is she coming back, sir?" – "The lady is dead," I replied. "Oh, sir, I hope not!" said the woman; "she was my best lodger. She paid me three guineas a week merely to sit in my drawing-rooms now and then." – "She met someone here?" I said; but the woman assured me that it was not so, that she always came alone, and saw no one. "What on earth did she do here?" I cried. "She simply sat in the drawing-room, sir, reading books, and sometimes had tea," the woman answered. I did not know what to say, so I gave her a sovereign and went away. Now, what do you think it all meant? You don't believe the woman was telling the truth?'

'I do.'

'Then why did Lady Alroy go there?'

'My dear Gerald,' I answered, 'Lady Alroy was simply a woman with a mania for mystery. She took those rooms for the pleasure of going there with her veil down and imagining she was a heroine. She had a passion for secrecy, but she herself was merely a sphinx without a secret.'

'Do you really think so?'

'I am sure of it,' I replied.

He took out the morocco case, opened it, and looked at the photograph. 'I wonder?' he said at last.

JAMES HOGG

James Hogg (1770–1835) was a Scottish poet who was known as the Ettrick Shepherd. He was so called because he was born in Ettrick and inherited the occupation of shepherd from his family. Largely self-educated, he is known for his verse celebrating Scottish rural scenes and pursuits and for his treatments of the Celtic folklore tradition. He was encouraged by Sir Walter Scott and in his later life was associated with *Blackwood's Magazine*.

Mary Burnet

The following incidents are related as having occurred at a shepherd's house, not a hundred miles from St Mary's Loch; but as the descendants of one of the families still reside in the vicinity, I deem it requisite to use names which cannot be recognised, save by those who have heard the story.

John Allanson, the farmer's son of Inverlawn, was a handsome, roving and incautious young man, enthusiastic, amorous and fond of adventure, and one who could hardly be said to fear the face of either man, woman or spirit. Among other love adventures, he fell a-courting Mary Burnet, of Kirkstyle, a most beautiful and innocent maiden, and one who had been bred up in rural simplicity. She loved him, but yet she was afraid of him; and though she had no objection to meeting with him among others, yet she carefully avoided meeting with him alone, though often and earnestly urged to it. One day, the young man, finding an opportunity, at Our Lady's Chapel, after mass, urged his suit for a private meeting so ardently, and with so many vows of love and sacred esteem, that Mary was persuaded to promise that perhaps she would come and meet him.

The trysting place was a little green sequestered spot, on the very verge of the lake, well known to many an angler, and to none better than the writer of this old tale; and the hour appointed, the time when the King's Elwand (now foolishly termed the Belt of Orion) set his first golden knob above the hill. Allanson came too early; and he watched the sky with such eagerness and devotion that he thought every little star that arose in the south-east the top knob of the King's Elwand. At last the Elwand did arise in good earnest, and then the youth, with a heart palpitating with agitation, had nothing for it but to watch the heathery brow by which bonny Mary Burnet was to descend. No Mary Burnet made her appearance, even although the King's Elwand had now measured its own equivocal length five or six times up the lift.

Young Allanson now felt all the most poignant miseries of disappointment; and, as the story goes, uttered in his heart an unhallowed wish – he wished that some witch or fairy would influence his Mary to come to him in spite of her maidenly scruples. This wish was thrice repeated with all the energy of disappointed love. It was thrice repeated, and no more, when, behold, Mary appeared on the brae, with wild and eccentric motions, speeding to the appointed place. Allanson's excitement seems to have been more than he was able to bear, as he instantly became delirious with joy, and always professed that he could remember nothing of their first meeting, save that Mary remained silent, and spoke not a word, either good or bad. In a short time she fell a-sobbing and weeping, refusing to be comforted, and then, uttering a piercing shriek, sprang up and ran from him with amazing speed.

At this part of the loch, which, as I said, is well known to many, the shore is overhung by a precipitous cliff, of no great height, but still inaccessible, either from above or below. Save in a great drought, the water comes to within a yard of the bottom of this cliff, and the intermediate space is filled with rough unshapely pieces of rock fallen from above. Along this narrow and rude space, hardly passable by the angler at noon, did Mary bound with the swiftness of a kid, although surrounded with darkness. Her lover, pursuing with all his energy, called out, 'Mary! Mary! my dear Mary, stop and speak with me. I'll conduct you home, or anywhere you please, but do not run from me. Stop, my dearest Mary – stop!'

Mary would not stop; but ran on, till, coming to a little cliff that jutted into the lake, round which there was no passage, and perceiving that her lover would there overtake her, she uttered another shriek and plunged into the lake. The loud sound of her fall into the still water rang in the young man's ears like the knell of death and if before he was crazed with love, he was now as much so with despair. He saw her floating lightly away from the shore towards the deepest part of the loch but, in a short time, she began to sink, and gradually disappeared, without uttering a throb or a cry. A good while previous to this, Allanson had flung off his bonnet, shoes and coat, and plunged in. He swam to the place where Mary disappeared but there was neither boil nor gurgle on the water, nor even a bell of departing breath, to mark the place where his beloved had sunk. Being strangely impressed, at that trying moment, with a determination to live or die with her, he tried to dive, in hopes either to bring her up or to die in her arms; and he thought of their being so found on the shore of the lake with a melancholy satisfaction; but by no effort of his could he reach the bottom, nor knew he what distance he was still from it. With an exhausted frame, and a despairing heart, he was obliged again to seek the shore, and, dripping wet as he was and half-naked, he ran to her father's house with the woeful tidings. Everything there was quiet. The old shepherd's family, of whom Mary was the youngest, and sole daughter, were all sunk in silent repose; and oh, how the distracted lover wept at the thought of wakening them to hear the doleful tidings! But waken them he must; so, going to the little window close by the goodman's bed, he called, in a melancholy tone, 'Andrew! Andrew Burnet, are you waking?'

'Troth, man, I think I be; or, at least, I'm half-and-half. What hast thou to say to auld Andrew Burnet at this time o' night?'

'Are you waking, I say?'

'Gudewife, am I waking? Because if I be, tell that stravaiger sae. He'll maybe tak' your word for it, for mine he winna tak'.'

'Oh, Andrew, none of your humour tonight; I bring you tidings the most woeful, the most dismal, the most heart-rending, that ever were brought to an honest man's door.'

'To his window, you mean,' cried Andrew, bolting out of bed, and proceeding to the door. 'Gude sauff us, man, come in, whatever you be, and tell us your tidings face to face; and then we'll can better judge of the truth of them. If they be in concord wi' your voice, they are melancholy indeed. Have the reavers come, and are our kye driven?'

'Oh, alas! waur than that – a thousand times waur than that! Your daughter – your dear beloved and only daughter, Mary –'

'What of Mary?' cried the goodman.

'What of Mary?' cried her mother, shuddering and groaning with terror; and at the same time she kindled a light.

The sight of their neighbour, half-naked and dripping with wet, and madness and despair in his looks, sent a chillness to their hearts that held them in silence, and they were unable to utter a word, till he went on thus, 'Mary is gone; your darling and mine is lost, and sleeps this night in a watery grave – and I have been her destroyer!'

'Thou art mad, John Allanson,' said the old man, vehemently, 'raving mad; at least I hope so. Wicked as thou art, thou hadst not the heart to kill my dear child. Oh yes, you are mad – God be thankful, you are mad. I see it in your looks and demeanour. Heaven be praised, you are mad. You are mad; but you'll get better again. But what do I say?' continued he, as recollecting himself. 'We can soon convince our own senses. Wife, lead the way to our daughter's bed.'

With a heart throbbing with terror and dismay, old Jean Linton led the way to Mary's chamber, followed by the two men, who were eagerly gazing, one over each of her shoulders. Mary's little apartment was in the farther end of the long narrow cottage; and as soon as they entered it, they perceived a form lying on the bed, with the bedclothes drawn over its head; and on the lid of Mary's little chest, that stood at the bedside, her clothes were lying neatly folded, as they were wont to be. Hope seemed to dawn on the faces of the two old people when they beheld this, but the lover's heart sank still deeper in despair. The father called her name, but the form on the bed returned no answer; however, they all heard distinctly sobs, as of one weeping. The old man then ventured to pull down the clothes from her face; and, strange to say, there indeed lay Mary Burnet, drowned in tears, yet apparently nowise surprised at the ghastly appearance of the three distracted figures. Allanson gasped for breath, for he remained still incredulous. He touched her clothes – he lifted her robes one by one – and all of them were dry, neat and clean, and had no appearance of having sunk in the lake.

There can be no doubt that Allanson was confounded by the strange event that had befallen him, and felt like one struggling with a frightful vision, or some energy beyond the power of man to comprehend. Nevertheless the assurance that Mary was there in life, weeping although she was, put him once more beside himself with joy; and he kneeled at her bedside, beseeching permission but to kiss her hand. She, however, repulsed him with disdain, saying with great emphasis, 'You are a bad man, John Allanson, and I entreat you to go out of my sight. The sufferings that I have undergone this night have been beyond the power of flesh and blood to endure; and by some cursed agency of yours have these sufferings been brought about. I therefore pray you, in his name, whose law you have transgressed, to depart out of my sight.'

Wholly overcome by conflicting passions, by circumstances so contrary to one another and so discordant with everything either in the works of nature or providence, the young man could do nothing but stand like a rigid statue, with his hands lifted up and his visage like that of a corpse, until led away by the two old people from their daughter's apartment. Then they lighted up a fire to dry him, and began to question him with the most intense curiosity; but they could elicit nothing from him but the most disjointed exclamations – such as, 'Lord in heaven, what can be the meaning of this?' And at other times: 'It is all the enchantment of the devil; the evil spirits have got dominion over me!'

Finding they could make nothing or him, they began to form conjectures of their own. Jean affirmed that it had been the mermaid of the loch that had come to him in Mary's shape, to allure him to his destruction; but Andrew Burnet, setting his bonnet to one side, and raising his left hand to a level with it, so that he might have full scope to motion and flourish, suiting his action to his words, thus began, with a face of sapience never to be excelled: 'Gudewife, it doth strike me that thou art very wide of the mark. It must have been a spirit of a great deal higher quality than a mere-maiden who played this extraordinary prank. The mere-maiden is not a spirit, but a beastly sensitive creature, with a malicious spirit within it. Now, what influence could a cauld clatch of a creature like that, wi' a tail like a great saumont-fish, hae ower our bairn, either to make her happy or unhappy? Or where could it borrow her claes, Jean? Tell me that. Na, na, Jean Linton, depend on it, the spirit that courtit wi' poor sinfu' Jock there has been a fairy; but whether a good ane or an ill ane, it is hard to determine.'

Andrew's disquisition was interrupted by the young man falling into a fit of trembling that was fearful to look at, and threatened soon to terminate his existence. Jean ran for the family cordial, observing by the way that 'though he was a wicked person, he was still a fellow-creature, and might live to repent'; and influenced by this spark of genuine humanity, she made him swallow two horn-spoonfuls of strong *aqua vitae*. Andrew then put a piece of scarlet thread round each wrist, and taking a strong rowan tree staff in his hand, he conveyed his trembling and astonished guest home, giving him at parting this sage advice: 'I'll tell you what it is, Jock Allanson – ye hae run a near risk o' perdition, and, escaping that for the present, o' losing your right reason. But take an auld man's advice – never gang again out by night to beguile ony honest man's daughter, lest a worse thing befall thee.'

Next morning Mary dressed herself more neatly than usual, but there was manifestly a deep melancholy settled on her lovely face, and at times the unbidden tear would start into her eye. She spoke no word, either good or bad, that ever her mother could recollect, that whole morning, but she once or twice observed her daughter gazing at her, as with an intense and melancholy interest. About nine o'clock in the morning, Mary took a hay-rake over her shoulder and went down to a meadow at the east end of the loch to coil a part of her father's hay, her father and brother engaging to join her about noon, when they came from the sheepfold. As soon as old Andrew came home, his wife and he, as was natural, instantly began to converse on the events of the preceding night; and in the course of their conversation Andrew said, 'Gudeness be about us, Jean, was not yon an awfu' speech o' our bairn's to young Jock Allanson last night?'

'Ay, it was a downsetter, gudeman, and spoken like a good Christian lass.'

'I'm no sae sure o' that, Jean Linton. My good woman, Jean Linton, I'm no sae sure o' that. Yon speech has gi'en me a great deal o' trouble o' heart; for d'ye ken, an' take my life – ay, an' take your life, Jean – nane o' us can tell whether it was in the Almighty's name or the devil's that she discharged her lover.'

'Oh fy, Andrew, how can ye say sae? How can ye doubt that it was in the Almighty's name?'

'Couldna she have said sae then, and that wad hae put it beyond a' doubt? And that wad hae been the natural way too; but instead of that she says, "I pray you, in the name of him whose law you have transgressed, to depart out o' my sight." I confess I'm terrified when I think about yon speech, Jean Linton. Didna she say too that "her sufferings had been beyond what flesh and blood could have endured"? What was she but flesh and blood. Didna that remark infer that she was something mair than a mortal creature? Jean Linton, Jean Linton! what will you say if it should turn out that our daughter *is* drowned, and that yon was the fairy we had in the house a' the night and this morning?'

'Oh, haud your tongue, Andrew Burnet, and dinna make my heart cauld within me. We hae aye trusted in the Lord yet, and he has never forsaken us, nor will he yet gie the Wicked One power ower us or ours.'

'Ye say very well, Jean, and we maun e'en hope for the best,' quoth old Andrew; and away he went, accompanied by his son Alexander, to assist their beloved Mary on the meadow.

No sooner had Andrew set his head over the bents, and come in view of the meadow, than he said to his son, 'I wish Jock Allanson maunna hae been east the loch fishing for geds the day, for I think my Mary has made very little progress in the meadow.'

'She's ower muckle ta'en up about other things this while to mind her wark,' said Alexander; 'I wadna wonder, father, if that lassie gangs a black gate yet.'

Andrew uttered a long and a deep sigh that seemed to ruffle the very fountains of life, and, without speaking another word, walked on to the hayfield. It was three hours since Mary had left home, and she ought at least to have put up a dozen coils of hay each hour. But, in place of that, she had put up only seven altogether, and the last was unfinished. Her own hay-rake, that had an M and a B neatly cut on the head of it, was leaning on the unfinished coil, and Mary was wanting. Her brother, thinking she had hid herself from them in sport, ran from one coil to another, calling her many bad names, playfully; but after he had turned them all up, and several deep swathes besides, she was not to be found. This young man, who slept in the byre, knew nothing of the events of the foregoing night, the old people and Allanson having mutually engaged to keep them a profound secret, and he had therefore less reason than his father to be seriously alarmed. When they began to work at the hay Andrew could work none; he looked this way and that way, but in no way could he see Mary approaching; so he put on his coat and went away home, to pour his sorrows into the bosom of his wife; and, in the meantime, he desired his son to run to all the neighbouring farming-houses and cots, every one, and make enquiries if anybody had seen Mary.

When Andrew went home and informed his wife that their darling was missing, the grief and astonishment of the aged couple knew no bounds. They sat down and wept together, and declared over and over that this act of providence was too strong for them, and too high to be understood. Jean besought her husband to kneel instantly, and pray urgently to God to restore their child to them; but he declined it, on account of the wrong frame of his mind, for he declared that his rage against John Allanson was so extreme as to unfit him for approaching the throne of his Maker. 'But if the profligate refuses to listen to the entreaties of an injured parent,' added he, 'he shall feel the weight of an injured father's arm.'

Andrew went straight away to Inverlawn, though without the least hope of finding young Allanson at home; but, on reaching the place, to his amazement, he found the young man lying ill of a burning fever, raving incessantly of witches, spirits and Mary Burnet. To such a height had his frenzy arrived, that when Andrew went there, it required three men to hold him in the bed. Both his parents testified their opinions openly, that their son was bewitched, or possessed of a demon, and the whole family was thrown into the greatest consternation. The good old shepherd, finding enough of grief there already, was obliged to confine his to his own bosom, and return disconsolate to his little family circle, in which there was a woeful blank that night.

His son returned also from a fruitless search. No one had seen any traces of his sister, but an old crazy woman, at a place called Oxcleuch, said that she had seen her go by in a grand chariot with young Jock Allanson, towards the Birkhill Path, and by that time they were at the Cross of Dumgree. The young man said he asked her what sort of a chariot it was, as there was never such a thing in that country as a chariot, nor yet a road for one. But she replied that he was widely mistaken, for that a great number of chariots sometimes passed that way, though never any of them returned. Those words appearing to be merely the ravings of superannuation, they were not regarded; but when no other traces of Mary could be found, old Andrew went up to consult this crazy dame once more, but he was not able to bring any such thing to her recollection. She spoke only in parables, which to him were incomprehensible.

Bonny Mary Burnet was lost. She left her father's house at nine o'clock on a Wednesday morning, 17th of September, neatly dressed in a white jerkin and green bonnet, with her hay-rake over her shoulder; and that was the last sight she was doomed ever to see of her native cottage. She seemed to have had some presentiment of this, as appeared from her demeanour that morning before she left it. Mary Burnet of Kirkstyle was lost, and great was the sensation produced over the whole country by the mysterious event. There was a long ballad extant at one period on the melancholy catastrophe, which was supposed to have been composed by the chaplain of St Mary's; but I have only heard tell of it, without ever hearing it sung or recited. Many of the verses concluded thus:

> But Bonny Mary Burnet
> We will never see again.

The story soon got abroad, with all its horrid circumstances (and there is little doubt that it was grievously exaggerated), and there was no obloquy that was not thrown on the survivor, who certainly in some degree deserved it, for, instead of growing better, he grew ten times more wicked than he was before. In one thing the whole country agreed, that it had been the real Mary Burnet who was drowned in the loch, and that the being which was found in her bed, lying weeping and complaining of suffering, and which vanished the next day, had been a fairy, an evil spirit or a changeling of some sort, for that it never spoke save once, and that in a mysterious manner; nor did it partake of any food with the rest of the family. Her father and mother knew not what to say or what to think, but they wandered through this weary world like people wandering in a dream. Everything that belonged to Mary Burnet was kept by her parents as the most sacred relics, and many a tear did her aged mother shed over them. Every article of her dress brought the once comely wearer to mind. Andrew often said, 'That to have lost the darling child of their old age in any way would have been a great trial, but to lose her in the way that they had done, was really mair than human frailty could endure.'

Many a weary day did he walk by the shores of the loch, looking eagerly for some vestige of her garments, and though he trembled at every appearance, yet did he continue to search on. He had a number of small bones collected, that had belonged to lambs and other minor animals, and, haply, some of them to fishes, from a fond supposition that they might once have formed joints of her toes or fingers. These he kept concealed in a little bag, in order, as he said, 'to let the doctors see them'. But no relic, besides these, could he ever discover of Mary's body.

Young Allanson recovered from his raging fever scarcely in the manner of other men, for he recovered all at once, after a few days' raving and madness. Mary Burnet, it appeared, was by him no more remembered. He grew ten times more wicked than before, and hesitated at no means of accomplishing his unhallowed purposes. The devout shepherds and cottagers around detested him; and, both in their families and in the wild, when there was no ear to hear but that of heaven, they prayed protection from his devices, as if he had been the Wicked One; and they all prophesied that he would make a bad end.

One fine day about the middle of October, when the days begin to get very short, and the nights long and dark, on a Friday morning, the next year but one after Mary Burnet was lost, a memorable day in the fairy annals, John Allanson, younger of Inverlawn, went to a great hiring fair at a village called Moffat, in Annandale, in order to hire a housemaid. His character was so notorious that not one young woman in the district would serve in his father's house; so away he went to the fair at Moffat, to hire the prettiest and loveliest girl he could there find, with the intention of ruining her as soon as she came home. This is no suppositious accusation, for he acknowledged his plan to Mr David Welch of Cariferan, who rode down to the market with him, and seemed to boast of it and dwell on it with delight. But the maidens of Annandale had a guardian angel at the fair that day, of which neither he nor they were aware.

Allanson looked through the hiring-market, and through the hiring-market, and at length fixed on one young woman, which indeed was not difficult to do, for there was no such form there for elegance and beauty. Mr Welch stood still and eyed him. Allanson took the beauty aside. She was clothed in green, and as lovely as a new-blown rose.

'Are you to hire, pretty maiden?'

'Yes, sir.'

'Will you hire with me?'

'I care not though I do. But if I hire with you, it must be for a long term.'

'Certainly. The longer the better. What are your wages to be?'

'You know, if I hire, I must be paid in kind. I must have the first living creature that I see about Inverlawn to myself.'

'I wish it may be me, then. But what do you know about Inverlawn?'

'I think I *should* know about it.'

'Bless me! I know the face as well as I know my own, and better. But the name has somehow escaped me. Pray, may I ask your name?'

'Hush! hush!' said she solemnly, and holding up her hand at the same time. 'Hush, hush, you had better say nothing about that here.'

'I am in utter amazement!' he exclaimed. 'What is the meaning of this? I conjure you to tell me your name!'

'It is Mary Burnet,' said she, in a soft whisper; and at the same time she let down a green veil over her face.

If Allanson's death-warrant had been announced to him at that moment, it could not have deprived him so completely of sense and motion. His visage changed into that of a corpse, his jaws fell down, and his eyes became glazed, so as apparently to throw no reflections inwardly. Mr Welch, who had kept his eye steadily on them all the while, perceived his comrade's dilemma, and went up to him. 'Allanson? Mr Allanson? What is the matter with you, man?' said he. 'Why, the girl has bewitched you, and turned you into a statue!'

Allanson made some sound in his throat, as if attempting to speak, but his tongue refused its office, and he only jabbered. Mr Welch, conceiving that he was seized with some fit, or about to faint, supported him into the Johnston Arms; but he either could not, or would not grant him any explanation. Welch being, however, resolved to see the maiden in green once more, persuaded Allanson, after causing him to drink a good deal, to go out into the hiring-market again in search of her. They ranged the market through and through, but the maiden in green was gone, and not to be found. She had vanished in the crowd the moment she divulged her name, and even though Welch had his eye fixed on her, he could not discover which way she went. Allanson appeared to be in a kind of stupor as well as terror, but when he found that she had left the market, he began to recover himself, and to look out again for the top of the market.

He soon found one more beautiful than the last. She was like a sylph, clothed in robes of pure snowy white, with green ribands. Again he pointed this new flower out to Mr David Welch, who declared that such a perfect model of beauty he had never in his life seen. Allanson, being resolved to have this one at any wages, took her aside, and put the usual question: 'Do you wish to hire, pretty maiden?'

'Yes, sir.'

'Will you hire with me?'

'I care not though I do.'

'What, then, are your wages to be? Come – say? And be reasonable; I am determined not to part with you for a trifle.'

'My wages must be in kind; I work on no other conditions. Pray, how are all the good people about Inverlawn?'

Allanson's breath began to cut, and a chillness to creep through his whole frame, and he answered, with a faltering tongue: 'I thank you – much in their ordinary way.'

'And your aged neighbours,' rejoined she, 'are they still alive and well?'

'I – I – I think they are,' said he, panting for breath. 'But I am at a loss to know whom I am indebted to for these kind recollections.'

'What,' said she, 'have you so soon forgot Mary Burnet of Kirkstyle?'

Allanson started as if a bullet had gone through his heart. The lovely sylphlike form glided into the crowd, and left the astounded libertine once more standing like a rigid statue, until aroused by his friend, Mr Welch. He tried a third fair one, and got the same answers, and the same name given. Indeed, the first time ever I heard the tale, it bore that he tried *seven*, who all turned out to be Mary Burnets of Kirkstyle; but I think it unlikely that he would try so many, as he must long ere that time have been sensible that he laboured under some power of enchantment. However, when nothing else would do, he helped himself to a good proportion of strong drink. While he was thus engaged, a phenomenon of beauty and grandeur came into the fair that caught the sole attention of all present. This was a lovely dame, riding in a gilded chariot, with two liverymen before, and two behind, clothed in green and gold; and never sure was there so splendid a meteor seen in a Moffat fair. The word instantly circulated in the market that this was the Lady Elizabeth Douglas, eldest daughter to the Earl of Morton, who then sojourned at Auchincastle, in the vicinity of Moffat, and which lady at that time was celebrated as a great beauty all over Scotland. She was afterwards Lady Keith; and the mention of this name in the tale, as it were by mere accident, fixes the era of it in the reign of James IV, at the very time that fairies, brownies and witches were at their rifest in Scotland.

Everyone in the market believed the lady to be the daughter of the Earl of Morton; and when she came to the Johnston Arms, a gentleman in green came out bareheaded, and received her out of the carriage. All the crowd gazed at such unparalleled beauty and grandeur, but none was half so much overcome as Allanson. He had never conceived aught half so lovely either in earth, or heaven, or fairyland; and while he stood in a burning fever of admiration, think of his astonishment, and the astonishment of the countless crowd that looked on, when this brilliant and matchless beauty beckoned him towards her! He could not believe his senses, but looked this way and that way to see how others regarded the affair; but she beckoned him a second time with such a winning courtesy and smile that immediately he pulled off his beaver cap and hasted up to her; and without more ado she gave him her arm and the two walked into the hostel.

Allanson conceived that he was thus distinguished by Lady Elizabeth Douglas, the flower of the land, and so did all the people of the market; and greatly they wondered who the young farmer could be that was thus particularly favoured; for it ought to have been mentioned that he had not one personal acquaintance in the fair save Mr David Welch of Cariferan. The first thing the lady did was to enquire kindly after his health. Allanson thanked her ladyship with all the courtesy he was master of; and being by this time persuaded that she was in love with him, he became as light as if treading on the air. She next enquired after his father and mother. Oho! thought he to himself, poor creature, she is terribly in for it! but her love shall not be thrown away upon a backward or ungrateful object. He answered her with great politeness, and at length began to talk of her noble father and young Lord William, but she cut him short by asking if he did not recognise her.

'Oh, yes! He knew who her ladyship was, and remembered that he had seen her comely face often before, although he could not, at that particular moment, recall to his memory the precise times or places of their meeting.'

She next asked for his old neighbours at Kirkstyle, and if they were still in life and health. Allanson felt as if his heart were a piece of ice. A chillness spread over his whole frame; he sank back on a seat, and remained motionless; but the beautiful and adorable creature soothed him with kind words, till he again gathered courage to speak.

'What!' said he; 'and has it been your own lovely self who has been playing tricks on me this whole day?'

'A first love is not easily extinguished, Mr Allanson,' said she. 'You may guess from my appearance that I have been fortunate in life; but, for all that, my first love for you has continued the same, unaltered and unchanged, and you must forgive the little freedoms I used today to try your affections, and the effects my appearance would have on you.'

'It argues something for my good taste, however, that I never pitched on any face for beauty today but your own,' said he. 'But now that we have met once more, we shall not so easily part again. I will devote the rest of my life to you, only let me know the place of your abode.'

'It is hard by,' said she, 'only a very little space from this; and happy, happy, would I be to see you there tonight, were it proper or convenient. But my lord is at present from home and in a distant country.'

'I should not conceive that any particular hindrance to my visit,' said he.

With great apparent reluctance she at length consented to admit of his visit, and offered to leave one of her gentlemen, whom she could trust, to be his conductor; but this he positively refused. It was his desire, he said, that no eye of man should see him enter or leave her happy dwelling. She said he was a self-willed man, but should have his own way; and after giving him such directions as would infallibly lead him to her mansion, she mounted her chariot and was driven away.

Allanson was uplifted above every sublunary concern. Seeking out his friend, David Welch, he imparted to him his extra-ordinary good fortune, but he did not tell him that she was not the Lady Elizabeth Douglas. Welch insisted on accompanying him on the way, and refused to turn back till he came to the very point of the road next to the lady's splendid mansion; and in spite of all that Allanson could say, Welch remained there till he saw his comrade enter the court gate, which glowed with lights as innumerable as the stars of the firmament.

Allanson had promised his father and mother to be home on the morning after the fair to breakfast. He came not either that day or the next; and the third day the old man mounted his white pony, and rode away towards Moffat in search of his son. He called at Cariferan on his way, and made enquiries of Mr Welch. The latter manifested some astonishment that the young man had not returned; nevertheless he assured his father of his safety, and desired him to return home; and then with reluctance confessed that the young man was engaged in an amour with the Earl of Morton's beautiful daughter; that he had gone to the castle by appointment, and that he, David Welch, had accompanied him to the gate, and seen him enter, and it was apparent that his reception had been a kind one, since he had tarried so long.

Mr Welch, seeing the old man greatly distressed, was persuaded to accompany him on his journey, as the last who had seen his son and seen him enter the castle. On reaching Moffat they found his steed standing at the hostel, whither it had returned on the night of the fair, before the company broke up; but the owner had not been heard of since seen in company with Lady Elizabeth Douglas. The old man set out for Auchincastle, taking Mr David Welch along with him; but long ere they reached the place, Mr Welch assured him he would not find his son there, as it was nearly in a different direction that they rode on the evening of the fair. However, to the castle they went, and were admitted to the earl, who, after hearing the old man's tale, seemed to consider him in a state of derangement. He sent for his daughter Elizabeth, and questioned her concerning her meeting with the son of the old respectable countryman – of her appointment with him on the night of the preceding Friday, and concluded by saying he hoped she had him still in safe concealment about the castle.

The lady, hearing her father talk in this manner, and seeing the serious and dejected looks of the old man, knew not what to say, and asked an explanation. But Mr Welch put a stop to it by declaring to old Allanson that the Lady Elizabeth was not the lady with whom his son made the appointment, for he had seen her, and would engage to know her again among ten thousand; nor was that the castle towards which he had accompanied his son, nor anything like it. 'But go with me,' continued he, 'and, though I am a stranger in this district, I think I can take you to the very place.'

They set out again; and Mr Welch traced the road from Moffat by which young Allanson and he had gone until, after travelling several miles, they came to a place where a road struck off to the right at an angle. 'Now I know we are right,' said Welch; 'for here we stopped, and your son entreated me to return, which I refused, and accompanied him to yon large tree, and a little way beyond it, from whence I saw him received in at the splendid gate. We shall be in sight of the mansion in three minutes.'

They passed on to the tree, and a space beyond it; but then Mr Welch lost the use of his speech, as he perceived that there was neither palace nor gate there, but a tremendous gulf, fifty fathoms deep, and a dark stream foaming and boiling below.

'How is this?' said old Allanson. 'There is neither mansion nor habitation of man here!' Welch's tongue for a long time refused its office, and he stood like a statue, gazing on the altered and awful scene. 'He only, who made the spirits of men,' said he, at last, 'and all the spirits that sojourn in the earth and air, can tell how this is. We are wandering in a world of enchantment, and have been influenced by some agencies above human nature or without its pale; for here of a certainty did I take leave of your son – and there, in that direction, and apparently either on the verge of that gulf or the space above it, did I see him received in at the court gate of a mansion, splendid beyond all conception. How can human comprehension make anything of this?'

They went forward to the verge, Mr Welch leading the way to the very spot on which he saw the gate opened, and there they found marks where a horse had been plunging. Its feet had been over the brink, but it seemed to have recovered itself, and deep, deep down, and far within, lay the mangled corpse of John Allanson; and in this manner, mysterious beyond all example, terminated the career of that wicked and flagitious young man. What a beautiful moral may be extracted from this fairy tale!

But among all these turnings and windings, there is no account given, you will say, of the fate of Mary Burnet; for this last appearance of hers at Moffat seems to have been altogether a phantom or illusion. Gentle and kind reader, I can give you no account of the fate of that maiden; for though the ancient fairy tale proceeds, it seems to me to involve her fate in ten times more mystery than what we have hitherto seen of it.

The yearly return of the day on which Mary was lost was observed as a day of mourning by her aged and disconsolate parents – a day of sorrow, of fasting and humiliation. Seven years came and passed away, and the seventh returning day of fasting and prayer was at hand. On the evening previous to it, old Andrew was moving along the sands of the loch, still looking for some relic of his beloved Mary, when he was aware of a little shrivelled old man, who came posting towards him. The creature was not above five spans in height, and had a face scarcely like that of a human creature; but he was, nevertheless, civil in his deportment and sensible in speech. He bade Andrew a good-evening, and asked him what he was looking for. Andrew answered that he was looking for that which he should never find.

'Pray, what is your name, ancient shepherd?' said the stranger; 'for methinks I should know something of you, and perhaps have a commission to you.'

'Alas! why should you ask after my name?' said Andrew. 'My name is now nothing to anyone.'

'Had not you once a beautiful daughter, named Mary?' said the stranger.

'It is a heart-rending question, man,' said Andrew; 'but certes, I had once a beloved daughter named Mary.'

'What became or her?' asked the stranger.

Andrew shook his head, turned round, and began to move away; it was a theme that his heart could not brook. He sauntered along the loch sands, his dim eye scanning every white pebble as he passed along. There was a hopelessness in his stooping form, his gait, his eye, his feature – in every step that he took there was a hopeless apathy. The dwarf followed him, and began to expostulate with him. 'Old man, I see you are pining under some real or fancied affliction,' said he. 'But in continuing to do so, you are neither acting according to the dictates of reason nor true religion. What is man that he should fret, or the son of man that he should repine, under the chastening hand of his Maker?'

'I am far frae justifying myself,' returned Andrew, surveying his shrivelled monitor with some degree of astonishment. 'But there are some feelings that neither reason nor religion can o'er-master; and there are some that a parent may cherish without sin.'

'I deny the position,' said the stranger, 'taken either absolutely or relatively. All repining under the Supreme decree is leavened with unrighteousness. But, subtleties aside, I ask you, as I did before, What became of your daughter?'

'Ask the Father of her spirit, and the framer of her body,' said Andrew solemnly; 'ask Him into whose hands I committed her from childhood. He alone knows what became of her, but I do not.'

'How long is it since you lost her?'

'It is seven years tomorrow!'

'Ay! you remember the time well. And you have mourned for her all that while?'

'Yes; and I will go down to the grave mourning for my only daughter, the child of my old age, and of all my affection. Oh, thou unearthly-looking monitor, knowest thou aught of my darling child? for if thou dost, thou wilt know that she was not like other women. There was a simplicity and a purity about my Mary that was hardly consistent with our frail nature.'

'Wouldst thou like to see her again?' said the dwarf.

Andrew turned round, his whole frame shaking as with a palsy, and gazed on the audacious imp. 'See her again, creature!' cried he vehemently. 'Would I like to see her again, sayest thou?'

'I said so,' said the dwarf, 'and I say further, Dost thou know this token? Look, and see if thou dost!'

Andrew took the token, and looked at it, then at the shrivelled stranger, and then at the token again; and at length he burst into tears, and wept aloud; but they were tears of joy, and his weeping seemed to have some breathings of laughter inter-mingled in it. And still as he kissed the token, he called out in broken and convulsive sentences, 'Yes, auld body, I *do* know it! – I *do* know it – I *do* know it! It is indeed the same golden Edward, with three holes in it, with which I presented my Mary on her birthday, in her eighteenth year, to buy a new suit for the holidays. But when she took it she said – ay, I mind weel what my bonny woman said – "It is sae bonny and sae ken-speckle," said she, "that I think I'll keep it for the sake of the giver." Oh dear, dear! Blessed little creature, tell me how she is, and where she is? Is she living, or is she dead?'

'She is living, and in good health,' said the dwarf; 'and better, and braver, and happier, and lovelier than ever; and if you make haste, you will see her and her family at Moffat tomorrow afternoon. They are to pass there on a journey, but it is an express one, and I am sent to you with that token, to inform you of the circumstance that you may have it in your power to see and embrace your beloved daughter once before you die.'

'And am I to meet my Mary at Moffat? Come away, little, dear, welcome body, thou blessed of heaven, come away, and taste of an auld shepherd's best cheer, and I'll gang foot for foot with you to Moffat, and my auld wife shall gang foot for foot with us too. I tell you, little, blessed and welcome crile, come along with me.'

'I may not tarry to enter your house, or taste of your cheer, good shepherd,' said the being. 'May plenty still be within your walls, and a thankful heart to enjoy it! But my directions are neither to taste meat nor drink in this country, but to haste back to her that sent me. Go – haste, and make ready, for you have no time to lose.'

'At what time will she be there?' cried Andrew, flinging the plaid from him to run home with the tidings.

'Precisely when the shadow of the Holy Cross falls due east,' cried the dwarf; and turning round, he hasted on his way.

When old Jean Linton saw her husband coming hobbling and running home without his plaid, and having his doublet flying wide open, she had no doubt that he had lost his wits; and, full of anxiety, she met him at the side of the kail-yard. 'Gudeness preserve us a' in our right senses, Andrew Burnet, what's the matter wi' you?'

'Stand out o' my gate, wife, for, d'ye see, I am rather in a haste, Jean Linton.'

'I see that indeed, gudeman; but stand still, and tell me what has putten you in sic a haste. Ir ye dementit?'

'Na, na, gudewife, Jean Linton, I'm no dementit – I'm only gaun away till Moffat.'

'Oh, gudeness, pity the poor auld body! How can ye gang to Moffat, man? Or what have ye to do at Moffat? Dinna ye mind that the morn is the day o' our solemnity?'

'Haud out o' my gate, auld wife, and dinna speak o' solemnities to me. I'll keep it at Moffat the morn. Ay, gudewife, and ye shall keep it at Moffat, too. What d'ye think o' that, woman? Too-whoo! ye dinna ken the mettle that's in an auld body till it be tried.'

'Andrew – Andrew Burnet!'

'Get awa' wi' your frightened looks, woman; and haste ye, gang and fling me out my Sabbath-day claes. And, Jean Linton, my woman, d'ye hear, gang and pit on your bridal gown, and your silk hood, for ye maun be at Moffat the morn too; and it is mair nor time we were awa'. Dinna look sae surprised, woman, till I tell ye that our ain Mary is to meet us at Moffat the morn.'

'Oh, Andrew! dinna sport wi' the feelings of an auld forsaken heart.'

'Gude forbid, my auld wife, that I should ever sport wi' feelings o' yours,' cried Andrew, bursting into tears; ' they are a' as sacred to me as breathings frae the Throne o' Grace. But it is true that I tell ye; our dear bairn is to meet us at Moffat the morn, wi' a son in every hand; and we maun e'en gang and see her aince again, and kiss her and bless her afore we dee.'

The tears now rushed from the old woman's eyes like fountains, and dropped from her sorrow-worn cheeks to the earth; and then, as with a spontaneous movement, she threw her skirt over her head, kneeled down at her husband's feet and poured out her soul in thanksgiving to her Maker. She then rose up, quite deprived of her senses through joy, and ran crouching away on the road towards Moffat, as if hasting beyond her power to be at it. But Andrew brought her back; and they prepared themselves for their journey.

Kirkstyle being twenty miles from Moffat, they set out on the afternoon of Tuesday, the 16th of September, slept that night at a place called Turnbery Shiel, and were in Moffat next day by noon. Wearisome was the remainder of the day to that aged couple; they wandered about conjecturing by what road their daughter would come, and how she would come attended. 'I have made up my mind on baith these matters,' said Andrew; 'at first I thought it was likely that she would come out of the east, because a' our blessings come frae that airt; but finding now that would be o'er near to the very road we hae come oursells, I now take it for granted she'll come frae the south; and I just think I see her leading a bonny boy in every hand, and a servant lass carrying a bit bundle ahint her.'

The two now walked out on all the southern roads, in hopes of meeting their Mary, but always returned to watch the shadow of the Holy Cross; and, by the time it fell due east, they could do nothing but stand in the middle of the street and look round them in all directions. At length, about half a mile out on the Dumfries road, they perceived a poor beggar woman approaching with two children following close to her, and another beggar a good way behind. Their eyes were instantly riveted on these objects, for Andrew thought he perceived his friend the dwarf in the one that was behind; and now all other earthly objects were to them as nothing, save these approaching beggars. At that moment a gilded chariot entered the village from the south, and drove by them at full speed, having two liverymen before, and two behind, clothed in green and gold. 'Ach-wow! the vanity of worldly grandeur!' ejaculated Andrew, as the splendid vehicle went thundering by; but neither he nor his wife deigned to look at it further, their whole attention being fixed on the group of beggars. 'Ay, it is just my woman,' said Andrew, 'it is just herself: I ken her gang yet, sair pressed down wi' poortith although she be. But I dinna care how poor she be, for baith her and hers sall be welcome to my fireside as lang as I hae ane.'

While their eyes were thus strained, and their hearts melting with tenderness and pity, Andrew felt something embracing his knees, and on his looking down, there was his Mary, blooming in splendour and beauty, kneeling at his feet. Andrew uttered a loud hysterical scream of joy, and clasped her to his bosom; and old Jean Linton stood trembling, with her arms spread, but durst not close them on so splendid a creature till her daughter first enfolded her in a fond embrace, and then she hung upon her and wept. It was a wonderful event – a restoration without a parallel. They indeed beheld their Mary, their long-lost darling; they held her in their embraces, believed in her identity and were satisfied. Satisfied, did I say? They were happy beyond the lot of mortals. She had just alighted from her chariot, and perceiving her aged parents standing together, she ran and kneeled at their feet They now retired into the hostel, where Mary presented her two sons to her father and mother. They spent the evening in every social endearment; and Mary loaded the good old couple with rich presents, watched over them till midnight, when they both fell into a deep and happy sleep, and then she remounted her chariot and was driven away. If she was any more seen in Scotland, I never heard of it; but her parents rejoiced in the thoughts of her happiness till the day of their death.

EDITH NESBIT

Edith Nesbit was born in 1858 and, like her fictional characters in *The Railway Children*, her middle-class family was one whose fortunes declined. After surviving a tough and nomadic childhood she made her first appearance in print in the *Sunday Magazine* in 1876. She married Hubert Bland in 1880 but financial hardship was to dog Nesbit again when Bland's business failed, forcing her to continue writing articles, stories and poems to support their burgeoning family. She only later in life focused on writing the children's stories for which she became so well known, including *The Story of the Treasure Seekers* (1899), *The Wouldbegoods* (1901), *Five Children and It* (1902) and *The Railway Children* (1906). She died in 1924.

The Detective

1

His mind was made up. There should be no looking back, no weakening, no foolish relentings. Civilisation had no place for him in her scheme of things; and he in his turn would show the jade that he was capable of a scheme in which she had no place, she and her pinchbeck meretricious substitutions of stones for bread, serpents for eggs. What exactly it was that had gone wrong does not matter. There was a girl in it, perhaps; a friend most likely. Almost certainly money and pride and the old detestation of arithmetic played their part. His mother was now dead, and his father was dead long since. There was no one nearer than a great-uncle to care where he went or what he did; whether he throve or went under, whether he lived or died. Also it was springtime. His thoughts turned longingly to the pleasant green country, the lush meadows, the blossoming orchards, nesting birds and flowering thorn, and to roads that should wind slowly, pleasantly, between these. The remembrance came to him of another spring day when he had played truant, had found four thrushes' nests and a moorhen's, and tried to draw a kingfisher on the back of his Latin prose; had paddled in a millstream between bright twinkling leaves and the bright twinkling counterfeits in the glassy water, had been caned at school next day, and his mother had cried when he told her. He remembered how he had said, 'I will be good, oh, mother, I will!' and then added with one of those odd sudden cautions that lined the fluttering garment of his impulsive soul, 'at least, I'll try to be good.'

Well, he had tried. For more than a year he had tried, bearing patiently the heavy yoke of ledger and costs book, the weary life of the office the great-uncle had found for him. There had been a caged bird at the cobbler's in the village at home that piped sweetly in its prison and laboured to draw up its own drinking water by slow chained thimblefuls. He sometimes thought that he was like that caged bird, straining and straining for ever at the horrible machinery which grudgingly yielded to his efforts the little pittance that kept him alive. And all the while the woods and fields and the long white roads were calling, calling.

And now the chief had been more than usually repulsive, and the young man stood at the top of the stairs, smoothing the silk hat that stood for so much, and remembering in detail the unusual repulsiveness of the chief. An error of two and sevenpence in one column, surely a trivial error, and of two hundred pounds in another, quite an obvious error that, and easily rectified, had been the inspiration of the words that sang discordantly to his revolted soul. He suddenly tossed his hat in the air, kicked it as it fell, black and shining, and sent it spinning down the stairs. The office boy clattered out, thin-necked, red-eared, slack mouth well open.

'My hat!' was his unintentionally appropriate idiom.

'Pardon me, *my* hat,' said the young man suavely.

But the junior was genuinely shocked. 'I say, Mr Sellinge,' he said solemnly, 'it'll never be the same again, that tile won't. Ironing it won't do it, no, nor yet blocking.'

'Bates,' the young man retorted with at least equal solemnity, 'I shall never wear that hat again. Remove your subservient carcase. I'm going back to tell the chief.'

'About your hat?' the junior asked, breathless, incredulous.

'About my hat,' Sellinge repeated.

The chief looked up a little blankly. Clerks who had had what he knew well they called the rough side of his tongue rarely returned to risk a second helping. And now this hopeless young incompetent, this irreverent trifler with the columns of the temple of the gods' pounds, shillings and pence, was standing before him, and plainly standing there to speak, not merely to be spoken to.

'Well, Sellinge,' he said, frowning a little, but not too much, lest he should scare away an apology more ample than that with which Sellinge had met the rough side. 'Well, what is it?'

Sellinge, briefly, respectfully, but quite plainly told him what it was. And the chief listened, hardly able to believe his respectable ears. 'And so,' the tale ended, 'I should like to leave at once, please, sir.'

'Do you realise, young man,' the head of the firm asked heavily, 'that you are throwing away your career?'

Sellinge explained what he did realise.

'Your soul, did you say?' The portly senior looked at him through gold-rimmed glasses. 'I never heard of such a thing in my life!'

Sellinge waited respectfully, and the Head of the House looked suddenly older. The unusual is the disconcerting. The chief was not used to hearing souls mentioned except on Sundays. Yet the boy was the grand-nephew of an old friend, a valued and useful business friend, a man whom it would be awkward for him to offend or annoy. This is the real meaning of friendship in the world of business. So he said, 'Come, come, now, Sellinge; think it over. I've had occasion to complain, but I've not complained unjustly, not unjustly, I think. Your opportunities in this office – what did you say?'

The young man had begun to say, quite politely, what he thought of the office.

'But, God bless my soul,' said the older man, quite flustered by this impossible rebellion. 'What is it you want? Come now,' he said, remembering the usefulness of that eminent great-uncle, and unbending as he remembered, 'if this isn't good enough for you, a respectable solicitor's office and every chance of rising, every chance,' he repeated pensively, oblivious now of all that the rough side had said; 'if this isn't good enough for you, what is? What would you like?' he asked, with a pathetic mixture of hopelessness, raillery, and the certitude that his question was unanswerable.

'I should like,' said Sellinge slowly, 'to be a tramp, or a burglar – '

('Great Heavens!' said the chief.)

' – or a detective. I want to go about and do things. I want – '

'A detective?' said the chief. 'Have you ever – '

'No,' said Sellinge, 'but I could.'

'A new Sherlock Holmes, eh?' said the chief, actually smiling.

'Never,' said the clerk firmly, and he frowned. 'May I go now, sir? I've no opening in the burgling or detective line, so I shall be a tramp, for this summer at least. Perhaps I'll go to Canada. I'm sorry I haven't been a success here. Bates is worth twice my money. He never wavers in his faith. Seven nines are always sixty-three with Bates.'

Again the chief thought of his useful city friend.

'Never mind Bates,' he said. 'Is the door closed? Right. Sit down, if you please, Mr Sellinge. I have something to say to you.'

Sellinge hesitated, looked round at the dusty leather-covered furniture, the worn Turkey carpet, the black, shiny deed-boxes, and the shelves of dull blue and yellow papers. The brown oblong of window framed a strip of blue sky and a strip of the opposite office's dirty brickwork. A small strayed cloud, very white and shining, began to cross the strip of sky.

'It's very kind of you, sir,' said Sellinge, his mind more made up than ever; 'but I wouldn't reconsider my decision for ten times what I've been getting.'

'Sit down,' said the chief again. 'I assure you I do not propose to raise your salary, nor to urge you to reconsider your decision. I merely wish to suggest an alternative, one of your own alternatives,' he added persuasively.

'Oh!' said Sellinge, sitting down abruptly, 'which?'

2

And now behold the dream realised. A young man with bare sun-bleached hair that looks as though it had never known the shiny black symbol of civilisation, boots large and dusty, and on his back the full equipment of an artist in oils; all a little too new the outfit, but satisfactory and complete. He goes slowly along through the clean white dust of the roads, and his glance to right and left embraces green field and woodland with the persuasive ardour of a happy lover. The only blot on the fair field of life outspread before him the parting words of the chief.

'It's a very simple job for a would-be detective. Just find out whether the old chap's mad or not. You get on with the lower orders, you tell me. Well, get them to talk to you. And if you find that out, well, there may be a career for you. I've long been dissatisfied with the ordinary enquiry agent. Yes, three pounds a week, and expenses. But in reason. Not first-class, you know.'

This much aloud. To himself he had said, 'A simpleton's

useful sometimes, if he's honest. And if he doesn't find out anything we shall be no worse off than we were before, and I shall be able to explain to his uncle that I really gave him exceptional opportunities. Exceptional.'

Sellinge also, walking along between the dusty powdered white-flowered hedges, felt that the opportunity was exceptional. All his life people had told him things, and the half-confidences of two people often make up a complete sphere of knowledge, if only the confidant possess the power of joining the broken halves. This power Sellinge had. He knew many things; the little scandals, the parochial intrigues and intricacies of the village where he was born were clearer to him than to the principal performers. He looked forward pleasantly to the lodging in the village alehouse, and to the slow gossip on the benches by the door.

The village (he was nearing it now) was steep and straggling, displaying its oddly assorted roofs amid a flutter of orchard trees, a carpet of green spaces. The Five Bells stood to the left, its tea-gardens beside it, cool and alluring.

Sellinge entered the dark sandy passage where the faint smell of last night's tobacco and this morning's beer contended with the fresh vigour of a bunch of wallflowers in a blue jug on the ring-marked bar.

Within ten minutes he had engaged his room, a little hot white attic under the roof, and had learned that it was Squire who lived in the big house, and that there was a lot of tales, so there was, but it didn't do to believe all you heard, nor yet more'n half you see, and least said soonest mended, and the house was worth looking at, or so people said as took notice of them old ancient tumbledown places. No, it wasn't likely you could get in. Used to be open of a Thursday, the 'ouse and grounds, but been closed to visitors this many year. Also that, for all it looked so near, the house was a good four-and-a-half miles by the road.

'And Squire's mighty good to the people in the village,' the pleasant-faced fat landlady behind the bar went on; 'pays good wages, 'e does, and if anyone's in trouble he's always got his hand in his pocket. I don't believe he spends half on himself to what he gives away. It'll be a poor day for Jevington when anything happens to him, sir, you take that from me. No harm in your trying to see the house, sir, but as for seeing him, he never sees no one. Why, listen' – there was the sound of hoofs and wheels in the road – 'look out, sir, quick!'

Sellinge looked out to see an old-fashioned carriage and pair sweep past, in the carriage a white-haired old man with a white thin face and pale clouded eyes.

'That's him,' said the landlady beside him, ducking as the carriage passed. 'Yes, four-and-a-half miles by the road, sir.'

Harnessed in his trappings of colour-box and easel, the young detective set out. There was about him none of the furtivity of your stage detective. His disguise was perfect, mainly because it was not a disguise. Such disguise as there was hung over his soul, which was pretending to itself that the errand was one of danger and difficulty. The attraction of the detective's career was to him not so much the idea of hunting down criminals as the dramatic attitude of one who goes about in the world with a false beard and a make-up box in one hand and his life in the other. To find out the truth about an old gentleman's eccentricities was quite another pair of sleeves, but of these, as yet, our hero perceived neither the cut nor the colour. He had wanted to be a tramp or a detective, and here he was, both. One has to earn one's bread, and what better way than this?

A smooth worn stile prefaced a path almost hidden in grass up for hay, a blaze of red sorrel, buttercups, ox-eyed daisies in the feathery foam of flowered grasses. The wood of the stile was warm to his hand, and the grasses that met over the path powdered his boots with their little seeds.

Then there was a wood, and a rabbit warren, and short crisp

grass dry on the chalk it thinly covered. The sun shone hardly in a sky of brass. The wayfarer panted for shade. It showed far ahead like a mirage in the desert, a group of pines, a flat whiteness of pond-water, a little house. One might ask the way at that house, and get – talk.

He fixed his eyes on it and walked on, the leather straps hot on his shoulders, his oak stick-handle hot in his hand. Then suddenly he saw on the hill, pale beyond the pines, someone coming down the path. He knew the magnet that a planted easel is to rustic minds. This might perhaps be, after all, the better way. Never did artist prepare so rapidly the scene that should attract the eye of the rustic gazer, the lingering but inevitable approach of the rustic foot.

In three minutes he was seated on his camp-stool, a canvas before him, his palette half-set. Four minutes saw a good deal of blue on the canvas. Purple, too, at the fifth minute, because the sky had turned that colour in the west, purple and, more-over, a strange threatening tint that called for burnt sienna and mid chrome and a dash of madder. The grey advancing figure had disappeared among the pines. He madly squeezed green paint on to the foreground: one must at least have a picture begun. And the sun searched intolerably every bit of him as he sat in the shadeless warren awaiting the passing of the other.

And then, more sudden than an earthquake or the birth of love, a mighty rushing wind fell on him, caught up canvas and easel, even colour-box and oak staff, and whirled them away like leaves in an autumn equinox. His hat went too, not that that mattered, and the virgin sketchbook whirled white before a wind that, the papers said next day, travelled at the rate of five-and-fifty miles an hour. The wonderful purple and copper of the west rushed up across the sky, a fierce spatter of rain stung face and hands. He pursued the colour-box, which had lodged in the front entry of a rabbit's house, caught at the canvas, whose face lay closely pressed to a sloe bush, and ran for the nearest shelter, the house among the pines. In a rain like that one has to run head down or be blinded, and so he did not see till he drew breath in the mouldering rotten porch of it that his shelter was not of those from which hospitality can be asked.

A little lodge it was, long since deserted; walls and ceiling were bulged and discoloured with damp, its latticed windows curtained only by the tapestry of the spider, its floors carpeted with old dust and drift of dry pine needles, and on its hearth the nests of long-fledged birds had fallen on the ashes of a fire gone out a very long time ago. A blazing lightning-flash dazzled him as he tried the handle of the door, and the door, hanging by one rusty hinge, yielded to his push as the first shattering peal of thunder clattered and cracked overhead. But a shelter it was, though the wind drove the rain almost horizontally through the broken window and across the room. He reached through the casement, and at the cost of a soaked coat-sleeve pulled to a faded green shutter and made this fast. Then he explored the upper rooms. Holes in the thatch had let through the weather, and the drop drop of the water that wears away stone had worn away the boards of the floor, so that they bent dangerously to his tread. The halfway landing of the little crooked staircase seemed the driest place. He sat down there with his back against the wall and listened to the cracking and blundering of the thunder, watched through the skylight the lightning shoot out of the clouds, rapid and menacing as the tongue from the mouth of a snake.

No man who is not a dreamer chooses as a symbolic rite the kicking of a tall black hat down the stairs of the office he has elected to desert. Sellinge, audience at first to the glorious orchestra, fell from hearing to a waking dream, and the waking dream merged in a dreamless sleep.

When he awoke he knew at once that he was not alone in the little forgotten house. A tramp perhaps, a trespasser almost certainly. He had not had time to move under this thought before the other overpowered it. It was he who was the tramp, the trespasser. The other might be the local police. Have you ever tried to explain anything to the police in a rural district? It would be better to lie quietly, holding one's breath, and so, perhaps, escape an interview that could not be to his advantage, and might, in view of the end he pursued, be absolutely the deuce-and-all.

So he lay quietly, listening. To almost nothing. The other person, whoever it was, moved hardly at all; or perhaps the movements were drowned in the mutter of the thunder and the lashing of the rain, for Sellinge had not slept out the storm. But its violence had lessened while he slept, and presently the great thunders died away in slow sulky mutterings, and the fierce rain settled to a steady patter on the thatch and a slow drip drip from the holes in the roof to the rotting boards below. And the dusk was falling; shadows were setting up their tents in the corners of the stairs and of the attic whose floor was on a level with his eyes. And below, through the patter of the rain, he could hear soft movements. How soft, his strained ears hardly knew till the abrupt contrast of a step on the earth without reminded him of the values of the ordinary noises that human beings make when they move.

The step on the earth outside was heavy and plashy in the wet mould; the touch on the broken door was harsh, and harshly the creaking one hinge responded. The footsteps on the boarded floor of the lower room were loud and echoing. Those other sounds had been as the half-heard murmur of summer woods in the ears of one half-asleep. This was definite, undeniable as the sound of London traffic.

Suddenly all sounds ceased for a moment, and in that moment Sellinge found time to wish that he had never found this shelter. The wildest, wettest, stormiest weather out under the sky seemed better than this little darkening house which he shared with these two others. For there were two. He knew it even before the man began to speak. But he had not known till then that the other, the softly moving first-comer, was a woman, and when he knew it, he felt, in a thrill of impotent resentment, the shame of his situation and the impossibility of escaping from it. He was an eavesdropper. He had not, somehow, thought of eavesdropping as incidental to the detective career. And there was nothing he could do to make things better which would not, inevitably, make them worse. To declare himself now would be to multiply a thousandfold everything which he desired to minimise. Because the first words that came to him from the two below were love-words, low, passionate and tender, in the voice of a man. He could not hear the answer of the woman, but there are ways of answering which cannot be overheard.

'Stay just as you are,' he heard the man's voice again, 'and let me stay here at your feet and worship you.'

And again, 'Oh, my love, my love, even to see you like this. It's all so different from what we used to think it would be; but it's heaven compared with everything else in the world.'

Sellinge supposed that the woman answered, though he caught no words, for the man went on: 'Yes, I know it's hard for you to come, and you come so seldom. And even when you're not here, I know you understand. But life's very long and cold, dear. They talk about death being cold. It's life that's the cold thing, Anna.'

Then the voice sank to a murmur, cherishing, caressing, hardly articulate, and the shadows deepened, deepened inside the house. But outside it grew lighter because the moon had risen and the clouds and rain had swept away and sunset and moonrise were mingling in the clear sky.

'Not yet; you will not send me away yet,' he heard. 'Oh, my love, such a little time, and all the rest of life without you. Ah! let me stay beside you a little while.'

The passion and the longing of the voice thrilled the listener to an answering passion of pity. He himself had read of love, thought of it, dreamed of it; but he had never heard it speak; he had not known that its voice could be like this.

A faint whispering sound came to him; the woman's answer, he thought, but so low was it that it was lost even as it reached him in the whisper of a wet ivy-branch at the window. He raised himself gently and crept on hands and knees to the window of the upper room. His movements made no sound that could have been heard below. He felt happier there, looking out on the clear, cold, wedded lights, and also he was as far as he could be, in the limits of that house, from those two poor lovers.

Yet still he heard the last words of the man, vibrant with the agony of a death-parting.

'Yes, yes, I will go.' Then, 'Oh, my dear, dear love; goodbye, goodbye!'

The sound of footsteps on the floor below, the broken hinged door was opened and closed again from without, he heard its iron latch click into place. He looked from the window. The last indiscretion of sight was nothing to the indiscretions of hearing that had gone before, and he wanted to see this man to whom all his soul had gone out in sympathy and pity. He had not supposed that he could ever be so sorry for anyone.

He looked to see a young man bowed under a weight of sorrow, and he saw an old man bowed with the weight of years. Silver-white was the hair in the moonlight, thin and stooping the shoulders, feeble the footsteps, and tremulous the hand that closed the gate of the little enclosure that had been a garden. The figure of a sad old man went away alone through the shadows of the pine trees.

And it was the figure of the old man who had driven by the Five Bells in the old-fashioned carriage, the figure of the man he had come down to watch, to spy upon. Well, he had spied, and he had found out – what?

He did not wait for anyone else to unlatch that closed door

and come out into the moonlight below the window. He thinks now that he knew even then that no one else would come out. He went down the stairs in the darkness, careless of the sound of his feet on the creaking boards. He lighted a match and held it up and looked round the little bare room with its one shuttered window and its one door, close latched. And there was no one there, no one at all. The room was as empty and cold as any last year's nest.

He got out very quickly and got away, not stopping to shut door or gate nor to pick up the colour-box and canvas from the foot of the stairs where he had left them. He went very quickly back to the Five Bells, and he was very glad of the lights and the talk and the smell and sight and sound of living men and women.

It was next day that he asked his questions; this time of the round-faced daughter of the house.

'No,' she told him, 'Squire wasn't married,' and, 'Yes, there was a sort of story.'

He pressed for the story, and presently got it.

'It ain't nothing much. Only they say when Squire was a young man there was some carryings on with the gamekeeper's daughter up at the lodge. Happen you noticed it, sir, an old tumbledown place in the pine woods.'

Yes, he had happened to notice it.

'Nobody knows the rights of it now,' the girl told him; 'all them as was in it's under the daisies this longtime, except Squire. But he went away and there was some mishap; he got thrown from his horse and didn't come home when expected, and the girl she was found drowned in the pond nigh where she used to live. And Squire he waren't never the same man. They say he hangs about round the old lodge to this day when it's full moon. And they do say – But there, I dunno, it's all silly talk, and I hope you won't take no notice of anything I've said. One gets talking.'

Caution, late born, was now strong in her, and he could not get any more.

'Do you remember the girl's name?' he asked at last, finding all assaults vain against the young woman's discretion.

'Why, I wasn't born nor yet thought of,' she told him, and laughed and called along the fresh-sanded passage: 'Mother, what was that girl's name, you know, the one up at the lodge that – '

'Ssh!' came back the mother's voice; 'you keep a still tongue, Lily; it's all silly talk.'

'All right, mother, but what was her name?'

'Anna,' came the voice along the fresh-sanded passage.

DEAR SIR [ran Sellinge's report, written the next day], I have made enquiries and find no ground for supposing the gentleman in question to be otherwise than of sound mind. He is much respected in the village and very kind to the poor. I remain here awaiting your instructions.

While he remained there awaiting the instructions, he explored the neighbourhood, but he found nothing of much interest except the grave on the north side of the churchyard, a grave marked by no stone, but covered anew every day with fresh flowers. It had been so covered every day, the sexton told him, for fifty years.

'A long time, fifty years,' said the man, 'a long time, sir. A lawyer in London, he pays for the flowers, but they do say – '

'Yes,' said Sellinge quickly, 'but then people say all sorts of things, don't they?'

'Some on 'em's true though,' said the sexton.

SAKI

Hector Hugh Munro (1870–1916), a novelist who wrote under the name Saki, was born at Akyab, Burma, son of a police official of Scottish extraction, and was brought up by aunts at Pilton in Devon. Educated at Exmouth and Bedford Grammar School, he travelled with his father in France, Germany and Switzerland, then was for a time in the police service in Burma but suffered badly from malaria. Returning to England, he wrote for the *Westminster Gazette,* and from 1902 to 1908 was a foreign correspondent for the *Morning Post.* In the First World War he served as a private with the Royal Fusiliers and was killed at Beaumont-Hamel. His books of humorous short stories include *Reginald* (1904), *Reginald in Russia* (1910), *The Chronicles of Clovis* (1912) and *Beasts and Super-Beasts* (1914); *The Unbearable Bassington* (1912) and *When William Came* (1914) are novels. His pseudonym Saki is the name of the cup-bearer in *The Rubáiyát of Omar Khayyám*.

The Cobweb

The farmhouse kitchen probably stood where it did as a matter of accident or haphazard choice; yet its situation might have been planned by a master-strategist in farmhouse architecture. Dairy and poultry-yard and herb garden, and all the busy places of the farm, seemed to lead by easy access into its wide flagged haven, where there was room for everything and where muddy boots left traces that were easily swept away. And yet, for all that it stood so well in the centre of human bustle, its long, latticed window, with the wide window-seat, built into an embrasure beyond the huge fireplace, looked out on a wild spreading view of hill and heather and wooded combe. The window nook made almost a little room in itself, quite the pleasantest room in the farm as far as situation and capabilities went. Young Mrs Ladbruk, whose husband had just come into the farm by way of inheritance, cast covetous eyes on this snug corner, and her fingers itched to make it bright and cosy with chintz curtains and bowls of flowers, and a shelf or two of old china. The musty farm parlour, looking out to a prim, cheerless garden imprisoned within high, blank walls, was not a room that lent itself readily either to comfort or decoration.

'When we are more settled I shall work wonders in the way of making the kitchen habitable,' said the young woman to her occasional visitors. There was an unspoken wish in those words, a wish which was unconfessed as well as unspoken. Emma Ladbruk was the mistress of the farm; jointly with her husband she might have her say, and to a certain extent her way, in ordering its affairs. But she was not mistress of the kitchen.

On one of the shelves of an old dresser, in company with chipped sauce-boats, pewter jugs, cheese-graters and paid bills, rested a worn and ragged Bible, on whose front page was the record, in faded ink, of a baptism dated ninety-four years ago. 'Martha Crale' was the name written on that yellow page. The yellow, wrinkled old dame who hobbled and muttered about the kitchen looking like a dead autumn leaf which the winter winds still pushed hither and thither, had once been Martha Crale; for seventy-odd years she had been Martha Mountjoy. For longer than anyone could remember she had pattered to and fro between oven and wash-house and dairy, and out to chicken-run and garden, grumbling and muttering and scolding, but working unceasingly. Emma Ladbruk, of whose coming she took as little notice as she would of a bee wandering in at a window on a summer's day, used at first to watch her with a kind of frightened curiosity. She was so old and so much a part of the place, it was difficult to think of her exactly as a living thing. Old Shep, the white-muzzled, stiff-limbed collie, waiting for his time to die, seemed almost more human than the withered, dried-up old woman. He had been a riotous, roystering puppy, mad with the joy of life, when she was already a tottering, hobbling dame; now he was just a blind, breathing carcase, nothing more, and she still worked with frail energy, still swept and baked and washed, fetched and carried. If there were something in these wise old dogs that did not perish utterly with death, Emma used to think to herself, what generations of ghost-dogs there must be out on those hills that Martha had reared and fed and tended and spoken a last goodbye word to in that old kitchen. And what memories she must have of human generations that had passed away in her time. It was difficult for anyone, let alone a stranger like Emma, to get her to talk of the days that had been; her shrill, quavering speech was of doors that had been left unfastened, pails that had got mislaid, calves whose feeding-time was overdue, and the various little faults and lapses that chequer a farmhouse routine. Now and again, when election time came round, she would unstore her recollections of the old names round which the fight had waged in the days gone by. There had been a Palmerston, that had been a name down Tiverton way; Tiverton was not a far journey as the crow flies, but to Martha it was almost a foreign country. Later there had been Northcotes and Aclands, and many other newer names that she had forgotten; the names changed, but it was always Libruls and Toories, Yellows and Blues. And they always quarrelled and shouted as to who was right and who was wrong. The one they quarrelled about most was a fine old gentleman with an angry face – she had seen his picture on the walls. She had seen it on the floor too, with a rotten apple squashed over it, for the farm had changed its politics from time to time. Martha had never been on one side or the other; none of 'they' had ever done the farm a stroke of good. Such was her sweeping verdict, given with all a peasant's distrust of the outside world.

When the half-frightened curiosity had somewhat faded away, Emma Ladbruk was uncomfortably conscious of another feeling towards the old woman. She was a quaint old tradition, lingering about the place, she was part and parcel of the farm itself, she was something at once pathetic and picturesque – but she was dreadfully in the way. Emma had come to the farm full of plans for little reforms and improvements, in part the result of training in the newest ways and methods, in part the outcome of her own ideas and fancies. Reforms in the kitchen region, if those deaf ears could have been induced to give them even a hearing, would have met with short shrift and scornful rejection, and the kitchen region spread over the zone of dairy and market business and half the work of the household. Emma, with the latest science of dead poultry dressing at her fingertips, sat by, an unheeded watcher, while old Martha trussed the chickens for the market-stall as she had trussed them for nearly four-score years – all leg and no breast. And the hundred hints about effective cleaning and labour-lightening and the things that make for wholesomeness which the young woman was ready to impart or to put into action dropped away into nothingness before that wan, muttering, unheeding presence. Above all, the coveted window corner, that was to be a dainty, cheerful oasis in the gaunt old kitchen, stood now choked and lumbered with a litter of odds and ends that Emma, for all her nominal authority, would not have dared or cared to displace; over them seemed to be spun the protection of something that was like a human cobweb. Decidedly Martha was in the way. It would have been an unworthy meanness to have wished to see the span of that brave old life shortened by a few paltry months, but as the days sped by Emma was conscious that the wish was there, disowned though it might be, lurking at the back of her mind.

She felt the meanness of the wish come over her with a qualm of self-reproach one day when she came into the kitchen and found an unaccustomed state of things in that usually busy quarter. Old Martha was not working. A basket of corn was on the floor by her side, and out in the yard the poultry were beginning to clamour a protest of overdue feeding-time. But Martha sat huddled in a shrunken bunch on the window seat, looking out with her dim old eyes as though she saw something stranger than the autumn landscape.

'Is anything the matter, Martha?' asked the young woman.

' 'Tis death, 'tis death a-coming,' answered the quavering voice; 'I knew 'twere coming. I knew it. 'Tweren't for nothing that old Shep's been howling all morning. And last night I heard the screech-owl give the death-cry, and there were something white as run across the yard yesterday; 'tweren't a cat nor a stoat, 'twere something. The fowls knew 'twere something; they all drew off to one side. Ay, there's been warnings. I knew it were a-coming.'

The young woman's eyes clouded with pity. The old thing sitting there so white and shrunken had once been a merry, noisy child, playing about in lanes and hay-lofts and farmhouse garrets; that had been eighty-odd years ago, and now she was just a frail old body cowering under the approaching chill of the death that was coming at last to take her. It was not probable that much could be done for her, but Emma hastened away to get assistance and counsel. Her husband, she knew, was down at a tree-felling some little distance off, but she might find some other intelligent soul who knew the old woman better than she did. The farm, she soon found out, had that faculty common to farmyards of swallowing up and losing its human population. The poultry followed her in interested fashion, and swine grunted interrogations at her from behind the bars of their sties, but barnyard and rickyard, orchard and stables and dairy, gave no reward to her search. Then, as she retraced her steps towards the kitchen, she came suddenly on her cousin, young Mr Jim, as everyone called him, who divided his time between amateur horse-dealing, rabbit-shooting and flirting with the farm maids.

'I'm afraid old Martha is dying,' said Emma. Jim was not the sort of person to whom one had to break news gently.

'Nonsense,' he said; 'Martha means to live to a hundred. She told me so, and she'll do it.'

'She may be actually dying at this moment, or it may just be the beginning of the break-up,' persisted Emma, with a feeling of contempt for the slowness and dullness of the young man.

A grin spread over his good-natured features.

'It don't look like it,' he said, nodding towards the yard. Emma turned to catch the meaning of his remark. Old Martha stood in the middle of a mob of poultry scattering handfuls of grain around her. The turkey-cock, with the bronzed sheen of his feathers and the purple-red of his wattles, the gamecock with the glowing metallic lustre of his Eastern plumage, the hens, with their ochres and buffs and umbers and their scarlet combs, and the drakes, with their bottle-green heads, made a medley of rich colour, in the centre of which the old woman looked like a withered stalk standing amid the riotous growth of gaily-hued flowers. But she threw the grain deftly amid the wilderness of beaks, and her quavering voice carried as far as the two people who were watching her. She was still harping on the theme of death coming to the farm.

'I knew 'twere a-coming. There's been signs and warnings.'

'Who's dead, then, old mother?' called out the young man.

' 'Tis young Mister Ladbruk,' she shrilled back; 'they've just a-carried his body in. Run out of the way of a tree that was coming down and ran hisself on to an iron post. Dead when they picked un up. Ay, I knew 'twere coming.'

And she turned to fling a handful of barley at a belated group of guinea-fowl that came racing towards her.

The farm was a family property, and passed to the rabbit-shooting cousin as the next-of-kin. Emma Ladbruk drifted out of its history as a bee that had wandered in at an open window might flit its way out again. On a cold grey morning she stood waiting with her boxes already stowed in the farm cart, till the last of the market produce should be ready, for the train she was to catch was of less importance than the chickens and butter and eggs that were to be offered for sale. From where she stood she could see an angle of the long latticed window that was to have been cosy with curtains and gay with bowls of flowers. Into her mind came the thought that for months, perhaps for years, long after she had been utterly forgotten, a white, unheeding face would be seen peering out through those latticed panes, and a weak, muttering voice would be heard quavering up and down those flagged passages. She made her way to a narrow barred casement that opened into the farm larder. Old Martha was standing at a table trussing a pair of chickens for the market stall as she had trussed them for nearly fourscore years.

GERTRUDE ATHERTON

Gertrude Atherton (1857–1948) was born Gertrude Franklin Horn in San Francisco and was a great-grand-niece of Benjamin Franklin. She started writing while still at school. In 1876 she married George H. B. Atherton, and when he died four years later she went to New York and began a writing career during which she produced some forty books. She lived for seven years in England and for six years in Munich, and was made a Chevalier of the Legion of Honour and an LLD of the University of California. Her most popular books were *The Conqueror* (1902), *Rezánov* (1906), *Black Oxen (1906), The Immortal Marriage* (1927) and *Dido, Queen of Hearts* (1929). *Adventures of a Novelist* (1932) is an autobiography of her earlier years.

Death and the Woman

Her husband was dying, and she was alone with him. Nothing could exceed the desolation of her surroundings. She and the man who was going from her were in the third-floor-back of a New York boarding-house. It was summer, and the other boarders were in the country; all the servants except the cook had been dismissed, and she, when not working, slept profoundly on the fifth floor. The landlady also was out of town on a brief holiday.

The window was open to admit the thick unstirring air; no sound rose from the row of long narrow yards, nor from the tall deep houses annexed. The latter deadened the rattle of the streets. At intervals the distant elevated lumbered protestingly along, its grunts and screams muffled by the hot suspended ocean.

She sat there plunged in the profoundest grief that can come
to the human soul, for in all other agony hope flickers, however
forlornly. She gazed dully at the unconscious breathing form of
the man who had been friend and companion and lover during
five years of youth too vigorous and hopeful to be warped by
uneven fortune. It was wasted by disease; the face was shrunken;
the night-garment hung loosely about a body which had never
been disfigured by flesh, but had been muscular with exercise
and full-blooded with health. She was glad that the body was
changed; glad that its beauty, too, had gone some other-where
than into the coffin. She had loved his hands as apart from
himself; loved their strong warm magnetism. They lay limp
and yellow on the quilt; she knew that they were already cold,
and that moisture was gathering on them. For a moment something convulsed within her. They had gone too. She repeated
the words twice, and after them, 'for ever'. And the while the
sweetness of their pressure came back to her.

She leaned suddenly over him. *He* was in there still, somewhere. Where? If he had not ceased to breathe, the Ego, the
Soul, the Personality was still in the sodden clay which had
shaped to give it speech. Why could it not manifest itself to
her? Was it still conscious in there, unable to project itself
through the disintegrating matter which was the only medium
its Creator had vouchsafed it? Did it struggle there, seeing her
agony, sharing it, longing for the complete disintegration which
should put an end to its torment? She called his name, she even
shook him slightly, mad to tear the body apart and find her
mate, yet even in that tortured moment realising that violence
would hasten his going.

The dying man took no notice of her, and she opened his
gown and put her cheek to his heart, calling him again. There
had never been more perfect union; how could the bond still
be so strong if he were not at the other end of it? He was
there, her other part; until dead he must be living. There was

no intermediate state. Why should he be as entombed and unresponding as if the screws were in the lid? But the faintly beating heart did not quicken beneath her lips. She extended her arms suddenly, describing eccentric lines, above, about him, rapidly opening and closing her hands as if to clutch some escaping object; then sprang to her feet and went to the window. She feared insanity. She had asked to be left alone with her dying husband, and she did not wish to lose her reason and shriek a crowd of people about her.

The green plots in the yards were not apparent, she noticed. Something heavy, like a pall, rested upon them. Then she understood that the day was over and that night was coming.

She returned swiftly to the bedside, wondering if she had remained away hours or seconds, and if he were dead. His face was still discernible, and Death had not relaxed it. She laid her own against it, then withdrew it with shuddering flesh, her teeth smiting each other as if an icy wind had passed.

She let herself fall back in the chair, clasping her hands against her heart, watching with expanding eyes the white sculptured face which, in the glittering dark, was becoming less defined of outline. If she lit the gas it would draw mosquitoes, and she could not shut from him the little air he must be mechanically grateful for. And she did not want to see the opening eye – the falling jaw.

Her vision became so fixed that at length she saw nothing, and closed her eyes and waited for the moisture to rise and relieve the strain. When she opened them his face had disappeared; the humid waves above the housetops put out even the light of the stars, and night was come.

Fearfully, she approached her ear to his lips; he still breathed. She made a motion to kiss him, then threw herself back in a quiver of agony – they were not the lips she had known, and she would have nothing less.

His breathing was so faint that in her half-reclining position she could not hear it, could not be aware of the moment of his death. She extended her arm resolutely and laid her hand on his heart. Not only must she feel his going, but, so strong had been the comradeship between them, it was a matter of loving honour to stand by him to the last.

She sat there in the hot heavy night, pressing her hand hard against the ebbing heart of the unseen, and awaited Death. Suddenly an odd fancy possessed her. Where was Death? Why was he tarrying? Who was detaining him? From what quarter would he come? He was taking his leisure, drawing near with footsteps as measured as those of men keeping time to a funeral march. By a wayward deflection she thought of the slow music that was always turned on in the theatre when the heroine was about to appear, or something eventful to happen. She had always thought that sort of thing ridiculous and inartistic. So had he.

She drew her brows together angrily, wondering at her levity, and pressed her relaxed palm against the heart it kept guard over. For a moment the sweat stood on her face; then the pent-up breath burst from her lungs. He still lived.

Once more the fancy wantoned above the stunned heart. Death – where was he? What a curious experience: to be sitting alone in a big house – she knew that the cook had stolen out – waiting for Death to come and snatch her husband from her. No; he would not snatch, he would steal upon his prey as noiselessly as the approach of Sin to Innocence – an invisible, unfair, sneaking enemy, with whom no man's strength could grapple. If he would only come like a man, and take his chances like a man! Women had been known to reach the hearts of giants with the dagger's point. But he would creep upon her.

She gave an exclamation of horror. Something was creeping over the window-sill. Her limbs palsied, but she struggled to her feet and looked back, her eyes dragged about against her own volition. Two small green stars glared menacingly at her just above the sill; then the cat possessing them leaped downward, and the stars disappeared.

She realised that she was horribly frightened. 'Is it possible?' she thought. 'Am I afraid of Death, and of Death that has not yet come? I have always been rather a brave woman; he used to call me heroic; but then with him it was impossible to fear anything. And I begged them to leave me alone with him as the last of earthly boons. Oh, shame!'

But she was still quaking as she resumed her seat, and laid her hand again on his heart. She wished that she had asked Mary to sit outside the door; there was no bell in the room. To call would be worse than desecrating the house of God, and she would not leave him for one moment. To return and find him dead – gone alone!

Her knees smote each other. It was idle to deny it; she was in a state of unreasoning terror. Her eyes rolled apprehensively about; she wondered if she should see It when It came; wondered how far off It was now. Not very far; the heart was barely pulsing. She had heard of the power of the corpse to drive brave men to frenzy, and had wondered, having no morbid horror of the dead. But this! To wait – and wait – and wait – perhaps for hours – past the midnight – on into the small hours – while that awful, determined, leisurely Something stole nearer and nearer.

She bent to him who had been her protector with a spasm of anger. Where was the indomitable spirit that had held her all these years with such a strong and loving clasp? How could he leave her? How could he desert her? Her head fell back and moved restlessly against the cushion; moaning with the agony of loss, she recalled him as he had been. Then fear once more took possession of her, and she sat erect, rigid, breathless, awaiting the approach of Death.

Suddenly, far down in the house, on the first floor, her strained hearing took note of a sound – a wary, muffled sound, as if someone were creeping up the stair, fearful of being heard.

Slowly! It seemed to count a hundred between the laying down of each foot. She gave a hysterical gasp. Where was the slow music?

Her face, her body, were wet – as if a wave of death-sweat had broken over them. There was a stiff feeling at the roots of her hair; she wondered if it were really standing erect. But she could not raise her hand to ascertain. Possibly it was only the colouring matter freezing and bleaching. Her muscles were flabby, her nerves twitched helplessly.

She knew that it was Death who was coming to her through the silent deserted house; knew that it was the sensitive ear of her intelligence that heard him, not the dull, coarse-grained ear of the body.

He toiled up the stair painfully, as if he were old and tired with much work. But how could he afford to loiter, with all the work he had to do? Every minute, every second, he must be in demand to hook his cold, hard finger about a soul struggling to escape from its putrefying tenement. But probably he had his emissaries, his minions; for only those worthy of the honour did he come in person.

He reached the first landing and crept like a cat down the hall to the next stair, then crawled slowly up as before. Light as the footfalls were, they were squarely planted, unfaltering; slow, they never halted.

Mechanically she pressed her jerking hand closer against the heart; its beats were almost done. They would finish, she calculated, just as those footfalls paused beside the bed.

She was no longer a human being; she was an Intelligence and an *ear*. Not a sound came from without, even the Elevated appeared to be temporarily off duty; but inside the big quiet house that footfall was waxing louder, louder, until iron feet crashed on iron stairs and the echo thundered.

She had counted the steps – one – two – three – irritated beyond endurance at the long deliberate pauses between. As they climbed and clanged with slow precision she continued to count, audibly and with equal precision, noting their hollow reverberation. How many steps had the stair? She wished she knew. No need! The colossal trampling announced the lessening distance in an increasing volume of sound not to be misunderstood. It turned the curve; it reached the landing; it advanced – slowly – down the hall; it paused before her door. Then knuckles of iron shook the frail panels. Her nerveless tongue gave no invitation. The knocking became more imperious; the very walls vibrated. The handle turned, swiftly and firmly. With a wild instinctive movement she flung herself into the arms of her husband.

*   *   *

When Mary opened the door and entered the room she found a dead woman lying across a dead man.

DEATH INTO THE WINDS

EDGAR WALLACE

Edgar Wallace (1875–1932) was one of the most prolific British writers of adventure stories and crime fiction of all time. In his short life he wrote 173 books and numerous short stories, thus earning the title 'king of thrillers'. He first found success with his novel *The Four Just Men*. As a publicity gimmick he offered a reward to any reader who could describe how the book's central murder was committed. Unfortunately he neglected to restrict the prize to the first person who worked it out. Although he lost a lot of money on the deal, the book became a bestseller and firmly established him as a popular author. He died in the United States *en route* to Hollywood to work on the screenplay of *King Kong*. Although he received a screen credit, he did no actual work on the film.

The Lone House Mystery

1

I am taking no credit out of what the newspapers called the Lone House Mystery. I've been long enough in the police force to know that the man who blows his own trumpet never gets into a good orchestra. So if anybody tells you that Superintendent Minter of Scotland Yard is trying to glorify himself, give them a dirty look for me.

'Superintendent' is a mouthful, and anyway, it is not matey. Not that I encourage young constables to call me 'Sooper' to my face. They never do. I want 'sir' from them and every other rank, but I like to overhear 'em talking about the old Sooper, always providing they don't use a certain adjective.

Mr John C. Field always called me Superintendent. I never

knew until he pronounced the word that there were so many syllables in it.

No man likes to admit he was in error, but I'm owning up that I broke all my rules when I liked him at first sight. It's all very well to go mad about a girl the first time you meet her, but it's wrong to file a man on your first impressions. Because a man who makes a hit the first time you meet him is going out of his way to make you think well of him. And normal men don't do that. Commercial travellers do and actors do, but they're not normal.

John C. Field was the type that anybody could admire. He was tall, broad-shouldered and good-looking, for all his fifty-odd years and his grey hair. He had the manners of a gentleman, could tell a good story and was a perfect host. He never stopped handing out the cigars.

I met him in a curious way. He lived in a smallish house on the banks of the Linder. I don't suppose you know the Linder – it's a stream that pretends to be a river until it runs into the Thames between Reading and Henley, and then it is put into its proper place and called the 'Bourne'. There is a house on the other side of the stream called Hainthorpe, and it was owned by a Mr Max Voss. He built it and had an electric power line carried from Reading. It was over this line that I went down to make enquiries. I was in the special branch of Scotland Yard at the time and did a lot of work that the county police knew nothing about. It is not an offence to use electric power, but just about this time the Flack brothers and Johnny McGarth and two or three of the big forgery gangs were terribly busy with private printing presses, and when we heard of a house-holder using up a lot of juice we were a bit suspicious.

So I went down to Hainthorpe and saw Mr Voss. He was a stout, red-faced man with a little white moustache, who had lost the use of his legs through frostbite in Russia. And that is how his new house came to be filled with electric contraptions.

He had electric chairs that ran him from one room to another, electric elevators, and even in his bathroom a sort of electric hoist that could lift him from his chair into his bath and out again.

'Now,' he said, with a twinkle in his eye, 'you'll want to see the printing presses where I make phoney money!' He chuckled with laughter when he saw he'd hit the right nail on the head.

I went there for an hour and stayed three days.

'Stay tonight, anyway,' he said. 'My man Veddle will give you any sleeping kit you require.'

Voss was an interesting man who had been an engineer in Russia. He wasn't altogether helpless, because he could hobble around on crutches, though it wasn't nice to see him doing it.

It was pretty late when I arrived, so I did not need any persuasion to stay to dinner, especially when I heard that young Garry Thurston was coming. I knew Garry – I'd met him half a dozen times at Marlborough Street and Bow Street and other police courts. He had more endorsements on his driving licence than any other rich young man I knew. His hobbies were speeding through police traps and parking in unauthorised places. A bright boy – one of the new type of criminals that the motoring regulations have created.

He had a big house in the neighbourhood and had struck up a friendship with Mr Voss. I suppose I'm all wrong, but I like these harum-scarum young men that the public schools and universities turn out by the thousand.

He stopped dead at the sight of me in the smoking-room.

'Moses!' he said. 'What have I done?'

When I told him that I was after mere forgers he seemed quite disappointed.

He was a nice boy, and if I ever have the misfortune to be married and have a son, he would be the kind that would annoy me less than any other. I don't know what novelists mean when they write about 'clean-limbed men', unless they're talking about people who have regular baths, but I have an idea that he was the kind of fellow they have in mind.

We were halfway through dinner when I first heard the name of Mr Field. It arose over a question of poaching. Voss remarked that he wished Field's policemen would keep to their own side of the river, and that was the first time I knew that Field was under police protection, and asked why. It was then that young Thurston broke in.

'He'll need a regiment of soldiers to look after him if something happens which I think is going to happen,' he said, and there was something in his tone which made me look at him. If ever I saw hate in a man's eyes I saw it in Garry Thurston's.

I noticed that Mr Voss changed the subject, and after the young man had gone home he told me why.

'Thurston is not normal about this man Field,' he said, 'and I needn't tell you it's about a girl – Field's secretary. She's a lovely creature, and so far as I can tell Field treats her with every respect and deference. But Garry's got it into his thick head that there's something sinister going on over at Lone House. I think it's the psychological result of poor Field living in a place called Lone House at all!'

That explained a lot to me. Young men in love are naturally murderous young animals. Whether it's normal or abnormal to want to murder the man who squeezes the hand of the young lady you've taken a fancy to, I don't know. I guess it's normal. Personally speaking, I've never been delirious except from natural causes.

'Field's policemen' rather puzzled me till Mr Voss explained. For some reason or other Field went in fear of his life, and paid a handsome sum per annum for individual police attention. There were usually two men on duty near the house all the time.

I couldn't have come to a better man than Max Voss to hear all the news of the neighbourhood. I think that red-faced old gentleman was the biggest gossip I have ever met. He knew the history of everybody for twenty miles round, could tell you all their private business, why engagements were broken off, what made Mrs So-and-So go to the Riviera in such a hurry last March, and why Lord What's-his-name was selling his pictures.

And he told me quite a lot about Field. He lived alone except for a few servants, and had no visitors, with the exception of a negro who came about once a month, a well-dressed young fellow, and a rather pretty black woman who arrived at rare intervals.

'Very few people know about this. She comes up river in a launch, sometimes with the negro and sometimes without him. They usually come in the evening, stay an hour or two and disappear. Before they come, Field sends all his servants out.'

I had to chuckle at this. 'Sounds to me like a mystery.'

Voss smiled. 'It is nothing to the mystery of Lady Kingfether's trip to North Africa,' he said, and began to tell me a long story.

It was a pretty interesting story. Every time I woke up something was happening.

I went to bed late and tired, and getting up at six o'clock in the morning, dressed and went out into the garden. Mr Voss had told me his man Veddle would look after me, but devil a sign of Veddle had I seen, either on the previous night or that morning, and I understood why when I came upon him suddenly on his way from the little cottage in the grounds where he lived. He tried to avoid me, but I've got pretty good eyesight for a man of sixty. No man who had ever seen Veddle could forget him. A heavy-looking man with a roundish face and eyes that never met you. I could have picked him out a mile away. When Voss had said 'Veddle', I never dreamed he was the same Veddle who had passed through my hands three times. Naturally, when criminals take on respectable employment they become Smith.

He knew me, of course.

'Why, Mr Minter,' he said in his oily way, 'this is a surprise!'

'Didn't know I was here, eh?' I said.

He coughed.

'Well, to tell you the truth, I did,' he said, 'but I thought it would be better if I kept out of your way. Mr Voss knows,' he went on quickly.

'About your previous convictions?'

He nodded.

'Does he know that two of them were for blackmail?' I asked.

He smiled lopsidedly at this.

'It's a long lane that has no turning, Mr Minter. I've given up all that sort of thing. Yes, Mr Voss knows. What a splendid gentleman! What a pity the Lord has so afflicted him!'

I didn't waste much time on the man. Blackmail is one of the crimes that makes me sick, and I'd sooner handle a bushel of snakes than deal with this kind of criminal. Naturally I did not mention the conversation to Voss, because the police never give away their clients. Voss brought up the subject himself at lunch.

'That man Veddle of mine is an old lag,' he said. 'I wondered if you'd recognise him. He's a good fellow, and I think I pay him enough to keep him straight.'

I didn't tell him that you couldn't pay any criminal enough to keep him straight, because there isn't so much money in the world, because I did not want to discourage him.

I saw Veddle again that afternoon in peculiar circumstances. He was always a bit of a dandy, and had considerable success with women of all classes. No man can understand the fascination which a certain kind of man exercises over a certain kind of woman. It isn't a question of looks or age, it's a kind of hypnotism.

I was taking a long walk by myself along the river bank. The river separated Mr Voss's property from the Lone House estate. Lone House itself was a square white building that stood on the crest of a rising lawn that sloped up from the river, which is almost a lake here, for the stream broadens into what is known locally as the Flash.

A small wood on Mr Voss's side of the river hides the house from view. I was coming out of Tadpole Copse, as it was called, when I saw Veddle waiting by the edge of the stream. A girl was rowing across the Flash. Her back was turned to the servant, and she did not see him till she had landed and tied up the boat. It was then that he approached her. I was naturally interested, and walked a little slower. If the girl did not see Veddle, Veddle did not see me, and I was within a dozen yards of the two when he went up to her, raising his hat.

I don't think I've ever seen anybody so lovely as this girl, Marjorie Venn, and I could quite understand why Garry Thurston had fallen for her. Except for police purposes, I can't describe women. I can write down the colour of their eyes and hair, their complexion and height, but I've never been able to say why they're beautiful. I just know they are or they're not; and she was.

She turned quickly and walked away from the man. He followed her, talking all the time, and presently I saw him grip her by the arm and swing her round. She saw me and said something, and Veddle turned and dropped his hand. She did not attempt to meet me, but walked off quickly, leaving the man looking a little foolish. But it's very difficult to embarrass a fellow who's done three stretches for felony. He met me with his sly smile.

'A nice little piece that,' he said – 'A friend of mine.'

'So it appears,' said I. 'Never seen anybody look more friendly than she did.'

He smiled crookedly.

'Women get that way if they like you,' he said.

'Who was the last woman you blackmailed?' I asked; but, bless you, you couldn't make him feel uncomfortable. He just smiled and went on his way.

I watched him, wondering whether he was trying to overtake

the girl. He hadn't gone a dozen paces when round the corner of a clump of trees came swinging a man who I guessed was Field himself. You can tell from a man's walk just what is in his mind, and I wondered if Veddle was gifted with second sight. If he had been he would have run, but he kept right on.

I saw Field stand squarely in his path. He asked a question, and in another second his fist shot out and Veddle went down. To my surprise he made a fight of it, came up again and took a left swing to the jaw that would have knocked out any ordinary man.

It wasn't any business of mine, but I am an officer of the law and I thought it was the right moment to interfere. By the time I reached Mr Field, Veddle was running for his life. I was a little taken aback when Field held out his hand.

'You're Superintendent Minter? I heard you were staying in the neighbourhood,' he said. 'I hope you're not going to prosecute me for trespass – this is a short cut to Hainthorpe Station and I often use it. I don't know whether Mr Voss objects.'

Before I could tell him I didn't know what was in Mr Voss's mind about trespassing he went on: 'Did you see that little fracas? I'm afraid I lost my temper with that fellow, but this is not the first time he has annoyed the young lady.'

He asked me to come over to his house for a drink and, going back to where the skiff was moored, he rowed me across. We landed at a little stage and walked together up the lawn to the open French windows of his study. I noticed then that in front of these the grass was worn and that there was a patch of bare earth – it's funny how a police officer can register these things automatically.

The little study was beautifully furnished, and evidently Mr Field was a man who had done a lot of travelling, for all the walls were covered with curios: African spears and assegais, and on the shelves was a collection of native pottery. He saw me looking round and, walking to the wall, picked down a broad-bladed sword.

'This will interest you if you know anything about Africa,' he said. 'It is the Sword of Tuna. It belonged to the Chief of Ituri – a man who gave me a lot of trouble and who predicted that it would never be sheathed till it was sheathed in my unworthy person.'

He smiled. 'I took it from him after a fight in the forest, so his prediction is not likely to be fulfilled.'

The blade was extraordinarily bright, and I told him that it must take a lot of work to keep it polished, but to my surprise he said that it was made from an alloy which always kept the blade shining – a native variety of stainless steel.

He replaced the sword, and for about a quarter of an hour we talked about Africa, where, he told me, he had made his money, and of the country, and only towards the end of our conversation did he mention the fact that he had a couple of detectives watching the house.

'I've made many enemies in my life,' he said, but did not go on any further to explain how he had made them.

He rowed me back to the other side of the Flash and asked me to dinner. I was going the following night. He was the kind of man I liked: he smoked good cigars, and not only smoked them but gave them to the right kind of people.

On my way back to Hainthorpe I met Mr Voss, or, rather, he nearly met me. The paths of his estate were as level as a billiard table and as broad as an ordinary drive, and they had need to be, for he drove his little electric chair at thirty miles an hour. It was bigger than a Bath chair and packed with batteries, and if I had not jumped into the bushes I should have known just how heavy it was.

I did not think it was necessary to hide anything about Veddle, and I told him what I had seen. He was blue with rage.

'What a beast!' he said. 'I have given that man his chance and I would have forgiven a little light larceny, but this is an offence beyond forgiveness.'

Every afternoon he was in the habit of driving to the top of Jollyboy Hill, which gave him a wonderful view of the surrounding country, and, as he offered to put his chair into low gear, I walked up by his side, though it was a bit of a climb. From the top of the hill you saw the river stretching for miles, and Lone House looked a pretty insignificant place to be the homestead of a thousand acres.

In the opposite direction I could see Dobey Manor, an old Elizabethan house where Garry Thurston's ancestors had lived for hundreds of years.

'A nice boy, Garry,' said Mr Voss thoughtfully. 'Don't tell him about Veddle – I don't want a murder on my hands.'

I dined with him that night, though I ought to have gone back to London, and he arranged that his car should pick me up at Lone House after my dinner there the following night and take me down.

'You are very much favoured,' he said. 'From what I hear, Field does not invite many people to his house. He is rather a recluse, and all the time I have been here he has not been to see me or asked me to pay him a visit.'

I saw Veddle that evening. He had the most beautiful black eye I had ever seen on a man, but, as he did not speak about the little scrap, I thought I'd be tactful and say nothing.

I was just a little bit uneasy because Veddle was marked on the police books as a dangerous man. He had twice fought off detectives who had been sent to arrest him and had once pulled a gun on them. I happen to know this because I was one of the detectives.

In the morning I was strolling in the garden when I saw him coming from his little cottage, and thought it wise to offer a few words of advice.

'You got what you asked for,' I said, 'and if you are a wise man you'll forget what happened yesterday afternoon.'

He looked at me a bit queerly. I'll swear it was one of the few times he ever looked any man in the eyes. 'He will get what is coming to him,' he said, and turned immediately away.

That afternoon I sat on the terrace at Hainthorpe. It was a warm, drowsy day after a heavy shower of rain, and I was half asleep when I saw Mr Voss move along the path in front of the terrace in his electric chair. He was going very fast. I watched him till he disappeared in the little copse near the river's edge and saw the chair emerge on the other side and come up the winding path towards Jollyboy Hill.

Mr Voss always wore a white bowler hat and grey check suit, and it was easy to pick these up even at a distance of a mile and a half, for, as I say, my eyesight was very good.

He was there longer than usual this day – he told me he never stayed more than ten minutes because he caught cold so easily. While he was there my eyes wandered to the copse, and I saw a little curl of smoke rising and wondered whether somebody had lit a fire. It was pretty hot – the sort of day when wood fires break out very easily. The smoke drifted away and presently I saw Mr Voss's chair coming down the hill and pass through the wood. A few minutes later he was waving his hand to me as he turned the chair on to the gentle incline which led to the front of the house. He guided the machine up to where I sat – the terrace was broad and stone-flagged.

'Did you see some smoke come over that wood? I thought the undergrowth was on fire.'

I told him I had seen it.

He shook his head. 'There was nothing there, but I was a little alarmed. Last year I lost a good plantation through gypsies lighting a fire and forgetting to put it out before they left.'

We talked for a little while and he told me he had made arrangements for his Rolls to pick me up at Lone House at ten.

'I hope you won't tell Garry about Veddle,' he said. 'I am getting rid of him – Veddle, I mean. I heard so many stories about this fellow in the village, and I can't afford to have that kind of man round me.' He questioned me about Veddle's past, but naturally I was cautious, for, no matter how bad a man is, the police never give him away. He knew, however, that Veddle had been charged with blackmail, and I thought it necessary that I should tell him also that this ex-convict was marked dangerous at headquarters.

He asked me to come into the house with him as Veddle had gone out for the afternoon, and I helped him into the lift and into the little runabout that he kept on the first floor. I was thoroughly awake by the time I got back to the terrace and sat down to read through a case which was fully reported in that morning's newspaper and in which I had an interest. I had hardly opened the paper before one of the maids came out and said I was wanted on the telephone. I didn't know the man who called me, but he said he was one of the detectives engaged to look after Mr Field. I didn't recognise the voice.

'Is that Superintendent Minter . . . Will you come over to Lone House? Mr Field has been murdered . . . '

I was so surprised that I could not speak for a moment.

'Murdered!' I said. 'Murdered?'

Then, hanging up the receiver, I dashed out of the house and ran along the path through the wood to the place immediately opposite Lone House. The detective was waiting in a boat. He was so agitated and upset that I could not make head or tail of what he was saying. He ran across the lawn and I followed him.

The French windows were wide open, and even before I entered the room I saw, on the damp, brown earth before the door, a distinct imprint of a naked foot. The man had not seen it, and I pushed him aside just as he was going to step on it.

I was first in the room and there I saw Field. He was lying in the centre of the floor, very still, and from his back protruded the hilt of the Sword of Tuna.

2

I didn't have to be a doctor to know that Field was dead. There was very little blood on the floor, considering the size of the sword blade, and the only disorder I could detect at the moment was a smashed coffee cup in the fireplace and a little table which had held the coffee service overturned on the floor. The second cup was not broken; the coffee pot had spilt on the carpet – when Field fell he might have overturned the table, as I remarked to the detective, whose name was Wills.

Now in a case like this a detective's work is usually hampered by a lot of squalling servants who run all over the house and destroy every clue that is likely to be useful to a police officer; and the first thing that struck me was the complete silence of the house and the absence of all servants. I asked Wills about this.

'The servants are out; they've been out since lunchtime,' he said. 'Mr Field sent them up to town to a charity matinee that he'd bought tickets for.'

He went out into the hall and I heard him call Miss Venn by name. When he came back: 'She must have gone out too,' he said, 'though I could have sworn I saw her an hour ago on the lawn.'

I sent him to telephone to his chief. I'm the sort of man who never asks for trouble, and there's no better way of getting trouble than interfering with the county constabulary. I don't say they are jealous of us at Scotland Yard, but they can do things so much better. They've often told me this.

While he was phoning, I had a look at Field. On his cheek was a wound about two inches long, little more than a scratch, but this must have happened before his death, because in his pocket I found a handkerchief covered with blood. There was nothing I could see likely to have caused this wound except a small paperknife which lay on a table against the wall. I examined the blade: it was perfectly clean, but I put it aside for microscopic examination in case one of these clever Berkshire detectives thought it was necessary. I believe in giving the county police all the help you can, and anyway it was certain they'd call in somebody from the Yard after they'd given the murderer time enough to get out of the country.

Leading from the study were two doors, one into the passage and the other into a room at the back of the house. On the other side of the passage was a sort of drawing-room and the dining-room. I say 'sort of drawing-room' because it was almost too comfortable to be a real drawing-room.

I tried the door of the back room: it was locked. Obviously there was another door into the same room from the passage, but I found this was locked too.

When Wills came back from phoning – he'd already had the intelligence to phone a doctor – he told me the story of the discovery. He was on duty single-handed that afternoon; the second detective attached to the establishment had gone to town in Mr Field's car to the charity matinee. Wills said that he had been told to hang around but keep well away from the house, and not to take any notice of anything he saw or heard. It was not an unusual instruction apparently.

'Sometimes,' said Wills, 'he used to have a coloured woman and a negro lad come down to see him. We always had the same instructions. As a matter of fact, I was watching the river, expecting them to turn up. They usually arrived in a motorboat from downstream, and moored off the lawn.'

'You didn't see them today?' I asked.

He shook his head.

'No; only the instructions I had today were exactly the same as I had when they were expected, and usually all the servants were sent out – and Miss Venn.'

I made a quick search of the house. I admit that curiosity is my vice, and I wanted to know as much about this case as was possible before the Surrey police came in with their hobnailed boots, laying their big hands over all the fingerprints. At least, that's what I felt at the time.

I was searching Field's bedroom when Wills called me downstairs.

'It's the deputy chief constable,' he said.

I didn't tell him what I thought of the deputy chief constable, because I am strong for discipline, and it's not my job to put young officers against their superiors. Not that I'd ever met the deputy chief constable, but I'd met others.

'Is that you, Minter? Deputy chief constable speaking.'

'Yes, sir,' I said, expecting some fool instructions.

'We've had particulars of this murder phoned to us by Wills, and I've been through to Scotland Yard. Will you take complete charge of the case? I have your own chief constable's permission.'

Naturally, I was very pleased, and told him so. He promised to come over later in the afternoon and see me. I must say this about the Berkshire constabulary, that there isn't a brighter or smarter lot in the whole of England. It's one of the best administered constabularies, and the men are as keen a lot of crime-hounds as you could wish to meet. Don't let anybody say anything against the Berkshire constabulary – I'm all for them.

My first search was of the desk in the study. I found a bundle of letters, a steel box, locked, and to which I could find no key, a loaded revolver, and, in an envelope, a lot of maps and plans of the Kwange Diamond Syndicate. I knew, as a matter of fact, that Field was heavily interested in diamonds, and that he had very valuable properties in Africa.

In another drawer I found his passbook and his bank deposit book and with these a small ledger which showed his investments. As near as I could gather, he was a half-a-million man. I was looking at this when Wills came in to tell me that Mr Voss was on the other bank and wanted to know if I could see him. I went down to the boat and rowed across. He was in his chair, and he held something in his hand which looked like a big gun cartridge.

'I've heard about the murder,' he said. 'I'm wondering whether this has got anything to do with it.'

I took the cartridge from him; it smelt of sulphur. And then, from under the rug which covered his knees, he took an awkward-looking pistol.

'I found them together in the copse,' he said, 'or at least, my servants found them under my directions. Do you remember the smoke, Minter – the smoke we saw coming from the trees?'

I'd forgotten all about that for the moment, but now I understood.

'This is a little smoke bomb. They used them in the war for signals,' said Voss.

His thin face was almost blue with excitement.

'The moment I heard of what had happened at Lone House, I remembered the smoke – it was a signal! I got my chair out and came straight away down with a couple of grooms, and we searched the copse thoroughly. We found these two things behind a bush – and something else.'

He dived again under the rug and produced a second cartridge, which, I could see, had not been discharged.

'Somebody was waiting there to give a signal. There must have been two people in it at least,' he said. And then: 'He is dead, I suppose?'

I nodded. He shook his head and frowned.

'It's queer. I always thought he would come to an end like that. I don't know why. But there was a mystery about the man.'

'Where is Veddle?' I asked, and he stared at me.

'Veddle? At the house, I suppose.'

He turned and shouted to the two grooms who were some distance away. They had not seen Veddle. He sent one of them in search of the man.

Veddle had been in my mind ever since I had seen the body of Field with the sword of Tuna sticking through his back. I hadn't forgotten his threat nor his police record, and if there was one man in the world who had to account for every minute of his time that man was Mr Veddle.

'I hadn't thought of him,' said Voss slowly.

He knitted his white eyebrows again and laughed.

'It couldn't have been Veddle: I saw him – now, when did I see him?' He thought for a little time. 'Now I come to think of it, I haven't seen him all the morning, but he's sure to be able to account for himself. He spends most of his time in the servants' hall trying to get off with my housemaid.'

A few yards beyond the copse was a small pleasure-house which had a view of the river, and this was equipped with a telephone, which the groom must have used, for he came back while I was talking and reported that Veddle was not in the house and had not been seen. Mr Voss brought his electric chair round, and I walked by its side back to the copse.

Locally it was called Tadpole Copse, and for a good reason, for it was that shape; large clumps that thinned off into a long tail, running parallel with the river and following its course downstream. It terminated on the edge of the property, where there was a narrow lane leading to the main road. It struck me at the time that it was quite possible for any man who had been hidden in the copse to have made a getaway without attracting attention even though the other bank of the river had been alive with policemen.

Voss went back to the house to make enquiries about his servant. He promised to telephone to me as soon as they were completed, and I returned to the boat and was ferried across to the house.

Two doctors were there when I arrived, and they said just the things you expect doctors to say – that Field had died instantly, that only a very powerful man could have killed him, and that it was a terrible business. They had brought an ambulance with them, and I sent the body away under Wills's charge and went on with my search of the desk.

I was really looking for keys. There were two locked rooms in the house, and at the moment I did not feel justified in breaking open any door until the servants returned.

I went round to the back of the house. The window of the locked room was set rather high and a blue blind was drawn down so that I could not see into it. Moreover, the windows were fastened on the inside. In all the circumstances I decided to wait till I found the key, or until the Berkshire police, who were on their way, brought me a pick-lock.

Why had he sent his servants out that afternoon, and what could Marjorie Venn tell me when she came back? Somehow I banked upon the secretary more than upon the servants, because she would know a great deal more of his intimate life.

I went back to the desk and resumed my search among the papers. I was turning over the pages of an engineering report dealing with the Kwange Mine when I heard a sound. Somebody was knocking, slowly and deliberately. I confess I am not a nervous man. Superintendents of police seldom are. If you're nervous you die before you reach the rank of sergeant. But this time I could feel my hair lift a little bit, for the knocking came from the door of the locked room.

3

There was no doubt about it: the sound of the knocking came from behind that locked door. I went over and tried the handle. I am a believer in miracles, and thought perhaps the knocker might have opened the door from the inside, but it was fast.

Then I heard a voice – the voice of a girl – cry 'Help!' and the solution of that mystery came at once. I didn't wait for the keys to come; outside the kitchen door I had seen a big axe – in fact,

I had thought that it might be useful in case of necessity. Going out, I brought in the axe and, calling to the girl to stand aside, I had that door open in two minutes.

She was standing by a large, oriental-looking sofa, holding on to the head for support.

'You're Miss Marjorie Venn, aren't you?'

She couldn't answer, but nodded. Her face was like death; even her lips were almost white.

I set her down and got a glass of water for her. Naturally, as soon as she felt better she began to cry. That's the trouble with women: when they can be useful they become useless. I had to humour her, but it was about ten minutes before she could speak and answer my questions.

'How long have you been there?'

'Where is he?' she asked. 'Has he gone?'

I guessed she was referring to Field. I thought at the moment it was not advisable to tell her that the late Mr Field was just then on his way to a mortuary.

'He's a beast!' she said. 'He gave me something in the coffee. You're a detective, aren't you?'

I had to tell her I was a superintendent. I mean, I'm not a snob, but I like to have credit for my rank.

It took a long time to get the truth out of her. She had lunched alone with Mr Field, and he had become a little too attentive. Apparently it was not the first time that this had happened; it was the first time she had ever spoken about it. And it was only then she discovered that all the servants had been sent out.

As a matter of fact, she had nothing to tell me except what I could already guess. He had not behaved himself, and then he had changed his tactics, apologised, and she thought that the incident was over.

'I'm leaving tonight,' she said. 'I can't stand it any more. It's been terrible! But he pays me a very good salary and I couldn't afford to throw up the work. I never dreamt he would be so base. Even when the coffee tasted bitter, I suspected nothing.' And then she shuddered.

'Do you live here, Miss Venn?' I thought she was a resident secretary, and was surprised when she shook her head. She lodged with a widow woman in a cottage about half a mile away. She had lived at the house, but certain things had happened and she had left. It was not necessary for her to explain what the certain things were. I began to get a new view of Mr Field.

She had heard nothing, could not remember being carried into the room. I think someone must have interrupted him and that he must have come out and locked her in.

Wills admitted to me afterwards that he had come down to the house and that Field had come out in a rage and ordered him to go to his post.

I thought, in the circumstances, as she was calmer, I might tell her what had happened. She was horrified; could hardly believe me. And then she broke into a fit of shuddering which I diagnosed as hysteria. This time it took her some time to get calm again, and the first person she mentioned was Wills, the detective.

'Where was he – when the murder was committed?' she asked.

I was staggered at the question, but she repeated it. I told her that so far as I knew Wills was on the road keeping watch.

'He was here, then!' she said, so emphatically that I opened my eyes.

'Of course he was here.'

She shook her head helplessly.

'I don't understand it.'

'Now look here, young lady,' said I – and although I am not a family man, I have got a fatherly manner which has been highly spoken of – 'what is all this stuff about Wills?'

She was silent for a long time, and then, womanlike, went off at an angle.

'It's dreadful . . . I can't believe it's true.'

'What about Wills?' I asked again.

She brought her mind back to the detective.

'Mr Field was sending him away today. He only found out this morning that he is the brother of that dreadful man – the convict.'

'Veddle?' I said quickly, and she nodded.

'Did you know that it was Mr Field who prosecuted Veddle the last time he went to prison? Or perhaps you didn't know he'd been to prison?'

I knew that all right, as I explained to her.

'But how did he find out that Wills was Veddle's brother?'

Field had found out by accident. He was rowing down the river, as he sometimes did, and had seen the two men talking together on the bank. They were on such good terms that he got suspicious, and when he returned he called Wills into his study and asked him what he meant by associating with a man of Veddle's character, and Wills had blurted out the truth. He hadn't attempted to hide the fact that his brother was an ex-convict. In fact, it was not until that moment really that Field remembered the man.

'Mr Field told me,' she went on, 'that his attitude was very unsatisfactory, and that he was sending him away.'

Just at that moment the deputy chief constable arrived by car and brought a crowd of bright young men, who had got all their detective science out of books. It was pitiful to see them looking for fingerprints and taking plaster casts of the naked foot, just like detectives in fiction, and measuring distances and setting up their cameras when there was nothing to photograph except me.

I told the chief all I knew of the case and got him to send the young lady back to her lodging in his car, and to get a doctor for her. One of his bright assistants suggested that we ought to hold her on suspicion, but there are some suggestions that I don't even answer, and that was one of them.

I went over with the deputy to see Mr Voss, who had sent a message to say that he had heard from Veddle. The man had telephoned him from Guildford. Halfway across the field he came flying down to meet us. I must say that that electric Bath chair of his exceeded all the speed limits, and the wonder to me was that he hadn't been killed years before.

There are some gentlemen who should never be admitted into police cases, because they get enthusiastic. I think they get their ideas of crime out of books written by this fellow whose name I see everywhere. He wanted to know if we'd got any fingerprints, and his red face got purple when I told him about the young lady locked in the room.

'Scandalous! Disgraceful! By gad, that fellow ought to be horsewhipped!'

'He's been killed,' I said, 'which is almost as bad.'

Then I asked him about Veddle.

'How he got to Guildford in the time I haven't the slightest idea. He must have had a car waiting for him. It's the most astounding thing that ever happened.'

'What did he say?' I asked him.

'Nothing very much. He said he would be away for two or three days, that he'd got a call from a sick brother. Before I could say anything about the murder he hung up.'

I decided to search the cottage where Veddle lived. It was on the edge of a plantation, and consisted of two rooms, one of which was a sort of kitchen-cum-dining-room, the other a bedroom. It was plainly but well furnished. Mr Voss, who couldn't get his machine through the door and shouted all his explanations through the windows, said he'd furnished it himself.

There was one cupboard, which contained an old suit and a

new suit of clothes and a couple of pairs of boots. But what I particularly noticed was that Veddle hadn't taken his pipe away. It was lying on the table and looked as if it had been put down in a hurry. Another curious thing was a long mackintosh hanging behind the door. It was the longest mackintosh I have ever seen. On top of it hung a black felt hat. I took down the mackintosh and, laying it on the bed, felt in the pockets – it is the sort of thing one does mechanically – and the first thing my fingers closed round was a small cylinder. I took it out. It was a smoke cartridge. I put that on the table and went on with the search.

One of the drawers of the bureau was locked. I took the liberty of opening it. It had a tin cash-box, which was unfastened, and in this I made a discovery. There must have been three hundred pounds in one-pound notes, a passport made out in the name of Wills – Sidney Wills, which was Veddle's real name – and a book of tickets which took him to Constantinople. There was a sleeper ticket also made out in the name of Wills, and the whole was enclosed in a Cook's folder, and, as I discovered from the stamp, had been purchased at Cook's West-End office the day before the murder.

There was a third thing in the drawer which I didn't take very much notice of at the time, but which turned out to be one of the big clues in the case. This was a scrap of paper on which was written: 'Bushes second stone's throw turn to Amberley Church third down.'

I sent this to the deputy chief constable.

'Very mysterious,' he said. 'I know Amberley Church well; it's about eight miles from here. It's got a very famous steeple.'

As I say, I didn't attach a great deal of importance to it. It was too mysterious for me. I put it in my pocket, and a few minutes afterwards, when I heard that Wills, the detective, was missing, I had forgotten it.

4

The disappearance of Wills rattled me. And I'm not a man easily rattled. Now and again you meet a crook detective, but mostly in books. I knew just what they'd say at Scotland Yard – they'd blame me for it. If a chimney catches fire, or a gas main blows up, the chief constable says to the deputy: 'Why isn't the Sooper more careful?'

Wills hadn't done anything dramatic: he'd just walked to the station, taken a ticket to London and had gone. I got on to the Yard by phone, but of course he hadn't turned up then, and I placed the chief constable in full possession of all the facts; and from the way he said: 'How did that come to happen, Minter?' I knew that I was halfway to a kick. If I wasn't one of the most efficient officers in the service, and didn't catch every man I was sent after, I should be blamed for their crimes.

I got one bit of evidence. After I'd finished telephoning and come out of the house, I found an assistant gardener waiting to see me. He had seen Veddle walking towards his cottage about the time of the murder. He had particularly noticed him because he wore a long mackintosh that reached to his heels and a black hat; the mackintosh had the collar up and the tab drawn across as though it were raining. This was remarkable because it was a fairly warm day. The gardener thought he was a stranger who was trying to find his way to the house, and had gone across towards him, when he recognised Veddle.

'From which way was he coming?'

'From Tadpole Copse,' said the man. 'I told Mr Voss and he sent me on to tell you.'

I liked Mr Voss: he was a nice man. But the one thing that rattles me is the amateur detective. I suppose the old gentleman found time hanging on his hands, and welcomed this murder as a farmer welcomes rain after a drought. He was what I would describe as a seething mass of excitement. His electric chair was dashing here and there; he was down in Tadpole Copse, with half a dozen gamekeepers and gardeners, finding clues that would have baffled the well-known Sherlock Holmes. He meant well, and that's the hardest thing you can say about any man.

He gave me one idea – more than one, if the truth be told. It was after I rowed across to Lone House and had come upon him and his searchers in the wood.

'Why do you trouble to row?' he said. 'Why don't you get Garry Thurston to lend you his submarine?'

I thought he was joking, but he went on: 'It's a motorboat. I call it the submarine because of its queer build.'

He told me that Garry had had the boat built for him to his own design. The river, though not an important one, is very deep, and leads, of course, to the Thames, where the Conservancy Board have a regulation against speeding. You're not allowed to use speedboats on the Thames, because the wash from them damages the banks and has been known to wreck barges.

As Garry was keen on speed, and had taken a natural science degree at Cambridge, he had designed a boat which offered him a maximum of speed with a minimum of wash.

'It honestly does look a submarine. There's only about four feet of it above water, and the driver's seat is more like a conning tower than a cockpit.'

'Where does he keep it?' I asked.

Apparently he had a boathouse about two hundred yards from the Flash. We afterwards measured and found that it was exactly two hundred and thirty yards in a straight line from Lone House.

Mr Voss was full of enthusiasm, and we went round the edge of the estate, touched a secondary road and in a very short time came to a big, green boathouse, but there was no boat there.

'He must be out in it,' said Mr Voss, a little annoyed, 'but when he comes in – there he is!'

He pointed to the river, and I'll swear to you that although my sight is as good as any man's I couldn't see it.

The boat was moving against a green background, and as it was painted green it was almost invisible. If I hadn't seen Garry Thurston's head and his big face I would never have seen it at all. The top was shaped like a sort of whaleback. The whole boat seemed to be awash and sinking.

It came towards us, moving very quickly, and Garry waved his hand to us, brought the boat alongside and stepped out.

'I've been down to the river,' he said, 'and nearly had an accident – Field's black friends were rowing up and they fouled my bow.'

I had heard about these strange negroes who came to see Field occasionally, and I was very much interested.

'When was this?' I asked.

He told me. It must have been half an hour before the murder was committed.

'They were lying under the bank, and the boy evidently decided to row across into one of the backwaters, and chose the moment I was hitting up a tolerable speed for this little river. I only avoided them by accident. Why doesn't Field bring his native pals here by road?'

I thought it was a bright moment to tell him that John Field had met his death that afternoon. He wasn't shocked, did not even seem surprised, and when he said, 'Poor devil!' I did not think he sounded terribly sincere. Then he asked quickly: 'Where was Miss Venn?'

'She was in the house,' I said, and I saw his face go pale.

'Good God!' he gasped. 'In the house when the murder was committed – '

I stopped him.

'She knew nothing about it – that's all I'm prepared to tell you. At least, she said she knew nothing about it.'

'Where is she now?' asked Garry. He looked absolutely ill

with worry. I told him that I had sent her to her lodgings, and I think he'd have started right away if I hadn't pointed out that it wasn't quite the thing to go worrying the girl unless she had given him some right.

'And anyway,' I said, 'she's a police witness, and I don't want her interfered with.'

I told him what I'd come for, and told him at the same time that his boat was quite useless for the purpose: it was too long and too full of odd contraptions for me to bother my head about. But he had what I had thought was a row-boat, under a canvas cover, but it proved to be a small motor dinghy, and with this he ran me down to the Flash, showing me in the meantime how to work it.

I hadn't by any means got through Field's papers. In his pocket had been a bunch of keys. There was one odd-looking key for which I could find no lock. I discovered it that evening, when I was trying the walls of his study. Behind a picture, which swung out on hinges, I found the steel door of a safe. It was packed with papers, mostly of a business nature, and I was going through these carefully when Miss Marjorie Venn arrived. About teatime I had sent her a note, telling her that when she was well enough I would like her assistance to sort out Field's papers. I didn't expect that she'd be well enough to come until the next day, but they telephoned, just before I began my search, to ask me if I would send the car for her.

She was quite calm; some of the colour had come back to her face; and I had a closer view of her than I had had that day on the bank, when Veddle had behaved like a blackguard. She was my ideal of what a woman should be: no hysterics, no swooning, just calm and sensible, which women so seldom are.

The servants had come back from the matinée, and I wanted to know exactly how I was to deal with them. She went out and saw them, and arranged that they were to stay on until further orders. A couple of the women, however, insisted on going home that night. She paid their wages out of money which she kept for that purpose.

There was no doubt about her being a help. She knew almost every document by sight, and saved me the trouble of reading through long legal agreements and contracts.

I sent for coffee when we were well into the work. It was while we were drinking this that she told me something about Field. He paid her a good salary, but she was in fear of him, and once or twice had been on the point of leaving him.

'I hate to say it of him, but he was absolutely unscrupulous,' she said. 'If he had not been a friend of my father's, and I was not obeying my father's wishes, I should never have stayed.'

This was a new one on me, but apparently Field and Miss Venn's father had been great friends in South Africa. Lewis Venn had died there – died apparently within a year of Field finding his gold-mine.

'When Mr Field came back I was about fifteen and at school. He paid for my education and helped my mother in many ways, and after dear mother's death he sent me to Oxford. I had never met him until then. He persuaded me to give up my studies and come and act as his private secretary. I was under that deep obligation to him – ' She paused. 'I think he has cancelled that,' she said quietly.

Her father and Field had been poor men, who had wandered about Africa looking for mythical gold-mines. One day they came to a native village and discovered, under a heap of earth, an immense store of raw gold, the accumulation of centuries, which the natives had won from a river and which had been handed on from chief to chief.

'The Chief of Tuna,' she said. 'This sword – ' She stopped and shuddered. It was this that had put them on the track of the gold-mine. 'Mr Field often spoke about it.'

She stopped rather abruptly.

'Now I think we ought to get on with our work,' she said.

It was five minutes after this that we made a discovery. There was a false bottom to the safe, and in this was a long envelope, and written on the outside: 'The Last Will and Testament of John Carlos Field'. The envelope was sealed; I broke the seal and opened it.

It was written on a double sheet of foolscap evidently in Field's own hand, and after the usual flim-flam with which legal documents began, it said: 'I leave all of which I die possessed to Marjorie Anna Venn, of Clive Cottage, in this parish – '

'To me?' Marjorie Venn looked as if she had seen a ghost. She evidently couldn't believe what I was reading.

'If you're Marjorie Anna Venn – '

She nodded. 'That is my full name.' She spoke like somebody who had been running and was out of breath. 'He asked me my full name one day, and I told him. But why – '

There was a big space under the place where he and the witnesses had signed, and here he had written a codicil, which was also witnessed.

'I direct that the sum of five hundred pounds shall be paid to my wife, Lita Field, and the sum of a thousand pounds to my son, Joseph John Field.'

We looked at one another.

'Then he was married!' she said.

At this minute one of my men came in to see me. 'There's a young man called. He says his name is Joseph John Field.'

I pushed back my chair, as much astonished as the girl.

'Show him in,' I said.

We didn't speak a word. And then the door opened, and there walked into the room a tall, young, good-looking negro.

'My name is Joseph John Field,' he said.

Did I say I was not easily rattled? Well, I'm not. But I'd been rattled twice in one day.

I looked at the negro, I looked at Marjorie.

The boy – he was about nineteen – stood there motionless; there was no expression on his face or in his brown eyes.

'Joseph John Field?' I said. 'You're not the son of John Field, who was the owner of this house?'

He nodded. 'Yes, I am his son,' he said quietly. 'My mother's father was the Chief of Tuna.'

I could only look at him. I thought these kinds of cases only existed in the minds of people who wrote cinema stories. But there was this negro, making a claim that was so preposterous that I simply couldn't believe him.

'Then your grandfather was the Chief of Tuna? I suppose you know that the Sword of Tuna – '

He interrupted me. 'Yes, I know that.'

'Who told you?' I asked sharply.

He hesitated.

'A detective. He telephoned to my mother tonight.'

'Wills?' I asked.

Again he hesitated.

'Yes, Mr Wills. He has been a good friend of ours. He once saved my mother from – from being beaten by Mr Field.'

He had the cultured voice of an English gentleman. I found afterwards that he had been educated at a public school, and was at that time at a university.

'Mr Wills thought that I should come and see you, because, as mother and I were in the neighbourhood today, and we were known to have visited the house recently, suspicion might attach to us.'

'It certainly does, young man,' said I, and it was only then that I asked him if he'd sit down.

I could see Marjorie was listening, fascinated. The young man drew up a chair on the other side of the desk. He wore dark gloves and carried an ebony cane. His clothes were made by a good West-End tailor. There was nothing ostentatious about his clothes, and, as I say, his voice was the voice of a gentleman.

He put his hand in his pocket, took out a leather case, opened it and handed me a folded paper. It was headed: 'March, 17th, being St Patrick's Day, 1907, at the Jesuit Mission, Kobulu'. Written in faded ink were the words:

> I have this day, and in accordance with the rites of Holy Church, performed the ceremony of marriage between John Carlos Field, English, and Lita, daughter of Kosulu, Chief of Tuna, and issue this certificate in proof thereof.
>
> MICHAEL ALOYSIUS VALETTI, SJ

Underneath was written: 'Confirmed – Morou, District Commissioner'.

I handed the document mechanically to Miss Venn.

She read it. 'This is your mother's marriage certificate,' she said.

He nodded. 'You are Miss Marjorie Venn? I've never seen you before, but I know you very well. My mother knew your father. They came to our village more than twenty years ago, my father and yours.'

I thought it was a pretty good moment to ask him about Field's life in Africa, but the boy would tell me nothing, except that Field behaved very badly to his mother and had brought a number of tribes with him to attack the village and had killed the chief – his father-in-law.

I was a little knocked out to find a young negro claiming to be the son of a white man, but if I'd had any sense, I'd have realised that this is one of the jokes that nature plays in marriages of mixed colour. It was understandable now why Field invariably sent his servants away when his wife and son called upon him.

My first inclination was to admire the man for having done the right thing by this coloured son of his, but then I realised that he could not very well do anything else. I didn't suppose his wife blackmailed him, but the possibility of the fact leaking out that this country gentleman was married to a negress would be quite sufficient to make him pay well to keep her quiet. He could not even divorce her or allow her to divorce him without creating a scandal. I mentioned this fact to the boy, who agreed and said that Field had offered his mother a large sum of money to apply in the District Courts – I think they were Belgian – for a divorce, but his mother, having been mission-trained a Catholic, would not hear of divorce.

I wanted to get his reaction to the will, so I told him that he had been practically cut off, except for a thousand pounds. He wasn't a bit surprised, except that he had been left anything at all.

'Where did my father die?' the girl asked suddenly, but Joseph Field would say very little about what happened in Africa twenty-two years before. Possibly he did not know very much, though I am inclined to believe that he knew more than he was prepared to tell.

He did throw some sort of light on the cause of the quarrel between Field and the Chief of Tuna.

'My father had difficulty in locating the diamond mine and came back again and again. He tried to persuade Kosulu – my grandfather – to let him have a share of the gold store which we kept in the village. Kosulu was paramount chief and the gold had been accumulating for centuries. It was to gain possession of this that he attacked the village – '

'Was my father in the attack?' asked the girl quickly.

Joseph Field shook his head.

'No, Miss Venn. The partnership had already been broken. Your father at the time was prospecting elsewhere. He did go back to the village after Kosulu was wounded and nursed him.

John Field was bitterly disappointed because he had not been given the gold. He thought when he married my mother he would be able to take possession of the store. Mr Venn at that time was a very sick man. My mother tells me he was planning to go to the coast to make his way back to what you call civilisation' – I saw him smile; I guess he had his own idea of civilisation. 'It was on his way to the coast your father died.'

I cross-examined him as to the number of times he and his mother had visited Lone House, but I could get nothing that helped me very much. They had only come once without invitation and that was the time that Wills had to intervene to save the woman from John Field's hunting crop.

There was nothing for me to do but to take his name and address. He and his mother lived in a flat in Bayswater and I told him that I would call to see them at the first available opportunity.

'What do you make of that?' I asked the girl when he had gone.

She shook her head.

I thought she looked rather sad and wondered why; not that I spend much time in analysing the emotions of females.

We did not do much more searching, but spent the next hour discussing Joseph John Field, and the part he may have played. I told her I knew that they had been in the neighbourhood that day and where I had my information from. When I mentioned Garry Thurston she went rather pink and started very quickly to talk about his boat.

'It's curious,' she said. 'Mr Field used to detest that motor-boat. I think it was because he hated being spied upon, as he called it, and he had an idea that Garry used to come down on to the Flash in it to – well, to see me.'

'And did you see him very often?' I asked.

'He is a great friend of mine,' she answered.

It's funny that you can never get a woman to give a straight answer to a straight question. However, it was not a subject that I wanted to pursue at that moment, so I let it drop.

The truth about John Field's marriage must come out at the inquest: I told Joseph that when I saw him off the premises, but he didn't seem much upset. It was clear to me that there was no love lost between him and his father. Generally when he referred to him he called him 'John Field'. I could see that the horsewhip incident was on his mind, and probably there were other incidents which nobody knew anything about.

It was easy to understand now why Wills was not popular with Field: he knew too much and probably presumed upon his knowledge. I guess that the woman must have told the detective that she was Field's wife.

An idea occurred to me suddenly. 'Do you mind if I ask you a delicate question. Miss Marjorie?' I said, and when she said no, I asked her if Field had proposed marriage to her.

'Three or four times,' she said quietly, and I did not pursue the subject, because it might have been a very painful one for the young lady.

From what she told me it seemed that Field had lived almost the life of a hermit: he knew nobody in the neighbourhood and made no friends.

'Mr Voss asked him to dinner once, but he refused. He tried to buy Hainthorpe – '

'Mr Voss's house?'

She nodded.

'He hated people living so close to him and he had an idea of building a house on top of Jollyboy Hill; in fact, he offered Mr Voss a very considerable sum of money through his agent for the hill alone, but the offer was not accepted.'

There wasn't much more to be done that night. Mr Voss had asked me to stay with him, and after seeing the young lady home, I got one of our men who understands engines to take me across the Flash. Here I found the little two-seater which

Mr Voss had put at my disposal: I don't understand motorboats, but I can drive a car.

As I think I have explained, the house stands in a little stretch of meadow which is wholly encircled by trees. The path to the house is just wide enough to take a small car. The road runs a little way through Tadpole Copse, through the thickest part of it. I was within a few yards of what I would call the exit, when I saw, in the light of my headlamps, somebody standing by the birch tree. Thinking it was one of the searchers, I slowed my car almost to a walk, and shouted: 'Do you want a lift?'

I had hardly spoken the words before the figure straightened itself and fired twice at me.

6

The bullets stung past me so close to my face that I thought I had been hit. For a moment I sat paralysed with astonishment. It was the sight of the figure running that sort of brought me to life. I was out of the car in a second, but by this time he was out of sight. If I'd had the sense to bring my car round on a full lock, the lamps would have made it possible for me to see. As it was I was stumbling about in the dark with no chance of following my gentleman friend.

I think I ought to explain that Mr Voss had made dozens of 'walks' in Tadpole Copse and there were paths running in all directions; it was a real laby – what's the word? Maze. I went back to the car and got my hand lamp, which I should have taken before. I ought to have known that any kind of search was a waste of time, but a man who's been fired at doesn't think as calmly as the chief constable sitting in his office (as I told him later). I hadn't any difficulty in finding where this bird had stood. I found the two shells of an automatic pistol lying on the grass. They were both hot when I found them. Naturally I kept them, because nowadays there is a new-fangled process by which you can identify from the cartridge the pistol that fired it, and I didn't think it was a satisfactory night's work. To go running through the wood was a waste of time – I realised that. The only hope was that the shots would have aroused one of Mr Voss's gamekeepers and that the man might be seen. Apparently it had aroused them, but in the wrong direction. Their cottages were on the other side of the house and I met them running over the ground on my way to Hainthorpe. By the time I told them what had happened, I remembered that I had two or three detectives at Lone House who would want to know all about the shooting, and I turned back to see them. I was giving instructions about notifying the police stations around, with the idea of putting a barrage on the roads, when I heard two more shots fired in quick succession. They came from the direction of Hainthorpe. I got into the car again and flew up the road, not so fast as I might have done because I had police officers and gamekeepers piled into the machine or hanging on to the footboards.

The entrance to Hainthorpe is a great portico, and the first thing I saw in the light of the motor lamps was a ladder lying across the drive. The house was in commotion. A servant, who looked scared sick, met me and asked me to come up to Mr Voss's room. He took me in the elevator. Mr Voss was sitting in bed. He was very red in the face, all his white hair was standing up and he was in his pyjamas.

'Look at that!' he roared and pointed to the curved bedhead.

It had been made of gilt wood, but now, for a space of about a foot, it was smashed to smithereens.

'They shot at me,' he said. (Did I say 'he said'? He yelled it.) 'Look at that!'

Over the bed was a square hole in the wall that had shivered the plaster and sent it flying in all directions. The damage was so great that it didn't look like an automatic bullet that had done the work.

When he pointed to the French windows leading to the portico I understood why.

One window was smashed to smithereens, one was neatly punctured with a hole – both bullets must have started somersaulting the moment they touched the obstruction of the glass. I went out on to the top of the portico. It was surrounded by a low balustrade and had over it a canvas awning – Mr Voss used to be pushed out here to enjoy the sunlight and sometimes, he told me, he had slept there.

One of the cartridge cases I discovered on the balustrade, the other on the drive below the next morning.

When I got Mr Voss quiet, he told me what had happened. He had not apparently heard the first two shots that were fired at me, but he was awakened by the sound of a ladder being put against the portico. He sat up in bed and switched on the light.

'It was the most stupid thing I could have done, for the devil could see his target. The light was hardly on before – bang! I actually saw the glass smash . . .'

Though he was always regarded as a man of iron nerve, he was trembling from head to foot. One of the splinters from the wood had cut his right hand, which was wrapped up in a handkerchief. I wanted him to see a doctor about it, but he pooh-poohed the idea. I went downstairs while he dressed himself with the assistance of a servant, and after a few minutes he came down in the lift and wheeled himself into the library. He was much calmer and had enough theories to last him for the rest of the night.

I had all the servants in the house brought into the library one by one and questioned them. Nobody had seen the man who had done the shooting. The ladder was one belonging to the gardeners and was used in the orchard, but kept hanging near the house. I questioned everybody closely as to whether they had seen a pistol in the possession of Veddle. They were all very vague, except a gardener who had actually seen an automatic in Veddle's cottage.

Mr Voss was very emphatic on the point.

'There was no doubt at all,' he said, 'he had a pistol: I saw him practising with it once and told him to throw it into the river.'

He told me then what he had never told me before: that in the course of the past year he had received two threatening letters written by anonymous correspondents.

'I didn't think it was worth while keeping them,' he said. 'They were written by some illiterate person, and I always suspected some gypsies I had turned off a corner of my land about this time last year.'

'They were not in Veddle's handwriting?'

'No,' he said slowly. 'I don't think I have ever seen Veddle's handwriting now that you mention it.'

I had the little scrap of paper in my pocket which I had taken from Veddle's cottage and I showed it to him. He examined the mysterious message it contained, reading out the words: 'Bushes second stone stop turn to Amberley Church third down.'

I took the paper from him. I could have sworn that the third and fourth words were 'stone's throw', but I saw I had made a mistake. Even with the change of the words it was as plain to me as it had been at first.

'I think that is Veddle's writing,' I said.

'What does it mean?'

'I haven't the slightest idea,' I said. 'The point is: is the writing anything like the anonymous letters you received?'

He shook his head. 'So far as I can remember, it isn't.' He pulled out a handful of letters from his pocket, trying to find some note which Veddle had written to him. He was one of those careless men who keep money, letters and odd memoranda all in one pocket. As he went through them he threw half of them away.

'I get my pockets full of this stuff,' he said. 'It is what I call a bachelor's wastepaper basket.'

I stooped and fished into the real wastepaper basket, and

handed him something he had thrown away. They might have been old bills, they were so sprinkled with ink, but I've got an instinct for money.

'You may be a rich man,' I said, 'but there is no reason why you should chuck your money into the wastepaper basket.'

They were bank notes, three for ten pounds and one for twenty pounds.

He chuckled at his carelessness.

'Perhaps that is why Veddle always took personal charge of my wastepaper basket. I wonder how much the rascal has made out of my carelessness.'

It was nearly four o'clock when I went up to my room, after a long talk with the chief constable on the wire.

I am one of those old-fashioned police officers who never have got out of their notebook habit. Give me a bit of a pencil and a sheet of paper and I can collect all my thoughts on one page. Here were the facts:

1 A very rich man, occupying a lonely house by the river, is killed. The only immediate clue is the impression on the earth outside of a naked footprint.

2 In the house at the time of the murder and locked up in a room is his private secretary, a girl to whom he had been making love although he was a married man. It was impossible that she could have locked the door herself, for the key of the room was found in the dead man's inside pocket when he was searched.

3 One of the detectives engaged to look after Field disappears, and we discover that he is the brother of Veddle – Mr Voss's servant, a man who had a quarrel and a fight with Field and who threatened to get even with him.

4 Veddle and Wills disappear, but on the night following the murder, some person unknown appears in the grounds and fires at me and attempts to assassinate Mr Voss.

5 Mr Garry Thurston, who is in love with the secretary, possesses a boat which could approach the house unseen. He states, and this is confirmed, he was cruising along the little river at or near the time of the murder, when he encounters a negress, who is Field's wife, and a young negro, who is Field's son, within striking distance of the house.

I wrote all this down, and the sun was shining through the windows by the time I had finished. I didn't feel like sleep. It's a queer thing – there is a point beyond which tiredness cannot go: you either drop into a heavy sleep where you sit, or you suddenly become as lively as a cricket. I had got to the cricket stage. I had a bath, shaved and, dressing myself, I went downstairs, unlocked the front door and stepped out. It was going to be a gorgeous day: the sun was up, the air was fresh and sweet. I decided to walk across the park towards Lone House. I knew the detectives would be there and some of them would be awake and could make me some coffee.

I stepped out very cheerfully, never dreaming that I was on the point of making a discovery which would change the whole complexion of the case.

As I think I told you, to reach the place where the river spreads out into a little lake one has to pass through Tadpole Copse. The birds were singing and it was the sort of morning that somehow you could not associate with police work, murders and midnight shootings.

I reached the spot where I had been fired at and, although I didn't expect to find anything, I had a sudden impulse to go off the path and make a search of the undergrowth. There was more than a possibility that I should find something which we had overlooked. I poked about with my stick without success and was turning to go when suddenly I saw two feet behind a bush; they were wide apart, the toes turned up. The man, whoever he was, must have been lying on his back.

I am not easily agitated, but there was something about these feet and their absolute stillness that sent a shiver down my spine. I walked quickly past the bush. Lying on his back was a man, his arms outstretched, his white face turned up to the sky. It was not necessary to see the blood on his throat to know that he was dead.

I stood looking at him, speechless. He was the one man I didn't expect to find murdered on that summer morning.

7

The dead man was Veddle. He had been shot at close quarters, and the doctor who saw him afterwards said he must have been killed instantaneously.

What struck me at the time was that he had not been killed in the place he was found. His attitude, the fact that there was little or no blood on the ground, and the obvious traces of a heavy body having been dragged to behind the bushes, all gave the OK to my first impression.

I didn't do any searching just then, but, running through the wood, I came to the water's edge, intending to call assistance from Lone House. The first thing I saw was Garry Thurston's queer-looking boat. It was moored to the bank, the painter tied to a tree, and its stern had drifted out so that it lay bow on to the bank. One of our men was on the lawn, and I shouted to him to come over. He travelled across in the little motor dinghy.

'How long has that boat been there?' I asked.

'I don't know. I saw it a quarter of an hour ago when I came out on to the lawn, and wondered what it was doing there. It belongs to Mr Thurston, doesn't it?'

I wasn't worrying about the ownership of the boat at the moment, but took him up to the place where the body lay, and together we began our search.

He had heard nothing in the night, except that, just before

daylight, he thought he heard the sound of a motor car back-firing. It seemed a long way off, and nothing like the sound of the shots he had heard earlier in the night.

Some rough attempt had been made to search Veddle's body, for the pockets of the jacket and the trouser pockets were turned inside out. It was in his hip pocket, on which he was lying, that we found the money – about two hundred pounds. The money was a bit of a shock to me, and upset all my previous calculations. It only shows how dangerous it is for an experienced police officer to make up his mind too soon.

'A hundred and eighty pounds,' said the sergeant, counting it.

I put it in my pocket without a word.

We began to comb the wood, and in ten minutes we had found the place where the murder was committed. We should have known this by certain signs had we not also found an already packed suitcase and an overcoat.

The place was about thirty yards from the drive which runs through Tadpole Copse, very near the spot where I had been shot at on the previous night.

There wasn't time to make more than a rough search of the suitcase, and that told us nothing.

I went down to the Flash and examined Garry Thurston's boat. The floor of the cockpit was covered with a rubber mat, of white and blue check, and on this were the marks of muddy footprints. They weren't so much muddy as wet; it looked as if somebody had been wading in the water before they got into the boat.

Taking the motor dinghy, I went up to the boathouse. The gates facing the river were wide open; the little door on the land side was locked. I knew, because Garry Thurston had told me, that the gates opened automatically at the pull of a lever on the inside of the boathouse, and they could only be opened from the inside. The boathouse itself was supported on piles, and I saw at once that it was possible for anybody who would take the risk to dive under its edge and climb up inside. I told the detective to take the suitcase across to Lone House, and, taking the police car, I drove up to Dobey Manor, where Mr Garry Thurston lived.

It was an old Elizabethan manor house, one of the show places of the county. I am not very well acquainted with the habits of the non-working classes, but I expected it would take me an hour to make anybody hear at that time of the morning. But the first person I saw when I got out of the car was Mr Thurston himself. He was up and dressed, and by the look of him I guessed he had not been to bed all night. He was unshaven, and his eyes had one of those tired, poker-party looks.

'You're up early, Mr Thurston,' I said, and he smiled.

'I haven't been to bed all night. In fact I've only just come in.' And then, abruptly: 'Have they found Veddle?'

That was the one question I didn't expect him to put to me, and I was a little taken aback. The one person I didn't think he would be interested in was Veddle.

'Yes, we've found him,' I replied.

I looked at his face pretty straightly, but it was like a mask and told me nothing. He didn't speak for a moment, and then: 'You found him, eh?' He spoke very slowly, as though he was thinking out every word carefully.

I expected him to ask me where Veddle had been found. I had an instinct that that was the question that was on his lips but that, for some reason, he dared not ask. I had come up to make enquiries about his motorboat. It was merely a precautionary enquiry to clear up any possibility that he might have an arrangement with somebody in the neighbourhood to use the boat. But his attitude and his appearance changed my angle.

'Yes,' I went on, not taking my eyes off him, 'I found Veddle shot dead in Tadpole Copse.'

He was a good-looking young fellow, but as I spoke his face went grey and old.

'You don't mean that!' It was almost in a whisper that he spoke. 'Shot dead! Good God! How – how awful!'

It wasn't a moment to try to carry on a polite conversation – I put my question to him without trimmings.

'Where have you been all night, Mr Thurston?'

The colour returned to his face in large quantities. He made no attempt to deny the fact that he hadn't been in bed.

'I was just wandering around,' he stammered. 'I couldn't sleep – Veddle dead! How perfectly ghastly!'

Why was he so interested in Veddle, dead or alive? That puzzled me; but so many things had puzzled me in the past twenty-four hours.

He stopped further enquiries by saying: 'Come inside and have some coffee,' and, turning abruptly, he walked ahead of me through the garden and up a broad flight of steps on to the terrace before the house.

The first thing I saw on the terrace was something under a canvas cover that looked like a machine gun. He saw my eyes go in that direction, and I noticed him frown. He would have passed on, but I was curious.

'Oh, that!' he said, and was a little embarrassed. 'That is a telescope. This house, as you see, is built on a rise, and on a clear day I can see objects forty miles away. If it wasn't for Jollyboy Hill one could see St Paul's well enough to tell the time by the clock.'

It was a fairly clear morning. I pointed to a church spire about five miles away.

'What church is that?' I asked.

'That's Amberley,' he said.

Amberley Church! I remembered the note that I had found in Veddle's room: 'Bushes second stone stop turn to Amberley Church third down.'

He seemed anxious to get me indoors, walked ahead of me, turning to see if I was following.

Generally speaking, I am not easily baffled, but the behaviour of this young man, his interest in Veddle, and the fact that he'd been out all night – the night that Veddle was murdered – upset quite a number of interesting theories that were beginning to sort themselves out in my mind.

It was when we were sitting in the big hall of his house, a room that looked like a small chapel, that I said why I had come. He stared when I told him about the boat. 'I can't understand that,' he said. 'No, I haven't used the boat since – well, I haven't used it since you saw me on the river. Will you tell me where you found it?'

I described the position where the boat had been moored, and then, to my surprise, he asked: 'Were any of Veddle's belongings on the bank or in the boat?'

When I told him about the suitcase I thought he turned a little pale. He certainly got up from the table quickly, leaving his coffee untouched, and paced up and down the room. I didn't know what to make of him. His agitation wasn't natural in a man who had nothing more than a casual interest in the death of Veddle.

I put the question again to him. 'What were you doing last night?'

'I went to town,' he said.

There was a 'you be damned' tone in his voice which was a little unexpected.

'Really, inspector, I don't see why my movements should be questioned.'

'What time did you go to town?'

'At seven o'clock last night – it may have been eight. I didn't dine here.'

I looked at his grey suit. He must have gone to town on pretty important business for it to have kept him up all night. I guessed then that he hadn't been back very long when I arrived at the house, but this guess was wrong, because I afterwards discovered he had returned at three o'clock.

There was no sense in alarming him. I put on my best jolly-good-fellow smile.

'Your coffee's getting cold, Mr Thurston,' I said, helping myself to another cup. 'If I've asked you any questions that I oughtn't to have asked I'm very sorry.'

I drank up the coffee.

'I think I'll toddle back to Lone House and see what they've found in Veddle's suitcase. Have you seen Miss Venn lately – '

I had hardly asked the question when I heard a woman's voice behind me say, 'Can I come in, please?'

I turned my head. Standing in the doorway was a woman. I guessed she was about forty. She was slim and tall, and dressed in a neat costume; and though she hadn't either the colour or the peculiar features of her race, I knew she was a negress and guessed she was John Field's wife.

8

The last person in the world I expected to see was the negress whom John Field had married in the wilds of Africa, and I was so taken by surprise that I hadn't a thing to say. You can't imagine anything more – what is the word? incongruous, is it? – than the sight of that young woman in this big, vaulted manor hall. She just didn't belong to the country and didn't belong to the house.

The queer thing was that I had made up my mind during the night that I would see her that day.

I turned to Garry Thurston. I expected him to look embarrassed, but he didn't.

'You don't know Mrs Field?' he said as calmly as you please. 'I brought her down from town early this morning – her and her son.'

It was one of those situations where a man can't exactly find the right word to break into a conversation. At least, I couldn't for a long time.

'Why did you bring her here?' I asked at last.

'Because I want to know something more about John Field – a great deal more than I know.'

Now it is a fact that until that moment I had never considered this young man very seriously. I know his boat was seen in the vicinity of the house about the time the murder was committed, and one of my subordinate officers had suggested he should be questioned. But also I know quite a lot about criminals, and when you get an educated man committing a murder he doesn't as a rule fall into any of the errors that upset the applecart of the half-wits.

I looked from him to the woman. She had just realised who I was, and she was looking at me in a curious and understanding way. Mr Thurston beckoned her in and pulled out a chair for her.

'Now, Mr Thurston,' I said, 'perhaps you'll tell me what it is you want to know about Field? I may be able to put you right.'

He shook his head.

'Nothing that I wanted to know about Field immediately concerns his murder,' he said. 'I was anxious to get particulars of his early life, and Mrs Field very kindly agreed to come down.'

'Did you have to bring her down here, Mr Thurston? Couldn't you have questioned her in London?'

He shook his head. 'The questions I wanted to put had to be asked here,' he said shortly, and I knew that nothing I could say would make him give me any further information, and I guessed from the look of the woman that she wasn't going to be helpful.

I put aside all the friend-of-the-family stuff, and began to ask him to account for his movements that night. And he had an alibi as fast as a rock. He'd been in town, and, what is more, his chauffeur had driven him and driven him back again. He couldn't have been anywhere near Tadpole Copse when the murder was committed. I don't think we were such good friends as we had been when I left, but he was the sort of young man who would know I was only doing my duty and would bear no malice.

I didn't go back straight to the house. It took my fancy to go up to the top of Jollyboy Hill. I've been too long in the police service to expect anything that looks or feels like inspiration, but I had an idea that once I got on top of that hill a lot of things would become clear that were at the moment a bit obscure.

Well, they didn't.

I walked down the other side of the hill, through Tadpole Copse, and stood there watching the local police while they were conducting a search which brought nothing to light except a towel. It was a curious thing to find in the bottom of a hollow tree. It hadn't been used very much, and looked to me as though it had not been long from the laundry, though it was crumpled and still damp. On the edge I found stitched one of those names that drapers sell to attach to laundry, and the name was 'Veddle'.

But the most important discovery of the morning was made by a detective officer of the Berkshire police, who took the dinghy down the river on the off-chance of finding some sort of clue. It's funny how amateurs expect to find clues strewn all over the face of the earth. But this fellow was lucky, for he found something that had a big bearing on the case. It was a sheet of paper floating on the water, and anybody who wasn't quite as enthusiastic as he was might have passed it by.

He took the dinghy up to it and fished it out. It was a large date sheet, evidently torn from a calendar, and the date on it was the 4th of August in the current year. He would have thrown it back again but he saw on the back some writing in pencil, and, having read it, he brought the paper to me.

The first thing that struck me when I saw it was that I had seen a calendar that size before, but for the minute I couldn't place it. The writing on the back was in copying pencil and the water had made it very messy, but it was as easy to read as print. On the top was the number '23', and evidently this was the number of a page, for the writing started in the middle of a sentence:

. . . have always kept my eyes open. And I kept my ears open too. I saw Field once in Tadpole Copse, but he saw me too and went back across the Flash. I went over two nights in succession and had a good look at the girl as she was leaving for her lodgings. I saw what I could do. If I married her my fortune would be made, and I did my best to make up to her. After all, she was only a secretary and she didn't know . . .

'She didn't know' were the last words on the paper. What didn't she know? To me it was fairly obvious. She didn't know that she was Field's heiress; but Veddle did.

What interested me about the sheet was that it was evidently part of a long story. Where were the other sheets? I sent the officer back in the dinghy to search the river as far as the Thames, and then I made my way up to the cottage where Veddle had lived.

Some busybody had been up to the house and wakened Mr Voss. I saw his mechanical chair whizzing down the path towards me, and from the fact that he still wore his pyjamas and a dressing-gown I guessed he'd only just got out of bed.

'Is it true about Veddle? When did it happen? Why didn't somebody wake me up?'

I couldn't answer all the questions he put to me, but I told him that I was going to search the cottage and asked him if he would lend me the key. He blew a whistle, and one of his gardeners came running forward and was sent back to the house to get the key, while we went on to the hut. I call it a hut although it was brick-made and was thatched. We had to wait a little time until the gardener returned, and I told Mr Voss as much as I thought he ought to know. He was very thoughtful.

'He must have been in the grounds last night. Do you think it was he who fired at us?'

I couldn't answer that question till the door of the cottage was opened. When I walked in, however, there was the answer on the table – a Browning pistol, the barrel still foul from the shot that had been fired, and seven unused cartridges in the magazine.

The room was just as I had left it, except (I remembered now) that the big calendar I had seen on one of the walls was lying on the table. The sheets had been torn off as far as September 7th. The back of the sheets were blank and could be used for writing paper. I had no doubt that Veddle had used it for that purpose. The pen and ink were still on the table. How had he obtained admission? I went to the door – Mr Voss could not come in because of the narrowness of the passage – and asked him if there was another key. He shook his head.

'He could easily have had one made, but I know of no other,' he said.

I was returning to the room when he called me back.

'It has just occurred to me that he may have been there all the time.'

'While I was searching before, you mean?'

He nodded.

'Yes. There's a large cellar underneath the house. I think it was used for storing wine in my predecessor's days. It's queer I never thought of that before. You'll find a trapdoor in the bedroom.'

I made a search of the bedroom, turned up the carpet, and sure enough there was the trap! A wooden ladder led to the bottom, and it only needed a casual examination to show that the cellar had been lived in and slept in, for there was a camp bed, half a dozen blankets and a small electric handlamp, the sort you can buy for five shillings at any store.

So that was where Veddle had hidden. The place was well ventilated, and he could have stayed there, without anybody being the wiser, for a week. I found a tin of biscuits, half a dozen bottles of mineral water, and the half of a Dutch cheese in a small cupboard behind the bed.

There was no other clue. I came up the steps, and closing the trap, whistled for an officer to stay on duty in the cottage until he was relieved. Mr Voss and I went back to the house together. I had to telephone to the chief constable and arrange for a couple more of my men to come down.

Mr Voss had to take his chair by another route. He ran up a long incline to the terrace, but he was waiting for me by the time I got up the steps. And then he made a suggestion which staggered me. When I say it staggered me, I am probably giving you a wrong impression. Nothing staggers me, but it was certainly unexpected.

'Is it possible to keep the story of the Veddle murder out of the newspapers?' he asked.

'Why on earth, Mr Voss?'

He looked at me very thoughtfully.

'You'll probably think that I'm not quite right in my head, but I have a theory that if this news is suppressed today, the murderer will be in your hands tomorrow morning.'

He would give me no reason. I hate people who are mysterious, because in nine cases out of ten they've nothing to be mysterious about. And then I told him about the piece of paper that was found on the river. I have been told by the chief constable that I am a talkative old man. Maybe I am; but I have found that the worst way to get through a case like this is keeping your mouth shut, and I thought this was the moment to talk.

He took the paper which I had in my pocket and examined it. 'Yes, that looks like Veddle's writing,' he said at last; 'obviously part of a long confession. I wonder what happened to the rest of it?'

That was the one thing I intended finding out.

9

I took the paper into his study and examined it carefully, and then, with Mr Voss's permission, I sent for his steward, or butler, or whatever he was called. I had seen a telephone in the cottage, and I had meant to ask before whether that phone was fixed up to the house exchange. When the steward told me it was not, a lot of light was thrown on the mystery of Veddle's death.

I got through to the local telephone supervisor and asked a few questions. Naturally he couldn't answer, because he'd only just come on duty; but an hour later, when I was having breakfast, I was informed the supervisor had got all the data I wanted. A call had come through at about ten o'clock on the previous night from the cottage phone, obviously from Veddle, who had asked for a London number and talked for six minutes, but the operator had no idea to whom he was speaking. There was a record of the call, and I got straight through to the number and found it was a small hotel near Paddington Station. Nobody named Wills was staying there, but the night porter had left a record that a 'Mr Staines' had been rung up at something after ten, and that it was a toll call. 'Mr Staines' himself was not in the hotel at the moment I phoned. I took no risks, but got through to the Yard immediately and sent a couple of officers to pick up 'Mr Staines' and see how much like Mr Wills he looked. When I came back I found Mr Voss had hatched out a brand-new theory, and it was so very much like my own that I wondered if I'd been talking aloud to myself.

'I'm sure this man Wills is in it,' he said. 'I shouldn't be surprised if he was the fellow who stole Garry Thurston's boat – my butler was telling me it was found moored on the Flash.'

'In that case,' said I, 'Mr Wills has got the last dying speech and confession of his brother. But why he went away without Veddle is a mystery to me.'

Voss returned to the subject of publicity, and he was very earnest.

'You have to realise, Sooper,' he said, 'that I have a scientific mind. I may not be a good detective, but I have the faculty of deduction. Since I lost the use of my legs I've spent my time working out problems more intricate than this, and I am more satisfied than ever that if you keep the shooting of Veddle out of the newspapers you'll have your man tomorrow morning.'

'Are you suggesting that Wills killed him?' I asked.

He shook his head.

'Of course not! Wills is obviously a confederate. He came up the river, probably by boat, last night, to get his brother away. You've been making enquiries at the exchange, haven't you? Without having stirred from this room or being told by any person who overheard your conversation, I can tell you you have been asking what were the messages that passed between the cottage and some unknown destination last night.'

I grinned at this.

'Oh, no, I'm not guessing, I'm telling you,' said Mr Voss, his face getting pinker and pinker, his white hair almost standing up on his head in his excitement. 'And I'll bet you found that it was his brother he called – or, if you haven't, I can tell you it was! He asked his brother to come down and get him away. His brother arrived by boat.'

'Why not by road?' said I.

'The roads are under observation, aren't they? What chance has a car of getting within a mile of this place? No, he came by river, probably by row-boat – he must have had a row-boat to have got out into the stream and stolen Garry Thurston's odd little launch. He brought that launch down to where you found it, and met his brother, who probably went back to the cottage for his suitcase or something of the sort. Did you find any suitcase, by the way? I see you did. He may have handed over the story of the crime to Wills, who rowed downstream ahead of the motorboat and got away, quite confident that his brother would escape.'

'I don't see the object of holding this story from the newspapers,' I said.

'Don't you?' Max Voss's voice was very quiet. 'I do! Two people have been killed, both by the same hand.' He tapped on the tablecloth, emphasising every point. 'The one person who knows the murderer is Wills. Publish the news that Veddle has been found killed and Wills will come into the open – and will go the same way as Field and his brother!'

That was a brand-new angle to me. It never occurred to me that Wills was hiding from anybody but Superintendent Minter. Personally, I don't like my theories upset by other people. Nothing annoys me more than to work out a case so that every little bit of the puzzle fits, and then for somebody to show me I've got one piece upside down. But Mr Voss was a man for whom I had a great respect, and the more I saw him the more I respected him. I don't believe in amateur detectives, the kind you read about in books, but if I had to work with one of those well-known sleuths I'd like him to be as near to Mr Voss as possible, because undoubtedly he had brains.

I thought Marjorie Venn was late when she turned up at Lone House that morning, but the truth was I had been up so early that ten o'clock seemed the middle of the day. I had taken a copy of the writing on the paper, and I showed it to her. She was puzzled, though she remembered several occasions when Veddle had tried to get acquainted with her. She had once paid a visit to a cinema house in Reading (it was on a Saturday afternoon and she had gone into Reading by the bus) and found Veddle sitting by her side.

I didn't tell her for some time about the man being dead. In fact, she got it from one of the servants in the house and came to me very distressed. I could see the business was getting on to her nerves, and I was wondering whether I couldn't get her away from the place to London. Mr Field's lawyer was coming that day, and as she inherited Field's money she could afford to stay at the best hotel in town, and I knew that the lawyer would advance the cash. When I made the suggestion, however, she wouldn't hear of it.

It was a casual reference I made to Garry Thurston which explained why she didn't want to leave the neighbourhood. I saw a flush come to her face, and I guessed that she and Garry were better friends than either of them had admitted.

I think she may have surmised my suspicion, for she very quickly got away from the subject of that young man.

'I'm not at all nervous, and I'd rather stay in the country till this ghastly murder is settled,' she said. 'And I wouldn't dream of leaving until I have all Mr Field's affairs in order.'

That afternoon I had a blow. Our chief constable is as kind a man as you'd meet in a day's march, but he is not what I would call a very sensitive man. Because, if he had been, he wouldn't have sent Superintendent Gurly to exercise, as he called it, a general supervision. Gurly is my senior. I've nothing to say against him; I dare say he's a good father and a moderately good husband. He's fat and I don't like fat men, but I've known fat men I could get on with. I never could get on with Gurly, ever since we were constables together. He was the sort of man who knew everything, except how little he knew; and naturally, the first thing he did when he came on the spot was to take charge of everything, give orders to my men and generally make himself conspicuously useless.

I have been on many cases with Superintendent Gurly, but never found a way of getting over him. If you threw up the case and went back to the Yard, it meant you had to go back to undo all his well-meaning work a few days later. If you complained to the chief constable, the chief would say: 'Well, you know what he is – just humour him.' He fussed about the house till late in the afternoon, and then he came into the study and said, 'I think I'll take a dinghy and row down the river, Minter.'

'Can you swim?' I asked, but even when he said no, I knew it was no good hoping, because fat men float.

I arranged to sleep at Lone House that night, and by the time dinner was over Gurly was back, as full of ideas as a bad egg is full of bouquet. Marjorie Venn had gone back to her lodgings, so that I could use all the bad language I wanted to use without hurting anybody's feelings. Anyway, you couldn't hurt Gurly with a hatchet. If ever I wanted to murder the man, it was when he said: 'I've got all the threads in my hand now, Minter – in fact, I think I could execute a warrant in the morning.'

'Fine,' I said. 'You naturally would know everything in half an hour. Who killed John Field?'

He looked at me and waggled his head, and I know that when Gurly waggles his head he's going to be so silly that you have to laugh or be sick.

'A girl,' he said.

I just gaped at him.

'Who? Miss Venn?'

He nodded.

'Is anything more obvious?' he asked. 'I wonder it hasn't occurred to you before, Minter.'

He leaned over the table, and he's so fat that the table creaked. I was creaking a bit myself.

'She was in the house when the murder was committed – you don't deny that. She was locked in the room, I grant you, but what was to prevent her from locking the door and throwing the key out of the window?'

'The only thing that was likely to prevent her was that the key was in the dead man's pocket,' I said, but that didn't choke him off.

'There may have been two keys, or three,' he said. 'Who benefited by his death? She did! It's pretty well established that she disliked him, Minter. She was having an affair with somebody in the neighbourhood – I haven't found out who it was – '

'You should have taken another five minutes,' I said; but, bless your soul, that kind of kick never reached him.

'He was killed by the Sword of Tuna – ' he began again, when I stopped him.

'The man who killed John Field left his naked footprint outside the door. It wasn't a woman, it was a man. Get that silly idea out of your head, Gurly.'

'There are one or two questions I'm going to ask her,' he said, and took out of his pocket a big notebook, which he must have spent hours filling up. 'Will you bring her in?'

'She's gone,' I said very coldly.

'Then she's got to be brought back.'

10

Now when Gurly is in that kind of mood there's no coping with him. He was perfectly within his rights in wanting to question Marjorie Venn, and I had no authority to stop him. For one thing, it would have looked pretty bad in his report if I had put any obstacle in his way; so, after trying to persuade him to leave the matter over till the morning, I agreed to go down with him to the cottage where she lived and see her.

'She may be gone in the morning,' said Gurly.

It was a waste of time answering.

A police car took us to the little village where Marjorie Venn lived with a widow woman who kept a small shop. Marjorie had the two best rooms in the house, and had furnished them herself, she told me.

The shop was shut, but we knocked up the landlady and told her what we had come about. She looked at us in surprise.

'Miss Venn has gone to London – she went half an hour ago, and took all her things with her – she's not coming back.'

I couldn't believe the news that Marjorie Venn had gone without saying a word to me, especially after all she had told me that afternoon. I had done my best to persuade her to go to London, but she had said she was staying until John Field's affairs were cleared up; and here, without the slightest warning, she had disappeared.

'What did I tell you?' said Gurly. 'I knew it, my boy. You oughtn't to have let her out of your sight – '

I didn't take any notice of him.

'How did she leave? When did she make up her mind?' I asked the widow.

According to her story, a note had been delivered to her and she had gone out immediately, not even putting on her hat. She was gone a quarter of an hour, and when she came back she seemed agitated and went straight up to her room and began packing. The landlady knew this because she had gone up with a glass of milk which the girl usually took before she went to bed. She found her putting her things into a suitcase, and Marjorie told her she had been called to London on very urgent business, and that a car was coming for her. It arrived a few minutes later.

Exactly what kind of car it was the landlady could not say, because it had driven through the village and had pulled up by the side of the road, and all that she saw was its tail light. Marjorie had carried her own suitcase to the car, and paid the woman her lodging money, and that was all the landlady knew.

I went to the village inn, but could find nobody who had seen the car. Even the village policeman could give me no information. Although the place was not on the highway to anywhere, cars frequently passed through the street. The news knocked me out, but old Gurly was chortling with joy.

'What did I tell you?' he shouted. ' She's bolted! She knew I was here, of course – '

'That's enough to make any woman bolt,' I snarled at him, 'but not a girl like Miss Venn.'

We took the car on to the first police control post, but they could tell us nothing. Any number of cars had passed, none of them so suspicious looking that the sergeant in charge felt called upon to pull it up.

'The car might have taken a circuitous route,' suggested Gurly, and for once in a way his was an intelligent suggestion.

There were half a dozen byways, but unless the car was moving in a circle it must pass one of the 'barrages'.

Driving back to the house, Gurly let himself go – he was more Gurlyish than ever I remembered him.

'It's the obvious things that always escape the ordinary police officer's attention,' he said. 'The moment I came into the house, my suspicions were on that girl. I worked it out a dozen ways, and I came to the conclusion that the only person who could have killed Field – '

'And shot Veddle?' I suggested.

'Why not?' said Gurly.

He was the sort of man who, when he gets into an argument and finds himself cornered, raises his voice to a shout. I kept him shouting all the way back to Lone House.

So far as I knew, the girl had no friends in London and the only thing to do was what Gurly did – circulate a description to the hotels and ask for notification of her arrival. Gurly would have sent out an 'arrest and detain' order, but I stopped that. After all, he's a member of the police force, and I didn't want Scotland Yard to look foolish.

From all our searchings and examinations that day, one or two important facts had come to light. The first of these was that Veddle was the man who had shot at me and at Max Voss. He had used an automatic; the back fire from the cartridge had burnt and blackened his hand. He had made some attempt to get the stain off, but it was very visible; and to prove my theory I found, on a re-search of the cottage, a spare box of ammunition.

We went over together, Gurly and I, and at Mr Voss's invitation went up to the house to supper. Before we went in I told the superintendent of Mr Voss's request, and naturally he took the opposite view from me.

'I quite agree – there's too much publicity about police affairs, Minter. The reporters would only have come down and got a sensational story, and taken away all the credit that's coming to me.'

Now, the curious thing about the Lone House murder was that we'd only had two local reporters on the job. As a rule, in cases like these the whole countryside is overrun with newspaper fellows; but you've got to remember that it wasn't called 'The Lone House Mystery' in the first two or three days. Only four people outside police circles knew how the murder had been committed – even the servants knew no more than that Mr Field had been found dead, for they were all out at the time of the murder, and we tied them all up to secrecy by promising them that they wouldn't lose their jobs (Miss Venn did that for me) if they kept quiet.

So I didn't think the story had reached the press, though I found later that one of the local reporters had phoned a column to an evening newspaper.

There was another reason why I thought the press would miss the Veddle killing. Big police cases usually go in threes, and just then the Tinnings case was holding down a lot of space in the newspapers – it was a poison murder, and a fashionable actress was in it, and, as I happened to know, most of the star men of the London press were quartered in a little town to the north of London, where the suspect lived. But, as I say, I was wrong.

One of the first questions Mr Voss asked me when I went in was whether there was anything about Veddle's murder in the evening newspapers. He had had them all sent down from London, and they contained no reference to the crime, but he was worried as to whether there was something in the later editions. I wasn't in a position to tell him, because I never read newspapers except when they contain the account of a trial where I have been specially commended by the judge.

It was the next day that I found that the murder had been splashed on the front page of an evening newspaper.

Naturally, Gurly and Mr Voss became best friends. Gurly has got a weakness for monied people. I had asked him not to discuss the case with Voss, because, as I told him, I didn't want him worried; but we hadn't been seated at the table for five minutes when Gurly started throwing off his theories and deductions.

'You know the girl, Mr Voss?'

Voss looked at him quickly.

'Miss Venn? Yes – why?'

Gurly smiled and spread out his fat hands. 'Who else could it be?'

I thought that Voss was going to have a fit. 'You don't mean to tell me that you suspect Marjorie Venn – '

I think he was going to say something rude, but he checked himself.

'Yes, I do,' said Gurly; 'and the fact that she's disappeared tonight – '

Voss pushed himself back from the table, staring at my thick-headed colleague.

'Disappeared? What do you mean – ?'

I thought it was time to step in.

'She's gone away, Mr Voss – left at a few minutes' notice.'

'When was this?'

He reached out his hands, gripped the edge of the table and pulled the wheelchair back to where it had been, and he seemed to have got the better of his annoyance.

Gurly told him, because Gurly is the sort of man who must speak or perish.

'Just tell me what happened to this young lady,' Voss interrupted him. 'I am very much interested in her; in fact, I had thought of asking you to introduce me. She may want work – '

'Work!' said Gurly. 'My dear fellow, that's the whole point – she's his heiress.'

'Field's?'

I never saw such a blank look of unbelief in a man's face.

'He left her all his money,' Gurly went on, rushing down the road marked 'Angels only'. 'That's my point! She had everything to gain by his death . . . '

He ambled on, but Voss wasn't listening to him. He was staring at me.

'You never told me this, Mr Minter,' he said. 'It is amazing news. Why did he leave her the money? Was there anything – wrong?'

Each question came like the snap of a whip, and as I didn't want Gurly to explain, I told him just as much as I thought an outsider ought to know. I saw the relief in his face before I had finished.

'Conscience, eh? The girl's father was his partner, you say? This rather complicates matters.'

'Upsets your pet solution?' I asked him, and he nodded.

Then without warning he switched on to another subject.

'Have you seen Garry Thurston? He hasn't been up today. I think he ought to know about Miss Venn's disappearance – have you told him?'

He snapped his fingers at the butler, who came back with a telephone; it had a long cord attached, and at the end a plug which he pushed into a socket in the wall.

I didn't say anything; I was anxious to know just what Mr Garry Thurston would say, and would have given anything to listen in and discover his reaction – that's the word, isn't it?

Voss jiggled the hook impatiently and presently he got through. He asked one or two questions, and I could tell he was talking to the servant.

'Garry's gone to bed.' He covered the receiver with his hand. 'Do you think I ought to get him up?'

Before I could reply he was speaking again.

'Yes. Tell him I want him. It's very urgent.'

He waited some time, and then: 'Hallo! Is that you, Garry? It's Voss speaking.'

He was silent for a while, evidently listening to what Thurston was saying at the other end.

'Yes,' he said at last, and then again: 'Yes.'

Once he started to interrupt Thurston, but he did not ask the question which I knew was on his lips. I saw his face go paler, and his bushy eyebrows meet, but he said nothing which would tell me what the conversation was all about. Then, to my surprise, he said, 'All right,' and hung up the receiver. He handed the instrument to the butler and met my eye.

'Well,' said I, 'you didn't seem to let him know very much about Miss Venn?'

He had no answer at once, but sat looking at me for quite a long time.

'No, I didn't ask him any questions: he told me all I wanted to know,' he said. 'Miss Venn went to London on Garry Thurston's advice. She went because he thought there was danger to her and – '

Bang!

The glass in the big oriel window smashed and splintered. Something hit the decanter in front of him and cut the neck off as though it had been sliced by a knife. For the second time in twenty-four hours somebody had shot at him.

11

How quickly can a man think? Not a second had passed between the shot being fired and the moment I jumped to my feet, but I had travelled nearly twelve thousand miles, I had lived over the life of Field and had gone over every aspect of his killing – and I knew the murderer. I knew him as I stood by that table, half twisted round towards the smashed window. I knew just why that smoke signal had been used in Tadpole Copse, and why I had found the print of the man's foot on the soft earth outside Field's study.

A second? It could not have been a tenth of a second. I'll do Gurly justice: he was out of that room before I could say 'knife', and I was not far behind him. We flew into the hall, over the terrace – there was nobody in sight. The grounds were as black as pitch; we could see nothing. Our only hope was that the couple of men we had left on duty patrolling the river bank near the copse would have heard the shot and might have seen the man who did the shooting, but although they hurried up to the house, they had met nobody.

It was nearly one o'clock before I left Voss. I intended putting my men inside the house, but Gurly wouldn't hear of it.

'I'll stay with Mr Voss,' he said, 'and if I am not as good as any two flat-footed policemen, then it's about time I resigned.'

I had my own views on that subject, but did not give them. What I did do was to take him aside and tell him that for the next twelve hours he must not let Voss out of his sight.

'You had better carry a gun,' I said.

He roared with laughter.

'If I see the gentleman who did the shooting, he will be sorry even if he carries two guns.'

Which was all very fine and large, but didn't impress me.

He went into Voss's bedroom and closed the curtains. He had a camp bed brought, and as soon as Max Voss was inside the room he had the camp bed put right across the door.

A lot of people think I am brave, but I'm not. I was in a bit of a funk when I walked down to the Flash, even though I had two police officers with me, for I knew that somewhere lurking in the darkness was the man who had tried to kill Voss.

I was absolutely dead for want of sleep, but before I lay down

I had several little jobs to do, and one of them was to go through the money I had found in Veddle's pocket, count it and seal it up ready to be sent to the Yard in the morning.

Counting that money took me longer than I had expected – it was two o'clock – because that money spoke and confirmed all that had come to me when the shot was fired.

At half-past two I lay down on the bed, but I could not sleep. Being over tired is almost as bad as not being tired at all. I lay there thinking about Veddle and John Field and the girl, Marjorie Venn, and she came into my thoughts more frequently than either of the other two.

Once I thought of getting up and making myself some tea, or pouring out something stronger, but I turned over again on to my other side and tried to drop off.

As a matter of precaution I had planted my two men halfway between the house and Tadpole Copse. I don't know whether I am sorry or glad I did that.

I couldn't sleep. I was absolutely like a wet rag, and getting up, I walked to the window. The dawn was beginning to break. There was just enough light to make shadows. I thought it was a tree in the middle of the lawn – a little tree I had overlooked – until I saw it move towards the water's edge.

'Who is that?' I shouted. 'Stop, or I'll fire.'

I didn't have a gun, but I thought the threat would be enough. Then I saw that it was a woman who was running towards the river, and my heart jumped, for I recognised the figure in the dawn light – it was Marjorie Venn!

I rushed out of the room, switching on the light as I went, and ran down the stairs. The front door leading to the lawn was wide open, so was the door of the study. When I got to the lawn I could see nothing. On the river's edge there was no sign of a boat.

I blew my whistle for the two men. Before they could come down I went back to the house and into the study. The safe door was wide open. The safe had contained a number of documents, and I could not see for the moment if any had been taken. Then, turning my head, I saw on the hearth a little bundle of ashes that was still smoking.

You know how paper burns: it leaves the letters all shiny and visible against the black background. I didn't need my glasses to know that the heap of ashes that was smouldering was the last will and testament of John Field, the will that had left all his money to Marjorie Venn.

I remembered it being in the safe. I remembered too that Marjorie had a key to the safe and a key to the front door.

By the time I finished my examination I heard my name called from the other side of the Flash. The two men had come down to the water's edge, and I ordered them to cross, as the motor-boat was on their side of the lake. They had seen nobody, heard nothing but my shout.

It was getting lighter and things were becoming visible. I was so certain that it was impossible to pick up the traces of Marjorie Venn that, having given the men some instructions, I went back to the study, lay down on the sofa and was asleep in a few minutes.

I suppose an old man does not require the amount of sleep that a youngster needs. The study clock was striking seven when I woke. I had taken a big glass cover which was over a piece of native carved ivory and had put it over the ashes in the grate before I lay down. The nature of the document was as plain as the daylight that showed it. There was the will, and I wondered if a burnt will could be proved. But would Marjorie Venn want to prove it? I wondered for a few minutes whether it was she or the negress who had burned away a fortune. No – I couldn't have mistaken Marjorie.

While the servants were getting breakfast I sat down at the table, took out some paper and wrote out the case as I saw it. That is a weakness of mine. I like to put A to B and B to C. In half an hour I had the whole of the case laid out as I understood it. Exactly what was the beginning of the trouble, and – to me – what was the end. It was not a very long document; it took me nine minutes to read to the chief constable (I got him out of his bed) and to receive my instructions from him.

Our chief constable is a very sensible man who trusts his subordinates, and apparently he did not send Gurly down, but Gurly had sent himself down on the promise that he would not interfere with me. Maybe the chief constable was lying when he said that, but it sounded true.

I finished the telephone talk, went up and had a bath and shaved. When I came down the two night watchers were on the lawn, waiting to be dismissed. If they expected me to put them to bed they were entitled to a grievance. I crossed the Flash with them and we went up to Mr Voss's house together.

He was an early riser, and his staff were usually up and about when most servants were thinking of turning over for their last little snooze. Even the butler was on his job.

'Mr Gurly is still asleep,' he said.

'What time does Mr Voss wake up as a rule?' I asked.

He told me that he usually took in the early-morning tea about eight o'clock when Mr Voss had a late night, and seven when he had an early one.

'I was bringing it up now,' he said.

Gurly was snoring like a pig. I didn't kick him, because he was my superior. I merely made a few faces at him – that didn't harm anybody.

He took a long time to wake up.

'Hello, Minter!' he growled. He was never at his brightest in the morning. 'What's doing?'

I told him I had come to see Voss, and, getting up, he cleared away his bed.

'I haven't heard from him all night long,' he said as I knocked at the door.

266

'He doesn't seem to hear us now,' I said, and knocked again. There was no reply.

I hammered on the panel, but still there was no answer. Peeping down through the keyhole, I saw that the key was still in the lock, and sent the butler to find a crowbar. I knew there was one hanging in a glass case with a fire hatchet farther along the corridor.

With the crowbar I forced the door open and walked in. The room was empty; the lights still burnt, and the closed curtains kept out whatever daylight there was. But the room was empty, and the bed had not been slept in. Max Voss had vanished as completely and as mysteriously as Marjorie Venn!

12

Pulling aside the curtains, I saw that the shutter was unfastened and that one of the windows was ajar. There was no ladder against the portico; I knew that, because I should have seen it when we came to the house.

Gurly was absolutely shaking with excitement.

'How did they get him away? He's a pretty heavy man to carry, and I heard no sound. Have a look at the balustrade – there'll probably be blood on it . . . '

He was firing off directions to the butler when I left him.

I had Voss's car brought round and went straight to Garry Thurston's house. I expected he would be up, and I wasn't disappointed. He was strolling on the lawn before the house, and he must have been out and about for some little time, for he was wearing tennis flannels, and told me as calmly as you please that he was cooling off after a set.

'Does Mrs Field play tennis?' I asked sharply, and he smiled.

'Mrs Field went to London last night,' he said very deliberately, 'and her son. She told me all I wanted to know. It wasn't very pleasant hearing for me, but then, I knew much worse before she came.'

I sort of scowled at him.

'That sounds like chapter one of a thrilling detective story,' I said.

'The last chapter,' he answered. 'I hope I haven't given you a lot of trouble, Mr Minter – I certainly didn't intend to. The fact is, I've had a perfectly dreadful few days, and I have been so engrossed in my own business that I haven't troubled very much about other people's feelings. How is Mr Voss?' I didn't answer him. 'Is there anything you want to see me about?'

'Yes, there is,' I said. 'Young man, I warn you that I'm out for blood. I've no respect for you nor your manor house nor your money nor – '

'Anything that is thy neighbour's,' he smiled. 'I realise that, superintendent. I can help you up to a point, and tell you the truth up to a point. Beyond that I am afraid I cannot promise either to be helpful or veracious.'

He pulled up two wicker chairs, and putting them facing each other, sat down in one of them. I didn't feel like sitting; besides, a man standing up has got an advantage when he's cross-examining a man who's sitting down. One of the best lawyers at the Bar told me that.

'Last night,' I said, 'Miss Marjorie Venn left her lodgings very hurriedly – '

'In a motor car,' said Garry Thurston coolly. 'Somebody sent a note for her, and that somebody was me. I wanted to see her very, very particularly, and I had something to tell her which induced her to go away with me.'

His frankness took my breath away.

'It was you who brought the car for her?'

He nodded.

'And took her to London?'

'No.'

'Where did you take her?' I asked.

He looked towards the house.

'She's there – in fact, she has been there since last night.'

'And she hasn't left the house all night?' I said sarcastically.

'As to that, I am not prepared to say,' said Garry Thurston. 'If she strolled with me in the night you may be sure she had a very good reason. She is not the sort of young lady who does things without a very good cause.'

His cheek was breathtaking.

'She's in the house – can I see her?'

He nodded. 'She's changing. We've been playing tennis all the morning.'

'Have you been near Voss's house?' I asked.

He shook his head. 'No.'

'Do you know where Voss is at this moment, and who took him away?'

He looked at me steadily.

'I've told you all that I'm going to tell you,' he said. 'Fortunately, you cannot put me in a torture chamber; more fortunately still, I am a very rich and influential young man. Not,' he added, 'that that makes a great deal of difference to you, Sooper. When I say that I am paying you a compliment. But your immediate superiors are not going to make the mistake of prosecuting me unless they have a very excellent basis for their prosecution. I did not murder John Field or Veddle; I did not fire at you – I have an idea Veddle did that. In fact, I have done nothing for which the law can touch me.'

I waited till he had finished, and then: 'Are you quite sure about that, Mr Thurston?' I asked quietly. 'Are you absolutely certain that in the past eight hours you have done nothing for which I can put you in the dock?'

He smiled again. 'Come along and have breakfast,' he said, but I wasn't going to allow him to blarney me.

I wanted to see the young lady, and he made no objection. She came down into the big library a few minutes after I had seated myself.

Marjorie Venn was very pale, but I never saw a girl who was more composed or surer of herself. There was a look in her face that I had never seen before, a sort of – what's the word? serenity, that's it – that made her like somebody new.

She gave me a little smile as she came in, and held out her hand. As I wasn't Gurly I took it.

'Now, young woman,' I said, 'will you explain why you came to my house in the middle of the night?'

'It was to be my house,' she said, her lips twitching. 'Yes, I'm not denying it, superintendent: I did come into the study, I did open the safe, and I did burn Mr Field's will.'

'Why on earth?' I asked her.

'Because I didn't want the money. It belongs to his wife. It was her devotion that helped Field to find the mine. Every penny of it belongs to her and her child. It would have been easy to have accepted the will and to have handed the money and property to her,' she went on, 'but I didn't want my name associated with Mr Field in any way.'

I didn't take my eyes off her.

'And so you prefer to be a poor woman?'

'Miss Venn will not be a poor woman,' Garry broke in. 'There are two reasons why she will not be, and one of them is that she and I are to be married next week.'

I played my trump card. 'With your father's consent?' I asked her, and her colour changed.

'Yes,' she said in a low voice, 'with my father's consent.'

Garry Thurston was looking at me. I felt his eyes searching my face, and I got a little kick out of the knowledge that I'd given him a bit of a shock.

And then I dropped all the friendly stuff and began to ask her questions. Any other girl would have been rattled, but she fenced with me so cleverly that after half an hour I knew no more than I had at the beginning, and, what was worse, she hadn't given me a handle that would help me to force her to speak.

When I got back to Hainthorpe I found Gurly had collected half the Berkshire constabulary and had organised a grand search of the grounds.

'I'm looking for a well. There must be one in the park somewhere . . . A gardener told me that he'd heard there was such a thing.'

'What do you want with a well?' I asked. 'Have the taps gone dry?'

But he was the sort of man who must have a well and a dead body to round off any case in which he was engaged. I often think that Gurly got most of his ideas of police work out of these sensational stories that are so popular nowadays.

I didn't trouble to look for the well, but put through a call supplementing the one I had sent from Garry Thurston's place. But I knew just how small my chance was, and I wasn't disappointed when by noon the County Police reported blank. But I knew London was working, that the ports were being watched, and that every train that drew out of town or pulled into a seaport was being combed for my man.

It was early in the afternoon that I got the message from the Bixton Cottage Hospital. Bixton lies on the river; it would be one of the healthiest places in England if it wasn't for the weir, which provides eighty per cent of the casualties that go into the red-brick cottage which is called a hospital. That weir is a pretty dangerous spot even in daylight, and doubly dangerous to a man who's rowing for his life in the dark and tries to land in order to avoid observation from the lock.

When they took him out of the water he was so near dead that the policeman who had heard him shout and went in after him didn't think he was worth artificial respiration; but being an amateur, and having just passed through his first-aid course, he had a cut at it, and nobody was more surprised than he when he heard the drowned man breathing.

He didn't recover consciousness till round about lunchtime,

and the first name he mentioned was that of Superintendent Minter.

They phoned me and I drove at top speed to the hospital. I had to wait for an hour, because the doctor wouldn't have him wakened, and I was taking tea with the matron when the nurse came for me, and I walked into the little ward and straight up to the bedside.

'Hello, Wills!' I said. Veddle's brother lay on the bed, looking more dead than alive. I could see he was frightened, and I knew why.

'You were a bit excited last night, weren't you?' I asked him. 'That shot you fired at Voss wasn't any too good. You shouldn't have missed him.'

He looked away.

'I didn't shoot at anybody,' he said sullenly. 'You can't prove that I shot at anybody.'

And this was true. If I was going to get a story out of Wills I'd have to hold off on that shooting charge until he did a little confessional work, and I rather fancied he was too wide awake to tell me much.

He didn't seem inclined to say anything, and for a long time he just lay, avoiding my eyes and ignoring my questions. Then, suddenly: 'You've got nothing on me, Sooper, except the disciplinary charge – did they give you my brother's statement? It was in my pocket – I don't think it's been thrown away. I've been carrying it ever since he handed it to me the other night. He knew something was going to happen, and he said he was taking no chances – he had the whole story written in case somebody got him, or they framed up a charge against him. It's written on the back of a calendar and one sheet's missing. But there's nothing against me in it, Sooper. You can talk about shooting as much as you like, and you can be as suspicious as you like, but you can prove nothing. I helped my brother because he's the only pal I ever had. I took the job down at

Lone House not to protect Field but to find out something my brother wanted to know.'

It was perfectly true, what Wills said: there was no evidence against him. We never found the gun he used when he shot at Voss; but in those loosely written pages that I read carefully that night I discovered the reason for the shooting.

13

I'm not giving you this document word for word. It was long, and a lot of Veddle's statements were wholly inaccurate.

Field and his partner Venn (he afterwards called himself Voss) located a mine in Africa. Venn, who was married to a charming colonial girl, sent her to England, where her child might be born, and the two partners continued their search. The mine was located through the instrumentality of a native chief, whose daughter Field married.

He tried also to secure from the chief, his father-in-law, a supply of raw gold that was in the village, and, when this was denied him, attacked the village, himself leading a hostile tribe. At the time Venn was living in the chief's hut, a very sick man. He cared little what became of him. News had reached him that his wife had died in childbirth. He did not know until many years afterwards that the letter which came to him was written by Field, designed to drive a sick man to suicide.

Field went back to England, an immensely wealthy man, quite confident that his sometime partner had died in the forest. He did not take his black wife with him – she followed, with her child, and located him. She was missionary-trained, spoke good English. Even she did not know that Voss was alive.

He had wandered from one tribe to another, careless of his fate, and quite ignorant of the fact that his partner had found and was working the mine they had sought, or that the attack upon the village had been instigated by Field. He only discovered this when, as a comparatively wealthy trader, he returned to the old village and received from the dying chief a legacy which made him a very rich man – the major portion of that store of crude gold which Field had taken such risks to procure. For the risks were very real. He was working his mine under charter from the Congo government, a charter which would have been instantly revoked if his share in the rebellion had been traced.

Without any very hard feeling against the man who had treated him shabbily, Venn came back to England, and again an accident revealed the truth. The letter he had received in the forest, telling him of his child's death, had been written by Field. Venn's wife had died in poverty a year before he arrived in England, and the child, he learned to his horror, was in Field's employment.

A property which was adjacent to Lone House was on the market, and Voss obviously sat down cold-bloodedly to plan the murder of the man who had allowed his wife to starve, and who now, for all he knew, was victimising Marjorie Venn. He must prepare his alibi in advance, and he appeared in the county as a man who had lost the use of his legs, could not move except in a mechanically propelled chair. He had the house altered, lifts installed, all the paraphernalia of infirmity were gathered, and the legend of the cripple who could not walk became very well known throughout the county.

He must have been something of an artist in his way. I have met men like that before, but Voss, or Venn, could give points to all of them. He reconnoitred the ground, decided exactly the dramatic manner in which his crime should be committed, and waited patiently for the right assistant to turn up.

Veddle was the man: an ex-convict, utterly dishonest, a man who read his employer's letters, and who, to Venn's consternation, surprised his secret. From that moment Veddle was doomed – from his statement it looked as though he was under the impression that his fortune was made.

Voss seized the opportunity to reveal his whole plan to his subordinate. It promised untold riches to this blackmailer – for Veddle had made another discovery, namely, that Marjorie Venn was his employer's daughter and would one day be a very rich woman. He kept his secret to himself, not even hinting to Voss that he knew as much, and in his clownish way he tried to make good with the young lady.

He had a grievance himself against Field, who had beaten him up, and he became the more willing to help his employer towards his revenge.

You will remember that Mr Voss always wore a grey check jacket and a white hat? On the day of the murder Veddle was waiting in the copse dressed exactly like his master. As the electric chair went into the wood it stopped, and the two men changed places. Veddle had received careful instructions – that was in the first clue I found. He was to go up the hill, stop at a certain bush, turn at a certain stone, so that he faced Amberley Church. In this position he would be visible for miles around. He would also have a commanding view of Tadpole Copse.

The moment he received the signal, he was to come down the hill in third speed. Voss had chosen his man well. Wills, the watching detective, had been got rid of through his brother. The moment the chair moved on, with Veddle in the seat, Voss threw off his check coat and slipped into the water, swam across the Flash and made his way over the lawn to the study.

He may have carried a knife; it is unlikely that he went without arms; but the Sword of Tuna was easy to grasp. Field must have had his back to him when he struck.

You must remember that Voss wore nothing but a bathing suit. He was in the water and across the Flash in a few minutes; he was a powerful swimmer. Arriving back in Tadpole Copse, he found the smoke pistol that Veddle had ready in his overcoat pocket and fired his signal. The moment Veddle saw this, he brought his car down the hill and through the wood. Here Voss was waiting – I don't know whether to call him Voss or Venn. He had dried his head and face roughly with a towel, which he had pushed into a hollow tree, and with his check coat and dummy collar, and a rug over his knees, nobody would have dreamed that the man in the chair that came out of one end of the wood was not the man who went in at the other.

Almost immediately Veddle got into his long coat and hid his clothes and made for his cottage. The moment a hue and cry was raised it was necessary to get Veddle out of the way. Full arrangements had been made, but Veddle was not taking any risks. He refused to leave the same night, and hid himself in his cellar.

I don't know how he discovered that his employer was double-crossing him. I think it may have been the fact that I was at the house.

The moment the hue and cry was raised Veddle lost his nerve and bolted. I found his money – the money that Voss had supplied him with and which was to get him out of England. I've reason to believe that he was actually hiding at Hainthorpe, in the house itself. It was afterwards that he went back to the cottage and hid himself in the cellar.

Voss was in a difficulty: he had to find a new supply of money. I knew exactly what had happened when I counted the money we had found on the dead body of Veddle, for one of the notes was splattered with ink; it was the same note I had seen in the possession of Max Voss.

The mystery of the shooting in the night was never thoroughly cleared up. I am satisfied in my own mind that Veddle was the would-be assassin, and that, believing his employer was trying to double-cross him, he had shot at him through his bedroom window. I don't like to think that Max Voss fired at me in the copse, and worked out a fake attack upon himself, but even this is possible.

There was somebody who knew his secret. The one man in the world he did not wish to know – that was Garry Thurston. Garry had a telescope on his terrace, and on the afternoon that Veddle, disguised as his master, went to the top of Jollyboy Hill, Mr Garry Thurston took a look at him through his telescope and immediately recognised the servant.

He was distracted because he was fond of Voss. He could not betray him. He was, I believe, bewildered, and then he heard that Field had a negro wife and wheedled the address where she was staying out of one of my men and went in search of her. It was she who told him the story of the two partners and in a second he guessed that Marjorie Venn was Voss's daughter. He wanted to get her out of the way. He wanted still more to save the life of the girl's father. Whether he assisted him to escape I cannot prove – escape he did and was never seen again in England.

That he killed Veddle in cold blood I am sure. Veddle had got on to his brother by telephone and arranged that they should meet in Tadpole Copse. He packed his suitcase, went down into the wood, handed over the statement to his brother, who was all along suspected. Wills rowed back to the Thames, never doubting that his brother would follow.

Naturally Voss didn't want the Veddle case to get into the papers: he knew that Wills would be on his track.

A queer case, an unsatisfactory case. I always look upon a murder case as unsatisfactory when nobody is hanged. At the same time I should not have liked Max Voss to have taken the nine o'clock walk: he was a decent fellow as murderers go.

MARY E. WILKINS FREEMAN

Mary Eleanor Wilkins Freeman was born in Randolph, Massachusetts in 1852. She passed the greater part of her life in Massachusetts and Vermont and for many years was the private secretary of Oliver Wendell Holmes. Freeman began writing stories and verse for children while still a teenager to help support her family and was quickly successful. Her best known work was written in the 1880s and 1890s while she lived in Randolph. She produced more than two dozen volumes of published short stories and novels. She is best known for two collections of stories, *A Humble Romance and Other Stories* (1887) and *A New England Nun and Other Stories* (1891), which deal mostly with New England life and are among the best of their kind. Freeman is also remembered for her novel *Pembroke* (1894), and she contributed a notable chapter to the collaborative novel *The Whole Family* (1908). In 1902 she married Dr Charles M. Freeman of Metuchen, New Jersey. In April 1926, Freeman became the first recipient of the William Dean Howells Medal for Distinction in Fiction from the American Academy of Arts and Letters. She died in 1930 and was interred in Hillside Cemetery in Scotch Plains, New Jersey.

The Shadows on the Wall

'Henry had words with Edward here in the study the night before Edward died,' said Caroline Glynn.

She was elderly, tall and harshly thin, with a hard colourlessness of face. She spoke not with acrimony, but with grave severity. Rebecca Ann Glynn, younger, stouter and rosy of face between her crinkling puffs of grey hair, gasped, by way of assent. She sat in a wide flounce of black silk in the corner of the sofa, and rolled terrified eyes from her sister Caroline to her sister Mrs Stephen Brigham, who had been Emma Glynn, the one beauty of the family. She was beautiful still, with a large, splendid, full-blown beauty; she filled a great rocking-chair with her superb bulk of femininity, and swayed gently back and forth, her black silks whispering and her black frills fluttering. Even the shock of death (for her brother Edward lay dead in the house) could not disturb her outward serenity of demeanour. She was grieved over the loss of her brother: he had been the youngest, and she had been fond of him, but never had Emma Brigham lost sight of her own importance amidst the waters of tribulation. She was always awake to the consciousness of her own stability in the midst of vicissitudes and the splendour of her permanent bearing.

But even her expression of masterly placidity changed before her sister Caroline's announcement and her sister Rebecca Ann's gasp of terror and distress in response.

'I think Henry might have controlled his temper, when poor Edward was so near his end,' said she with an asperity which disturbed slightly the roseate curves of her beautiful mouth.

'Of course he did not *know*,' murmured Rebecca Ann in a faint tone strangely out of keeping with her appearance.

One involuntarily looked again to be sure that such a feeble pipe came from that full-swelling chest.

'Of course he did not know it,' said Caroline quickly. She turned on her sister with a strange sharp look of suspicion. 'How could he have known it?' said she. Then she shrank as if from the other's possible answer. 'Of course you and I both know he could not,' said she conclusively, but her pale face was paler than it had been before.

Rebecca gasped again. The married sister was now sitting up straight in her chair; she had ceased rocking, and was eyeing them both intently with a sudden accentuation of family likeness in her face. Given one common intensity of emotion and similar lines showed the three sisters to be of one race.

'What do you mean?' said she impartially to them both. Then she, too, seemed to shrink before a possible answer. She even laughed an evasive sort of laugh. 'I guess you don't mean anything,' said she, but her face wore still the expression of shrinking horror.

'Nobody means anything,' said Caroline firmly. She rose and crossed the room towards the door with grim decisiveness.

'Where are you going?' asked Mrs Brigham.

'I have something to see to,' replied Caroline, and the others at once knew by her tone that she had some solemn and sad duty to perform in the chamber of death.

'Oh,' said Mrs Brigham.

After the door had closed behind Caroline, she turned to Rebecca.

'Did Henry have many words with him?' she asked.

'They were talking very loud,' replied Rebecca evasively, yet with an answering gleam of ready response to the other's curiosity in the quick lift of her soft blue eyes.

Mrs Brigham looked at her. She had not resumed rocking. She still sat up straight with a slight knitting of intensity on her fair forehead, between the pretty rippling curves of her auburn hair.

'Did you – hear anything?' she asked in a low voice with a glance towards the door.

'I was just across the hall in the south parlour, and that door was open and this door ajar,' replied Rebecca with a slight flush.

'Then you must have – '

'I couldn't help it.'

'Everything?'

'Most of it.'

'What was it?'

'The old story.'

'I suppose Henry was mad, as he always was, because Edward was living on here for nothing, when he had wasted all the money father left him.'

Rebecca nodded with a fearful glance at the door.

When Emma spoke again her voice was still more hushed. 'I know how he felt,' said she. 'He had always been so prudent himself, and worked hard at his profession, and there Edward had never done anything but spend, and it must have looked to him as if Edward was living at his expense, but he wasn't.'

'No, he wasn't.'

'It was the way father left the property – that all the children should have a home here – and he left money enough to buy the food and all if we had all come home.'

'Yes.'

'And Edward had a right here according to the terms of father's will, and Henry ought to have remembered it.'

'Yes, he ought.'

'Did he say hard things?'

'Pretty hard from what I heard.'

'What?'

'I heard him tell Edward that he had no business here at all, and he thought he had better go away.'

'What did Edward say?'

'That he would stay here as long as he lived and afterwards, too, if he had a mind to, and he would like to see Henry get him out; and then – '

'What?'

'Then he laughed.'

'What did Henry say.'

'I didn't hear him say anything, but – '

'But what?'

'I saw him when he came out of this room.'

'He looked mad?'

'You've seen him when he looked so.'

Emma nodded; the expression of horror on her face had deepened.

'Do you remember that time he killed the cat because she had scratched him?'

'Yes. Don't!'

Then Caroline re-entered the room. She went up to the stove in which a wood fire was burning – it was a cold, gloomy day of fall – and she warmed her hands, which were reddened from recent washing in cold water.

Mrs Brigham looked at her and hesitated. She glanced at the door, which was still ajar, as it did not easily shut, being still swollen with the damp weather of the summer. She rose and pushed it together with a sharp thud which jarred the house. Rebecca started painfully with a half exclamation. Caroline looked at her disapprovingly.

'It is time you controlled your nerves, Rebecca,' said she.

'I can't help it,' replied Rebecca with almost a wail. 'I am nervous. There's enough to make me so, the Lord knows.'

'What do you mean by that?' asked Caroline with her old air of sharp suspicion, and something between challenge and dread of its being met.

Rebecca shrank.

'Nothing,' said she.

'Then I wouldn't keep speaking in such a fashion.'

Emma, returning from the closed door, said imperiously that it ought to be fixed, it shut so hard.

'It will shrink enough after we have had the fire a few days,' replied Caroline. 'If anything is done to it it will be too small; there will be a crack at the sill.'

'I think Henry ought to be ashamed of himself for talking as he did to Edward,' said Mrs Brigham abruptly, but in an almost inaudible voice.

'Hush!' said Caroline, with a glance of actual fear at the closed door.

'Nobody can hear with the door shut.'

'He must have heard it shut, and – '

'Well, I can say what I want to before he comes down, and *I* am not afraid of him.'

'I don't know who is afraid of him! What reason is there for anybody to be afraid of Henry?' demanded Caroline.

Mrs Brigham trembled before her sister's look. Rebecca gasped again. 'There isn't any reason, of course. Why should there be?'

'I wouldn't speak so, then. Somebody might overhear you and think it was queer. Miranda Joy is in the south parlour sewing, you know.'

'I thought she went upstairs to stitch on the machine.'

'She did, but she has come down again.'

'Well, she can't hear.'

'I say again I think Henry ought to be ashamed of himself. I shouldn't think he'd ever get over it, having words with poor Edward the very night before he died. Edward was enough sight better disposition than Henry, with all his faults. I always thought a great deal of poor Edward, myself.'

Mrs Brigham passed a large fluff of handkerchief across her eyes; Rebecca sobbed outright.

'Rebecca,' said Caroline admonishingly, keeping her mouth stiff and swallowing determinately.

'I never heard him speak a cross word, but perhaps he spoke cross to Henry that last night. I don't know, but he did from what Rebecca overheard,' said Emma.

'Not so much cross as sort of soft, and sweet, and aggravating,' sniffled Rebecca.

'He never raised his voice,' said Caroline; 'but he had his way.'

'He had a right to in this case.'

'Yes, he did.'

'He had as much of a right here as Henry,' sobbed Rebecca,

'and now he's gone, and he will never be in this home that poor father left him and the rest of us again.'

'What do you really think ailed Edward?' asked Emma in hardly more than a whisper. She did not look at her sister.

Caroline sat down in a nearby armchair, and clutched the arms convulsively until her thin knuckles whitened.

'I told you,' said she.

Rebecca held her handkerchief over her mouth, and looked at them above it with terrified, streaming eyes.

'I know you said that he had terrible pains in his stomach, and had spasms, but what do you think made him have them?'

'Henry called it gastric trouble. You know Edward has always had dyspepsia.'

Mrs Brigham hesitated a moment. 'Was there any talk of an – examination?' said she.

Then Caroline turned on her fiercely.

'No,' said she in a terrible voice. 'No.'

The three sisters' souls seemed to meet on one common ground of terrified understanding through their eyes. The old-fashioned latch of the door was heard to rattle, and a push from without made the door shake ineffectually. 'It's Henry,' Rebecca sighed rather than whispered. Mrs Brigham settled herself after a noiseless rush across the floor into her rocking-chair again, and was swaying back and forth with her head comfortably leaning back, when the door at last yielded and Henry Glynn entered. He cast a covertly sharp, comprehensive glance at Mrs Brigham with her elaborate calm; at Rebecca quietly huddled in the corner of the sofa with her handkerchief to her face and only one small reddened ear, as attentive as a dog's, uncovered and revealing her alertness for his presence; at Caroline sitting with a strained composure in her armchair by the stove. She met his eyes quite firmly with a look of inscrutable fear, and defiance of the fear and of him.

Henry Glynn looked more like this sister than the others.

Both had the same hard delicacy of form and feature, both were tall and almost emaciated, both had a sparse growth of grey blond hair far back from high intellectual foreheads, both had an almost noble aquilinity of feature. They confronted each other with the pitiless immovability of two statues in whose marble lineaments emotions were fixed for all eternity.

Then Henry Glynn smiled and the smile transformed his face. He looked suddenly years younger, and an almost boyish recklessness and irresolution appeared in his face. He flung himself into a chair with a gesture which was bewildering from its incongruity with his general appearance. He leaned his head back, flung one leg over the other, and looked laughingly at Mrs Brigham.

'I declare, Emma, you grow younger every year,' he said.

She flushed a little, and her placid mouth widened at the corners. She was susceptible to praise.

'Our thoughts today ought to belong to the one of us who will never grow older,' said Caroline in a hard voice.

Henry looked at her, still smiling. 'Of course, we none of us forget that,' said he, in a deep, gentle voice, 'but we have to speak to the living, Caroline, and I have not seen Emma for a long time, and the living are as dear as the dead.'

'Not to me,' said Caroline.

She rose, and went abruptly out of the room again. Rebecca also rose and hurried after her, sobbing loudly.

Henry looked slowly after them.

'Caroline is completely unstrung,' said he. Mrs Brigham rocked. A confidence in him inspired by his manner was stealing over her. Out of that confidence she spoke quite easily and naturally.

'His death was very sudden,' said she.

Henry's eyelids quivered slightly but his gaze was unswerving.

'Yes,' said he; 'it was very sudden. He was sick only a few hours.'

'What did you call it?'

'Gastric.'

'You did not think of an examination?'

'There was no need. I am perfectly certain as to the cause of his death.'

Suddenly Mrs Brigham felt a creep as of some live horror over her very soul. Her flesh prickled with cold, before an inflection of his voice. She rose, tottering on weak knees.

'Where are you going?' asked Henry in a strange, breathless voice.

Mrs Brigham said something incoherent about some sewing which she had to do, some black for the funeral, and was out of the room. She went up to the front chamber which she occupied. Caroline was there. She went close to her and took her hands, and the two sisters looked at each other.

'Don't speak, don't, I won't have it!' said Caroline finally in an awful whisper.

'I won't,' replied Emma.

That afternoon the three sisters were in the study, the large front room on the ground floor across the hall from the south parlour, when the dusk deepened.

Mrs Brigham was hemming some black material. She sat close to the west window for the waning light. At last she laid her work on her lap.

'It's no use, I cannot see to sew another stitch until we have a light,' said she.

Caroline, who was writing some letters at the table, turned to Rebecca, in her usual place on the sofa.

'Rebecca, you had better get a lamp,' she said.

Rebecca started up; even in the dusk her face showed her agitation.

'It doesn't seem to me that we need a lamp quite yet,' she said in a piteous, pleading voice like a child's.

'Yes, we do,' returned Mrs Brigham peremptorily. 'We must

have a light. I must finish this tonight or I can't go to the funeral, and I can't see to sew another stitch.'

'Caroline can see to write letters, and she is farther from the window than you are,' said Rebecca.

'Are you trying to save kerosene or are you lazy, Rebecca Glynn?' cried Mrs Brigham. 'I can go and get the light myself, but I have this work all in my lap.'

Caroline's pen stopped scratching.

'Rebecca, we must have the light,' said she.

'Had we better have it in here?' asked Rebecca weakly.

'Of course! Why not?' cried Caroline sternly.

'I am sure I don't want to take my sewing into the other room, when it is all cleaned up for tomorrow,' said Mrs Brigham.

'Why, I never heard such a to-do about lighting a lamp.'

Rebecca rose and left the room. Presently she entered with a lamp – a large one with a white porcelain shade. She set it on a table, an old-fashioned card-table which was placed against the opposite wall from the window. That wall was clear of book-cases and books, which were only on three sides of the room. That opposite wall was taken up with three doors, the one small space being occupied by the table. Above the table on the old-fashioned paper, of a white satin gloss, traversed by an in-determinate green scroll, hung quite high a small gilt-and-black-framed ivory miniature taken in her girlhood of the mother of the family. When the lamp was set on the table beneath it, the tiny pretty face painted on the ivory seemed to gleam out with a look of intelligence.

'What have you put that lamp over there for?' asked Mrs Brigham, with more of impatience than her voice usually revealed. 'Why didn't you set it in the hall and have done with it. Neither Caroline nor I can see if it is on that table.'

'I thought perhaps you would move,' replied Rebecca hoarsely.

'If I do move, we can't both sit at that table. Caroline has her paper all spread around. Why don't you set the lamp on the study table in the middle of the room, then we can both see?'

Rebecca hesitated. Her face was very pale. She looked with an appeal that was fairly agonising at her sister Caroline.

'Why don't you put the lamp on this table, as she says?' asked Caroline, almost fiercely. 'Why do you act so, Rebecca?'

'I should think you *would* ask her that,' said Mrs Brigham. 'She doesn't act like herself at all.'

Rebecca took the lamp and set it on the table in the middle of the room without another word. Then she turned her back upon it quickly and seated herself on the sofa, and placed a hand over her eyes as if to shade them, and remained so.

'Does the light hurt your eyes, and is that the reason why you didn't want the lamp?' asked Mrs Brigham kindly.

'I always like to sit in the dark,' replied Rebecca chokingly. Then she snatched her handkerchief from her pocket and began to weep. Caroline continued to write, Mrs Brigham to sew.

Suddenly Mrs Brigham as she sewed glanced at the opposite wall. The glance became a steady stare. She looked intently, her work suspended in her hands. Then she looked away again and took a few more stitches, then she looked again, and again turned to her task. At last she laid her work in her lap and stared concentratedly. She looked from the wall around the room, taking note of the various objects; she looked at the wall long and intently. Then she turned to her sisters.

'What *is* that?' said she.

'What?' asked Caroline harshly; her pen scratched loudly across the paper.

Rebecca gave one of her convulsive gasps.

'That strange shadow on the wall,' replied Mrs Brigham.

Rebecca sat with her face hidden: Caroline dipped her pen in the inkstand.

'Why don't you turn around and look?' asked Mrs Brigham in a wondering and somewhat aggrieved way.

'I am in a hurry to finish this letter, if Mrs Wilson Ebbit is going to get word in time to come to the funeral,' replied Caroline shortly.

Mrs Brigham rose, her work slipping to the floor, and she began walking around the room, moving various articles of furniture, with her eyes on the shadow.

Then suddenly she shrieked out: 'Look at this awful shadow! What is it? Caroline, look, look! Rebecca, look! *What is it?*'

All Mrs Brigham's triumphant placidity was gone. Her handsome face was livid with horror. She stood stiffly pointing at the shadow.

'Look!' said she, pointing her finger at it. 'Look! What is it?'

Then Rebecca burst out in a wild wail after a shuddering glance at the wall: 'Oh, Caroline, there it is again! There it is again!'

'Caroline Glynn, you look!' said Mrs Brigham. 'Look! What is that dreadful shadow?'

Caroline rose, turned, and stood confronting the wall.

'How should I know?' she said.

'It has been there every night since he died,' cried Rebecca.

'Every night?'

'Yes. He died Thursday and this is Saturday; tonight makes three nights,' said Caroline rigidly. She stood as if holding herself calm with a vice of concentrated will.

'It – it looks like – like – ' stammered Mrs Brigham in a tone of intense horror.

'I know what it looks like well enough,' said Caroline. 'I've got eyes in my head.'

'It looks like Edward,' burst out Rebecca in a sort of frenzy of fear. 'Only – '

'Yes, it does,' assented Mrs Brigham, whose horror-stricken tone matched her sister's, 'only – Oh, it is awful! What is it, Caroline?'

'I ask you again, how should I know?' replied Caroline. 'I see it there like you. How should I know any more than you?'

'It *must* be something in the room,' said Mrs Brigham, staring wildly around.

'We moved everything in the room the first night it came,' said Rebecca; 'it is not anything in the room.'

Caroline turned upon her with a sort of fury. 'Of course it is something in the room,' said she. 'How you act! What do you mean by talking so? Of course it is something in the room.'

'Of course, it is,' agreed Mrs Brigham, looking at Caroline suspiciously. 'Of course it must be. It is only a coincidence. It just happens so. Perhaps it is that fold of the window curtain that makes it. It must be something in the room.'

'It is not anything in the room,' repeated Rebecca with obstinate horror.

The door opened suddenly and Henry Glynn entered. He began to speak, then his eyes followed the direction of the others' gaze. He stood stock still staring at the shadow on the wall. It was life size and stretched half across the white parallelogram of a door, half across the wall space on which the picture hung.

'What is that?' he demanded in a strange voice.

'It must be due to something in the room,' Mrs Brigham said faintly.

'It is not due to anything in the room,' said Rebecca again with the shrill insistency of terror.

'How you act, Rebecca Glynn,' said Caroline.

Henry Glynn stood and stared a moment longer. His face showed a gamut of emotions – horror, conviction, then furious incredulity. Suddenly he began hastening hither and thither about the room. He moved the furniture with fierce jerks, turning ever to see the effect upon the shadow on the wall. Not a line of its terrible outline wavered.

'It must be something in the room!' he declared in a voice which seemed to snap like a lash.

His face changed. The inmost secrecy of his nature seemed evident until one almost lost sight of his lineaments. Rebecca stood close to her sofa, regarding him with woeful, fascinated eyes. Mrs Brigham clutched Caroline's hand. They both stood in a corner out of his way. For a few moments he raged about the room like a caged wild animal. He moved every piece of furniture; when the moving of a piece did not affect the shadow, he flung it to the floor, his sisters watching.

Then suddenly he desisted. He laughed and began straightening the furniture which he had flung down.

'What an absurdity,' he said easily. 'Such a to-do about a shadow.'

'That's so,' assented Mrs Brigham, in a scared voice which she tried to make natural. As she spoke she lifted a chair near her.

'I think you have broken the chair that Edward was so fond of,' said Caroline.

Terror and wrath were struggling for expression on her face. Her mouth was set, her eyes shrinking. Henry lifted the chair with a show of anxiety.

'Just as good as ever,' he said pleasantly. He laughed again, looking at his sisters. 'Did I scare you?' he said. 'I should think you might be used to me by this time. You know my way of wanting to leap to the bottom of a mystery, and that shadow does look – queer – and I thought if there was any way of accounting for it I would like to without any delay.'

'You don't seem to have succeeded,' remarked Caroline dryly, with a slight glance at the wall.

Henry's eyes followed hers and he quivered perceptibly.

'Oh, there is no accounting for shadows,' he said, and he laughed again. 'A man is a fool to try to account for shadows.'

Then the supper bell rang, and they all left the room, but Henry kept his back to the wall, as did, indeed, the others.

Mrs Brigham pressed close to Caroline as she crossed the hall. 'He looked like a demon!' she breathed in her ear.

Henry led the way with an alert motion like a boy; Rebecca

brought up the rear; she could scarcely walk, her knees trembled so.

'I can't sit in that room again this evening,' she whispered to Caroline after supper.

'Very well, we will sit in the south room,' replied Caroline. 'I think we will sit in the south parlour,' she said aloud; 'it isn't as damp as the study, and I have a cold.'

So they all sat in the south room with their sewing. Henry read the newspaper, his chair drawn close to the lamp on the table. About nine o'clock he rose abruptly and crossed the hall to the study. The three sisters looked at one another. Mrs Brigham rose, folded her rustling skirts compactly around her, and began tiptoeing towards the door.

'What are you going to do?' enquired Rebecca agitatedly.

'I am going to see what he is about,' replied Mrs Brigham cautiously.

She pointed as she spoke to the study door across the hall; it was ajar. Henry had striven to pull it together behind him, but it had somehow swollen beyond the limit with curious speed. It was still ajar and a streak of light showed from top to bottom. The hall lamp was not lit.

'You had better stay where you are,' said Caroline with guarded sharpness.

'I am going to see,' repeated Mrs Brigham firmly.

Then she folded her skirts so tightly that her bulk with its swelling curves was revealed in a black silk sheath, and she went with a slow toddle across the hall to the study door. She stood there, her eye at the crack.

In the south room Rebecca stopped sewing and sat watching with dilated eyes. Caroline sewed steadily. What Mrs Brigham, standing at the crack in the study door, saw was this:

Henry Glynn, evidently reasoning that the source of the strange shadow must be between the table on which the lamp stood and the wall, was making systematic passes and thrusts all over and through the intervening space with an old sword which had belonged to his father. Not an inch was left unpierced. He seemed to have divided the space into mathematical sections. He brandished the sword with a sort of cold fury and calculation; the blade gave out flashes of light, the shadow remained unmoved. Mrs Brigham, watching, felt herself cold with horror.

Finally Henry ceased and stood with the sword in hand and raised as if to strike, surveying the shadow on the wall threateningly. Mrs Brigham toddled back across the hall and shut the south-room door behind her before she related what she had seen.

'He looked like a demon!' she said again. 'Have you got any of that old wine in the house, Caroline? I don't feel as if I could stand much more.'

Indeed, she looked overcome. Her handsome placid face was worn and strained and pale.

'Yes, plenty,' said Caroline; 'you can have some when you go to bed.'

'I think we had all better take some,' said Mrs Brigham. 'Oh, my God, Caroline, what – '

'Don't ask and don't speak,' said Caroline.

'No, I am not going to,' replied Mrs Brigham; 'but – '

Rebecca moaned aloud.

'What are you doing that for?' asked Caroline harshly.

'Poor Edward,' returned Rebecca.

'That is all you have to groan for,' said Caroline. 'There is nothing else.'

'I am going to bed,' said Mrs Brigham. 'I shan't be able to be at the funeral if I don't.'

Soon the three sisters went to their chambers and the south parlour was deserted. Caroline called to Henry in the study to put out the light before he came upstairs. They had been gone about an hour when he came into the room bringing the lamp which had stood in the study. He set it on the table and waited a few minutes, pacing up and down. His face was terrible, his fair complexion showed livid; his blue eyes seemed dark blanks of awful reflections.

Then he took the lamp up and returned to the library. He set the lamp on the centre table, and the shadow sprang out on the wall. Again he studied the furniture and moved it about, but deliberately, with none of his former frenzy. Nothing affected the shadow. Then he returned to the south room with the lamp and again waited. Again he returned to the study and placed the lamp on the table, and the shadow sprang out upon the wall. It was midnight before he went upstairs. Mrs Brigham and the other sisters, who could not sleep, heard him.

The next day was the funeral. That evening the family sat in the south room. Some relatives were with them. Nobody entered the study until Henry carried a lamp in there after the others had retired for the night. He saw again the shadow on the wall leap to an awful life before the light.

The next morning at breakfast Henry Glynn announced that he had to go to the city for three days. The sisters looked at him with surprise. He very seldom left home, and just now his practice had been neglected on account of Edward's death. He was a physician.

'How can you leave your patients now?' asked Mrs Brigham wonderingly.

'I don't know how to, but there is no other way,' replied Henry easily. 'I have had a telegram from Dr Mitford.'

'Consultation?' enquired Mrs Brigham.

'I have business,' replied Henry.

Dr Mitford was an old classmate of his who lived in a neighbouring city and who occasionally called upon him in the case of a consultation.

After he had gone Mrs Brigham said to Caroline that after all Henry had not said that he was going to consult with Dr Mitford, and she thought it very strange.

'Everything is very strange,' said Rebecca with a shudder.

'What do you mean?' enquired Caroline sharply.

'Nothing,' replied Rebecca.

Nobody entered the library that day, nor the next, nor the next. The third day Henry was expected home, but he did not arrive and the last train from the city had come.

'I call it pretty queer work,' said Mrs Brigham. 'The idea of a doctor leaving his patients for three days anyhow, at such a time as this, and I know he has some very sick ones; he said so. And the idea of a consultation lasting three days! There is no sense in it, and *now* he is not returned. I don't understand it, for my part.'

'I don't either,' said Rebecca.

They were all in the south parlour. There was no light in the study opposite, and the door was ajar.

Presently Mrs Brigham rose – she could not have told why; something seemed to impel her, some will outside her own. She went out of the room, again wrapping her rustling skirts around that she might pass noiselessly, and began pushing at the swollen door of the study.

'She has not got any lamp,' said Rebecca in a shaking voice.

Caroline, who was writing letters, rose again, took a lamp (there were two in the room) and followed her sister. Rebecca had risen, but she stood trembling, not venturing to follow.

The doorbell rang, but the others did not hear it; it was on the south door on the other side of the house from the study. Rebecca, after hesitating until the bell rang the second time, went to the door; she remembered that the servant was out.

Caroline and her sister Emma entered the study. Caroline set the lamp on the table. They looked at the wall. 'Oh, my God,' gasped Mrs Brigham, 'there are – there are *two*– shadows.' The sisters stood clutching each other, staring at the awful things on the wall. Then Rebecca came in, staggering, with a telegram in her hand. 'Here is – a telegram,' she gasped. 'Henry is – dead.'

JACK LONDON

John Griffith London (1876–1916), a novelist who wrote under the name Jack London, was born in San Francisco, the illegitimate son of an Irish vagabond and an American girl who afterwards married John London, a grocer. Brought up in poverty, he worked at all sorts of odd jobs, but read omnivorously. About the age of nineteen he attended Oakland High School for a short time and then had a year at the University of California. But an ordered existence was impossible for him. The open sea and the open road were his passions, and at one time he was arrested as a vagrant. In 1897 he took part in the Klondike gold rush; he got no gold, but from his experiences he afterwards wrote *The Call of the Wild* (1903), which sold nearly a million and a half copies. In 1904 he was a special correspondent in the Russo-Japanese War, and in 1907 he set off with his wife on a world cruise; after visiting Honolulu they abandoned the voyage in Australia, and he wrote of it in *The Cruise of the Snark* (1911). In 1912 he sailed round the Horn. At this time he was reckoned the best paid and most popular writer in America, but drink and extravagance caused his work to deteriorate, and he finally committed suicide. He is best remembered for such stories as *The God of his Fathers* (1901), *The Sea Wolf* (1904), *White Fang* (1905), *Before Adam* (1906), *Smoke Bellew* (1912), *John Barleycorn* (1913), *The Star Rover* (1914) and *Jerry of the Islands* (1917).

All Gold Canyon

It was the green heart of the canyon, where the walls swerved back from the rigid plan and relieved their harshness of line by making a little sheltered nook and filling it to the brim with sweetness and roundness and softness. Here all things rested. Even the narrow stream ceased its turbulent down-rush long enough to form a quiet pool. Knee-deep in the water, with drooping head and half-shut eyes, drowsed a red-coated, many-antlered buck.

On one side, beginning at the very lip of the pool, was a tiny meadow, a cool, resilient surface of green that extended to the base of the frowning wall. Beyond the pool a gentle slope of earth ran up and up to meet the opposing wall. Fine grass covered the slope – grass that was spangled with flowers, with here and there patches of colour, orange and purple and golden. Below, the canyon was shut in. There was no view. The walls leaned together abruptly and the canyon ended in a chaos of rocks, moss-covered and hidden by a green screen of vines and creepers and boughs of trees. Up the canyon rose far hills and peaks, the big foothills, pine-covered and remote. And far beyond, like clouds upon the border of the sky, towered minarets of white, where the Sierra's eternal snows flashed austerely the blazes of the sun.

There was no dust in the canyon. The leaves and flowers were clean and virginal. The grass was young velvet. Over the pool three cottonwoods sent their snowy fluffs fluttering down the quiet air. On the slope the blossoms of the wine-wooded manzanita filled the air with springtime odours, while the leaves, wise with experience, were already beginning their vertical twist against the coming aridity of summer. In the open spaces on the slope, beyond the farthest shadow-reach of the manzanita, poised the mariposa lilies, like so many flights of jewelled moths suddenly arrested and on the verge of trembling into flight again. Here and there that woods' harlequin, the madrone, permitting itself to be caught in the act of changing its pea-green trunk to madder-red, breathed its fragrance into the air from great clusters of waxen bells. Creamy white were these bells, shaped like lilies-of-the-valley, with the sweetness of perfume that is of the springtime.

There was not a sigh of wind. The air was drowsy with its weight of perfume. It was a sweetness that would have been cloying had the air been heavy and humid. But the air was sharp and thin. It was as starlight transmuted into atmosphere, shot through and warmed by sunshine, and flower-drenched with sweetness.

An occasional butterfly drifted in and out through the patches of light and shade. And from all about rose the low and sleepy hum of mountain bees – feasting Sybarites that jostled one another good-naturedly at the board, nor found time for rough discourtesy. So quietly did the little stream drip and ripple its way through the canyon that it spoke only in faint and occasional gurgles. The voice of the stream was as a drowsy whisper, ever interrupted by dozings and silences, ever lifted again in the awakenings.

The motion of all things was a drifting in the heart of the canyon. Sunshine and butterflies drifted in and out among the trees. The hum of the bees and the whisper of the stream were a drifting of sound. And the drifting sound and drifting colour seemed to weave together in the making of a delicate and intangible fabric which was the spirit of the place. It was a spirit of peace that was not of death but of smooth-pulsing life, of quietude that was not silence, of movement that was not action, of repose that was quick with existence without being violent with struggle and travail. The spirit of the place was the spirit of the peace of the living, somnolent with the easement and content of prosperity and undisturbed by rumours of far wars.

The red-coated, many-antlered buck acknowledged the lord-ship of the spirit of the place and dozed knee-deep in the cool, shaded pool. There seemed no flies to vex him and he was languid with rest. Sometimes his ears moved when the stream awoke and whispered; but they moved lazily, with foreknow-ledge that it was merely the stream grown garrulous at discovery that it had slept.

But there came a time when the buck's ears lifted and tensed with swift eagerness for sound. His head was turned down the canyon. His sensitive, quivering nostrils scented the air. His eyes could not pierce the green screen through which the stream rippled away, but to his ears came the voice of a man. It was a steady, monotonous, singsong voice. Once the buck heard the harsh clash of metal upon rock. At the sound he snorted with a sudden start that jerked him through the air from water to meadow, and his feet sank into the young velvet, while he pricked his ears and again scented the air. Then he stole across the tiny meadow, pausing once and again to listen, and faded away out of the canyon like a wraith, soft-footed and without sound.

The clash of steel-shod soles against the rocks began to be heard, and the man's voice grew louder. It was raised in a sort of chant and became distinct with nearness, so that the words could be heard:

> 'Tu'n around an' tu'n yo' face
> Untoe them sweet hills of grace
>   (D' pow'rs of sin yo' am scornin'!).
> Look about an' look aroun',
> Fling yo' sin-pack on d' groun'
>   (Yo' will meet wid d' Lord in d' mornin'!).'

A sound of scrambling accompanied the song, and the spirit of the place fled away on the heels of the red-coated buck. The green screen was burst asunder, and a man peered out at the meadow and the pool and the sloping side-hill. He was a deliberate sort of man. He took in the scene with one embracing glance, then ran his eyes over the details to verify the general impression. Then, and not until then, did he open his mouth in vivid and solemn approval: 'Smoke of life an' snakes of purgatory! Will you just look at that! Wood an' water an' grass an' a side-hill! A pocket-hunter's delight an' a cayuse's paradise! Cool green for tired eyes! Pink pills for pale people ain't in it. A secret pasture for prospectors and a resting-place for tired burros. It's just booful!'

He was a sandy-complexioned man in whose face geniality and humour seemed the salient characteristics. It was a mobile face, quick-changing to inward mood and thought. Thinking was in him a visible process. Ideas chased across his face like wind-flaws across the surface of a lake. His hair, sparse and unkempt of growth, was as indeterminate and colourless as his complexion. It would seem that all the colour of his frame had gone into his eyes, for they were startlingly blue. Also, they were laughing and merry eyes, within them much of the naivety and wonder of the child; and yet, in an unassertive way, they contained much of calm self-reliance and strength of purpose founded upon self-experience and experience of the world.

From out the screen of vines and creepers he flung ahead of him a miner's pick and shovel and gold-pan. Then he crawled out himself into the open. He was clad in faded overalls and black cotton shirt, with hobnailed brogans on his feet, and on his head a hat whose shapelessness and stains advertised the rough usage of wind and rain and sun and camp-smoke. He stood erect, seeing wide-eyed the secrecy of the scene and sensuously inhaling the warm, sweet breath of the canyon-garden through nostrils that dilated and quivered with delight. His eyes narrowed to laughing slits of blue, his face wreathed itself in joy, and his mouth curled in a smile as he cried aloud: 'Jumping dandelions and happy hollyhocks, but that smells good to me! Talk about your attar o' roses an' cologne factories! They ain't in it!'

He had the habit of soliloquy. His quick-changing facial expressions might tell every thought and mood, but the tongue, perforce, ran hard after, repeating, like a second Boswell.

The man lay down on the lip of the pool and drank long and deep of its water. 'Tastes good to me,' he murmured, lifting his head and gazing across the pool at the side-hill, while he wiped his mouth with the back of his hand. The side-hill attracted his attention. Still lying on his stomach, he studied the hill formation long and carefully. It was a practised eye that travelled up the slope to the crumbling canyon-wall and back and down again to the edge of the pool. He scrambled to his feet and favoured the side-hill with a second survey.

'Looks good to me,' he concluded, picking up his pick and shovel and gold-pan.

He crossed the stream below the pool, stepping agilely from stone to stone. Where the side-hill touched the water he dug up a shovelful of dirt and put it into the gold-pan. He squatted down, holding the pan in his two hands, and partly immersing it in the stream. Then he imparted to the pan a deft circular motion that sent the water sluicing in and out through the dirt and gravel. The larger and the lighter particles worked to the surface, and these, by a skilful dipping movement of the pan, he spilled out and over the edge. Occasionally, to expedite matters, he rested the pan and with his fingers raked out the large pebbles and pieces of rock.

The contents of the pan diminished rapidly until only fine dirt and the smallest bits of gravel remained. At this stage he began to work very deliberately and carefully. It was fine washing, and he washed fine and finer, with a keen scrutiny and delicate and fastidious touch. At last the pan seemed empty of everything but water; but with a quick semicircular flirt that sent the water flying over the shallow rim into the stream, he disclosed a layer of black sand on the bottom of the pan. So thin was this layer that it was like a streak of paint. He examined it closely. In the midst of it was a tiny golden speck. He dribbled a little water in over the depressed edge of the pan. With a quick flirt he sent the water sluicing across the bottom, turning the grains of black sand over and over. A second tiny golden speck rewarded his effort.

The washing had now become very fine – fine beyond all need of ordinary placer-mining. He worked the black sand, a small portion at a time, up the shallow rim of the pan. Each small portion he examined sharply, so that his eyes saw every grain of it before he allowed it to slide over the edge and away. Jealously, bit by bit, he let the black sand slip away. A golden speck, no larger than a pin-point, appeared on the rim, and by his manipulation of the water it returned to the bottom of the pan. And in such fashion another speck was disclosed, and another. Great was his care of them. Like a shepherd he herded his flock of golden specks so that not one should be lost. At last, of the pan of dirt nothing remained but his golden herd. He counted it, and then, after all his labour, sent it flying out of the pan with one final swirl of water.

But his blue eyes were shining with desire as he rose to his feet. 'Seven,' he muttered aloud, asserting the sum of the specks for which he had toiled so hard and which he had so wantonly thrown away. 'Seven,' he repeated, with the emphasis of one trying to impress a number on his memory.

He stood still a long while, surveying the hillside. In his eyes was a curiosity, new-aroused and burning. There was an exultance about his bearing and a keenness like that of a hunting animal catching the fresh scent of game.

He moved down the stream a few steps and took a second panful of dirt.

Again came the careful washing, the jealous herding of the golden specks, and the wantonness with which he sent them flying into the stream.

'Five,' he muttered, and repeated, 'five.'

He could not forbear another survey of the hill before filling the pan farther down the stream. His golden herds diminished. 'Four, three, two, two, one,' were his memory tabulations as he moved down the stream. When but one speck of gold rewarded his washing, he stopped and built a fire of dry twigs. Into this he thrust the gold-pan and burned it till it was blue-black. He held up the pan and examined it critically. Then he nodded approbation. Against such a colour-background he could defy the tiniest yellow speck to elude him.

Still moving down the stream, he panned again. A single speck was his reward. A third pan contained no gold at all. Not satisfied with this, he panned three times again, taking his shovels of dirt within a foot of one another. Each pan proved empty of gold, and the fact, instead of discouraging him, seemed to give him satisfaction. His elation increased with each barren washing, until he arose, exclaiming jubilantly: 'If it ain't the real thing, may God knock off my head with sour apples!'

Returning to where he had started operations, he began to pan up the stream. At first his golden herds increased – increased prodigiously. 'Fourteen, eighteen, twenty-one, twenty-six,' ran his memory tabulations. Just above the pool he struck his richest pan – thirty-five colours.

'Almost enough to save,' he remarked regretfully as he allowed the water to sweep them away.

The sun climbed to the top of the sky. The man worked on. Pan by pan, he went up the stream, the tally of results steadily decreasing.

'It's just booful, the way it peters out,' he exulted when a shovelful of dirt contained no more than a single speck of gold. And when no specks at all were found in several pans, he straightened up and favoured the hillside with a confident glance.

'Ah, ha! Mr Pocket!' he cried out, as though to an auditor hidden somewhere above him beneath the surface of the slope. 'Ah, ha! Mr Pocket! I'm a-comin', I'm a-comin', an' I'm shorely gwine to get yer! You heah me, Mr Pocket? I'm gwine to get yer as shore as punkins ain't cauliflowers!'

He turned and flung a measuring glance at the sun poised above him in the azure of the cloudless sky. Then he went down the canyon, following the line of shovel-holes he had made in filling the pans. He crossed the stream below the pool and disappeared through the green screen. There was little opportunity for the spirit of the place to return with its quietude and repose, for the man's voice, raised in ragtime song, still dominated the canyon with possession.

After a time, with a greater clashing of steel-shod feet on rock, he returned. The green screen was tremendously agitated. It surged back and forth in the throes of a struggle. There was a loud grating and clanging of metal. The man's voice leaped to a higher pitch and was sharp with imperativeness. A large body plunged and panted. There was a snapping and ripping and rending, and amid a shower of falling leaves a horse burst through the screen. On its back was a pack, and from this trailed broken vines and torn creepers. The animal gazed with astonished eyes at the scene into which it had been precipitated, then dropped its head to the grass and began contentedly to graze. A second horse scrambled into view, slipping once on the mossy rocks and regaining equilibrium when its hoofs sank into the yielding surface of the meadow. It was riderless, though on its back was a high-horned Mexican saddle, scarred and discoloured by long usage.

The man brought up the rear. He threw off pack and saddle, with an eye to camp location, and gave the animals their freedom to graze. He unpacked his food and got out frying-pan and coffee-pot. He gathered an armful of dry wood, and with a few stones made a place for his fire.

'My!' he said, 'but I've got an appetite. I could scoff iron-filings an' horseshoe nails an' thank you kindly, ma'am, for a second helpin'.'

He straightened up, and, while he reached for matches in the pocket of his overalls, his eyes travelled across the pool to the side-hill. His fingers had clutched the matchbox, but they relaxed their hold and the hand came out empty. The man wavered perceptibly. He looked at his preparations for cooking and he looked at the hill.

'Guess I'll take another whack at her,' he concluded, starting to cross the stream. 'They ain't no sense in it, I know,' he mumbled apologetically. 'But keepin' grub back an hour ain't goin' to hurt none, I reckon.'

A few feet back from his first line of test-pans he started a second line. The sun dropped down the western sky, the shadows lengthened, but the man worked on. He began a third line of test-pans. He was cross-cutting the hillside, line by line, as he ascended. The centre of each line produced the richest pans, while the ends came where no colours showed in the pan. And as he ascended the hillside the lines grew perceptibly shorter. The regularity with which their length diminished served to indicate that somewhere up the slope the last line would be so short as to have scarcely length at all, and that beyond could come only a point. The design was growing into an inverted V. The converging sides of this V marked the boundaries of the gold-bearing dirt.

The apex of the V was evidently the man's goal. Often he ran his eye along the converging sides and on up the hill, trying to divine the apex, the point where the gold-bearing dirt must cease. Here resided 'Mr Pocket' – for so the man familiarly addressed the imaginary point above him on the slope, crying out: 'Come down out o' that, Mr Pocket! Be right smart an' agreeable, an' come down!'

'All right,' he would add later, in a voice resigned to determination. 'All right, Mr Pocket. It's plain to me I got to come right up an' snatch you out bald-headed. An' I'll do it! I'll do it!' he would threaten still later.

Each pan he carried down to the water to wash, and as he went higher up the hill the pans grew richer, until he began to save the gold in an empty baking-powder can which he carried carelessly in his hip-pocket. So engrossed was he in his toil that he did not notice the long twilight of oncoming night. It was not until he tried vainly to see the gold colours in the bottom of the pan that he realised the passage of time. He straightened up abruptly. An expression of whimsical wonderment and awe overspread his face as he drawled: 'Gosh darn my buttons! If I didn't plumb forget dinner!'

He stumbled across the stream in the darkness and lighted his long-delayed fire. Flapjacks and bacon and warmed-over beans constituted his supper. Then he smoked a pipe by the smouldering coals, listening to the night noises and watching the moonlight stream through the canyon. After that he unrolled his bed, took off his heavy shoes, and pulled the blankets up to his chin. His face showed white in the moonlight, like the face of a corpse. But it was a corpse that knew its resurrection, for the man rose suddenly on one elbow and gazed across at his hillside.

'Good-night, Mr Pocket,' he called sleepily. 'Good-night.'

He slept through the early grey of morning until the direct rays of the sun smote his closed eyelids, when he awoke with a start and looked about him until he had established the continuity of his existence and identified his present self with the days previously lived.

To dress, he had merely to buckle on his shoes. He glanced at his fireplace and at his hillside, wavered, but fought down the temptation and started the fire.

'Keep yer shirt on, Bill; keep yer shirt on,' he admonished himself. 'What's the good of rushin'? No use in gettin' all het up an' sweaty. Mr Pocket'll wait for you. He ain't a-runnin' away before you can get your breakfast. Now, what you want, Bill, is something fresh in yer bill o' fare. So it's up to you to go an' get it.'

He cut a short pole at the water's edge and drew from one of his pockets a bit of line and a draggled fly that had once been a royal coachman.

'Mebbe they'll bite in the early morning,' he muttered, as he made his first cast into the pool. And a moment later he was gleefully crying: 'What'd I tell you, eh? What'd I tell you?'

He had no reel, nor any inclination to waste time, so by main strength, and swiftly, he drew out of the water a flashing ten-inch trout. Three more, caught in rapid succession, furnished his breakfast. When he came to the stepping-stones on his way to his hillside, he was struck by a sudden thought, and paused.

'I'd just better take a hike downstream a ways,' he said. 'There's no tellin' who may be snoopin' around.'

But he crossed over on the stones, and with a, 'I really oughter take that hike,' the need of the precaution passed out of his mind and he fell to work.

At nightfall he straightened up. The small of his back was stiff from stooping toil, and as he put his hand behind him to soothe the protesting muscles, he said: 'Now what d'ye think of that? I clean forgot my dinner again! If I don't watch out, I'll sure be degeneratin' into a two-meal-a-day crank.'

'Pockets is the hangedest things I ever see for makin' a man absent-minded,' he communed that night, as he crawled into his blankets. Nor did he forget to call up the hillside, 'Good-night, Mr Pocket! Good-night!'

Rising with the sun, and snatching a hasty breakfast, he was early at work. A fever seemed to be growing in him, nor did the increasing richness of the test-pans allay this fever. There was a flush in his cheek other than that made by the heat of the sun, and he was oblivious to fatigue and the passage of time. When he filled a pan with dirt, he ran down the hill to wash it; nor could he forbear running up the hill again, panting and stumbling profanely, to refill the pan.

He was now a hundred yards from the water, and the inverted V was assuming definite proportions. The width of the pay-dirt steadily decreased, and the man extended in his mind's eye the sides of the V to their meeting place far up the hill. This was his goal, the apex of the V, and he panned many times to locate it. 'Just about two yards above that manzanita bush an' a yard to the right,' he finally concluded.

Then the temptation seized him. 'As plain as the nose on your face,' he said, as he abandoned his laborious cross-cutting and climbed to the indicated apex. He filled a pan and carried it down the hill to wash. It contained no trace of gold. He dug deep, and he dug shallow, filling and washing a dozen pans, and was unrewarded even by the tiniest golden speck. He was enraged at having yielded to the temptation, and berated himself blasphemously and pridelessly. Then he went down the hill and took up the cross-cutting.

'Slow an' certain, Bill; slow an' certain,' he crooned. 'Short-cuts to fortune ain't in your line, an' it's about time you knew it. Get wise, Bill; get wise. Slow an' certain's the only hand you can play; so go to it, an' keep to it, too.'

As the cross-cuts decreased, showing that the sides of the V were converging, the depth of the V increased. The gold-trace was dipping into the hill. It was only at thirty inches beneath the surface that he could get colours in his pan. The dirt he found at twenty-five inches from the surface, and at thirty-five inches yielded barren pans. At the base of the V, by the water's edge, he had found the gold colours at the grass roots. The higher he went up the hill, the deeper the gold dipped. To dig a hole three feet deep in order to get one test-pan was a task of no mean magnitude; while between the man and the apex intervened an untold number of such holes to be dug. 'An' there's no tellin' how much deeper it'll pitch,' he sighed, in a moment's pause, while his fingers soothed his aching back.

Feverish with desire, with aching back and stiffening muscles, with pick and shovel gouging and mauling the soft brown earth, the man toiled up the hill. Before him was the smooth slope, spangled with flowers and made sweet with their breath. Behind him was devastation. It looked like some terrible eruption breaking out on the smooth skin of the hill. His slow progress was like that of a slug, befouling beauty with a monstrous trail.

Though the dipping gold-trace increased the man's work, he found consolation in the increasing richness of the pans. Twenty cents, thirty cents, fifty cents, sixty cents, were the values of the gold found in the pans, and at nightfall he washed his banner pan, which gave him a dollar's worth of gold-dust from a shovelful of dirt.

'I'll just bet it's my luck to have some inquisitive one come buttin' in here on my pasture,' he mumbled sleepily that night as he pulled the blankets up to his chin.

Suddenly he sat upright. 'Bill!' he called sharply. 'Now, listen to me, Bill; d'ye hear! It's up to you, tomorrow mornin', to mosey round an' see what you can see. Understand? Tomorrow morning, an' don't you forget it!'

He yawned and glanced across at his side-hill. 'Good-night, Mr Pocket,' he called.

In the morning he stole a march on the sun, for he had finished breakfast when its first rays caught him, and he was climbing the wall of the canyon where it crumbled away and gave footing. From the outlook at the top he found himself in the midst of loneliness. As far as he could see, chain after chain of mountains heaved themselves into his vision. To the east his eyes, leaping the miles between range and range and between many ranges, brought up at last against the white-peaked Sierras – the main crest, where the backbone of the Western world reared itself against the sky. To the north and south he could see more distinctly the cross-systems that broke through the main trend of the sea of mountains. To the west the ranges fell away, one behind the other, diminishing and fading into the gentle foothills that, in turn, descended into the great valley which he could not see.

And in all that mighty sweep of earth he saw no sign of man nor of the handiwork of man – save only the torn bosom of the hillside at his feet. The man looked long and carefully. Once, far down his own canyon, he thought he saw in the air a faint hint of smoke. He looked again and decided that it was the purple haze of the hills made dark by a convolution of the canyon wall at its back.

'Hey, you, Mr Pocket!' he called down into the canyon. 'Stand out from under! I'm a-comin', Mr Pocket! I'm a-comin'!'

The heavy brogans on the man's feet made him appear clumsy-footed, but he swung down from the giddy height as lightly and airily as a mountain goat. A rock, turning under his foot on the edge of the precipice, did not disconcert him. He seemed to know the precise time required for the turn to culminate in disaster, and in the meantime he utilised the false footing itself for the momentary earth-contact necessary to carry him on into safety. Where the earth sloped so steeply that it was impossible to stand for a second upright, the man did not hesitate. His foot pressed the impossible surface for but a fraction of the fatal second and gave him the bound that carried him onward. Again, where even the fraction of a second's footing was out of the question, he would swing his body past by a moment's hand-grip on a jutting knob of rock, a crevice or a precariously rooted shrub. At last, with a wild leap and yell, he exchanged the face of the wall for an earth-slide and finished the descent in the midst of several tons of sliding earth and gravel.

His first pan of the morning washed out over two dollars in coarse gold. It was from the centre of the V. To either side the diminution in the values of the pans was swift. His lines of cross-cutting holes were growing very short. The converging sides of the inverted V were only a few yards apart. Their meeting-point was only a few yards above him. But the pay-streak was dipping deeper and deeper into the earth. By early afternoon he was sinking the test-holes five feet before the pans could show the gold-trace.

For that matter, the gold-trace had become something more than a trace; it was a placer mine in itself, and the man resolved to come back after he had found the pocket and work over the ground. But the increasing richness of the pans began to worry him. By late afternoon the worth of the pans had grown to three and four dollars. The man scratched his head perplexedly and looked a few feet up the hill at the manzanita bush that marked approximately the apex of the V. He nodded his head and said oracularly: 'It's one o' two things, Bill; one o' two things. Either Mr Pocket's spilled himself all out an' down the hill, or else Mr Pocket's so rich you maybe won't be able to carry him all away with you. And that'd be an awful shame, wouldn't it, now?' He chuckled at contemplation of so pleasant a dilemma.

Nightfall found him by the edge of the stream, his eyes wrestling with the gathering darkness over the washing of a five-dollar pan.

'Wisht I had an electric light to go on working,' he said.

He found sleep difficult that night. Many times he com-posed himself and closed his eyes for slumber to overtake him; but his blood pounded with too strong desire, and as many times his eyes opened and he murmured wearily, 'Wisht it was sun-up.'

Sleep came to him in the end, but his eyes were open with the first paling of the stars, and the grey of dawn caught him with breakfast finished and climbing the hillside in the direction of the secret abiding-place of Mr Pocket.

The first cross-cut the man made, there was space for only three holes, so narrow had become the pay-streak and so close was he to the fountainhead of the golden stream he had been following for four days.

'Be ca'm, Bill; be ca'm,' he admonished himself, as he broke ground for the final hole where the sides of the V had at last come together in a point.

'I've got the almighty cinch on you, Mr Pocket, an' you can't lose me,' he said many times as he sank the hole deeper and deeper.

Four feet, five feet, six feet, he dug his way down into the earth. The digging grew harder. His pick grated on broken rock. He examined the rock. 'Rotten quartz,' was his conclusion as, with the shovel, he cleared the bottom of the hole of loose dirt. He attacked the crumbling quartz with the pick, bursting the disintegrating rock asunder with every stroke.

He thrust his shovel into the loose mass. His eye caught a gleam of yellow. He dropped the shovel and squatted suddenly on his heels. As a farmer rubs the clinging earth from fresh-dug potatoes, so the man, a piece of rotten quartz held in both hands, rubbed the dirt away.

'Sufferin' Sardanopolis!' he cried. 'Lumps an' chunks of it! Lumps an' chunks of it!'

It was only half rock he held in his hand. The other half was virgin gold. He dropped it into his pan and examined another piece. Little yellow was to be seen, but with his strong fingers he crumbled the rotten quartz away till both hands were filled with glowing yellow. He rubbed the dirt away from fragment after fragment, tossing them into the gold-pan. It was a treasure-hole. So much had the quartz rotted away that there was less of it than there was of gold. Now and again he found a piece to which no rock clung – a piece that was all gold. A chunk, where the pick had laid open the heart of the gold, glittered like a handful of yellow jewels, and he cocked his head at it and slowly turned it around and over to observe the rich play of the light upon it.

'Talk about yer too-much-gold diggin's!' the man snorted contemptuously. 'Why, this diggin' 'd make it look like thirty cents. This diggin' is All Gold. An' right here an' now I name this yere canyon "All Gold Canyon", b' gosh!'

Still squatting on his heels, he continued examining the fragments and tossing them into the pan. Suddenly there came to him a premonition of danger. It seemed a shadow had fallen upon him. But there was no shadow. His heart had given a great jump up into his throat and was choking him. Then his blood slowly chilled and he felt the sweat of his shirt cold against his flesh.

He did not spring up nor look around. He did not move. He was considering the nature of the premonition he had received, trying to locate the source of the mysterious force that had warned him, striving to sense the imperative presence of the unseen thing that threatened him. There is an aura of things hostile, made manifest by messengers too refined for the senses to know; and this aura he felt, but knew not how he felt it. His was the feeling as when a cloud passes over the sun. It seemed that between him and life had passed something dark and smothering and menacing; a gloom, as it were, that swallowed up life and made for death – his death.

Every force of his being impelled him to spring up and con-front the unseen danger, but his soul dominated the panic, and he remained squatting on his heels, in his hands a chunk of gold. He did not dare to look around, but he knew by now that there was something behind him and above him. He made believe to be interested in the gold in his hand. He examined it critically, turned it over and over, and rubbed the dirt from it. And all the time he knew that something behind him was looking at the gold over his shoulder.

Still feigning interest in the chunk of gold in his hand, he listened intently and he heard the breathing of the thing behind him. His eyes searched the ground in front of him for a weapon, but they saw only the uprooted gold, worthless to him now in his extremity. There was his pick, a handy weapon on occasion; but this was not such an occasion. The man realised his predicament. He was in a narrow hole that was seven feet deep. His head did not come to the surface of the ground. He was in a trap.

He remained squatting on his heels. He was quite cool and collected; but his mind, considering every factor, showed him only his helplessness. He continued rubbing the dirt from the quartz fragments and throwing the gold into the pan. There was nothing else for him to do. Yet he knew that he would have to rise up, sooner or later, and face the danger that breathed at his back. The minutes passed, and with the passage of each minute he knew that by so much he was nearer the time when he must stand up, or else – and his wet shirt went cold against his flesh again at the thought – or else he might receive death as he stooped there over his treasure.

Still he squatted on his heels, rubbing dirt from gold and debating in just what manner he should rise up. He might rise up with a rush and claw his way out of the hole to meet whatever threatened on the even footing above ground. Or he might rise up slowly and carelessly, and feign casually to discover the thing that breathed at his back. His instinct and every fighting fibre of his body favoured the mad, clawing rush to the surface. His intellect, and the craft thereof, favoured the slow and cautious meeting with the thing that menaced and which he could not see. And while he debated, a loud, crashing noise burst on his ear. At the same instant he received a stunning blow on the left side of the back, and from the point of impact felt a rush of flame through his flesh. He sprang up in the air, but halfway to his feet collapsed. His body crumpled in like a leaf withered in sudden heat, and he came down, his chest across his pan of gold, his face in the dirt and rock, his legs tangled and twisted because of the restricted space at the bottom of the hole. His legs twitched convulsively several times. His body was shaken as with a mighty ague. There was a slow expansion of the lungs, accompanied by a deep sigh. Then the air was slowly, very slowly, exhaled, and his body as slowly flattened itself down into inertness.

Above, revolver in hand, a man was peering down over the edge of the hole. He peered for a long time at the prone and motionless body beneath him. After a while the stranger sat down on the edge of the hole so that he could see into it, and rested the revolver on his knee. Reaching his hand into a pocket, he drew out a wisp of brown paper. Into this he dropped a few crumbs of tobacco. The combination became a cigarette, brown and squat, with the ends turned in. Not once did he take his eyes from the body at the bottom of the hole. He lighted the cigarette and drew its smoke into his lungs with a caressing intake of the breath. He smoked slowly. Once the cigarette went out and he relighted it. And all the while he studied the body beneath him.

In the end he tossed the cigarette stub away and rose to his feet. He moved to the edge of the hole. Spanning it, a hand resting on each edge, and with the revolver still in the right hand, he muscled his body down into the hole. While his feet were yet a yard from the bottom he released his hands and dropped down.

At the instant his feet struck bottom he saw the pocket-miner's arm leap out, and his own legs knew a swift, jerking grip that overthrew him. In the nature of the jump his revolver hand was above his head. Swiftly as the grip had flashed about his legs, just as swiftly he brought the revolver down. He was still in the air, his fall in process of completion, when he pulled the trigger. The explosion was deafening in the confined space. The smoke filled the hole so that he could see nothing. He struck the bottom on his back, and like a cat's the pocket-miner's body was on top of him. Even as the miner's body passed on top, the stranger crooked in his right arm to fire; and even in that instant the miner, with a quick thrust of elbow, struck his wrist. The muzzle was thrown up and the bullet thudded into the dirt of the side of the hole.

The next instant the stranger felt the miner's hand grip his wrist. The struggle was now for the revolver. Each man strove to turn it against the other's body. The smoke in the hole was clearing. The stranger, lying on his back, was beginning to see dimly. But suddenly he was blinded by a handful of dirt deliberately flung into his eyes by his antagonist. In that moment of shock his grip on the revolver was broken. In the next moment he felt a smashing darkness descend upon his brain, and in the midst of the darkness even the darkness ceased.

But the pocket-miner fired again and again, until the revolver was empty. Then he tossed it from him and, breathing heavily, sat down on the dead man's legs.

The miner was sobbing and struggling for breath. 'Measly skunk!' he panted; 'a-campin' on my trail an' lettin' me do the work, an' then shootin' me in the back!'

He was half crying from anger and exhaustion. He peered at the face of the dead man. It was sprinkled with loose dirt and gravel, and it was difficult to distinguish the features.

'Never laid eyes on him before,' the miner concluded his scrutiny. 'Just a common an' ordinary thief, hang him! An' he shot me in the back! He shot me in the back!'

He opened his shirt and felt himself, front and back, on his left side.

'Went clean through, and no harm done!' he cried jubilantly. 'I'll bet he aimed all right; but he drew the gun over when he pulled the trigger – the cur! But I fixed 'm! Oh, I fixed 'm!'

His fingers were investigating the bullet-hole in his side, and a shade of regret passed over his face. 'It's goin' to be stiffer 'n hell,' he said. 'An' it's up to me to get mended an' get out o' here.'

He crawled out of the hole and went down the hill to his camp. Half an hour later he returned, leading his packhorse. His open shirt disclosed the rude bandages with which he had dressed his wound. He was slow and awkward with his left-hand movements, but that did not prevent his using the arm.

The bight of the pack-rope under the dead man's shoulders enabled him to heave the body out of the hole. Then he set to work gathering up his gold. He worked steadily for several hours, pausing often to rest his stiffening shoulder and to exclaim: 'He shot me in the back, the measly skunk! He shot me in the back!'

When his treasure was quite cleaned up and wrapped securely into a number of blanket-covered parcels, he made an estimate of its value.

'Four hundred pounds, or I'm a Hottentot,' he concluded. 'Say two hundred in quartz an' dirt – that leaves two hundred pounds of gold. Bill! Wake up! Two hundred pounds of gold! Forty thousand dollars! An' it's yourn – all yourn!'

He scratched his head delightedly and his fingers blundered into an unfamiliar groove. They quested along it for several inches. It was a crease through his scalp where the second bullet had ploughed.

He walked angrily over to the dead man.

'You would, would you!' he bullied. 'You would, eh? Well, I fixed you good an' plenty, an' I'll give you decent burial, too. That's more 'n you'd have done for me.'

He dragged the body to the edge of the hole and toppled it in. It struck the bottom with a dull crash, on its side, the face twisted up to the light. The miner peered down at it.

'An' you shot me in the back!' he said accusingly.

With pick and shovel he filled the hole. Then he loaded the gold on his horse. It was too great a load for the animal, and when he had gained his camp he transferred part of it to his saddle-horse. Even so, he was compelled to abandon a portion of his outfit – pick and shovel and gold-pan, extra food and cooking utensils, and divers odds and ends.

The sun was at the zenith when the man forced the horses at the screen of vines and creepers. To climb the huge boulders the animals were compelled to uprear and struggle blindly through the tangled mass of vegetation. Once the saddle-horse fell heavily and the man removed the pack to get the animal on its feet. After it started on its way again the man thrust his head out from among the leaves and peered up at the hillside.

'The measly skunk!' he said, and disappeared.

There was a ripping and tearing of vines and boughs. The trees surged back and forth, marking the passage of the animals through the midst of them. There was a clashing of steel-shod hoofs on stone, and now and again a sharp cry of command. Then the voice of the man was raised in song:

'Tu'n around an' tu'n yo' face
Untoe them sweet hills of grace
(D' pow'rs of sin yo' am scornin'!).
Look about an' look aroun',
Fling yo' sin-pack on d' groun'
(Yo' will meet wid d' Lord in d' mornin'!).'

The song grew faint and fainter, and through the silence crept back the spirit of the place. The stream once more drowsed and whispered; the hum of the mountain bees rose sleepily. Down through the perfume-weighted air fluttered the snowy fluffs of the cottonwoods. The butterflies drifted in and out among the trees, and over all blazed the quiet sunshine. Only remained the hoof-marks in the meadow and the torn hillside to mark the boisterous trail of the life that had broken the peace of the place and passed on.